A WOMAN INVOLVED

John Gordon Davis was born in what was then
Rhodesia of English parents, and was educated
in South Africa. He became a member of the
Seamen's Union, spending his university va-
cations at sea with the Dutch whaling fleet in the
Antarctic, and on British merchantmen. He
took degrees in political science and law and
joined the Rhodesian Civil Service before becoming a barrister in Hong Kong. The success
of his first novel allowed him to take up writing
full time. He and his wife Rosemary live in
Southern Spain.

JOHN GORDON DAVIS

A Woman Involved

FONTANA/Collins

First published by William Collins Sons & Co. Ltd 1987
First issued in Fontana Paperbacks 1988

Copyright © John Gordon Davis 1987

Made and printed in Great Britain by
William Collins Sons & Co. Ltd, Glasgow

To Minna and Max Lucas

VOLUME 1

Rome, 1978

'Who murdered you?' people cried at the corpse.

There was no autopsy to find out why he died. Yet he had been in excellent health. No death certificate was ever published. And when he was embalmed, within twelve hours of his death, the morticians were forbidden to draw one drop of blood off his body. For three days Pope John Paul I lay in state in the Basilica of Saint Peter's, and thousands of people filed past the coffin to pay their last homage to the Pope who had reigned for only thirty-three days. At seven o'clock on the third day the doors of Saint Peter's were closed, and the body lay in flickering candlelight for the last night, Swiss guards standing vigil at each corner of the catafalque. But at seven-thirty, through a side door, entered some more pilgrims. They came from the Pope's birthplace, and they had received special permission to come late to pay their last respects. They began to file past the body, mourning. Then something strange happened.

Suddenly a group of Vatican officials and doctors appeared. The pilgrims were told to leave immediately. They did so, bewildered. Then the Swiss guards were ordered to leave. Then big crimson screens were erected around the body, so that nobody who had chanced to hide inside the massive basilica could see what was happening. The officials and the doctors began an examination of the Pope's body, behind the screens.

The examination lasted one and a half hours. The press demanded to know whether this had been a belated autopsy, but the Vatican announced that it had been a routine examination, lasting only twenty minutes, by the morticians and a professor of medicine to check on the state of preservation of the body.

But neither the morticians nor the professor were even present.

11

Rome, May 1980

He was probably the most popular man in the world when they tried to murder him.

There were thousands of people in Saint Peter's Square to attend the papal audience in front of the basilica. At about five pm Pope John Paul II appeared in his popemobile and a roar went up from the crowd. He stood in his vehicle, beaming, dressed in white, his arms outstretched, waving and leaning out to touch people as he rode slowly between them. Then suddenly the shocking shots rang out.

They were fired from seven feet away. Two bullets struck Pope John Paul II in the abdomen, three more grazed him. He clutched himself and lurched, then he fell back into the arms of his private secretary. There was pandemonium. The screams from the crowd, the shock, the horror, the surging. A young man was trying to race away, dodging and shoving, but within moments outraged people overwhelmed him.

He was a Turk. His name was Mehmet Ali Agca, and he claimed he had been hired by the Bulgarian secret service to assassinate the Pope.

Falkland Islands, 1982

It was bitterly cold. The windswept South Atlantic was icy. On the archipelago of hard, bleak islands the Royal Marines were outfighting the Argentinian soldiers who had invaded the far-flung British colony. But it was in the skies that the outcome of this war could be determined, since the British forces were over seven thousand miles from home and their troop ships and lines of supply were very vulnerable to aerial attack.

The fighter plane of the Argentinian Air Force came screaming out of the bleak west, and suspended under its wings were deadly exocet missiles. Out on the black ocean the British warship steamed towards the rocky beaches. When the Argentinian aircraft was still miles away from the ship the pilot pressed the button and the exocet's rocket fired, and it unleashed itself.

The rocket went streaking over the sea, its electronic equipment unerringly telling it where to go, homing in on the man'o'war. On board the British warship they hardly knew what hit them.

It hit them with a mighty blinding crash that rent through the ship, steel and machinery flying midst flesh and blood and bone, and within minutes the ship was engulfed in terrible fire and killer smoke, and men were jumping into the freezing sea to escape the flames.

London, 18th June 1982

It was before dawn when they found him.

The man hung from the ironwork of Blackfriars Bridge, his arms limp by his side, the rope gouging into his neck. He was podgy and smallish, with a bristling black moustache and black, thinning hair. His eyes were bulging, and he was very dead. The police hauled him up, and when they searched through his well-cut suit, they found ten kilos of bricks in his pockets, and over fifteen thousand dollars in cash.

His name was Roberto Calvi. He had a forged passport, and he had recently been convicted of serious currency offences in Italy. He was the president of Banco Ambrosiana, financial adviser to the Vatican Bank, and he was called 'God's Banker'.

Grenada, Caribbean, October 1983

There were still some pockets of resistance in the jungled mountains, but the island was quiet for the first time since the war began. There was a curfew.

On the runway, an aeroplane stood ready to fly the bodies of soldiers back to America for burial. In the mortuary the coffins stood in rows, labelled, ready to go. In the dispensary, Medical Corporal Smythe was drinking Coca-Cola and surgical alcohol. His portable radio was on, but he was drunk and hardly interested in it; but then he heard something that made him pay attention:

'It has been officially announced by the Pentagon that the number of American servicemen killed in the recent invasion of Grenada is only eighteen. Their bodies are being flown home from Grenada tonight . . .'

13

Corporal Smythe wondered if he had heard right.

Eighteen? . . . But he *knew* there were only seventeen! He had laid the poor bastards out.

Corporal Smythe felt a flash of self-importance. He was in the news – they were talking about *his* job! . . . Millions of people across the world were being misinformed, and only *he* knew the Pentagon was wrong! He wanted to tell people. And he couldn't. Then frustration turned to indignation – the goddam Pentagon had made a boo-boo . . .

Corporal Smythe sat there, then he got up aggressively. He opened the dispensary door, and started down the corridor.

He came to the mortuary door, and unlocked it.

There were the coffins, in three silent rows. Corporal Smythe pointed at the first one, and started to count.

He had only counted half when he realized that the radio had been right: there were *six* coffins in each row!

He stared. He counted again. *Six* times three makes eighteen . . .

Corporal Smythe stood there, astonished. Where had the other one come from?

He walked indignantly to the first coffin. He peered at the typewritten details fixed onto the lid.

He went down the row, reading each label. He remembered each name. Halfway down the second row he stopped.

This label he certainly did not remember . . . This label he was absolutely sure he had not typed!

Name: Steven M. Jackson
Sergeant, Delta Force . . .

Corporal Smythe was astonished.

Who had put another body in his mortuary without telling him?

If he had not been drinking surgical alcohol, perhaps Corporal Smythe might not have been so indignant; perhaps, but for the surgical alcohol, he might not have found it extraordinary that at the end of a war, in the middle of the night, another body was found and encoffined without anybody waking him to tell him; perhaps, but for the surgical alcohol, he might not have been so aggressively disappointed to find out that he was not in the news after all; but Corporal Smythe began to unscrew the coffin lid.

He stared down into the open coffin.

There was no corpse in the coffin. No Sergeant Jackson. Only sea sand.

Part One

1

The sun shone bright and the sea was like glass.

A launch lay at anchor near a coral reef off the Caribbean island of Grenada. A man sat on the after deck, in swimming trunks, drinking a bottle of beer. Near him lay an airtank, goggles and flippers. His name was Max Hapsburg, and he was half German with big blue eyes that were very intelligent, but his dark good looks came from his Greek mother. He was about thirty-eight, and he was known to most big bankers of the world.

He was alone on his boat at the moment. His guests and his wife were somewhere along the reef, under the water.

Anna Hapsburg did not know where the others were. She had not seen them for almost half an hour.

She swam slowly along the magnificent coral reef, fifteen feet below the surface. The sunshine shafted down onto the multitude of beautiful shapes, onto growths and flowers and animals all the colours of the rainbow: the kaleidoscope rambled, rugged and smooth, sparkling and dark, with bays and grottos, going on and on, fading into mistiness. Anna loved the reefs. She swam slowly in her underwater wonder-world, her long golden legs gently flipping, her long blonde hair streaming silkily behind her.

When she was about two hundred yards from the boat, she saw the sharks.

There were two. They were indistinct, to her right, on the surface. Her heart missed a beat and her stomach contracted; she stared at them a terrified, heart-pounding moment, then she frantically turned for the boat.

She swam desperately, resisting her screaming instinct to thrash her legs. She swam and she swam, her heart knocking, her eyes wide: she glanced back frantically, and she could not see them any more, and that was worse: she swam and swam and swam for what seemed an eternity; then she saw the keel of the launch ahead, and it seemed the sweetest sight she had ever seen. She looked back desperately over her shoulder again; then the keel was coming up, the swimming ladder gleaming. She rose, arms upstretched, and she grabbed the ladder and broke surface and she began to scramble up. She spat out the mouthpiece and gasped: '*Sharks* . . .'

Max got to his feet. '*Where?*'

She pointed behind her. Max saw the fins on the surface. He snapped: 'Have you warned the others?'

She was halfway out of the water.

'No . . .'

'Go and warn them! I'll follow.' He snatched up his flippers.

She stared at him, horrified, her hair plastered to her head. *But oh God yes of course they had to warn the others* . . . She clung to the ladder a terrified moment more, then she crossed herself and rammed the airhose back into her mouth, and she sank, with dread, back into the water.

She swam back the way she had come. And her fear was the purest she had ever known.

She did not see the sharks on the way back. Within two hundred yards she saw Bill and Janet Nicols. She signalled to them desperately, *Shark* . . . She turned back towards the boat.

The keel came into view again. They swam and they swam, hearts pounding. Anna made for the swimming ladder and grabbed it, and heaved. She scrambled up onto the sun-beaten deck. Janet came up the ladder frantically behind her. Anna grabbed her hand and heaved her onto the deck. Bill came scrambling up after her.

'Where's Max?' Anna swept her eyes over the sea.

'Here I am . . .'

Anna spun around. Max Hapsburg was coming out of the saloon, a grin all over his handsome face. 'Anyone for tennis?'

She looked at him incredulously, and he burst out laughing.

'They were dolphins! *Dolphins* . . .'

She was absolutely shocked.

Max laughed. '*You should have seen the look on your face – but any fool could have seen they were dolphins* . . .'

She screamed: '*You beast!*'

She ripped her goggles off her head and hurled them at him:
'*You beast –!*'

2

It was five years since Jack Morgan had seen Anna Hapsburg.
But he still dreamt of her often; and they were always intense
and beautiful dreams, and his heart sang because he was with
her again at last; and when he woke up he was filled with
yearning. He tried to go back to sleep so he could be with her
again, but he could not, and she was gone.

Only three months they had had together. In those lovely
days her name was Anna Valentine, and she was in her final year
at Exeter University; he was a young lieutenant-commander
in the Royal Navy on ninety days study-leave at the same
university. She lived in a women's residence on the campus;
he had digs nearby in town, a bedsitter with a gasring.
'We have not yet met,' he had said on the telephone, 'but
I'm the ardent admirer who sent you those flowers this
morning.'

'Oh, yes . . . Well, thank you, Mr Morgan, they're lovely
roses and I'm very flattered,' she had replied, 'but as it happens
I am engaged to be married.'

This was terrible news. '*Married? When?*'

'At the end of this term, Mr Morgan.'

'This is very depressing news, Miss Valentine. But where is
this painfully fortunate man?'

'In Grenada. That's a small island in the Caribbean, you
mightn't have heard of it.'

Relief. 'Certainly. A spice island. You grow nutmeg.'

'Correct! Most people think it's a city in Spain.'

'So did I, but when I heard you speak at the Debating Society
last night, I made enquiries about you, then looked up Grenada
in the *Encyclopaedia Britannica*, so I would impress you
over dinner. I know all about Grenada, Gross National Pro-
duct, per capita income, birth rate, electricity problems, the
works.'

She smiled. 'I am impressed, Mr Morgan. But I'm afraid dinner together wouldn't be appropriate, because I'm getting married in three months' time.'

'On the contrary, all the more urgency about this dinner, Miss Valentine. Because I'm going back to sea in three months' time and I think it highly important that we have the opportunity to consider each other before then, because it's a crystal-clear case of love at first sight, Miss Valentine. I've never resorted to the *Encyclopaedia Britannica* and a florist in the same context before . . .'

And, oh, why, *why* had they not done it? *Why*, after three glorious months of love and laughter and absolute happiness, that made them want to dance in the streets, that made the whole world seem a bowl of cherries and terribly amusing, happiness that made the whole world laugh with them, and envy them, happiness that gave them daydreams in the middle of lectures, that gave them the giggles every night as he smuggled her up to his digs past his landlady (House Rules: No Visitors of Opposite Gender, No Drink, No Cooking for Visitors, No Curries, No Music, No Pets, No Confabulations, By Order, Mrs Garvey), happiness that made them make love all night when they should have been cramming for final examinations, the happiness of talking talking talking about everything under the sun, and the rapture, *rapture*, of each other's bodies – oh why, at the end of those three glorious months, when the examinations had somehow been written and passed (though not with the flying colours expected of both of them), *why* had they not just walked into the nearest registry office and married and lived joyously ever after? – Oh how different the world would have been.

But, they had not. Because she was a Catholic and she wanted a proper church wedding, with her family around her. So they had flown back to Grenada for their last few days together, to introduce him to her parents and tell them that their darling daughter was going to live in darkest England for the rest of her life. They were going to be married on his next leave, four months hence. Then he had gone back to sea in his goddam submarine.

He had never seen her again.

It was that shark story that had finally made up his mind to go back to Grenada, after five long years. Janet Nicols had looked him up on her last visit to England, and the tale had come out.

So now here he sat in a dark aeroplane, staring out of the window at the moonlight, at long last doing what he had so often dreamt of doing, flying across the Atlantic to try to see the woman he had once loved so madly. He had no idea what was going to happen. He had not told anybody he was coming, not even Janet Nicols. He did not know if he would set eyes on Anna, even from a distance. Maybe she would refuse to see him. And now that he was actually doing it at last, fulfilling his dream, he was not even sure what he wanted to happen. Did he really still love her so madly? Or was she just a dream? And if so, was it not best that he just keep her as that, his lovely dream-girl? When you're lying in your lonely bunk in your submarine, or sitting in your lonely farmhouse drinking whisky in front of the fire, home is the sailor home from the sea but the home is empty, it is easy to be sure that you still love her with all your heart, you are even glad to be sad, thinking of what might have been – but now that he had finally made up his mind to go, he was not so sure. It was unreal. He was very excited, but wasn't all this foolishness? What the hell are you doing? he asked himself many times that long night – why are you flying halfway round the world just for the chance of seeing, of only glimpsing maybe, the woman who once loved you and left you and married another man? What right have you got to try to interfere with her marriage now? What makes you think you've got a chance? The shark story? Because Janet Nicols cautiously admitted, under cross-examination, that Anna's marriage to Max had not been going well? But had Janet said that Anna ever spoke of him? No. Indeed, Janet had said that Anna would never leave Max because she was a devout Catholic, marriage is for better or worse . . . What makes you think she'll even *want* to see you? So, what foolishness is this? – and now that you are actually on this aeroplane at last, are you even sure you really still love her? Don't you really prefer to be free to be glad to be sad? . . . Don't you even resent her, for breaking your heart? . . .

Many times in that long, unreal night it was like that. But then, a little later, it was different again. Because you had another dream about her, he said. Because she came to you again, and she was beautiful and smiling, and you felt her whole loveliness pressed against you again, and you smelt her scent and you looked into her lovely eyes and oh God yes you still loved her, and oh yes she still loved you, and when you woke up your heart was breaking and you desperately tried to go back to sleep, to be with her again. And for days afterwards you could not stop thinking about her, and there was such yearning . . .

And then the sun came up, glorious and red and gold, and the Caribbean was born below him, the turquoise waters, and the reefs, and the white beaches, and the palms, and he glimpsed again the golden girl; this was *her* part of the world, where *she* lived, he glimpsed her hair swirling across her laughing face as she ran across the white sands into his arms, he felt her warm-cool body against him, and he knew that he did still love her, that she was in his blood. He was very excited when the plane began its descent and the island of Grenada came up out of the sea, mauve and brooding in the sun, the blue sea fading to turquoise around it; and his heart was beating deliciously, and he knew he still loved her.

3

There had been a revolution here since his last visit, a coup by the New Jewel Movement; there were some tattered posters proclaiming its glory and he saw Cuban soldiers around Pearls airfield, but otherwise it was just like he remembered: the sun shining big and bright, the sky so blue; everything so green, the air fragrant with spices: it was a beautiful day to be doing the wonderful thing he had yearned to do for so long. He was grinning inside with excitement as he strode into the hot airport building, he wanted to smile at everybody, and he loved every black face. He rented a car. It seemed he remembered everything, and he loved every mile of the road into town. *This was her island in the sun* . . . He was grinning when he turned his car into the gates of the Victoria Hotel.

It was somewhat run-down, and he did not remember it like that, but he did not care. He checked in, carried his bag to his room. It was unreal, and beautifully real. The gardens out there beyond his balcony, the bar, palms, the beach beyond, the sparkling sea. *Her sea.* He showered, and shaved carefully. He looked at his face in the mirror. How much change would she see? There were no grey hairs yet – and most of his colleagues had plenty of those. He brushed his teeth thoroughly. Then he did not know what to do with himself.

It was only breakfast time, too early to do anything yet. He went down to the empty bar in the garden. It was sultry-quiet. He ordered a cold beer, and just gave himself up to the delicious excitement of waiting.

He had drunk half of the beer when a voice behind him said: 'Hullo, Jack.'

He turned, taken by surprise. '*Janet Nicol* . . .'

He stood up. He took her hands, grinning, and kissed her cheek. 'What a coincidence! I was going to contact you . . .'

She said, 'Not a coincidence at all. I've known for three days that you were coming back to Grenada.'

She sat beside him, drinking fruit juice. She said: 'I work for British West Indies Airways, remember. BWIA has strict instructions to report if ever a Jack Morgan books a seat to our fair island.'

He was astonished. 'Good God . . .'

She said: 'Max is extremely jealous, Jack. And one of his many sidelines is that he's a director of BWIA. And the immigration department is under instructions to report the arrival of any Mr Morgans.'

'Good God! Does he run the Post Office as well?'

Janet did not smile. 'Grenada is a small island. And Max has a lot of clout.' She added significantly: 'With the police, included.' Before he could ask what the hell that meant she went on soberly: 'And he's not just a big fish in a small Caribbean pond.' She raised her eyebrows. 'And big fish can bite.'

'Are you saying that he'd use the *police*?'

'He might.'

Morgan said incredulously: 'For what bloody offence? . . .'

She said, 'I don't know what he'd do. But your offence is that you're in love with his wife.'

'I haven't seen Anna for five years!'

'And they haven't stopped having arguments about you for five years.'

He was amazed. 'Arguments?'

Janet said, 'Hell-fire rows. Max is obsessed with the belief that Anna is still in love with you.'

Morgan wanted to throw his arms wide to the sky in joy. 'And? Is she?'

She ignored the question. 'He even says that you have lovers' trysts every time she goes to New York and London.'

He wanted to throw back his head and laugh, because she loved him. '*Would that we had* . . .'

Janet said: 'That's why he did that shark hoax. To punish her.' She looked at him: 'So don't you think you should stay away from the island?'

Morgan put his hands on his chest.

'I should stay away from the island because Max . . . ?' He shook his head. 'Look, in five years I haven't so much as sent her a Christmas card. And I wouldn't be here now, if you hadn't looked me up and told me how he punishes her with shark hoaxes.' He shook his head in wonder. 'Why doesn't he put detectives onto her and find out the truth?'

She said: 'Oh, he's done that. And had detectives following you.'

He was incredulous. 'I don't believe it.'

Janet said, 'You have a grey Ford station-wagon. Three years ago you bought a farmhouse outside Plymouth. You've had a number of girlfriends but the last one I heard of was a blonde bombshell called Ingrid something.' She raised her eyebrows.

He was amazed. 'Then he knows I've been at sea every time she came to England.'

She said, 'No, you spent a year ashore. With the Special Boat Service.'

Morgan was astonished. The Special Boat Service is a very secretive branch of the Royal Navy. 'He must be out of his mind to go to such lengths.'

'Is he?' She gave a little smile. 'Tell me – why have you come back to the island?' Before he could answer, she said: 'After all these years, you come to take his wife away from him.'

His heart turned over like a porpoise.

'I've come to lay a ghost,' he said.

Janet nodded at the sea.

'So he's not out of his mind, is he? He loves her, you see. Obsessed with her, if you like.' She turned to him. 'Like you are. And so he's obsessed with the notion that she's still in love with you.'

He felt his pulse flutter. 'And? Is she?'

Janet turned back to the sea.

'He says she dreams about you.'

Morgan stared at her. *Dreams* . . . And he felt joy.

'How would he know what she dreams?'

'She speaks your name.'

Morgan slumped against the bar happily. Janet went on: 'So you should go away and not cause any more trouble and pain, Jack.'

'Trouble? I haven't uttered a murmur since that awful day she sent me a telegram saying she was marrying Max.'

'You don't know what it was like for her to send you that telegram . . . You don't know the agony of indecision she went through.' Janet sighed, and shook her head. 'The pressure upon her – the last-minute pressure from friends and family alike to think again, was enormous.' She turned to him earnestly. 'She will never leave Max. She believes she's made her bed and must lie in it. So all you can do is cause emotional confusion. And endless trouble.'

Oh God, he was so happy.

'And if I don't leave, what is Max going to do? Burst in here with the police?'

She shook her head. 'He's not even here at the moment – he's in New York. But don't underestimate him.' She paused. 'You must leave.'

He squeezed her hand. 'Is that the message she sent me?'

She said, 'She's not going to see you, Jack.'

He did not believe that. 'But her message?'

She hesitated, then she said, reluctantly: '"Tell him I love him. And goodbye."'

He wanted to shout for joy. *I love him* . . . Janet sighed, as if she regretted telling him. 'And now I must go.'

He was deliciously happy.

'Will you give Anna a message from me?'

Janet waited, noncommittal.

'Tell her that I'm not leaving until I've seen her.'

4

Oh yes, he was in love.

It seemed the longest day of his life, and the happiest. He thought through what Janet had said, and he tried to caution himself, against causing pain, against being optimistic, but he did not quite make it. He dared not leave the hotel, he dared not sleep off his jet-lag, in case she came and went while he was asleep. He sat alone at the crowded bar in the garden, slowly drinking beer, watching the hotel lobby, just feeling the excitement, of her, of being back here where she lived. Finally the sun went down, blazing red and gold through the palms; after dinner he could resist it no longer. He got into his rented car. He drove through Saint George's, out onto the winding coastal road, through the heavy tropical foliage, past the grand houses; then he came to hers, on the seashore. He had never seen it before, but he knew the address from the telephone directory. He drove slowly past it. He stopped two hundred yards beyond. He walked down onto the beach.

The big house was across a little bay. There were lights on, twinkling between the trees. *Her* house. He stood, looking at it. Imagining her inside it, imagining what she was thinking and feeling; she knew that he was here, he *knew* what she was feeling, and with all his happiness and his yearning he willed her and willed her to come to him tomorrow. He sat on the dark beach for over an hour, just watching her house, imagining her, remembering her. Finally he drove back to the hotel, and went to bed, very tired but too happy to go to sleep easily.

That first night, five long years ago, their dinners had gone cold whilst they talked and laughed and talked. She had said:

'Saint Thomas Aquinas will prove it to you, Jack Morgan,

by pure Aristotelian logic, even if he cannot prove by logic what *kind* of God He is – read his *Summa in Theologica*. He gives five proofs of God's existence, though it's his third argument I like best, his Actuality–Potentiality proof of a Prime or Un-moved Mover. "And this all men call God." No intelligent man could read that book and remain an agnostic, Jack . . .'

And when the floorshow came on, a troupe of limbo dancers from Jamaica, she had been unable to resist it when the pole was only twenty inches above the floor and she had kicked her shoes off and gone dancing under it, to roars of applause, her long blonde hair sweeping the floor, her arms upstretched, her jerking feet wide apart, a grin all over her lovely face; and when she had come back to the table, flushed and laughing, he had known with absolute certainty that he was going to marry this marvellous girl; he had taken her hand, and what he wanted to say with all his heart was 'Let's check into this hotel and make love', but instead he said:

'Tomorrow, you're coming on a picnic, Ms Valentine, and reading Saint Thomas Aquinas to me, it's this Actuality–Potentiality theory I'm really wild about . . .'

'Oh? What about my lectures, Jack Morgan?'

'What about my immortal soul, Ms Valentine?'

She had agreed to try to save his soul, though not to kiss him goodnight (nor had he tried too hard, in order to impress her), but he had driven back to his digs on air, wanting to whoop and holler and toot his horn, and he had blown Mrs Garvey a big kiss instead when she came out complaining about him disturbing the house by coming in late. *'Mrs Garvey, be joyful, tomorrow I'm taking the most wonderful girl in the world on a picnic to read* Summa in Theologica! . . .'

'What about your lectures, Lieutenant-Commander?'

'What about my immortal soul, Mrs Garvey? – What about my immortal soul? . . .'

And what a picnic it was! He bought *Summa in Theologica* as soon as the shops opened and he swotted up Saint Thomas' third proof while the delicatessen packed up the hamper. It was an absolutely beautiful spring day for saving his soul! The sun shone bright and the birds sang and the bees buzzed and butterflies fluttered and he sang her 'The Surrey with the Fringe

29

on Top' as he tootled her down the Cornish lanes in his beat-up old Volkswagen, absolutely on top of the world. And he knew he was going to live deliriously happily ever after with this wonderful girl, and it was a wonderful feeling to be totally self-confident and very, very amusing. He spread their blanket on the soft grass by the stream and popped the champagne, and the cork flew and went dancing away over the sparkling rapids and he said:

'That's how our life's going to be, Anna Valentine!'

And he took her in his arms and toppled her over onto the blanket, and she grinned up at him:

'What about your immortal soul, Jack Morgan? That's what I'm bunking lectures for . . .'

'Ms Valentine, I've got a complete arm-lock already on the Third Proof and I know that good Saint Thomas would approve entirely of my honourable intentions towards you . . .'

And she had laughed up at him, and let him kiss her. But she had not made love to him. They really *did* read *Summa in Theologica*. While the birds sang and the bees buzzed and the stream twinkled, and the champagne tasted like nectar.

She had not made love to him for five long, deliciously nerve-racked days, five more days of walking on air, of singing in the rain, of *Summa in Theologica* and everything from Karl Marx and Adam Smith to the Beatles and Beethoven, from P. G. Wodehouse to Franz Kafka, five more delightfully anguished days of lovely Cornwall country pubs, bangers and mash and cream teas, of Cornish moors and coves and beaches, long tracks along the sand, five more days of delicious frustration and almost no lectures at all; on the sixth day he had fetched her at her residence, and she had solemnly announced:

'I wrote to Max this morning. I've told him.'

It was the most important moment in his life, the happiest and the most solemn. He had taken her hand, and turned and led her silently down the steps to his old car. They drove in silence through the town. He parked the car, and opened the door for her. They walked hand in hand, by unspoken agreement, into the hotel. His hand was shaking as he signed the register. They rode up in the elevator wordlessly. Hand in hand, down the corridor. Room 201.

He closed the door, and leant back against it. They looked at each other. They were both very nervous. Then he took her in his arms, and crushed her against him, and his hands were trembling as he undressed her. They toppled wordlessly onto the bed, and, and, oh, the bliss of each other's bodies at last.

He was awake before dawn. For a few moments, at his lowest ebb; Janet's words flashed through his mind, and he tried to caution himself; then he was properly awake and he knew that she was awake too, lying in this same pre-dawn unreality. He got up and pulled on his swimming trunks. He went down onto the beach, and he started to run. To run, to run, to appease his yearning in the humid dawn, sweating out the booze and cigarettes of yesterday, with each rasp of his breath just thinking of her, thinking of her. When he had run two miles he turned into the sea, splashing and pounding, and he plunged. He swam and he swam underwater until his lungs were bursting, then he broke surface with a gushing gasp. And he flung his arms full wide to the horizon where she lived, and he bellowed to the early morning:
'*Come today my love . . .*'

She came in the middle of the day.

He was sitting at the bar, in the dappled shade, where he could see the lobby. He saw her suddenly appear in the front door, a splash of blonde hair, her willowy silhouette against the outside light, and his heart turned over and all his self-caution was forgotten. He stood up; she walked through the lobby, out onto the verandah, and she took his breath away. She stood for a moment at the top step, tall and blonde and elegant, frowning slightly in the sunlight, looking about the shadowed garden with half a smile of expectation on her mouth; then she saw him striding towards her out of the shadows, and her lovely face broke into her dazzling Anna smile, and she started down the steps.

He strode towards her, his heart pounding, and there was nothing else in the world but her coming towards him, smiling. Then his hands took hers, and then her face was next to his, for a fleeting moment their bodies touching as he kissed her cheek, and he got the delicious scent of her, and in that instant

31

he felt all the passion of five long years. Then they were standing back from each other a laughy, shaky: *'Hullo'* – she grinned, *'– Hullo . . .'*

Afterwards, when he would try to remember the details, it was all confused, like a dream; he would remember just wanting to crush her in his arms, and her backing off, laughing, saying, 'We better sit down, but I can only stay a moment . . .' which was the most ridiculous statement in the world, because no way was this wonderful thing going to be stopped. He remembered taking her hand and leading her back up the steps into the hotel, laughy and shaky and saying God knows what, and she let him lead her through the lobby, up the staircase, and it did not occur to him that he was compromising her, they were just naturally hurrying away together to a private place to be alone with their excitement; then they were inside his room, and they just stood a moment, looking at each other, grinning, and it seemed the happiest thing in the world, he could hardly believe that this was happening at last, and she was more beautiful than he remembered her: she grinned: 'I can hardly believe this . . .'

'Nor can I . . .'

And he took her in his arms, and she put her arms tight around his neck, and they kissed each other, mouths crushed together, and oh, God, God the sweet taste of her again, the glorious feel of her body against him again, the warmth, and she clawed him tight and cried: 'Oh why didn't you come back five years ago?' – and he did not care about any of that, all he cared about was now, *now*, and his hand went joyfully to her breast and, oh, the wonderful feel of her, and she kissed him fiercely and then broke the embrace.

She backed out of his arms, her hair awry, her face smouldering. He stepped after her, recklessly happy, to take her in his arms again, possess her, to carry her off and she held up her hand to stop him. 'I didn't mean this to happen . . .'

She turned away and ran her fingers through her hair. 'Wow . . .' she breathed, 'Oh boy . . .' She walked to the window shakily; then she turned to him. She said ardently:

'Of course I want to make love to you! With all my heart! But I'm not going to . . . I came to tell you . . .' She stopped, then shook her head. 'I came to see you – I had to just *see* you again. And then tell you that you had to go away . . .'

He was deliciously happy. 'You love me.'

She tried to say it seriously, but she could not help grinning. '*Do* I? Or am I only in love with that magic *memory* of you – those wonderful days? . . .'

'You love me.'

She closed her eyes. 'I'm *married*, Jack. For better or worse . . .'

He said relentlessly, 'The magic is still there.'

She ran her hand through her hair again and turned away.

'And I want to keep it as magic, Jack. To be cherished . . .' She turned back to him, then held out her hand to him: 'Come,' she appealed. 'Walk with me. Openly, for all the world to see. Along the beach, in the sunshine. And tell me all about your wonderful life. *Talk* to me . . . Let me *feast* upon your story. So I can take it away with me . . .'

He held out a happy finger at her: 'No more *Summa in Theologica!* . . .'

They burst out laughing. It seemed the most tragically hilarious thing to say.

5

And oh he was in love!

They walked out into the dappled sunshine of the garden, walking on air, out onto the long white beach, oh so happy. He wanted to remember every detail, each step beside her, each glance, each laugh, each word; they talked constantly, laughy, seriously, urgently, and he wanted to throw his arms wide to the sky and rejoice – *He was here, back in paradise, and she was with him, just like in the dreams!* And he knew with absolute certainty that it was nonsense that he was never going to see her again – *she was his and this was just the beginning!* And he wanted to fling his arms around her and laugh into her beautiful face that this business of her Catholic vows was absolute nonsense because she was going to be married to him every day for the rest of her beautiful life! She said, pacing along beside him, her hands locked behind her back:

'I went to one of the best psychiatrists in New York. I said to him: I only want to ask you one question: "What does it mean when you keep dreaming repeatedly about one man?" And he said to me: "Tell me about him?"' She shot him a laughing glance. 'So I told him. And he said: "Well, clear as day, you're in love with this paragon of virtue. Describe these dreams," he said. So I did. And do you know what he said?'

'What?' He was grinning.

'He said: Correction: You don't love this man – you're *obsessed* by him!' She flung her arms wide: '*Obsessed!*'

And Morgan laughed and made to grab her and she skipped aside: 'And I said, "So what the hell does one do about such an obsession, Doctor?"' She was walking backwards in front of him: 'He said: "It depends on how you look at it, Mrs Hapsburg . . . To sensible people it is just a romantic memory which they get into perspective . . ."'

And he tried to grab her again. 'But to other lucky people?'

'"To other *un*lucky people – *it seems better than real life!* Because it is unspoilt by life. But they're unlucky because dreams never come true and if they're not careful it can screw up their lives" –'

'But ours are going to come true!'

She walked backwards in front of him, the laughter suddenly gone out of her eyes.

'No, darling Jack. Please believe me. But, yes, we *are* lucky, because we can cherish our dreams – they will stay with us forever . . .'

And he wanted to laugh and holler, '*Bullshit, Anna Valentine! . . .*'

She shook her head firmly as she paced beside him.

'Please don't ask me that. I want to talk about *you*.'

He said, 'I have a right to know.'

'Do you? For better or worse, Jack. That's what the preacher-man said.'

He knew it was nonsense. 'You also made a vow to me.'

'Yes, I did. And I'm truly sorry.'

34

'Because you still love me,' he said.

She looked at the horizon, her hands clasped behind her back. 'You are entitled only to know what happened five years ago.'

This was very important information but he cared about Now, not five years ago. She breathed deep and said:

'I was a coward . . .' She paced, formulating it. 'You were so clever. So well-read, and . . . *learned*. And so damn . . . *funny*. You had done so much with your life. And we had such an intense, crazy time together. It seemed as if I had packed everything I had ever learned, and felt, into those three glorious months. All my worldly experience had been paraded and brought into service. And so when you were gone back to sea, and all the chips were down, and the pressure was mounting . . . I became afraid that when you came back you'd find that you'd burnt me out. That I had nothing new to offer you – that I wasn't the soulmate you'd thought I was . . . And then you wouldn't love me any more.'

Morgan was truly amazed. And he did not believe her. She was one of the strongest-willed persons he had known. And she had spoken as if rehearsed. And as for him being more learned than her – they had had countless discussions about everything under the sun.

'Bullshit, Anna.'

She said resolutely: 'And Max didn't demand anything like that from me, you see. And I had known him for years – I was *safe* with Max. He's very clever but he was no intellectual.'

He did not believe for one moment that she would have married Max or anybody for those reasons. Something else had happened. 'Nor was I an intellectual.'

She insisted, 'You *were*. Master of Science. Only twenty-nine years old and already second-in-command of one of Her Majesty's submarines! Oh, that was a pretty tough act for poor Max to follow.' She half-laughed. 'And when I wrote and told him I was in love with you, he had the nerve to write back and say that it would not last because submariners are notoriously *dull* people.'

He knew she was trying to get away from the question. 'Well, maybe he was right.'

'*Dull?* God, anything but dull! You were the funniest man

35

alive! You made me laugh! And all that derring-do submarine stuff?' She smiled, and her eyes smarted a moment. 'Even Dad slapped Max down on that one. Dad didn't want me to marry you, either, but he said to Max: "I'll have you know that every submariner is an extremely likeable and absolutely first-class fella! He *has* to be – you can't afford to have a dislikeable man on a dangerous job like that!"'

He laughed. He knew that she had not told him the truth, that something else had happened to stop her marrying him, but right now he did not care. He was happy.

She sat on the rocks, hugging her knees, her smoky-blue eyes feasting on him. He said:

'That was the first thing you ever asked me. Between limbo dances and morbid interest in my soul. You see, all your crew are experts at their different jobs. And you rely on them completely, and you do your own job. It's a matter of complete mutual trust.'

She asked: 'Are you still a Christian, Jack?'

He smiled. 'Of sorts. Thanks to you and Saint Thomas. In that order.'

She smiled. 'But a Catholic?'

'Once a Catholic, always a Catholic, you can't expect too much of us. I still live in fear secretly. It's the only way I know how.'

'Do you pray?'

'I have a crack at it once a day.' He added: 'I don't think I sound very convincing.'

She grinned. 'But why do you live in secret fear?'

'The Jesuits say, Give me a child till age seven, and you've got him for life.'

'But you weren't brought up by Jesuits.'

'My father was.'

She smiled and got back to her original question. 'But now that you're the commander of the submarine, all that responsibility for this multi-multi-million-pound machine. So huge, in that dark, hostile environment – sailing *blind* . . . How do you feel?'

He said: 'I still rely completely on my crew. And our equipment is so very sophisticated. I know exactly where we are. I know the depth to the ocean bed, my charts and radar tell me what obstacles lie ahead, the contours of the sea bed, even if there's a shoal of fish. Our nuclear fuel and oxygen will keep us going for months. And it's always calm down there, even if there're mountainous waves on the surface. It's really very safe.'

She sighed, unconvinced. 'And what about the Special Boat Service you're in?'

He was surprised again that she knew.

'I was never *in* the Special Boat Service. Max's detective got that one wrong. The Special Boat boys are far too hot-shot for me. They're the crack underwater warriors, Navy's equivalent to the SAS. But they sometimes work in conjunction with submarines, and a couple of years ago I was made Submarine Liaison Officer for a year, at Poole, where the Special Boat Service has its headquarters. Submarine Liaison Officer is a boring desk job, nothing to do most of the time. So I asked if I could join in some of the training the Special Boat boys do, for the hell of it. My admiral thought it was a good idea. But I wasn't much good. I'm a submariner, not a commando.'

She looked unconvinced. 'What did you learn?'

'Oh, some parachuting. Water jumps. Then some ground jumps. Then a few night jumps.' He shook his head. 'I got my little certificates, but I didn't like it, I'm scared of heights.'

She smiled. 'Then what?'

'Then I went back to Lympstone, where I'd done my basic training years ago. I joined in some commando courses with the SBS boys. Assault courses. Unarmed combat. Weaponry. That was good fun.'

'Then what?'

'That's it. I applied to learn to fly, but they thought that was a bit extravagant for a submariner. So I tried to take my private pilot's licence, at my own expense. I got halfway through, but had to go back to sea before I finished.'

'What a pity. Will you finish it?'

'Yes, but only because I don't like leaving jobs half-done. I don't like flying.'

'Oh, I love it. I've got my private pilot's licence, now.'

He was impressed. 'Have you?'

'Max has a plane. A Cessna. I decided to do it, and it's great fun. However – what else did you learn?'

'That's it. My year ashore was up and I went back to my nice safe submarine.'

She smiled. 'Safe, huh? And what are your submarines doing for their living?'

'Defence patrols. Shadowing Russian fleets. And shadowing Russian submarines that are shadowing NATO fleets.'

'And isn't there a Russian submarine shadowing you?'

'Yes, but there's usually another of our submarines shadowing *him*.'

'And if there's a war you all bang torpedoes into each other?'

'Ah, war,' he said. 'Well, we're all afraid of war, that's why we're all shadowing each other, to prevent it.'

She said, 'Were you in the Falklands War?'

'Yes, my sub was down there.'

She sighed deeply. 'I thought you were. Was it you who sank the *Belgrano*?'

He grinned. 'No.'

'And? Were you afraid?'

'At times. It was the first time I'd gone to war, you see.' He added: 'Not that I saw much of it, from down there.'

She sighed deeply. 'Oh God, war . . . What a terrible way to die, deep under the hostile ocean, the water pouring in. At least in ordinary ships you have lifeboats.' She sighed again. 'You know, I've said a prayer for you every night for five years.'

'Have you? . . .' And oh, he was so happy, and he knew with absolute certainty that she was going to be his.

She walked beside him, her hands clasped behind her back.

'Very well. I'll try. What do you want to know?'

He said: 'Why did he put you through that ordeal with the dolphins?'

She paced. She did not want to talk about it.

'We'd had another row. He did it to punish me.'

'Jesus. What a terrible thing to do. What about?'

'Never mind.'

'You were very courageous.'

'Not really. I didn't have time to think, I just thought I had

38

to do it, to save the others. I was stupid. I should have realized he wouldn't send me back if they were sharks.'

'But he sent you back knowing you were terrified. And so? Have you forgiven him?'

She said: 'I understand him.'

'What is your understanding?'

She took a breath.

'In some ways he is insecure. In other ways he is a charming, mature, brilliant man. It is the insecure man who has the tantrums. Who sent me back into the water.'

'Has he done similar things to you?'

'Please, Jack. I'm only talking about the dolphin incident because Janet told you.'

He let it go, for the time being.

'And does Max love you?'

'Oh, yes. Of that I have no doubt.'

'Or just want to possess you?'

'Both. No doubt. But he certainly loves me, in his demanding way.' She added: 'He's always had everything his own way, you see. Complete success. School. Business. High-finance. Everything. You were the only one who ever stood in his way for long.'

'For long? Only for six months. Five years ago. Why is he still insecure?'

She said firmly: 'It's a long story, Jack. And I don't want to tell it.'

He frowned. 'Are you saying he's impotent?'

'He's certainly not that. But we haven't made love for years.'

He wanted to say *For God's sake, don't live like this any more! – come live with me!* 'And? Do you love him?'

'I married him for better or worse.'

He did not believe this determined Catholic loyalty. There was some other reason why she stayed with him. She said, getting away from the question:

'God, he's a clever man with money. I've never known him to lose on a deal. Before the revolution, the old government relied on him enormously. He could have been Minister of Finance if he'd wanted, despite his youth and white skin. But he saw the New Jewel revolution coming. He sold everything he owned in Grenada. And now the revolutionary government also relies on him. His know-how. Or the Prime Minister does, Maurice Bishop. And the banks rely on him. The overseas banks and the International Monetary Fund.'

'But how does he reconcile his wealth with being a socialist? He's a hot-shot capitalist.'

She smiled. 'Ah, but we socialists want *every*body to be wealthy – with the *people* owning the means of production.' She added, more seriously: 'He's not a socialist. But he's an economist. If the government wants to be socialist, he'll help them run their economy efficiently.' She added defensively, 'It's a perfectly moral attitude. The old government *was* corrupt. The revolution here is a *fait accompli*. He wants to stay here. He can help.'

Morgan said: 'There seems to be a big Cuban influence here. I saw them at the airport. What does Max think about that?'

'Russian influence too. They're building a big new airport.' She sighed. 'Max is a moderating influence. He's persuading the Prime Minister to mend some of his fences with America.'

He said: 'And you? You're still a socialist?'

She looked at the sand as she walked.

'Yes. Though I'm a bit more practical than when you knew me. I certainly don't like what this government has done – nor what the communists are doing worldwide. But, yes, I want to see the wealth spread down to the workers who create it. Not stay in the hands of the fat shareholders who pay miserable wages. And, as far as I can see, the only way to achieve that, in cases where capitalism is entrenched and unfair, is for the workers' government to take over and own the source of wealth.' She smiled sadly. 'We had many an argument about this at university, didn't we? So now can we talk about you? . . .'

The sun was getting low. They lay under the palms, a yard apart; she traced a pattern in the sand while he said:

'We were cruising happily up the Channel, back to Plymouth. We were going to dock before sunset. Your telegram was handed to me. And . . .' He shook his head, half-smiling: 'I couldn't believe it. I just *couldn't* believe it . . . I thought maybe it was some kind of bad practical joke from my mates ashore. Then I believed it – but I still didn't. I had to concentrate on my job, and I kept thinking I was still marrying you in three days' time.' He smiled, because it didn't matter now, everything was wonderful again now. 'Anyway, we slogged on up the Channel. It seemed the longest passage of my life. I was bursting to get off the boat and go charging up the jetty to leap on the next aeroplane to Grenada.'

She closed her eyes. 'Oh, why didn't you? . . .'

He was happy. 'Your telegram said: "Marrying Max tomorrow." It was dated the day before.'

Her eyes were moist. 'I didn't marry him until several days later . . . But you wouldn't have found me, anyway. I was in Las Vegas. He persuaded me to get the hell off the island. He was scared you'd show up. But . . .' She breathed deep: 'I couldn't marry him for days.' She shook her head. 'Oh, I was in such a mess. Each day he wanted to drag me off to one of those ghastly wedding chapels. But I *couldn't*, because I was still in a nightmare about you. Oh my, you don't know how many times I nearly jumped on a plane and went screaming over to England.'

He sighed. 'Why didn't you?'

'I was in a much worse way than you because I was the one who had made all the heavy-duty decisions! I had taken it unto myself to change the course of the universe – I had been through all that agony of decision to turn my back on my knight in shining armour! . . .' She laughed tearfully: 'You only had to *accept* the decision without pranging the submarine!'

Morgan grinned. She smiled wanly. 'I did kind of love Max. I was *in* love with you but I loved him. I had known him for *years*, he was part of the establishment. And he adored me. But you? . . . Oh my . . .' She lay back in the sand and smiled up at the sky. 'Lieutenant-Commander Jack Morgan, RN, who went down to the sea in ships. So handsome, so brave, so expert, so charming, so sexy, who made me laugh so much, who made me *think* so much – I was only so *in* love with you. And the pressure on me was enormous – from my family, and Max. "You hardly *know* him . . . You don't really know what he's *like* . . ." And I'd have to go and live in rainy England – they really rubbed that in. Leave this lovely island, my whole way of life, and be a Navy wife, alone half the time – you won't even know *where* he is because it's all so bloody secret, you

41

won't even be able to *write* to him because he's underwater, and you won't even get any letters . . . And, of course, they said, he's got no money.'

Morgan smiled. He believed this, but he knew that something else had happened too. But he was too happy to press her. 'They were right on that one.'

'Oh,' she said, 'what a mean little argument that was – and I told them so. Ah, they said, but you're accustomed to so much, this life here, your trips to Miami and New York and Caracas . . . I shouted, "He'll be a goddam admiral soon!"'

Morgan laughed. She smiled at him. 'Which is true. Oh, but it was an intense war that was waged against you. And it all slowly added up to a terrible doubt growing in my mind.' She took a deep breath. 'And you were thousands of miles away, underwater. I couldn't contact you, to get reassurance, just talk it out with you, explain my fears . . .'

He reached out and took her hand.

'Well, now I've come to you.'

She looked at him; then two tears welled over her eyelids. 'Far, far too late . . .'

He pulled her gently towards him; she watched his mouth as he whispered: 'It's never too late to be happy.'

And their mouths touched; and then crushed together; and, oh, the sweet taste and scent of her again, the joy, and he felt her tremble once, and then her arm went around his neck and she kissed him fiercely; then she bit his mouth and twisted out of his arms, and jumped up. She walked away, running her fingers through her hair.

He lay a moment, watching her, the lovely line of her, and oh, he loved her. Then he got up and followed her. They were a hundred yards from the hotel lights. He caught up with her and turned her towards him.

'Come away with me.'

She looked at him with absolute longing, rigid against him; she started to shake her head, then she closed her eyes and her body went soft against him and she crushed her mouth against his again. And she kissed him and kissed him, as if she wanted to bite him, and he felt the bliss well up, the utter joy, her strong softness and smoothness, her breasts and her belly and her loins pressed against him; then she broke the kiss, and

42

backed off, her face smouldering with emotion and her eyes full of tears.

'I'm going now . . . And I'm never coming back . . .'

He took a pace towards her and she stepped backwards. 'Never coming back!' She shook her head at him: '*Do you believe that?*'

He felt his eyes burn and he wanted to laugh. 'No.'

She cried: 'Never! Believe that! I cannot! I dare not! I'm still a coward, don't you see? Goodbye, darling Jack! I love you – and goodbye . . .'

She turned and walked away fast, up the path towards the road, her head up, and the tears running down her face.

He stood in the dusk and watched her; and his heart was singing. Because he knew she was coming back.

6

It was dark when he got back to the hotel. He was so happy he did not know what to do with himself. Gone, gone were the cautions he had given himself – *he was in love!* He went upstairs, to his room. Out onto his balcony. He filled his breast with balmy air and stretched out his arms to the night, and to her. Then there was a knock on his door.

He whirled around. He knew it was her. He strode to the door and flung it open joyfully.

He stared. Two black policemen stood there.

'You come with us, Mr Morgan.'

His heart was suddenly hammering. 'What on earth for?'

One of the policemen put his hand on his shoulder. 'Do you come quietly, man, or do we drag you out in front of every-body?' The other policeman pushed past him, into the room. He snatched up Morgan's bag.

'*What the hell* –' Morgan lunged at him. The first man seized his wrist and glared into his eyes. For an instant Morgan was about to lash out at them; then furious common sense came back. He shook his wrist free.

'Very well! We'll find out what this is about!'

He strode down the corridor between them, his face like thunder.

Down the stairs, into the lobby. They went through the front doors, out into the drive.

A police car was waiting.

He strode furiously into the police station.

A room led off the charge office. One constable went into it, with Morgan's bag. Morgan waited, seething. The constable reappeared at the door and beckoned. Morgan strode through.

A black inspector sat behind the desk, the bag on it. Morgan said furiously: '*I demand to know what the hell this is about!*'

The inspector put his hand into the bag, and slowly pulled out a black plastic package. It had a rubber band wrapped around it. He held it out. 'What is this?'

Morgan stared at it. He had never set eyes on it before.

'I've no idea!'

'Open it.'

Morgan snatched it from him. He ripped open the plastic bag. Inside was a plastic box. He snatched it out and opened the lid.

Inside was fine white powder. He stared at it, aghast.

'*You bastards*,' he whispered.

The officer said, 'I think that's cocaine, Mr Morgan. About half a kilo. Worth a lot of money.'

'*You bastards planted that stuff on me!*'

The officer said: 'Your fingerprints are on the box.'

'*You've just made me touch the box and put my fingerprints on it!*'

The officer took the box, and carefully replaced the lid. He nodded to the constables.

Morgan spun around, his fists bunched, as the constables bounded at him and seized each arm.

They shoved him in a cell. He paced up and down. Then a voice said: 'Morgan? . . .'

He spun around.

He recognized him immediately, from a photograph Anna had shown him years ago. It was Max Hapsburg who was on the other side of the bars, heavier in the face, with greying temples. Morgan stared at him, then whispered furiously: 'What have you done with her? If you lay a finger on her, I'll kill you one day.'

Max said quietly: 'No need for such gallantry. She is safe and sound and as free as the air. And she wants nothing whatsoever to do with you.' His eyes had not left Morgan's.

Morgan clenched his fist. 'I demand to see a lawyer. I'm going to blow this story sky-high.'

'I don't think you'll do that. I doubt anybody will believe a man who was found in possession of half a kilo of cocaine.' He held up a finger, and went on softly, his big eyes unwavering: 'But what you *are* going to do is stay away from my wife . . .' He took a controlled, angry breath. 'Now, you're going to get off this island, Morgan. In a moment you're going to find this door to be inexplicably unlocked. And you're going to *escape* from lawful custody. There's a taxi outside. And at the airport is a plane, flying to Miami in an hour. You're going to board that plane, Morgan. If you don't, you'll be re-arrested, and put on trial for possession of drugs. And from Miami you'll fly back to England. And . . .' His big Greek eyes widened: 'You will never . . . *never* set foot on the island of Grenada again. And you will *never* contact my wife again. Because if you do . . .' He pointed at the office down the corridor, 'The police have evidence to extradite you back from England to face trial here. And you'll go to jail for the rest of your life.'

He glared; then turned and strode away.

Part Two

7

When Jonathan Morgan, nicknamed Jack, was eight years old, his mother, for whom everything British was unquestionably best, had insisted that he learn boxing, though the family could ill afford the additional cost on top of the exorbitant fees for the excellent public school she insisted he attend. It was essential, she said, that an English gentleman could put up his dukes and defend himself in an efficient and sportsmanlike manner. So, every Wednesday and Saturday, Jonathan Morgan went along to the school gymnasium to get himself terrorized by other little boys whose demented mothers felt the same as his. He had little natural aptitude for fisticuffs, but this bi-weekly ordeal soon developed a certain cunning in the unhappy young sportsman, a strategy that went like this: Come charging murderously out of your corner like a bull at a gate and knock the living shit out of the other little boy before he hurts you. Render him *hors de combat*, then he can't hit you. This strategy back-fired because he won all his bouts, he was put on the school team, and term after term, year after year, he had to be terrorized by boys from other good public schools at boxing tournaments, extravaganzas of bloodshed and brain-damage which the mothers attended with great pride. By the time he left school he had been unbeaten champion for two years, had hated every minute of it, and he vowed never to fight again. But he brought the same bull-at-a-gate strategy to his university days. Jack Morgan was not a born sportsman, but he earned his rugby blue with suicidal tackling and fanatical fitness, and his cricket blue with sledge-hammer batting. He was brighter than most, certainly, but not sufficiently so to explain his sparkling results: he earned his Bachelor of Science degree *cum laude* only by unrelenting hard, hard work. And when he chose the Royal Navy as his career, he tackled the gruelling Marine training courses with the same grim determination, and passed with flying colours; but when it came to settling down in the service he knew that he was not a warrior at heart: he was an

49

academic, and he applied to join Submarines. It is more restful down there. It was nice to use just his head, and no brawn. And when, at the age of thirty-five, he was thrown out of the Royal Navy, or 'compulsorily retired', as a result of The Cocaine Affair, he had refused a commission in the Sultan of Oman's navy and declined to join the lucrative company of former SAS and Special Boat boys who undertake contracts for highly paid derring-do for which they have been so well trained by Her Majesty, even though he badly needed the money. Instead he sold his house, commuted his pension, bought a second-hand freight-ship and doggedly began a precarious civilian career in merchant shipping.

It was a small freighter, only six thousand tons, in good condition but only profitable because Jack Morgan was both owner and master and he lived permanently aboard, ate from the ship's stores and had no wife. The only other asset he owned was a little farm in the mountains of France which he had never even seen and which he had been forced to accept as payment of Makepeace's debts when that scatterbrain had decided that being a shipping tycoon was dead boring after the Special Boat Service and decided to join the shady company of the ex-SAS and SBS boys. 'They make such good *money*,' Makepeace had cajoled, his triangular face all plaintive. 'Let's sell the ship and *both* go.'

'No way.'

'But it's not necessarily *killing* people,' Makepeace appealed '– it's *looking after* people. Like bodyguard work for these Arab guys. There's a *fortune* to be made in security work in Europe – all these high-ups coming here. And training their armies. And arranging arms and ammunition, all that good stuff – pay a *fortune*, they do. It's mostly official, you know.'

'I'm a seaman, Makepeace, not a hired gun. If you don't like the merchant marine, pay your debts and go.'

'But how do I pay the money I owe you?'

'In cash.'

'That's the difficulty,' Makepeace mused. 'Look, there's this little place I've got in France. Lovely spot, bought it from my brother-in-law for my old age . . .'

'Sell it. If you're joining Danziger and the boys, you're not going to have any old age.'

'I wondered if you'd take it as payment –'

'No way.'

So he took the rock-farm in France, because that was the only way he'd ever get anything from Makepeace, and he had not seen it to this day because he was so busy surviving. He was doing carpentry on his bridge when the Navy car drew up on the quay in Plymouth and the ensign scrambled out. He came clattering up the companionway to the bridge. He was a red-headed young man with a white, earnest face. He saluted and panted:

'Captain S/M's compliments, sir, he wants to see you immediately, this moment, sir.'

Morgan looked at him angrily. Ensign Phillips, who thought he dined with kings because he was a four-ring captain's flunky . . . 'The Captain of Submarines wants to see me immediately, does he, Phillips?'

'Yes, sir.'

'This moment, you say?'

'Yes, sir.'

Morgan breathed deep. 'What about?'

'Don't know, sir.'

Morgan took another angry breath.

'Phillips,' he said, 'please do *not* convey my compliments to the Captain S/M. But *do* remind him that I am *no* longer in Her Majesty's Navy. And that if for some extraordinary reason he wants to see me, *he can bloody well come here! And request permission to come aboard first!*'

'Sir –'

'Do you think you can remember all that, Phillips?'

Ensign Phillips blinked. 'But please, sir –'

'Thank you, Phillips, that will be all.'

Morgan picked up his saw elaborately. Phillips blinked, then saluted worriedly and turned and clattered down off the bridge.

Twenty minutes later Morgan saw the car coming back along the jetty. It stopped opposite the freighter. He had been wondering what all this was about, but he studiously ignored the car. Two minutes later the Captain of Submarines clambered up onto the bridge. 'Permission to come aboard?'

Morgan straightened, and glared at him.

'You're already aboard, Carrington. You can go back and holler from the jetty.'

Carrington looked thoroughly peeved. He was tall, aristo-cratic, immaculate in his uniform; the man did not move, he flowed. 'Now look here, Jack – this is top priority.'

Morgan put down his saw.

'I'll never understand the Navy. Or you. You know I hate your guts. And yet, when for some extraordinary reason you want to see me, you send a flunky with a curt message. "This moment", quote, unquote.' He frowned in wonder. 'You're so puffed up with your own importance that you don't even know that's dumb behaviour – it seems perfectly normal to you to wave your wand and command.'

'Have you quite finished?'

'No. You can go and get *fucked*, Carrington!'

Carrington enquired: 'The whole Navy as well?'

'Yes! Because not one of you bastards stood by me!'

Carrington said, 'We haven't got time to go over all that again, but let me say that I didn't ruin your career, Jack – you did. You shouldn't have been fooling around with a married woman. Indeed, I saved your bacon. You could have been court-martialled on the story we were given about that cocaine. Instead you were quietly retired.'

'Because you believed my version?'

'Of course. We wouldn't let a man we believed guilty of such a serious offence walk free.'

'Then if you believed me you should have stood by me! But, no. The Navy couldn't stand a whiff of scandal. Oh dear me no, we can't have the public saying there's no smoke without fire, et cetera, can we? So, to save your precious image you sacrifice an innocent man!'

Carrington said, 'If you play with fire you must expect to get your fingers burnt. And married women are fire. You can't expect the Navy to pull you out of that soup. Now, we've got a very important job for you to do.'

Morgan wondered if he had heard right.

'The Navy's got a job for me?'

'And it's very urgent. So will you please be so kind as to accompany me back to Headquarters?'

Morgan almost wanted to laugh. 'This moment? And what on earth makes the Navy think I'll do a job for them?'

Carrington said: 'I could hand you your Call-up papers. As

a retired officer you're still subject to call-up and the Naval Discipline Act.'

Morgan held out his hand angrily. 'So? Hand me my Call-up papers.'

Carrington said crisply, 'We want this to be unofficial.'

Morgan was completely taken aback.

'*Unofficial*?' he said. 'You mean, "Deniable"?'

'Exactly.'

Morgan stared. Jesus Christ. 'I repeat, what makes the Navy think I'll do an unofficial and deniable job for them?'

'Money,' Carrington said.

Morgan could hardly believe this. He picked up his saw again. 'Carrington, please tell the Navy to stick their money right up their arse.'

'Big money, in this case.'

'The Navy's got a big arse. Particularly in its Captain of Submarines!'

'You're not coming?'

'How very perspicacious.'

Carrington sighed. 'Then I must tell you, Jack, that the Navy will reconsider legal proceedings in respect of that cocaine report.' He added: 'I'll deny I ever said that.'

Morgan wondered if he had heard right.

'Jesus Christ . . . Not only does the Navy submit to blackmail, it now *practises* blackmail! . . . Jesus Christ,' he said again. 'Now I've heard everything.'

8

He grimly followed the Captain of Submarines into his office. A lanky middle-aged man with spectacles heaved himself up from an armchair as they entered. Carrington suddenly seemed in good humour.

'Jack, this is somebody hardly anybody knows. Anthony Brink-Ford. In his indefinable way he's one of the gentlemen who controls poor mortals like me. Anthony – Jack Morgan.'

'How do you do?' Morgan nodded briefly. He said to Carrington: 'You're mortal?'

'Alas, I sometimes suspect so.' He went behind his desk and picked up a form and a Bible. 'Hold that, raise your right hand and repeat after me.' He prepared to read the form.

'You're joking.'

'Just the usual Official Secrets Oath, Jack, got to take it.'

'But I'm no longer an official.'

'As a retired Royal Navy officer, you're still in the Reserves, Jack.'

'Then if I'm still an officer I haven't got to take the Oath again!'

'We can require you to do so, under certain circumstances.'

'Where my continued loyalty is questionable? Are you handing me my Call-up papers?'

'No.'

'Then if my loyalty is questioned, I'm going back to my boat.' He turned to go.

'Jack . . .' Carrington sighed. 'All right.' He put the Bible down. He said wearily: 'You're still familiar with the Oath?'

'I don't suffer from amnesia!'

'All right,' Carrington sighed. He waved his hand. 'Please sit down.'

Morgan sat, pleased with his little victory. 'This doesn't mean I'm going to do a bloody thing.'

'Now, then.' Carrington sat. He crossed his legs. 'Officially Anthony draws the salary of a Permanent Under-Secretary of State. In fact, he's one of the senior chaps in MI6. He wants to talk to you.' He waved a hand. 'And I want you to know I think it stinks. But it's got to be done.'

Morgan frowned. '*You* think it stinks? . . .' He sat back. 'Boy, then it must be really bad.'

It was water off Carrington's back. 'I want you to know that I'm on your side, Jack.'

Morgan shook his head.

'Now,' he said, 'I've *really* heard everything.'

Anthony Brink-Ford's rimless spectacles made his eyes look unusually large. He sat forward and said:

'You've heard about the state of emergency in Grenada, Mr Morgan? It's been in the newspapers.'

Morgan felt his pulse trip. *So it was about Grenada*. He nodded. Brink-Ford went on:

'In short, there's been another coup. The Prime Minister, Maurice Bishop, who was a communist but changed his tune somewhat and began to make overtures to America again – he was placed under house arrest by his army. The hard-line communists in his cabinet wanted to get rid of him, but they dared not do so, because of his popular support.'

Morgan was trying to think ahead – and all he could think was *Anna* . . .

'Well,' Brink-Ford said, 'today Bishop's supporters stormed his house, and set him free. They marched into town. Bishop had four or five of his loyal cabinet ministers and advisers with him.' He raised his eyebrows at Morgan. 'One of them was a well-known financier called Max Hapsburg.'

Morgan stared at him. Brink-Ford went on: 'They confronted the army. Then the hard-line communist leaders arrived. Bishop and five of his leading friends were seized. They were dragged into the army headquarters, and shot.'

Morgan stared. 'And Max Hapsburg was one of those shot?'

Brink-Ford nodded. 'Yes.' He added significantly: 'His wife was definitely not present.' He paused, then went on soberly: 'The United States of America is about to invade Grenada.'

America about to invade Grenada? Morgan's mind was fumbling, with the beat in his chest. Brink-Ford continued:

'The official reason is the safety of one thousand American medical students who are living on the island. In a state of siege in the university, while civil war's raging. After the hostage crisis in Iran and Jimmy Carter's bungling of that, and the recent bombing of American military in Beirut, President Reagan is not taking any chances with American lives. Or America's reputation.' He added: 'Or his own. There's a presidential election next year. Another reason is the usual one: the Russians. The Reds are on the island in a big way, Soviets and Cubans. Amongst other things, they are building a huge new airport, capable of taking any planes. Why? Little Grenada's tourist traffic is handled quite satisfactorily by the existing airport. So obviously the Russians intend making Grenada

55

another military base, like Cuba. America is not going to tolerate that.'

Morgan was thinking hard. 'And the other reason?'

'Those are good enough reasons, in our book. Even though Mrs Thatcher is going to scream blue murder about America's interference – because Grenada is a member of the British Commonwealth. Just like Reagan made a big show of complaining about Thatcher's Falklands War. So he could keep in sweet with Latin America.' He paused. 'There *is* no other reason for America's invasion officially. But there is an important spin-off, as the Americans say.'

'And that is?'

Brink-Ford pressed his fingers together. He said:

'Max Hapsburg died today, with certain information in his head. Highly important, of a secret nature.' He paused. 'And we believe – that is to say, Her Majesty's government, and the United States believe, that Max Hapsburg may have told his wife the information . . . That she either *knows* it, or knows where it is to be found.'

Morgan stared at the man. He could not believe this was happening. 'What makes you think that?'

Brink-Ford said, 'Suffice it to say that Max Hapsburg was a prominent man in banking circles. He was involved in many – or several – top level negotiations on behalf of certain Caribbean and Latin American countries, about their international debts. It appears that, to that end, he was possibly not above applying a little pressure in certain areas.'

Morgan said slowly: 'And you want me to get Anna . . . to his widow, and get this information from her.'

Brink-Ford's eyes were big behind his spectacles.

'Commander – Mr Morgan . . . We have a most important task which only *you* can carry out.' He paused. 'You are the *only* person, because of your – er – association, with Mrs Hapsburg.' He took an uncomfortable breath. 'Mr Morgan, it is of the utmost importance that you proceed to Grenada and get to see Anna Hapsburg immediately. That you . . . *win* her complete confidence.' He cleared his throat. 'And persuade her to come away with you, to a place of safety. In fact, to England.'

Morgan was astonished. Brink-Ford went on:

'And if for some reason she will not do that voluntarily, you must *make* her come to England . . .'

Morgan could not believe his British ears.

'Good God,' he said. 'Ab*duct* her? . . . Against her will? So you can . . . *extract* the information out of her? And if I refuse to be a party to this . . . *kidnapping*, you'll exert a little blackmail on *me*? Jesus.' He could not believe it. He got up and walked to the window. He looked out elaborately. He turned back to them. 'Am I in England? Or Russia?' He walked back to his chair. He sat down incredulously. 'Half an hour ago *this* sanctimonious prick –' he pointed at Carrington – 'was telling me that it all served me right for playing with married women – with *fire*, he said. Now you want to *use* that . . .'

'A different thing entirely. This is for Queen and Country.'

Morgan half-laughed. 'Now I've heard *absolutely* everything. Seduction and abduction for Queen and Country! . . .'

Brink-Ford sat forward earnestly. 'Have you been in touch with Mrs Hapsburg since that incident a year ago?'

Morgan snorted. 'No, I have not.'

'Has she attempted to be in touch with you?'

'No, she has not.'

'Do you know why not?'

'I've a pretty good idea! Her husband threatened to have me extradited to Grenada to face trial, if she did. And for the same reason I haven't dared contact her!'

Brink-Ford said: 'That suggests . . . Or rather, may I ask – are you still enamoured of Anna Hapsburg?'

Morgan glared at him. 'You may not. And may I ask what this red-hot information is which I have to extract from her?'

Brink-Ford sat back.

'First I'll tell you how we're going to get you into Grenada.' He looked at his watch. 'At this moment American battleships are steaming towards Grenada. Meanwhile troops are being assembled in nearby Barbados. Now, this afternoon you will fly to Barbados on a scheduled flight. With a false passport. You will be met by an officer of the United States Navy – a SEAL officer. That's their specialized Sea Air Land forces, like our Special Boat Service. He will equip you with the uniform and weapons of an American SEAL.' He glanced at his file. 'Your name will be Steven M. Jackson. The M is for Matheson.

You will be drilled on your new temporary identity. Family, training courses, military history. He'll familiarize you with your weapons, et cetera. I'm told you've been trained to parachute?'

Morgan was staring at him. 'Years ago. And I hated every jump.'

'Well, I believe you may be parachuting into the sea, near the capital of St George's, to start your search for Anna Hapsburg.' He paused, collecting his notes. 'We don't know where she is. The island is in chaos. The telephones are cut. She may be barricaded in her home. Her parents are deceased, as you probably know. We think she may have fled to Government House. We know that about thirty civilians have taken refuge there, but we don't know who they are. The governor is a British appointee, a black man called Scoon. Or she may be in one of the embassies. Anyway, you and your squad of SEALs will first look for her in her home. Then you will storm the rabble army that is besieging Government House, get inside and see if she's there. If she is, you will all simply hold the fort until the invasion is over. Which should only be a matter of two days or so. And you, personally, will stay in Anna Hapsburg's company all the time.'

Morgan could hardly believe this was happening.

'And if she isn't in Government House?'

'You go back over the wall and look for her,' Carrington said. 'First in the obvious places, like foreign embassies. You'll take some SEALs with you. When you find her, report by radio to Command. If you're in a safe place, like an embassy, sit tight until the bun-fight's over. If you're in a dangerous situation, radio for help.'

Brink-Ford said: 'Above all, you've got to keep Anna Hapsburg safe. Avoid risks as far as possible, avoid confrontation with the enemy, but give nobody the benefit of the doubt. Shoot to kill anybody who looks like endangering her. And the same applies to yourself – it is vital that you stay alive.'

Carrington smiled: 'We thought you might like that part of it.'

Morgan was in no mood for jokes.

'So that I can win her confidence for you bastards.'

Brink-Ford said earnestly: 'For Queen and Country. Mr

Morgan, you are the only person who *can* win her confidence . . .'

'And if she doesn't divulge the information to me, you'll get it out of her by hook or by crook?'

'Mr Morgan, the whole purpose in sending you is so that we do *not* have to get it out of her by hook or by crook. And to get her away from people who would *certainly* not hesitate to use force to get the information. And then kill her afterwards. Namely, the Russians.'

Morgan stared. He thought, Jesus . . . 'And the Americans also want this information?'

'Indeed. They're collaborating with us. But only the SEALs in your immediate squad will know that your special assignment is to find Anna Hapsburg. They won't know *why*. They'll ask no questions. And only a couple of people in the whole armed services will know you've been put there by us.'

Morgan was grappling with all this.

'But rather than disguise me as an American soldier, where my true identity may be discovered, why not send me disguised as a British journalist, or diplomat?'

'Because,' Carrington said, 'officially Great Britain is keeping out of this. That's why we're asking you to do this unofficially, not serving Call-up papers on you. And *because* this is a highly military situation, you need the cover and facilities of the military to do the job properly. Journalists can't run around with machine guns, can they?'

Morgan sat back. And took a deep, tense breath. Bemused. Anna had come back into his life? . . . And for a moment he felt a flash of anger. 'You'll cause endless trouble,' Janet Nicols had said. She was right. He said: 'Tell me what information I'm after.'

Brink-Ford sat back. 'I can tell you only as much as you *need* to know.' He paused. 'You have probably heard of Klaus Barbie?'

Morgan said, wonderingly: 'Klaus Barbie? The "Butcher of Lyons"?'

Brink-Ford said: 'Exactly. He is a Nazi war criminal who has recently been found in Bolivia, extradited back to France, and he's presently in prison awaiting trial for murdering hundreds of French during the war. The French authorities have enough

59

evidence to guillotine him a dozen times. Yet they are stalling on the prosecution. Why?' He raised his eyebrows. 'The theory is that Klaus Barbie knows certain facts that he is threatening to reveal if he is brought to trial. Those facts, if he could prove them to be true, would be . . . terribly damaging to certain institutions in the West.'

Morgan was even more amazed. Anna was involved in this?
'What institutions?'

'That is the only detail I will tell you. You *need* to know that much, to help you . . . unravel Mrs Hapsburg's mind. Because that information which Klaus Barbie possesses was also possessed by Max Hapsburg. Indeed, we believe Max Hapsburg actually possessed the *evidence*. We believe it is in the form of an intelligence file, acquired by the Nazis during the war, or possibly in the form of a microfilm of that file.'

Morgan was amazed. 'How did Max Hapsburg get hold of that file? He's my age, born after the war.'

'Good question. How much do you know of Hapsburg's history?'

'Only what his wife told me. That his father was a wealthy German who lived in South America after the war, married a Greek woman. He wasn't a Nazi war criminal, was he?'

'No. He was a Nazi, undoubtedly, but not a war criminal. Have you heard of Admiral Canaris?'

'Yes,' Morgan said. 'He was the head of German Intelligence during the war, wasn't he?'

'Correct,' Brink-Ford said. 'Dietmar Hapsburg, Max's father, worked with Admiral Canaris in Intelligence. It may be that when Germany crumbled, Dietmar Hapsburg fled to South America with this file – as insurance. When he died, Max came into possession of it. Somehow, Klaus Barbie got to hear of it, presumably.' Brink-Ford held up his palm. 'That's as much as you need to know. We know – or we *think* we know – the general *nature* of the information. What we haven't got is the *proof* – the file, or the microfilm, that shows it to be true. Or false.' He added: 'We sincerely hope, by the way, that it is false.' He sighed briskly. 'Max Hapsburg was a very wealthy man, with many connections. Maybe he kept the evidence in a bank vault somewhere. Or in a hole in the ground. We don't know.' He nodded at Morgan. 'But we think Mrs Hapsburg knows. And that's what we want you to find out. But more than that. We want you to get Mrs Hapsburg to a place of complete safety while we get hold of this evidence, and check it out.' He pointed at the floor. 'Right here, where we can look after her. Because, I assure you, Mr Morgan, a number of other people will be after her too.' Brink-Ford elaborated: 'In fact, I do not exaggerate when I say that Mrs Hapsburg's life is in extreme danger. Mercifully, for us – and for her – *and* for you – we have the might of the United States military behind us. If Anna Hapsburg were on her own in the middle of this Russian-inspired coup in Grenada, she wouldn't survive a day. And after this invasion, they'll still be trying to get her.'

Morgan felt a stab of fear for her. But he could hardly believe all this. Carrington said, 'As regards your freighter, she'll sail on schedule, with a captain provided by us. While officially you are on a hiking holiday in Scotland.'

Morgan felt feverish. For Anna's safety. He looked at them, bemused. The civil service faces he once upon a time thought were incorruptible.

He took a deep breath. Then he held a shaky finger out at them.

'Now let me make one thing abundantly clear.' He glared. 'I'm going on this operation for *her* sake – not for Queen and so-called Country!' He shook his finger once. 'And after I get her off that island, if you so much as lay a finger upon her . . .' He raised his eyebrows: 'I'll blow this story sky-high. Do you understand that? Blow Queen and Country and Margaret Thatcher . . .'

Part Three

9

In the middle of that rainy night several groups of SEALs landed on the north-eastern shores of Grenada from their rubber boats, to reconnoitre landing beaches for the assault at dawn. They radioed back to their ships that there were many dangerous coral reefs and the old grass airport of Pearls was heavily defended by the People's Revolutionary Army and Cubans. At the same time a Specter helicopter gunship was flying high over the new airport at Point Salines, where the US Rangers would land, and the report they radioed back was worse: the runway was blocked with vehicles, construction equipment and metal spikes.

At the same time, two more parties of SEALs were approaching the western shore of the island, near the capital of Saint George's, in their raiding boats, twenty-two men counting Jack Morgan. They ran up the beach for the blackness of the palms. Eight of them started along the dark treeline towards the big house of Max Hapsburg on the point of the bay.

There were no lights burning. There was a double garage, both doors open, one car visible inside. The big house was surrounded by trees and shrubs and lawns. The front door was ajar.

Morgan crouched in the rain beside the commander, his heart knocking. Two SEALs broke cover and ran at the door, and flung themselves on either side of it. Then they burst inside and disappeared.

Morgan waited. He could still hardly believe he was here. Then a light snapped on in the hall. A figure reappeared, and signalled. Morgan and the commander ran for the door

'Empty. But there's signs of a fight.'

Morgan looked around feverishly. The rugs in the hall were bunched, and a chair was knocked over. He crouched and examined the marble floor for blood. He saw none. 'Come upstairs,' the SEAL said.

Morgan followed him, bounding up the wide staircase. The rugs on the landing were also bunched. They strode down the corridor. Into a bedroom.

It was obviously hers. It was the first time he had seen it, of course, and it was unreal that he was standing in it now. A big double bed, elegant furniture. There was another bedroom leading off this one, with another double bed. There were two dressing rooms. There was the sound of running water, coming from a bathroom. A wall safe stood agape; it was empty. Some wardrobe doors stood open. Morgan strode into the next bedroom. A drawer from a bedside table lay on the floor. He strode for the bathroom.

The shower was beating down into the tub. *Why?* He felt the water: cold. A towel lay in one corner, a stool had been kicked over. He crouched and examined the tiled floor, looking for blood. There was none. He stood up. Then he saw it.

His heart missed a beat, and he feverishly crouched and examined it. It was on one corner of the bathtub: one small smear of blood. He strode out of the room.

He ran down the staircase, back to the hall. 'Definitely nobody in the house?'

'Nor in the gardens. No new graves either, as far as we can see in this light.'

'Then let's get the hell on to Government House.'

The dark rain wept down.

Government House stands on a hill, overlooking the old harbour of Saint George's. Nearby is Fort Ruppert, headquarters of the People's Revolutionary Army. Government House is an old colonial building, set in gardens, with a big iron gate bearing the royal coat of arms. Surrounding the walls were the soldiers of the People's Revolutionary Army, holding the people inside hostage.

At dawn the Marines landed at the old Pearls airport in the north, midst teaming rain and anti-aircraft fire; at the same time the Rangers flew in from Florida over New airport midst even heavier anti-aircraft fire; at dawn a party of SEALs attacked the Radio Free Grenada station. At dawn the twenty-one SEALs and Jack Morgan stormed Government House.

They came fighting up the streets towards the hilltop, midst

66

the clatter of guns and the stink of cordite, and they stormed the perimeter of Government House.

Morgan frantically threw himself at the wall midst the cacophony of gunfire, swung his leg up, and rolled over the top. He landed with a crash in a flowerbed. He scrambled up and crouched there, rasping, thanking God, getting his breath. Over the wall came the others. They ran off in different directions to cover different aspects of the house; the commander rasped '*Go*' and Morgan ran.

He ran flat out across the lawn, for the kitchen. The commander flung himself at the door handle. It was locked. He stepped backwards and kicked, and the door crashed in. They burst through the door together.

'*Freeze! – US soldiers! – Freeze!*'

The dark kitchen was empty. The commander bounded for the door to the corridor, stood flat against the wall. Morgan crouched, dry-mouthed. The commander shouted:

'*Freeze! – We're US soldiers! – Freeze!*'

Nothing. Only the crack and thud of gunfire out there. The commander burst through the door. He ran up the corridor, to the hall.

It was empty. He looked into the dining room. There was nobody. Morgan came running up the corridor. The commander bounded up to the living room door, and flung it open.

'*Freeze! US soldiers! –*'

There was a mass of shocked faces, black and white, people on the floor. There was a moment's silence; then an elderly black man got to his feet shakily.

'Praise the Lord . . .' he said.

'Are you the Governor, sir?'

The black man nodded his head. 'I am, Paul Scoon . . .'

Morgan's eyes were sweeping every face in the darkened room. He rasped, 'Is Mrs Anna Hapsburg in the house?'

The Governor was saying to the commander, 'Our radio was shot out –'

'*Anna Hapsburg! Is she in the house?*'

'Oh,' the Governor said distractedly – 'She must be upstairs . . .'

Morgan's heart turned over. He turned and hurried out of the room. He bounded up the stairs.

The thud of gunfire was muffled. Morgan strode down the upstairs passage, looking into each room. They were all empty, the curtains drawn, mattresses on the floor. His mouth was dry. He came to the last room.

'Anna?' He twisted the door handle.

The door moved, then it was stopped by an armchair.

'*Anna?*' He shoved. The armchair slid.

The room was in half-darkness.

He looked in at. A pistol, pointed straight at him. Behind it, a woman crouched, at the end of the bed. He could only see her forehead, and her two white hands.

His heart was pounding. It was unreal. He lowered his gun.

'Anna? Put the gun down. This is Jack Morgan.'

She stared incredulously at the blackened face smiling uncertainly at her, her frightened eyes wide, the gun still tremblingly pointing at him. Morgan put his hand to his head, and pulled off his cap.

'It's Jack.'

She stared at him, the gun still pointing. Then, slowly, incredulously she straightened up.

'I don't believe it . . .'

Morgan was grinning at her, shaky with relief. 'Well, it's me . . .'

She put one hand to her head incredulously. But the other still held the gun at him. 'I don't believe it . . .'

He said: 'I've come to get you out of here. Now put the gun down.'

She slowly lowered the gun, staring. Shakily he stepped around the armchair, a smile all over his face. He stepped over the mattress towards her. She stood there, astonished, gaunt. Then she dropped the gun, and closed her eyes.

10

In the north the guns and mortars stuttered and thudded as the marines fought it out at old Pearls airport. In the south the Cuban anti-aircraft fire was so heavy, pounding the sky, that the commander of the Rangers aborted the first jump, but he knew from photographs that the positioning of the guns was such that they could not be lowered to hit a target under six hundred feet, so he brought his men in at five hundred. They hit the ground almost immediately after their parachutes opened, and they went running into action, guns blazing against heavy Cuban rifle fire. Over near Grand Anse beach the SEALs fought their way into the Radio Free Grenada broadcasting station, and the other party of SEALs attacked Richmond Hill Prison, supported by helicopter gunships. At strategic points within Government House the SEALs waited, ready to blast the heads off anybody who tried to breach the walls.

In the bedroom, Morgan sat on the mattress with Anna Hapsburg. There was nothing he could do about the war raging out there, there was nothing he wanted to do but sit here with her and just thank God she was safe, that the might of the entire United States was out there fighting their battles for them. He was still shaky at seeing her, and, oh, he just wanted to take her in his arms; but there was nothing like that in the air. She was a very different woman from the one he had seen a year ago. She was thinner, her long legs seemed longer, her shoulders more angular, her smoky blue eyes bigger, and there was no sparkle in them. She said grimly:

'I'm sorry, I don't believe you, Jack. It's just too much of a coincidence.' She looked at him: 'They sent you to get me, didn't they?'

'They?' And he felt like laughing, he was so happy.

She said, 'The Americans, obviously. You're here with the American army.' She shook her head at him. 'After what Max did to you, you disappear off the face of the earth. Suddenly Max is killed in a coup, and you reappear in an American invasion, like a knight in shining armour. They *sent* you, didn't they? Because they know we were lovers once.'

Oh God, he wanted to tell her the truth, he didn't owe a damn thing to the Royal bloody Navy but he did not want to turn her against himself.

He said: 'Look, once you've been in the Navy you're never really free of them, they'll call you up in emergencies. And this was an emergency. The Americans needed local knowledge of Grenada. They didn't even have up-to-date plans of the island

69

– they came in with tourist maps. So they called on the British, because this used to be a British colony. And so the Navy pulled me out of retirement. But my only job was to brief them on the features of the island, especially around Government House, because we knew civilians were under siege here.' He smiled and shook his head. 'I didn't know you were in this house until I asked the Governor.'

She said: 'So the *British* sent you? To find me?'

'I told *them* I was going to find you. Come hell or high water.'

'But how can you tell the British anything?'

He said: 'They needed me. They had to agree. Told me to be careful. No heroics. This is America's war.'

She didn't believe him. 'I hope they're paying you well. They didn't tell you to question me?'

And oh God he wanted to tell her the truth and be done with this! 'About what, for God's sake?'

Her nerves were strung tight. 'Are the British paying you to find me?'

'Oh Jesus . . .' But his anger was with himself and the Royal goddam Navy.

She closed her exhausted eyes. She put her hand to her brow and massaged. 'I'm sorry . . .'

He wanted to take her in his arms and claim her, tell her *he* was sorry. She opened her eyes and said:

'The Russians are after me, you see.'

Brink-Ford had told him, but it was shocking all over again. 'The Russians? How do you know?'

She took a trembly breath, and massaged her forehead.

'I know something.' She shook her head. 'They *think* I know something. That Max told me.'

This was what he was supposed to be here for. 'What did Max tell you?'

She sat quite still, controlling her tension.

'He didn't tell me anything conclusive – he only hinted at it. In a rage.' He waited. It seemed she was not going to continue. Then: she took another deep breath. 'Oh God, it became a miserable, cat-and-dog relationship . . . After your last visit.' She shook her head again. 'Oh, he was a good man in so many ways. But . . . Maybe I'm in shock, maybe I can't believe that he's dead . . . And God knows I don't wish him dead . . .' She breathed, then it came out as a sob: '*But God knows I also don't feel any grief either* . . .'

He wanted to take her in his arms.

'That's probably normal, in the circumstances.'

She sat there, steeped in guilt. And he wanted to squeeze her tight, and squeeze the story out of her, and get it over with. 'But what is it that Max told you?'

She shook her head in refusal. 'He was drunk. He screamed it at me . . .'

He waited.

She lifted her head. And suddenly she looked more under control again. She said:

'I won't tell you. I won't tell anybody. Because I don't believe it, and it can only do tremendous damage.' She gave a trembly sigh; then said bleakly: 'But the Russians are after me.' She jerked her head at the gun on the mattress. 'That's why I was hiding up here. When I heard you breaking into the house, I thought you were Russians.' She paused. Then she said: 'They tried to kidnap me. And I killed a man.'

He stared at her. *Killed a man?*

He said: 'Tell me, from the beginning, Anna. Everything.'

She slumped back against the wall, her elbows on her knees. Her forehead in her hands.

'Then don't interrupt me. Let me tell it straight.'

He waited, his nerves stretched.

She looked at the wall, then said flatly: 'I was all in favour of Maurice Bishop at first – he looked like he was going to be a new broom that swept the corrupt old government clean. But he turned so hostile to the West. And Moscow got him in their pocket, they were turning Grenada into another Cuba. Max did his best to talk Maurice Bishop out of all this – and persuaded him to patch it up with America. So the hard-line communists turned on Bishop, They placed him under house arrest and they put the whole island under twenty four-hour curfew. Anybody breaking it was shot on sight.' She massaged her forehead. Morgan waited. She continued: 'But a mob of Bishop's supporters got him out of his house. Somebody telephoned Max and he left home to go there. So I was alone.

71

All our servants had disappeared, because of the curfew. An hour later I got a frantic phone call from the Russian embassy. Telling me that Max and Bishop and some others had been shot by the Revolutionary Army – executed . . .'

She closed her eyes. She took a trembly breath. 'I was absolutely shocked. I . . . There was no love lost any more between Max and me, but this was terrible . . .'

Morgan waited. She massaged her temples.

'Ten minutes later, a car arrives. I had locked myself in the house. It was a white man. He beat on the door, saying he had come to take me to the Russian embassy for my own protection. That's why I let him in. But I told him I wasn't going to go.' She breathed. 'I don't trust the Russians. He began to shout.' She glanced at him. 'He told me to get all the documents out of Max's safe and come with him. Now I was really frightened. I told him Max had no safe – I told him to get out. He shouted that I'd better show him where it was or he'd drag me back to the embassy and they'd get it out of me. He shouted, "Tell me the names of the foreign banks where he has safety-deposit boxes!" He tried to grab me and I ran up the stairs. He chased me. I ran into the bedroom . . .' She closed her eyes and breathed: 'I grabbed the gun Max kept in his bedside drawer . . . I ran into the bathroom. But he was right behind me. He shoved the door open and I staggered backwards. He lunged at me . . .'

Morgan waited, in suspense. She took a quivering breath.

'It was . . . instinctive. I was frantic. I fired blindly.' She closed her eyes again. 'I hit him in the forehead. He crashed into the bath.'

'Jesus . . .' He leant out and squeezed her hand once.

She sat up and wiped her eyelids.

'I was in shock. All I knew was I had to get out of the house . . . Get away from the island. And take whatever was in Max's safe. I knew the combination, though I hadn't used it for years. I opened it. There was a pile of documents, and keys and things. And some money. I just stuffed it into a handgrip.'

'Everything?'

She nodded. 'And the gun. I started to run out of the house. To drive to the airport. I was going to get Max's aeroplane and fly away. Then I remembered the body.' She put her fingertips to her eyes. 'Oh God, I was frightened. I was going to be shot by the Revolutionary Army for murder . . . I had to get rid of the body. But *where*? I dragged him out of the bath. There was blood in the bath, so I turned on the shower, to wash it away. I tied a towel tight around his head to stop getting blood on the floor.' She pressed her eyes. 'And I dragged him. Through the bedroom. Down the stairs. Oh God, it was horrible . . .'

He squeezed her knee.

She continued bleakly: 'I got him downstairs. I somehow got him into the car. The front passenger seat. Then . . . Then I didn't know where to take him.' She shook her head. '*Where?* And where was I going to run to afterwards? The mobs. The curfew. The army would be at the airport. Then I knew the only place I could run to was the Governor's house.' She breathed deep. 'So I drove the car into town.'

'The Russian car?'

She nodded. 'It was dark now. I drove without lights. If I was stopped, I was going to say I was taking an injured comrade to the hospital.' She sighed deeply. 'I took back roads, through the shacks. Everything was deserted because of the curfew. But then I could hear the sounds of mobs. I stopped the car in a lane. I pulled the towel off his head. I . . . I had the presence of mind to remember my fingerprints. I wiped the steering wheel. Then I abandoned the car . . .'

Morgan sighed grimly. 'Then?'

'Then I walked. Through the back streets. Then up the hill, to Government House.'

'And nobody challenged you?'

'No. All the action was several blocks away.'

'Did anybody see you abandon the car?'

'It was a dark lane. Nobody would have seen me until I was a hundred yards away.' She added: 'I hope.'

'What did you do with the towel?'

'I threw it down a drain. Half a mile away.'

'And the gun is the one you were pointing at me?'

She nodded.

He picked it up, and put it in his pocket. 'We must get rid of that. At the bottom of the ocean.'

She looked at him. 'But the Russian embassy knows one of their men went to my house. What's going to happen?'

He took a tense breath.

'I'm not a lawyer. But with all the mayhem on this island, one dead Russian is not particularly surprising. And even if you are implicated, you have the argument of self-defence.'

'Do you think the Revolutionary Army will listen to *that?*'

'There's not going to be any Revolutionary Army after this, the Yanks aren't here on a goodwill tour.' He ran his hand through his hair. 'And the things from the safe?'

She waved her hand. The handgrip stood in the corner.

'Have you read the documents?'

She nodded.

'And? Is there anything significant? That the Russians would be so interested in?'

'No.' He knew she was lying. She said: 'There's Max's will. *Un*signed, by the way. In which he leaves everything to me.'

'What about the keys? What locks are they for?'

She said, 'Probably his safety-deposit boxes. They're not labelled.'

He put his finger on her chin and turned her face to him. He said: 'What is it the Russian wanted to know?'

She held his eye. 'I've told you – No.'

He hardly cared, as long as he was with her.

'Can I look through those documents?'

She demanded, 'Why?'

'Because the Russians are after you. Because you know something that Max knew. I want to know what that is.'

She demanded again, 'Why?'

He didn't care a damn about his assignment, or about deceiving her – all he was worried about was her safety. 'So I know what we're up against, Anna! The Russians have tried once to kidnap you, to get this information. After they'd got it they might have murdered you! I need to know what they're after so we can evade them next time.'

Her eyes were steady. She said slowly:

'The British sent you to get the same information, didn't they?'

He hardly cared what lies he told her.

'Bullshit! My job is over! I gave the Americans my local knowledge, and we've secured Government House! The only reason I need to know what Max told you is to protect you!'

She looked at him grimly. He went on: 'You've got to tell me sometime, Anna! Because when you're off this island you're coming to live with me. And if I've got to deal with Russians I need to know *why*.'

Her nerves near breaking; she said softly:

'Oh, no, Jack – I can't live with you. I'm not involving you in this.' She clenched her fist in her lap. 'I'm not letting you fight my battles for me. When we get off this island I've got my own thing to do and I'm going to politely disappear until it's done.'

He said: 'You're not going anywhere without me, Anna.'

She clenched her fist. 'I'm a marked man! – I'm red-hot, and they'll kill you too if you're in their way!'

It was all still staggering to him. He held up both hands, to calm her. Outside there was the thud of gunfire. He said:

'We'll cross the bridges as we come to them . . .' He sighed angrily. 'All right, now, why don't you try to sleep?'

She closed her eyes.

'I haven't slept for days.' She breathed, 'Will you stay here if I sleep? And guard that handgrip?'

The handgrip. 'Yes, of course.'

She massaged her forehead. She said, 'And you'll examine the contents, I suppose.' She shrugged wearily. 'You won't find anything. Because I've destroyed it. But the keys must be guarded.'

He frowned at her. 'What have you destroyed?'

She shook her head, rubbing her forehead. 'It doesn't matter.'

'Of course it matters! Or the Russians wouldn't be after it.'

Her nerves cracked and she cried: 'One page from his notebook! Containing a list of numbers, that's all!'

'Numbers? Of what? Safety-deposit boxes?'

She cried, 'Of course! If you were Max where else would you keep something that could destroy the whole Roman –'

She opened her eyes, aghast. She stared at him; then she dropped her head, and held it.

'Oh God, forgive me . . .' she whispered.

Morgan stared at her. *Destroy the whole Roman what? The whole Roman Catholic Church?* . . . She sat tensely, then she flung her head up. She waved her hand angrily at the bag.

'Go ahead! The box numbers are listed in his will, anyway.'

He frowned. 'But, if the numbers are listed in the will, why did you destroy the numbers in the notebook?'

Suddenly tears were glistening.

'All the numbers except two are listed in the will! And those are the numbers I've destroyed! They are in my head! I memorized them!'

'But tell me *why* . . .'

She cried at him: 'Because I'm going to destroy what's in those two boxes, that's why!'

And she threw herself on the mattress and put her hands over her face. She sobbed once. And he came down beside her and put his arms around her. She cried: '*I'm not going to tell anybody . . . I'll die first, like God's Banker hanging from Blackfriars Bridge! . . . And if you try to take me anywhere I'll fight you tooth and nail!*' . . .

His exhausted mind was racing. *God's Banker hanging from Blackfriars Bridge in London? Two months ago? The Italian banker?* . . . He held her, his mind fumbling.

'I won't try to take you anywhere you don't want to go.'

She lay, racked, sobbing her exhaustion into her hands; he held her, and oh God he hated this whole stinking business; then she twisted in his arms.

'Do you swear?'

His heart turned over for her. 'Yes.'

She lay still a moment; then she sat up abruptly. She looked at him hard. 'And you're not here to trick me – do you swear to that?'

He said: 'I swear it . . .'

11

Over at old Pearls airport there was still scattered gunfire as the Marines mopped up the Revolutionary Army and the Cubans. The Rangers were still clearing the new airfield of the earth-moving equipment and spikes under sniper fire; they hot-wired the bulldozers and steamrollers and they used them as tanks to charge Cuban positions, and there were running battles and counter-attacks, and all the time the thudding of the mortars and the stench of cordite. The Revolutionary Army retreated back through the town, commandeering houses for defence positions and setting up barricades; they swarmed around the True Blue medical campus, and the American students lay low in their rooms, the bullets smashing and whining and ricocheting everywhere. And now helicopter gunships came clattering through the sky to take on the People's Revolutionary Army surrounding Government House, but first they had to take on the anti-aircraft guns at Fort Frederick and Fort Ruppert, and the thudding and thundering and clattering and chattering filled the sky and shook the windows.

Upstairs, Anna Hapsburg was in an exhausted sleep at last.

Once upon a time, when he was a schoolboy, Jack Morgan had been deeply religious, and a Catholic. But university and the rough-and-tumble of the Navy had changed that. He found he could no longer believe in a God who would damn him to eternal flames, if only because no twentieth-century judge would sentence anybody to such a punishment for anything; nor could he believe in a God who logged up millions of prayers a minute like a mighty computer and tried to rearrange the world on request, if only because such a God cannot be persuaded to change His mind because, being omniscient, He already knew whether He was going to change His mind or not. And so Jack Morgan, scientist, had reluctantly become an atheist. But then he had the good fortune to meet Anna Valentine and read a book called *Summa in Theologica*, written in the fourteenth century. And, to his relief, the good Saint Thomas had proved to him, through pure, invincible Aristotelian logic, that a God existed – even if he could not, by logic, prove what kind of God He was. And Morgan had been able to believe again. It was a long way from the Holy Roman Church that he used to believe so completely, but Jack Morgan had the comfort of being able to pray again, at least in homage.

But it was different for Anna Hapsburg. She believed completely.

He looked at her. She lay on her stomach, one leg bent, her long hair matted across her face.

77

Her beloved Roman Catholic Church? Was that what this secret, this Nazi file was all about? 'Something that could destroy the whole Roman . . .' she had said. And she had been aghast that it had slipped out.

An important Western institution, Brink-Ford had said.

Well, if the authority of the Catholic Church were suddenly destroyed, many governments would be in trouble. Latin America – the power of the Church there was enormous, it was the opium of the masses. If the Russians had the ability to undermine the Catholic Church, to destroy its authority, it would enormously help their policy of world-wide revolution, of 'liberating the world from the capitalist yoke'.

Morgan dragged his hands down his face. But all this was guess-work.

He was too tired to think straight. Oh, to sleep. To just take her in his arms and sleep, sleep, sleep. But he could not. It had all been go go go, so much action, so much tension, that the enormity of it hadn't fully sunk in until now. *The Russians had sent a man to get her and she had killed him* . . . And if she hadn't she would probably be dead herself now – the information extracted from her, her body dumped midst the ruins out there. And if the British couldn't get the information out of her politely? He was bloody sure they'd get it somehow. And then what? Do they just turn her loose afterwards, to tell every newspaper what the terrible British had done to her, to shout her story from the rooftops? Including perhaps the very information they so desperately wanted to get their hands on. Or did even the pukka British make sure people didn't talk?

God, it was like a bad dream. Gone was the euphoria of finding her, of knowing she was safe for the moment.

Something Klaus Barbie, the Butcher of Lyons, a Nazi war criminal, knew.

Something the Catholic Church had done during the Second World War?

Collaborated with the Nazis? But it was common knowledge that the Catholic Church had not raised its voice to stop the Nazi extermination of the Jews, that the Pope of that time made a concordat, a live-and-let-live deal with Hitler to ensure that the Holy Roman Church was allowed to survive. But would that, so long after the event, shake the Church to its foundations, destabilize the Western world?

Something that God's Banker had died over? . . .

He gave an exhausted sigh and looked down at the contents of her handgrip, spread on the floor.

The notebook. Passports. The will. Some share certificates. Some newspaper and magazine articles. A wad of money. The keys.

The passports. Three. At least one was false. It was an American passport, it bore Max's photograph, but it was in the name of Maxwell Constantine. The next was Grenadan, the other West German, both in Max's real name. It was not very unusual that he should have had two nationalities. But why the false American passport? It had a good number of immigration stamps in it, but mostly Max had used the German passport. Morgan had made a list of every entry and exit stamp in every passport, and had arranged them in date order. Max had travelled a good deal. South America, United States, Europe. Morgan could not remember the date when God's Banker had been found hanging from Blackfriars Bridge but Max had been to England several times every year.

The will. It left everything to 'my darling wife, Anna Louise Hapsburg, on condition that she does not remarry nor cohabit with any man . . .'

What did all that mean? Morgan knew nothing about wills, but were those conditions legally enforceable? When would she get the inheritance? – only *after* she had *not* remarried nor cohabitated? How long would she have to wait to prove her virtue? And if, having inherited, she *then* remarried or commenced to live in sin, would she then be *dis*inherited?

But it showed an insecure, jealous man – who would try to intimidate his wife. Was such a man to be believed if he claimed to have something that could destroy the Roman Catholic Church? Or was he so unstable that he invented his story? The bastard had once concocted a terrifying case against him . . .

Morgan stared across the room.

No. *She* believed it. And so did the British who had sent him here. And the Americans. And the Russians.

Attached to the will was a schedule of principal assets. The man was extremely wealthy. Real estate, shares, bonds. There was a list of safety-deposit boxes, and the banks in which they were. Banks in Miami, Venezuela, Liechtenstein, and London.

Morgan squeezed his eyes.

But the microfilm or file probably was *not* in any of those banks. It was probably in one of the other banks listed on the page that she had torn from the notebook. And even if he found out which banks those were, how do you get into a man's safety-deposit box?

He sighed, and picked up the keys again.

Some of them had numbers stamped on them, some of them were blank. Some of the box numbers mentioned in the will corresponded with numbers on keys. So, at least some of the keys were eliminated. But that didn't help much.

And then the cash. Twenty thousand dollars.

That was a lot of money to Jack Morgan, but not to Max Hapsburg. Why shouldn't he keep twenty thousand bucks in his safe, in case he had to jump on an aeroplane suddenly?

Yes, but twenty thousand? All in used fifty-dollar bills? It made a bulky wad. Why not travellers cheques? In case he had to run and be anonymous? Not leave a trail of travellers cheques and credit card deals for the authorities to follow?

That left the newspaper and magazine cuttings.

They all concerned the Third World debt. Max was mentioned in several pieces. In short, most Third World countries, including Grenada, were in serious trouble because they had borrowed so heavily at high interest rates. They could not repay their loans, partly because of mismanagement, waste and corruption, and partly because the commodities which they produced had recently dropped drastically in value. The dollar was too high, the interest rates too high; the loans were now crushingly burdensome and the terms should be renegotiated. Some debtor countries were threatening to declare themselves bankrupt, to form a cartel, defy the banks and refuse to pay; but saner countries, and leading figures like Max Hapsburg, had dissuaded them from this suicidal course for the time being. There were lists of big banks and the frightening amounts they had loaned and could not recover. The overall picture was frightening; if the crisis was not resolved, if the debtor countries did not repay the loans, many big Western banks would go bankrupt. So millions of depositors would lose their money, the bankrupt banks would have to call in the other loans they had made so many industries would go bankrupt too, so millions of workers would become unemployed and unable to repay *their* debts – in short, there would be an international depression which would make the Wall Street crash of 1929 look like a Sunday-school picnic. And the inherent political dangers were spelled out.

If the debtor countries did not improve their economies, if the masses were kept poor, as in most of South America, if a strong, sensible middle class did not emerge, these countries were vulnerable to communist-inspired revolution. Russia stood to gain everything from this economic crisis. If the Western banks collapsed because of the Third World debt, it could bring about the collapse of the capitalist system the Russians were working for. And, in the final result, it was the capitalist system which was to blame. Greed. The banks were to blame, for greedily lending vast sums of money at high interest rates to these corrupt banana republics during the good times of high commodity prices . . .

Morgan stared across the gloom. Outside were the sounds of war. '*I'd rather die like God's Banker . . .*'

So banking, high finance, had something to do with this Nazi secret that could destroy the Roman Catholic Church, to quote Anna, this important institution that could destabilize the West, to quote Brink-Ford. And so Vatican banking might be involved. And God's Banker hanging from Blackfriars Bridge might look like suicide, but obviously Anna knew he had been murdered . . .

Murdered by whom? By Max Hapsburg?

By the Vatican? He could hardly believe that.

And murdered for what? What had God's Banker gone to London for? For the secret which Max Hapsburg possessed? The same secret that was now locked in Anna's head?

He sighed in frustration. This was all conjecture. Maybe God's Banker had nothing to do with it, maybe she had used it as a figure of speech.

But no, he did not believe that either. Not in the context. The murder of God's Banker had everything to do with this.

81

And, looking at the facts so far, he had no doubt that she was in grave danger of being murdered too. And not necessarily by the Russians alone.

12

In the afternoon the 82nd paratroopers and the Caribbean Peace-keeping Force began to arrive at the new airport, the planes coming in under heavy sniper fire. In Saint George's the helicopter gunships and fighter planes were still taking on the anti-aircraft guns of Fort Frederick and Fort Ruppert. In the medical schools the American students were still nailed down, mattresses stuffed in windows, the bullets crashing and smashing and ricocheting about them. In the late afternoon the Rangers fought their way to the True Blue campus and cleared a landing zone for helicopters on the basketball court and started evacuating them. And darkness came down on the thudding and the smoke and the dust and the cracking of the guns.

The sounds of war awoke Anna. She sat up. He said:

'It's all right, they won't bomb us by mistake. It'll all be over soon.'

She was wide awake. And full of hard distrust again. She said:

'And then what happens? They're going to fly us out of here by helicopter onto the aircraft carrier?'

'Right.'

'And then what is going to happen to the civilians?'

'They'll go wherever they want, once order is reestablished. Most of them will come back here.'

'And me?'

He hated this subterfuge. He said, 'We're going to live happily ever after, Anna.'

She was incredulous.

'Nonsense!' She pointed at the sea. 'Once we're safely out of here, they'll fly me to America! And then they question me, don't they? About the same thing the Russians wanted . . .'

She cried at him: 'Well, I'm not going, Jack! I'll scream bloody blue murder if they try to take me!'

His nerves were going. 'Anna? –'

'You don't deny it, do you? You're after the same thing, aren't you? . . .' She glared at him: '*Do* you deny it?'

And then, through his tension, seeing that angry anguish in her eyes, it was easier to lie. He loved her, and pitied her, and he wasn't going to let anybody do anything to her.

'I deny it,' he said quietly.

There was no electricity; the whole island was blacked out. Over near the airfield the Cubans and People's Revolutionary Army forces regrouped in the darkness, and there was sniper fire and the clatter of helicopter gunships dealing with it.

'Did you read what's in the bag?' Her voice was flat as she hung on to her self-control.

'Yes.'

'And?' She said it bitterly.

He sat back against the wall in the flickering candlelight. He did not want to talk about it now, but he had to.

'Last night you said that this thing could destroy the whole Catholic Church.'

She blinked. She waved her hand in dismissal. Then sighed. 'Oh, what's the use, you won't believe me. Yes, it's about the Catholic Church. And that's all I'm going to tell you . . .' She sighed angrily. 'Look, I know you're not a Catholic any more –'

'But I have great respect for the Church. All churches.'

'All right. But to me it's much more than that. It's . . . God's corporeal representative. God is the most important thing in life, and therefore His Church is the most important thing on this earth . . .' She paused then made the point with slow emphasis: 'I *believe*. I believe that the Pope is God's vicar. That he is infallible. I believe in transubstantiation, in the Holy Trinity, in Heaven and Hell – the whole nine yards.'

Morgan nodded.

She went on, as if rehearsed: 'I know the Church can make mistakes, but that's because of human frailty. You get mistakes in any profession. And I know that many people *resent* the Catholic Church.' She didn't take her eyes off him. 'It's wealth, for example. The . . . *grip* it's got on the people. The fear, if you like. Okay. Arguments can be made against all that. But I sincerely believe that the power of the Church works for the *good* of mankind. It is *good* for mankind to be under the thumb of the Church, because man is an irresponsible, cruel, thoughtless creature. Man *needs* a big stick. And the Church is God's stick. The Church is *vital* to the stability of mankind, let alone to his immortal soul.'

Morgan waited. He nodded.

'It follows that if anybody attempts to . . . damage the Church, I will do everything in my power to stop him. Not only as a Christian but as an honourable person.' She paused. 'That is my solemn duty. And if I didn't do it, I would be . . . Judas Iscariot.'

Morgan watched her. And loved her. She went on:

'And believe me, if these people who're chasing me succeed . . .' She tailed off. Then: 'I don't believe what Max told me is true. I believe it's a vile fabrication. But the fabricated evidence exists. And Max got his hands on it.'

'Did he say how he got hold of it?'

She shook her head. 'But Max was everywhere, knew just about everybody. Fingers in all pies.'

He said: 'You've heard of Klaus Barbie?'

She was taken by surprise. Then said dismissively: 'Of course, it's been in the newspapers recently. The Butcher of Lyons. He's in jail in France.'

'Awaiting trial. Did Max know Barbie?'

She looked mystified. 'Not to my knowledge.'

He did not believe her. 'Did Max know any old Nazis? Hiding in South America?'

'He might have. They're all over South America.'

'Did he go to South America much?'

'Often. He had business deals all over. Look, Max had many failings. If you're wondering if Max was a Nazi, you're quite wrong. Why're you asking these questions?'

'If you won't tell me I've got to try to figure this out for myself.' He went on: 'Roberto Calvi, God's Banker? Did Max know him?'

She stared at him an instant.

'I don't know. He knew a lot of people in international banking. I only met a few of them.'

'What do you know about God's Banker?'

'Only what was in the newspapers.'

He said: 'Why did Max keep those magazine articles about the Third World debt in his safe? One could find them in any public library.'

'I don't know.'

'Was God's Banker involved in Max's negotiations over the Third World debt?'

'No.'

'How do you know?'

She closed her eyes. 'Oh Jack, Jack . . . Here!' She thrust her hand into her pocket and tossed a wad of newspaper cuttings onto the mattress. 'You might as well read it for yourself, if you can get it in any public library! This was also in the safe. He wasn't *murdered*, he committed suicide.'

He unfolded the cuttings. There were three. She said: 'They sometimes contradict each other, like bloody newspapers do. I might as well summarize them for you.'

'Okay.'

She sighed tensely, and looked away.

'Nothing to it. Roberto Calvi, God's so-called Banker, owned the Banco Ambrosiano in Italy. Thought to be very respectable. He also became a financial adviser to the Vatican Bank – that's why he was nicknamed God's Banker. But, unbeknown to the Vatican, he also did a lot of shady deals. The Vatican found itself innocently involved. There was a financial scandal. God's Banker was eventually prosecuted in Italy, fined ten million dollars and sentenced to four years in jail. He got bail, pending appeal, and fled to England on a false passport. The next morning he committed suicide by hanging himself from Blackfriars Bridge. End of story.'

Morgan said: 'Suicide? With ten kilos of bricks in his pockets?'

'Exactly. If it was murder, they wouldn't have weighted him – hanging was enough. He weighted himself to ensure a quick death. He also had a lot of money on him – fifteen thousand dollars. A murderer wouldn't have left that.'

'Last night you cried: "I'd rather die like God's Banker than tell anybody". You must believe it's murder.'

She waved a hand. 'I was hysterical last night. And completely flabbergasted by you showing up.' She turned away. 'When Wall Street crashed in 1929 bankers and stockbrokers jumped out of windows like lemmings.'

He did not believe her. 'When was it that you had this drunken row with Max?'

'On my birthday. Last year.'

'That's the twentieth of June?'

'So you remember.'

He looked at the newspaper cuttings. 'And God's Banker was found hanging on the eighteenth of June. Two days before. And when Max had his drunken outburst he taunted you with God's Banker, to prove he had the evidence?'

She turned away. 'Oh, he was *drunk*. He was going away the next day and he was insanely jealous. And he . . . *despised* the Church. He was just saying anything to hurt me. He used to ask me if I confessed my adulteries, got absolution and then did it again. And so on.'

'And *did* he go away the next day?'

She closed her eyes. 'Oh Jack, I'm not going to answer any more questions. This is *my* business!'

He picked up the list he had made of entries and exits from Max's passports. 'The next day, the twenty-first of June, he flew to New York. On the same day, to Switzerland. And, two days later, back to Grenada.'

She got up. And paced across the room. 'I can't remember. He was always flying everywhere. Why the hell am I answering these questions? No more!'

He held out a finger at her. 'Listen, Anna. The Russians are after you. I'm trying to protect you.' He pointed at the window. 'In a few hours this Mickey Mouse war is going to be over. And the Yanks are going to airlift us out of here. What are you going to do? You'll have no choice but to go with them –'

'And then the CIA start questioning me!' She shook her head fiercely: 'No way! I've committed no crime! I'm refusing to go with them to America!'

'Anna, you're going to have no choice! You're under martial law. But at least you'll be safe from the Russians.' He sighed angrily. 'So, we'll get you a lawyer. He'll protect your legal rights. As you say, you've committed no crime, they'll *have* to leave you alone.'

'A lawyer?' She shook her head incredulously. 'I'll have to get half a dozen lawyers before Max's estate is wound up and legally mine, because he didn't sign the will! But I'm *not* –' she shook her head – 'going to tell a lawyer what Max told me. Because if the Russians can screw the story out of me they can get it out of a lawyer too – *easier*! *And* so could the CIA! And how long does this lawyer business take – a couple of days? And you don't think that in that time the CIA will have got the story out of me? And even *after* the lawyer gets me free, you think they'll quit? Will they, hell!' She snorted angrily: 'Don't think I haven't thought it all through, Jack!' Suddenly her exhausted eyes filled with tears. 'I'm not going to let those people get their hands on me!'

His nerves were going. And oh God, God, what she said was probably true but he was still too much of a Royal Navy man at heart to believe that of the British, even though he believed almost anything now. He got to his feet, and he took her in his arms.

'Anna, you're coming with me to England. A British lawyer will be able to protect you.'

She flung her head back and looked up at him. 'That's why you're here, isn't it? . . .'

He sighed. 'I'm here because of my local knowledge.'

She stared at him. 'You're not going to make me go to England, Jack . . . I know a hell of a lot more about this than you do, and I don't trust your pukka British either! . . .' She shook her head fiercely. 'You're *naive* to think they're any different! . . . *And you're not going to make me go there!* . . .'

He closed his eyes, and his heart welled.

'I'm not going to make you go anywhere . . .'

She was rigid in his arms. Desperate to believe him.

'Do you swear that you haven't been sent to get me?'

And oh God, God, she had all the legal rights in the world on her side. He held her tight and said: 'I swear it.'

'To God? . . .'

He felt his nerves almost crack.

'To God . . .'

13

In the small hours the Marines lifted off in helicopters from Pearls airport and went clattering over the island to Saint George's; at the same time another company of Marines was coming ashore from the aircraft carrier in thirteen amtracks, with five tanks, to raise the siege of Government House. And the furious sounds of battle filled the darkness. At seven o'clock the Marines came bursting into the grounds and there was cheering and clapping and laughing. Then came the thudding of a helicopter above the house, dust and leaves blasting away.

The big machine came clattering down onto the lawn. The hostages were already assembled outside. The SEAL commander shouted in Morgan's ear: '*You and the lady first, right in the back!*'

Morgan grabbed Anna's elbow and they ran for the helicopter. They scrambled into the big fuselage. Then the other people came running, doubled up in the roaring blast. Anna sat, clutching the handgrip. The helicopter filled up, people scrambling over each other.

The helicopter roared, and rocked, then rose up into the air. Up, up. The sounds of battle were drowned but now the devastation came into view below, smoke and dust and rubble and bodies. Over to the south the battle to rescue the American students in the Grand Anse campus was still going on. The helicopter swung away and went chopping across the harbour, out towards the sea.

The Guam lay huge and grey, her decks stacked with aircraft. The helicopter came chopping down, down, the steel decks loomed up; then she touched down and applause broke out from the passengers. The doors opened and out they scrambled, and sailors hustled them across the deck. Morgan began to crouch towards the door, but the pilot twisted in his seat and beckoned to him. He handed him a headset and said over the intercom: 'You're the guy from Delta Force guarding Mrs Hapsburg?'

'Right.'

'Then hold tight.'

The helicopter roared, then it rose up rockily off the deck again. It wheeled and went chopping away. Morgan looked back at Anna. She tried to shout something to him, but he could only see her lips moving. He rasped to the pilot: *'Where the hell are we going?'*

'To Trinidad. Don't ask me why, buddy, I just do as I'm told in this game.'

'On whose orders?'

'The Admiral himself.'

Anna came scrambling angrily across the fuselage. She grabbed Morgan's shoulders and shouted: *'Where're we going?'*

'What's her problem?' the pilot said.

'She wants to know why the hell we're going to Trinidad.'

'Tell her I ain't much good at arguing with admirals. Commanders, sure, lieutenant-commanders, a piece of cake, but admirals? – forget it.'

Anna shouted something furiously. Morgan took off the headset and grabbed her hand. He crouched down to the rear of the aircraft with her. He cupped his hands to her ear and shouted: *'Calm down! We're going to Trinidad. I don't know why but we have no goddam option! You're subject to American martial law! When we get to Trinidad, leave it to me – don't make a fuss until I've found out what's happening! Right now I'm responsible for your safety. If you make a fuss they'll put somebody else onto looking after you!'*

He glared at her, then squeezed her hand hard and he scrambled back to the pilot. He rammed on the headset, and tried to think.

Trinidad . . . Were they going to try to debrief her there? . . . Who? Brink-Ford himself? . . .

He looked back at Anna. She had her eyes closed, trying hard to control her fury and her nerves.

He put his hand in his pouch, and felt the gun. The gun with which she had killed the Russian, the gun he was supposed to drop in the sea.

The helicopter came chopping over the airport, towards the far corner. Down there a car was waiting. When the helicopter settled on the ground, two men got out of the car.

Morgan scrambled out of the helicopter and held out his hand for Anna. She came clambering out, hair flying. They hurried under the downblast towards the car. A third man was getting out, his hand clutching his hat. One man held open the back door for them. Before they reached it, the helicopter was taking off again. Morgan stopped at the car door. '*Who are you?*' he shouted.

The man indicated the open door and pointed at the helicopter. Then the noise abated as it rose away. 'Who are you?' Morgan repeated.

'Thompson, Security, British Consulate, and that's Edwards. Get in please, sir.'

'Identification, please. For all I know you're KGB.'

The man pulled out a wallet and flipped it open. 'This' – he indicated the man with the hat – 'is Mr Gillespie, the British consul.'

'How do you do?' the consul called. 'Do let's go.'

Anna held back angrily. 'May I ask where?'

The consul said, 'Can we discuss that en route?'

'No, we cannot!' She turned to Morgan. 'Can I have a word?'

She walked away angrily. Morgan followed equally angrily. She turned to him: '*So it's the bloody British who want me!*'

He gripped her arm and whispered:

'Anna, at least we're not on the aircraft carrier! You couldn't have swum off! Now those two security guys aren't stage props! We've got to go with them and figure it out from there!' He seized her elbow and led her back to the car.

She got in, furiously. Morgan got in beside her, Thompson beside him.

The consul started the car. He said airily: 'We're going to my residence.' He drove off across the grass. 'I dare say you could use a hot bath and a decent meal?'

They drove out of the airport, through security gates without stopping, onto the highway. Anna seethed, her hand clammy in Morgan's, her face averted. They drove through tropical island countryside. Then through seashore suburbs. The car swung into a gateway.

A Union Jack hung from a pole. The iron gates opened electronically. They drove through, and stopped outside the front door. The garden was beautiful. The consul's wife opened the door, beaming.

She bustled out, and took charge of Anna. The consul led Morgan straight into his study. He closed the door and faced him. He was a nice, bookish man.

'Now we can speak. Thompson and Edwards are utterly reliable, of course, but we don't know much about the cloak-and-dagger business here. Now, then, you'll be perfectly safe, the house is well secured. And comfortable, I hope. Please make yourselves at home. You needn't worry about being seen, because I was given strict instructions to give the servants the day off –'

'How long are we here for?'

Mr Gillespie said busily, 'An RAF plane is coming to fetch you. It arrives after midnight, for reasons of secrecy.'

'To take us where?'

The consul lifted a white hand. 'One of your people will be coming here shortly and he'll answer –'

'Who?'

'One of your people. I've no idea where the plane's coming from or going to. Mine not to reason why. All I know is that I am to look after you till then.'

'I'd like some civilian kit.'

'Indeed. I have already bought some for you, they knew your size. I was authorized to buy Mrs Hapsburg a change of dress and – er . . . underwear, but if it doesn't fit my daughter's clothing may do so. Oh, and you're to stay indoors, please. And you're not to use the telephone.' He added: 'All calls go through our central switchboard.' He rubbed his hands. 'Now, then, business over, what can I get you to drink?'

'I'm allowed to drink, am I? A beer, please. But I'll take it upstairs and drink it while I bath.'

'Of course. My wife will serve luncheon shortly.'

Morgan said firmly: 'Thank you, but we'll skip lunch. We're both exhausted. I think we'll just have a bath, a drink and a sleep.'

'Of *course*,' Mr Gillespie said, apparently relieved. 'Would you like my wife to bring a tray to your respective rooms?'

'That would be a better idea, thank you.' He added firmly: 'Mr Gillespie, I don't know how much head office has told you, but Mrs Hapsburg and I will be sleeping in the same room.'

Mr Gillespie blinked. 'You mean, for security reasons? . . .'

'Both.'

'Oh . . .' Mr Gillespie touched his spectacles. 'Well, of course.' He added with a rush of joviality: 'Beer . . .' He bustled for the door. Then stopped. 'Oh, I'm told to relieve you of your weapons. Evidently they're not Her Majesty's.'

Morgan would have liked to toss the gun at the man, like they do in the movies, except it would have alarmed Mr Gillespie. He placed his machine gun on the desk. Just then there was a smart knock, and the door opened.

'Ah . . .' the consul said, even more relieved.

'Good morning,' Christopher Carrington said, with his crooked grin. He was carrying a briefcase.

Morgan stared at him.

Carrington propped himself against the bookshelves, pipe in hand, a picture of masculine elegance. In civilian clothes. 'Arrived yesterday,' he said – 'thought the Yanks might spring you from jolly old G.H. yesterday, but no such luck. They made a bit of a mess of it, if you ask me. All that sweat just to disperse a few fuzzy-wuzzies? After all, they're not exactly Zulus, are they? We could have done it with one hand tied behind our backs. Still, I must congratulate you, most sincerely, Jack.'

'What the hell are you here for, Carrington?'

Carrington lit his pipe.

'Officially, I'm a naval observer of what the Yanks are up to. Officially Maggie Thatcher's as sore as a gumboil with Ronnie. Unofficially, I'm here to hold your hand.'

'You, of all people?'

'Why not? We're old shipmates.'

Jesus. 'Well, I don't need you to hold my hand. Or Anna's.'

'Delighted to hear it. As I say, congratulations, Jack.' He wagged his eyebrows, gave his jolly smirk: 'I hope it wasn't all work and no play?'

Jesus, he could hit the bastard. 'Meaning?'

Carrington took his pipe from his mouth, and examined it.

'Meaning how are you and Mrs Hapsburg getting along, Jack?'

'Mind your own bloody business!'

'Oh, I'm sorry,' Carrington said. He meant it. 'I've offended you, I'm truly sorry, but what I really mean is, it *is* my business you see. How Mrs Hapsburg has taken to you coming back into her life is most important to us. That's why we sent you. May I ask – are you two – er – close?'

Morgan glared at him. 'Very. Now go to hell.'

'Excellent. I will presently, but excellent. And? What has she told you, Jack?'

'Nothing.'

'Nothing?' Carrington moved to the consul's desk, and sat down. He opened his briefcase. 'Sit down, we'll start the debriefing.'

'We will not! I'm going to sleep. And so is Anna.'

'She has told you nothing at all? I don't believe you.'

'Gee, that's tough, Carrington. What I want to know is what you plan for Anna Hapsburg.'

Carrington put a match to his pipe. He puffed out smoke.

'We fly tonight in an RAF jet to England. You and Anna will be comfortably accommodated in a safe house. She'll be debriefed. And you.' He shrugged. 'After that, she's free to do what she likes.'

Morgan resisted saying: She's free to do what she likes right now! Carrington went on: 'What we need to know is, is she going to give trouble?'

'Trouble?' Morgan said dangerously.

'Is she going to cooperate?'

'And if she doesn't?'

Carrington sighed. 'That's the tricky part.'

Oh Jesus . . . He had to bite his tongue.

'She'll cooperate. She's glad to be off the island. She very much wants to go to England with me.'

'*Good*,' Carrington said with relief '– we're *so* pleased. We're relying on you to reassure her – that's why we sent you, and jolly well done, too, Jack.'

Morgan jabbed an angry finger at the man. 'Then get off my back! Don't you *dare* burst in here like a bull in a china shop with your big tactless mouth and your supercilious smirk and start demanding answers! Or in addition to getting your nose flattened you'll frighten her off, you big prick! You'll make her suspicious! So leave us severely alone until we get to England! And then if you try any tricks on her . . .' He held up his finger. 'I'll break your neck.' He jabbed his finger at the ceiling. 'Now I'm going upstairs to sleep! Don't you *dare* come near us until it's time to leave!'

He glared at the man, then strode out of the room.

Carrington smiled and raised his hands in peace.

Morgan strode up the stairs with four bottles of beer and the civilian clothes the consul had given him. Mrs Gillespie was coming down, clutching a bundle of Anna's clothing. She shook the bundle gaily as she darted past him: 'Just going to stick these in the washing machine – do give me anything of yours, they'll be dry in a jiffy! Just leave them outside your door . . .'

'Thank you.'

He climbed the stairs, and opened the door to the first bedroom. It had a private bathroom and there was the sound of the shower. He closed the bedroom door behind him. There was a key. He locked the door.

He went to the window. The air conditioner was humming. He twisted the catch and slid the window open. He looked out.

The room was on the side of the house. It was a straight-forward drop from the window, onto lawn. And the window immediately below was the consul's study. Beyond the lawn were flowerbeds, tropical trees, then a garden wall. About eight feet high. Beyond a road led down to the beach. The other way was the suburban road. Heavily treed. Lampposts.

He turned to the bathroom door. The shower suddenly stopped; the curtain swept back. The door opened and Anna came out.

She was wearing Mrs Gillespie's bathrobe. Water was still running off her. Her washed hair hung in long tresses. She looked at him angrily.

'You lied to me.'

He held up a finger, then pointed at the door. He walked into the bathroom, and switched on the shower again. He beckoned her back into the bathroom. She came. He said softly:

'Anna, this is your last opportunity to think about this. Now, at midnight they're flying us to England on an RAF plane. The

94

British intend to interrogate you about this evidence. If you cooperate, I believe you'll be safe. They'll protect you from the Russians. Now, do you want to do so?'

Her eyes flashed. 'You lied to me! And I'm telling you loud and clear that I'm *not* going! They have no legal right to make me go anywhere – I'm an American citizen and I demand to see the American consul!'

He closed the door.

'Yes, I lied to you! But it'll do you no good screaming for the American consul because the American government is in on this! How do you think the British got me into an American uniform in an American war? Why did the American admiral have you flown to the British authorities in Trinidad?'

'Why *indeed*? I think you better start telling me the *truth*!'

'The truth is yes, I was sent by the British to find you and get you to England! Because yes, the British and Americans want to find this information of Max's! Just like the Russians want to!'

She hissed, 'And what are the noble British going to do with it?'

'I don't know!'

'You're lying to me again!'

He closed his eyes angrily. 'I am not lying now, Anna. I don't know what the information is, so I don't know what they'll do with it. They'll exploit it, yes! Now, you've got two options –'

'*Why did you lie to me?*'

'Goddammit, because you were overwrought! You didn't trust me! I had to figure out what this was about and what to do about it!'

'No – you lied to me because that was your assignment! The British told you to get the story out of me –'

'Correct! But I was also lying to win your trust so *I* could figure out what to do! Now I'm trying to help *you*.' He glared at her. 'Now, you've only got two options, Anna. You can fly with them to England, and hire a lawyer to protect your rights. But I don't think you'll have a chance to do that. You'll be whisked from some military airfield to some unknown destination to be interrogated –'

'I'm not going with them to England!'

He looked at her. 'Is that final?'

'Yes!'

He took a breath. 'Then your only option is to trust me and go out by that window with me after dark. And escape.'

'*Or*,' she said angrily, 'I can walk out by the front door! As I'm fully legally entitled to do!'

He stood aside and waved his hand.

'Try it. See how far you get. You won't get *near* the front door! They'll forcibly detain you. They haven't gone to all this trouble just to let you stroll away. But go ahead, try it!'

'But they can't detain me – that's illegal!'

'Of course it's illegal! But whatever it is you've got in your head they want so badly that they'll do it! And a hell of a lot more!' He glared at her, then took a deep, tense breath. 'Look, Anna, right now they're off their guard because I've told them that you're cooperative. So this moment, *I'm* your only jailer. There're two security men in the house, plus a bastard called Carrington who's supposed to be my controller. But they're all entrusting your safe-keeping to me because I'm the only one who can keep you happy. But if you try to walk out and kick up a fuss, they'll politely lock you up with the two security men as your jailers and at midnight they'll put you on that plane in a straitjacket!' He glared at her. 'But if you trust *this* jailer' – he banged his chest – 'we've got a chance of escaping, because *they* trust me and won't be watching! Then we can get you a lawyer.'

She stared at him. The shower gushing down.

'Why are you doing this?'

'Because you are legally entitled to do what you like! They have no rights over you. And I'm not going to stand by and let them force you to do something. And I believe they *will* use force if necessary – it's that important to them. And worse than that – I'm by no means sure that if you've been uncooperative they'll let you walk out and tell the world what the beastly British did to you. Or let you blow your secret information to the wide world!' He took a tense breath. 'I'm doing this because I believe you're in serious danger.' He added: 'And because I love you.'

She looked at him angrily.

'And what'll the British do to you? For helping me escape their clutches?'

He said: 'To *me*? Nothing! What can they do? I'm here on an *illegal* assignment of kidnapping Anna Hapsburg. What can they legally do to me for refusing to be an accomplice to a crime? They daren't court-martial me, because I'm here unofficially and deniably, quote unquote, and I've committed no crime. And I'll be a terrible embarrassment when I tell the court what the British were up to in Grenada. That would make lovely reading in the press.' He waved his hand impatiently. 'They daren't do a damn thing to me.'

She said, 'They could kill you. To keep your mouth closed.'

He snorted. 'They won't dare do anything once we've got a lawyer.' He pointed grimly at the window. 'That's the only way out, Anna. We're committing no crime and you've got nothing to lose.'

She looked at him. Exhausted. 'And where do we go?'

'You have to tell me. I don't know where this precious information is, remember. First we have to get off this island. To South America, obviously, only a hundred miles away. From there, you have to tell me.' He held out a warning finger. 'I don't want you to tell me now. I don't want you to think I may tip-toe downstairs and tell those bastards what you've told me.'

She took a big, tremulous breath.

'Oh, thank God,' she whispered.

And he knew she really was thanking God.

14

He was suddenly awake, just as it was getting dark. She was still deep asleep. He went into the bathroom, dashed cold water onto his face. He pulled on the clothes Mr Gillespie had provided. He unzipped Anna's handgrip and took some money. Then he sat down, to wait for dark.

He parted the curtain. For a minute he watched. There was nobody to be seen in the garden. There was no light in the study window below.

He slid the window open. He swung his leg over the sill. He dropped onto the lawn below. He scrambled up and ran for the trees.

He ran at the wall, and jumped. He gripped the top and swung his leg up. He straddled it, then he rolled over.

He dropped into the road below. He scrambled up.

He walked down the road fast for a hundred yards, then he came to the beach. He started running.

The taxi dropped him off along the waterfront.

He walked feverishly towards the harbour. There were sailing boats, sport-fishing boats. He came to a handpainted sign. It read: *Big King for Big Fish*. It gave a telephone number. There were more signs. He pulled out his wallet and made a note.

Ahead there was a bar, overlooking the harbour. He made for it. He went in and signalled to the black barman. 'Beer, please.'

He paid for it with one of Max Hapsburg's fifty-dollar bills and got the change. 'Have you got a telephone?'

'Nope. Don't work.'

Morgan pushed a dollar bill across the bar. 'Where do I find Big King? I want to go fishing.'

The barman took the dollar. He jerked his head. 'He's anchored out there aways. See that hot-water boat?'

Morgan peered across the harbour. The launch was about forty feet long, with a flying bridge.

'How do I get out there? Is there a rowboat?'

'Sounds like five bucks to me.'

He would gladly have paid fifty.

The barman turned and yelled: 'Take this gennelman to Big King . . .'

A black boy rowed him out. There were lights burning in Big King's portholes. There was a rubber dinghy tied to the stern. Morgan grabbed the gunnel. He called, 'Mr King?'

A head appeared at the aft hatch. It wore a baseball cap and the face was round and heavy. 'Yeah?'

'Can I rent your boat tomorrow?'

'Nope,' Big King said, 'she's already rented. For the next three days. After that, okay.'

'Can you take me to Saint Vincent, day after tomorrow?'

'Saint Vincent?'

Morgan gave the boy ten dollars, so he would remember him. And, hopefully, Saint Vincent. 'Okay, son, Mr King will row me ashore.' He climbed aboard the *Kingfisher*. He extended his hand. 'My name is Smithers.'

Big King's hand was big and rough.

'Smithers, huh? Or Jones? What do you want to go to Saint Vincent for? Cos I don't smuggle dope no more, got my ass burned.'

Morgan was measuring the man. Old, out of condition. 'No dope. What do you charge a day?'

'A hundred and fifty bucks, counting the rods and bait. Bring your own food and booze, cos I run no gin palace.'

Morgan said: 'Can you get me and my wife to Saint Vincent tonight?'

'Nope. Because I won't be back by dawn to pick up my party.'

'Six hundred dollars, to forget your party.'

'Nope. Big King's got a reputation to maintain.'

'How much?'

'Nope. There's plenty of boats who'll take you but they'll cost you plenty more than six hundred bucks if you're running grass.'

'We'll be carrying no drugs. You can search us.'

'Yeah? – you going to let me look up your wife's vagina? You can carry a lot of cocaine up there, in a condom. Sorry, mister, I got a party anyways.'

Morgan said, 'Okay, Mr King, I'm sorry but it looks like we're going to do this the hard way.' He pulled out the gun.

He felt shaky. It was the first time he had ever used a gun unlawfully. 'Start your engines and pull up your anchor, please.'

The *Kingfisher* chugged out of the harbour, into the small swells. Big King sat at the helm, big and sweaty, with a face like thunder. Morgan stood behind him. This had been so easy so far he desperately regretted not having brought Anna with him in the first place. He said: 'Turn along the coast. Top speed.'

Big King said, 'Jesus, you could have got a dozen guys to do this voluntary. What happens up the coast?'

'You're going to anchor while I fetch my wife.' He could see Big King's mind working on that one. 'I'm going to tie you up while I do that, Mr King. I'm sorry to have to do this. I wish you *were* doing it voluntarily.'

Big King growled, 'Okay, so I'll do it voluntary.'

'Too late, Mr King, I don't trust you now.'

'Jesus,' Big King said. 'The pot calling the kettle black.'

Morgan smiled, despite himself. It seemed the first time he had smiled in years.

The trees were silhouetted against the lamplights on the coast road, the houses twinkling between them. But the beach looked empty. When they were three hundred yards offshore, Morgan said: 'Okay, douse your lights. Then drop the anchor.'

Big King put the engines into neutral. 'Why don't *you* drop the fuckin' anchor? . . .' He clambered along the gunnel, to the bows. He let the anchor go, with a splash. He came clambering back sullenly. 'Now what, Admiral?'

'Lie down, please. On your stomach.'

Big King muttered, 'You not one of those, too, are you?' But he lowered himself.

'Hands together behind your back, please.' Big King groaned and obeyed. Morgan pocketed the pistol. 'Now, if you try anything funny it's going to hurt. You, not me.'

He lashed Big King's wrists together feverishly, then ran the rope down to his ankles. He lashed them together. Big King said bitterly, 'Don't cut the rope, it's good rope.'

Morgan hurried to the locker, and snatched out a flag. It was American.

'Open wide.'

'Look,' Big King moaned. 'I won't holler. Nobody'll hear me, anyways.'

'*Open.*'

'Oh, *shit* . . .'

Morgan bound the gag around Big King's bristly mouth.

He turned and hurried to the stern. He pulled the dinghy alongside and clambered down into it. He untied the painter, grabbed the oars and started rowing hard.

He feverishly pulled the dinghy up onto the sand. The dark beach seemed deserted.

He ran through the palms. To the road at the side of the consular residence. There was nobody to be seen. He took a run at the wall, and swung himself up.

He dropped into the dark garden below. He crouched, panting, peering.

There was no light in the consul's study. He slipped through the trees, down the side of the house. His heart was knocking. He came opposite Anna's window. He took a pebble out of his pocket. He carefully threw it against the window.

She appeared immediately, her face white. She opened the window. She swung her leg over the sill, then the other, clutching the bag. For a moment she sat, then she jumped.

She hit the grass, her knees bent, and she rolled. She scrambled up and ran into the darkness of the trees. Morgan grabbed her hand.

He leant against the wall, and laced his hands together. She put her foot into his hands, and she sprang. She clambered up on top of the wall; then she disappeared. Morgan jumped, and grabbed the top. He swung his leg up, and rolled over.

'*Walk naturally.*'

He gripped her hand. It was clammy. She walked erect, her heart pounding, looking to neither left nor right. Ahead were the palms of the beach.

'*Now run!*'

They ran through the dark palms. They came out onto the beach, panting. Out there was the unlit shape of the *Kingfisher*. They ran along the beach, to the dinghy. Morgan grabbed the painter and went splashing out into the sea.

'*Jump in.*'

She splashed out to it, and clambered in. He climbed aboard, snatched up the oars and started to row.

She clambered shakily aboard the launch. Big King glowered at her from his horizontal position, bulging-eyed.

Morgan hurried to the wheel and started the engines. His hands were trembly. Then he clambered up to the bows. He heaved up the anchor, hand over hand. He lashed it down then came scrambling back to the wheelhouse. He put the engines into gear and opened the throttles. The boat eased forward, *doem – doem – doem.*

'Take the wheel.'

She took it. Her face was gaunt in the glow of the instrument panel. Morgan snatched up a chart, and looked at it. Then grabbed the parallel rulers. He marked off a course for Venezuela.

'Three-zero-five.'

He took back the helm and swung the boat onto the course. Then gave the helm back to her.

He looked behind, at the land. His mouth was dry.

There was not a sign of movement. He sighed out. *They had made it . . .* For a moment he felt euphoric. He turned and went back to Big King.

He squatted beside him. 'Now, Mr King, are we going to be friends?'

Big King gargled into his gag and rolled his eye at him.

Morgan said: 'That's Mrs Smithers. She doesn't like bad language. Or bloodshed. Now, I'm going to untie you, Mr King. But you must be polite.'

Big King looked at him murderously and growled something through his stars and stripes.

'Or do I leave you tied up, Mr King?'

Big King groaned and closed his eyes.

'Okay,' Morgan said. 'But first I must find your gun.'

He clambered down the hatch to the accommodation. He started in the obvious places.

Five minutes later he had found an FN rifle and a 12 bore shotgun, and the ammunition. He locked the guns in the forward cabin. He took the ammunition with him, up to the helm. He said to Anna:

'Untie his hands. Let him untie his own feet.'

Anna went to Big King. She knelt and wrestled the knot undone. She stood up, and came back to Morgan.

Big King wrestled his hands free. He sat up with a groan, flexing his hands. Then his big fingers wrestled loose the knot of his gag. He spat out the stars and stripes. He sat there, flexing his jaw.

'You sonofabitch . . .'

Morgan picked up Anna's bag and placed it at Big King's feet. 'Search it. For drugs.'

Big King scowled: then rummaged through the bag. He shoved it aside. 'So what? I can't look in the other place, can I?' He started untying his feet.

'Where?' Anna demanded.

Big King suddenly looked embarrassed. 'Ask your boyfriend,' he muttered. He untied his feet, grunting. He sat there, massaging his big ankles.

Morgan said, 'Get him a drink. What have you got, Mr King?'

'Rum,' Big King growled. 'Straight,' he added.

'And the same for us,' Morgan said. 'And now will you please take the helm, Mr King?'

'And will you please please please for Christ's sake quit calling me Mr King?'

He lumbered over to the helm and snatched it. He looked at the compass, then looked at the receding shore lights. 'Hey! – we're going the wrong way for Saint Vincent's!'

'We're going to Venezuela, Mr King.'

Big King stared at him. He whispered:

'You're gonna load this ship up with cocaine and run it back up the islands to Miami . . . You're going to kill me and use my ship for one drug run?'

'If I was going to kill you, why did I untie you?'

Big King glared. 'What happens when we get to Venezuela?'

'Mrs Smithers and I get off. You do what you like.'

Big King said slowly:

'Pirates, *Mister* Smithers . . .' He pointed west with a fat, gnarled finger. 'Those waters are *full* of pirates! They board you, they murder you, they steal your boat, use it for one drug run up to Miami, then sink the boat to destroy the goddam evidence! Then start again . . .'

'Mr King, I *am* the pirate, remember.'

Anna came up the hatch, with three glasses of dark rum. She put one in front of Big King. Morgan turned, and sat down at the dining table behind him. Anna slumped down beside him. She looked aft at the sea. Morgan said: 'Nothing's following us.'

He dragged his hands down his face. They were still trembly.

Anna took a mouthful of rum, threw back her head, and swallowed. It burned down into her gut, and she shuddered.

She took his hand, and squeezed it hard.

'Thank you,' she said.

15

They saw only some distant fishing craft all night. Before dawn the *Kingfisher* dropped anchor two hundred yards off the black, jungled coast of Venezuela.

It was humid, oily hot. A mile away the lights of Garrucha twinkled. Anna climbed down into the dinghy. Big King followed. Morgan climbed in, untied the painter and shoved off. Big King took up the oars and started rowing.

The dinghy crunched onto the beach and Morgan and Anna climbed out.

'Well,' Morgan said, 'many thanks, Mr King.'

'Oh, a pleasure,' Big King glowered, 'an absolute pleasure. Any time.'

'I'll send you a cheque for a thousand dollars to cover expenses and to compensate for the loss of your charter party. Care of the Heron Bar. I'm afraid I need all the cash I've got right now.'

'Oh, sure. Send me a Get Well card, too.'

'Goodbye, Mr King,' Anna said, 'and thank you.'

'Oh sure,' Big King said. 'And will you do something for me?'

'What?'

'Don't call me, I'll call you. But if you ever do, will you please please please not call me Mr King?'

'What do we call you, then?'

'I'm hoping you'll never have to call me any goddam thing.'

'What name do I put on the cheque?' Morgan said.

Big King looked at him. 'You really gonna send me a cheque?'

'Yes.'

Big King looked away. He dug the oars into the water.

'Morris Longbottom,' he muttered.

Local knowledge, that's what he desperately needed.

Big King had told him there was a railway station in Garrucha. There must also be a bus station. The port was only for fishing boats. There was no airport. But the jungle was full of airstrips used by smugglers for flipping drugs out of the country, Big King had said.

They walked fast along the beach towards the town. By now the British and the Yanks would have their people throughout the Caribbean looking for them. And so would the Russians.

In the sunrise they climbed up a rocky path, onto the road leading into Garrucha.

The town was not yet awake. They walked through the shacks on the outskirts. Then they were entering town. The shops were still shut. A woman in black was mopping the pavement. Down sidestreets, they could glimpse the harbour, fishing boats, nets. Ahead was a plaza, silent in the early morning.

It was lined with old buildings. On the opposite side of the square, a man was wiping down tables outside a café. They walked in and sat down in a far corner. The barman called, '*Sí?*'

Anna ordered coffee and brandy.

The drinks came. Morgan swallowed his brandy, in one go. Anna did the same, and shuddered. She gave a bleak smile. Morgan held up two fingers at the barman and called:

'*Coñac, por favor.*'

They sipped the coffee. It was good and strong. He sat there, feeling the balm of it. He was about to speak, and she put her hand on his. She said:

'Thank you. From my heart. For what you've done.'

'Because I love you,' he said.

She closed her eyes and squeezed his hand. 'But you also did it because you believe it morally *right*.'

He smiled. 'All right . . .' He hunched forward on the table. 'We're in South America. Now tell me where we go from here.'

She held his hand across the table.

'New York,' she said. 'Manhattan.'

He was relieved. 'Both safety-deposit boxes recorded on the page you tore out of the notebook are in New York?'

She shook her head. 'Only one. But that's the most likely.'

'And where is the other box?'

'Switzerland.'

He stroked his eyebrow. *Opposite sides of the world.*

'Why do you think New York is the most likely place?'

'Because the night Max and I had the drunken row – he said he had the evidence in New York. In very safe custody, were his words. And he had no other bank in New York that I know of. And no New York bank is listed in his will. Only in the notebook.'

'What did the note say?'

'Just the box number, plus the letters H.K.S.B. Which stand for Hongkong and Shanghai Bank. That safety-deposit box is in our joint names. We opened it together last year. He'd bought me some expensive jewellery, he was on one of his spending sprees. We had to go up-state for a week. So he rented a deposit box for all this loot.'

'In your *joint* names? So you can walk into the bank and open that box?'

'Yes. I never did it. Max got the jewellery out for me a week later. But I remember he rented it for one year.'

Morgan sat back. Relief. 'Well, this is easy. We just go to the bank and you open the box. Then get a lawyer. No lies, no forged signatures.'

He unzipped her bag, and pulled out the list he had made of all entries and exits from Max's three passports. He studied it.

'You had your drunken row on your birthday, the twentieth of June last year. Two days before that, on the eighteenth, God's Banker was found hanging in London. The same day Max arrived in London. The same day he flew to New York. The next day he flew back to you in Grenada. The day after that was your birthday.' He thought he was getting somewhere. 'When Max had this outburst did he mention God's Banker being hanged? As proof that he had the evidence?'

'No. I've told you that already.'

He did not believe her. He consulted the list again.

'The next day he went to Switzerland. Via New York.' He tapped the list. 'He may have gone to New York to get the microfilm out of the deposit box – because you had access to it. And gone to Switzerland to put it in a new box.'

'But we *have* to check out New York.'

'Oh, yes.' He hesitated; then turned her face towards him. 'Anna? It's time you told me what's on this microfilm.'

Her exhausted eyes were the most beautiful he had ever seen. She said:

'Jack? . . . Darling Jack. I do trust you. But I'm not going to tell you. Because what you don't know you cannot be made to tell.'

He sat back wearily. All right, that would have to wait, he was too tired to argue with her now. He said:

'We must dye your hair. And buy some clothes. The British know what we're wearing.'

She nodded, eyes pressed closed. 'And then?'

He said, 'We can't go to America from Caracas airport. Or any airport. They'll be watching for us at obvious places like that.' He rubbed his chin. 'I haven't got a passport. Except Max's. I can change his photograph for mine. But they'll be watching for the name of Hapsburg.'

The waiter came with two more steaming coffees. He spoke something in Spanish and Anna translated: 'You want anything to eat?'

He couldn't think of eating. 'No, you have something.'

She shook her head. The waiter went away. She said: 'We could buy forged passports in Caracas.'

'But that'll take time. And time's our problem.' He sighed. 'We must assume that every available British, American and KGB agent in the Caribbean area is looking for us in the obvious places. Therefore, we've got to get out without going through immigration formalities anywhere.'

She massaged her forehead. 'So, we must charter an aeroplane.'

'But where? Go to a flying club? By now the Brits and Yanks will have places like that covered too. And how do you persuade the guy to charter you his aeroplane without going through normal immigration formalities?'

'With money. We're in South America, remember.'

He said: 'Big King put me onto a guy in this town called José Luis.'

107

'Who?'

'José Luis, the local Mr Big if you want to buy a ton of cocaine. He's also into "wet-backs", smuggling people illegally into the States to work. When it comes to anything in this town, José Luis is your man.'

'Lord – we can't go in an aircraft that's running drugs.'

'Of course not. We're in enough difficulty without having the Drug Enforcement Agency on our backs. No, we either charter an aircraft to ourselves through José Luis, or go with a bunch of wet-backs.'

She stroked her eyebrows worriedly. 'How do we find this guy?'

'Big King says we ask at a joint called Bar García.'

'And if he won't help us?'

'Then we take a train to Caracas. And start again.'

She pressed her eyebrows. 'Maybe we should do that first. Instead of flirting with drug runners?'

'Time. In Caracas we'd have to start from scratch. Asking round the underworld. Attracting attention. Here, at least we know of José Luis.'

She sighed. 'Oh God, what have I got you into?'

'So far it's been plain sailing. A laugh-a-minute. But if it isn't in New York? Then, it's Switzerland. We won't be able to do it without false passports. And competent people helping us.'

'Like who?'

He took a breath. 'You've got to get a very respectable lawyer. And get your story down on affidavit.' He held up a hand to silence her. 'As much as you need to tell. So that if we're caught, we've got somebody who can leap into action on our behalf. *Habeas corpus*, or whatever it's called. Lawyers are bound to secrecy, Anna –'

'Jack, I'm not telling this story to any lawyer until I absolutely have to. Because although the lawyer himself may treat it as confidential, what about his secretary who types it – how do we know what *her* security-rating is?'

'Oh, Jesus, Anna . . .'

'I'm sorry, Jack.' She passed over that one. 'And the forged passports? How do we get those?'

He had to control his anger. He said: 'I'll have to get somebody like Makepeace to help us.'

'Makepeace?'

'Used to be in the Navy with me. He was in the Special Boat Service. He quit and went into private practice, as it were. Security work. Bodyguarding.' He added: 'He was my partner for a while in my steamship company. But there wasn't enough money in it for him.'

'And now he does what, exactly?'

'A bit of everything. He runs a hang-gliding and parachute school in the Midlands of England most of the time. And teaches karate – he was on the Navy's karate team.' He waved his hand. 'He does private military-type work. These SAS and SBS guys, they never really quit the game, until they're too old. They're too accustomed to action to do a desk job. There's a fraternity of them, guys who're available for special assignments.' He added: 'The government hires them sometimes. "Unofficially and deniably".'

'And what will Makepeace do for us?'

God, he was tired, now.

'We haven't had time to think this all through. New York seems easy. But if we've got to go to a bank in Switzerland –' he shook his head – 'we're into a whole new ball-game. Because that Swiss box will not be in your name, but Max's. You may be able to forge Max's signature, but you can't impersonate him. So? How're you going to get into that box? Who's going to impersonate Max Hapsburg and forge his signature?'

She said firmly: 'Not you. I'm not letting you take that risk.'

'Then who? Hire a forger? An actor?'

She said: 'I don't know yet.'

Morgan sighed again.

'Anna,' he said, 'if we've got to go to Switzerland, into a Swiss bank, then you really need a good lawyer. Hand the problem to him. He'll protect your legal rights, against the British and Americans.'

'And against the Russians too?' She raised her eyebrows. 'I've also thought about it, Jack. And if you knew as much about the integrity of lawyers as I do after living with Max for five years, you wouldn't be so confident of them.'

Morgan sighed, and let it go for the time being.

'Anyway, we'll need Makepeace: To get us passports. To charter us an aircraft in Europe. We can't just fly into Switzerland by scheduled airline. They will be watching for us there too.' He shook his head. Tired. 'Consider what happens after you've found the right box. What do you intend to do with the microfilm? Destroy it, then and there? Or take it with you? But whatever you do, it's when you leave the bank that the danger really starts. *They* won't know you've destroyed it. So that's when they'll really need to pounce on you – before you've gone a hundred yards, before you can slip it to somebody else.' He spread his hands. 'We'll need somebody like Makepeace to make a getaway. A car. Give us cover. And then fly us out. Once we leave the bank we've *got* to shake them off.' He sighed. 'That's the sort of thing we need Makepeace for. And a few more of the boys, probably.' He added: 'These guys don't come cheap. But they're pretty damn good.'

She massaged her forehead. 'Don't you think the British government could find out which banks Max used, simply by asking the Swiss government? And the same in America?'

Morgan shook his head. 'Not Switzerland. Banking secrecy is sacred there. If the British could have done that they hardly needed to send me to Grenada to find you. No, they would have to apply to the Swiss courts for a special court order to get that information. They'd have to prove that a crime had been committed and the proof lay in the box. Tell the whole story. And what crime can they prove has been committed?' He shook his head. 'And I doubt they could do it in America, either. It would be unconstitutional.'

'That wouldn't stop the CIA.'

'But they'd have to break the law to do it. And there'd be hell to pay. You could sue the American government for millions. Then the whole secret would come out, be public knowledge. They wouldn't want that.'

She sat, thinking.

'I don't like the sound of this José Luis. Max knew a lot of important people all over South America. I think I know somebody who'd help us.'

Morgan had the feeling she had been testing his views before putting forward a better plan of her own. 'Who? And would you trust him?'

'I wouldn't tell him the truth. But I would trust him to keep his mouth shut. He's a very powerful man. Called Horst

Vasquez. Half German, half Spanish. A friend of Max's father. He's mixed up in politics, and he's a Mason, like Max was. He's got a huge ranch here in Venezuela. He's about sixty, I suppose. He's always been very fond of me.' She added: 'Always flirts with me.'

'Could he get us false passports?'

'Probably. And he's got his own aeroplane. Two, in fact.'

'But is he a crook, or just well connected, or what?'

'He's like Max, fingers in lots of pies. No, he's not a crook, but everything is for sale in South America. I'm sure he can grease the right palms to get us passports.'

Morgan sat back in his chair.

'Excellent. That would solve half our problems. But what story are you going to tell him? Those passports must be in false names, remember. He'll be very curious to know why.'

'I simply tell him that I'm on the run because of the coup in Grenada – I need to lie low. He knows Max was involved with the revolutionary government, it's credible therefore that I'm in trouble too. And you're helping me.'

Morgan sat forward, his hands laced. 'You think he'll buy that?'

'He knows Max was politically active all over the place. String-pulling, wheeling, dealing. Horst is the same sort of man. South America is run like that. He won't find it incredible. Particularly if I act frantic and tearful.' She added bleakly: 'Which won't be hard.'

Morgan thought. 'Could you tell him that we've been lovers for years? That now that Max is gone your new name is – or is going to be . . . Anna Armstrong?'

She shook her head. 'He wouldn't like that. He respected Max, though he thought he was a heel for treating me badly.'

Morgan sat back.

'And your other friends in the region?'

She said: 'Several. But Horst is the best bet.'

'Where's his ranch?'

'Without looking at a map, I'd say about three hundred miles from here.' She added: 'Stupendous place. Vast plains. Thousands of cattle.'

Morgan said: 'And these aeroplanes of his? You think he would fly us to some point in America?'

111

'It's possible. He's got a pilot. I've flown his planes myself. But I could hardly steal one.'

'Why not? We hijacked Big King's boat. You could send Horst an apologetic telegram from Florida telling him where it is. What fuel range has it got?'

'The big one's a Cessna Twin. About a thousand miles.'

Morgan visualized the map. 'We'd have to refuel some-where.' He sat back in his chair. 'If it works, this is the answer to our immediate problems. Even if we don't get his plane, just the passports. Well – we better get our story straight, so we don't contradict each other. And the next job is to find a car to rent. Can you telephone Horst first, to make sure he's there?'

'Yes. Though South American telephones are not the most reliable.' She looked at her watch. 'He'll be up by now.'

Morgan said, 'Don't say anything compromising. Just find out whether he's there.'

There was an antique telephone in the café.

Morgan sat in the far corner, watching Anna repeatedly dial, wait, then hang up and dial again. Finally her face lit up and he heard her speak in Spanish, her free hand over her ear.

She spoke, then listened, then spoke again. Then she re-placed the receiver in exasperation. She dialled again.

It rang and it rang. He saw her speak again. Then she slowly replaced the receiver.

She turned and walked back to the table. She was pale.

'He won't talk to me.'

Morgan looked at her. 'Tell me the whole conversation.'

She took a breath.

'He answered the phone himself. I said, "Hullo, Horst, know who this is?" There was a surprised silence. Then he said, "Is that you?" I said "Yes, dearest, can I come to see you today?" He sounded shocked. He stuttered. Then he said "No, imposs-ible!" And he hung up.'

'Oh, Jesus . . .'

'So I thought he had misunderstood who I was. So I dialled again. It rang a long time. Finally the maid answered, María. I said, "María, this is Anna, let me speak with the señor." She sounded flustered. She said "He cannot speak with you." I said

"Tell him it's *Anna*." She said, "He knows nobody by that name." And she hung up.'

Morgan rested his forehead in his hand and sighed.

'Oh Jesus . . . So they've already been onto him. Was your friendship with him that well known?'

'He came to Grenada sometimes. Always stayed with us. The Russians know, because Max introduced Horst to Bishop ages ago. But I'm surprised if the British know.'

'On an island that size everybody knows everybody's business. What's surprising is if the Russians already know we've escaped from British custody – it was only twelve hours ago.'

She said, 'Big King?'

Morgan shook his head. 'He's still in the middle of the ocean right now. And I took the valve out of his two-way radio.' He breathed angrily. 'Well, we better not try any of your other friends.'

She said grimly: 'So it's José Luis.'

'And find a place to hide. A pensión. And get some hairdye and clothes.'

16

Bar García is on a corner overlooking the harbour of Garrucha, a nice old place spoilt with a new chrome counter and formica-top tables. Morgan had hoped for a more private place, but José Luis felt that private business was best done in public.

'This is my campo,' he said, 'my town.' He spoke no English, so Anna did the talking. He waved his hand. 'Some people, like Big King, think I am a gangster, but I am merely a simple businessman. I do not sell drugs.'

'Good,' Anna said. 'All we want is to get on an aeroplane to America.'

José Luis looked puzzled, very puzzled. 'At Caracas airport there are many airlines.'

'They're no good to us.'

José Luis went on: 'Now, some of my *friends* sometimes deal in drugs, I believe.'

Morgan was frustrated that he did not understand the Spanish. Anna said, 'We won't want anything to do with drugs. I only want to charter a small plane. With pilot. Or get on a plane that is taking people to America.'

José Luis looked regretful. 'Ah, some of my friends do deal in passengers. But they do not talk to strangers. But maybe I could give them a message for you?'

'That's very kind of you.'

'I'm a very kind person, Señora. But, alas, my friends do not do passenger work to America, they feel that is too risky. The United States Coastguard have planes too, you know, and much radar. My friends only carry passengers as far as the Bahamas. But that is only a short distance by boat from Florida.'

Morgan understood the last part. He visualized the map. The Bahamas – hundreds of tropical islands, a hundred miles or so off the Florida coast.

'And how much does it cost?'

'Three thousand dollars each person.'

Anna translated to Morgan. He said, 'Okay. Ask him when we go. It must be tonight. Or tomorrow at the latest.'

Anna translated. José Luis said: 'I must ask my friends. But next week, I think.'

'Next *week*? That's impossible.'

José Luis shrugged.

Anna said, 'A *chartered* plane. There must be dozens for charter, with all this drug-running.'

José Luis shrugged. 'Impossible.'

Of course it wasn't impossible. 'How much?'

José Luis shrugged. 'My friends? . . . Thirty thousand dollars.'

Anna glared at him. They had less than twenty thousand. And they were going to need it. She said: 'Ten.'

José Luis rolled his eyes. 'Pff . . . Impossible.'

She was inclined to believe him – ten thousand might be cheap for a job like that. 'Eleven.'

'Impossible.'

Anna slapped both hands on the table and stood up. So, it was to be Caracas after all. Start all over again.

114

'What's happening?' Morgan demanded.

Anna told him.

José Luis said: 'Maybe my friends will listen to twenty.'

'Sorry, José, I've only got twelve.' Anna turned to go.

José Luis said: 'Twelve thousand dollars, and maybe my friends will fetch you at your pensión after darkness.'

Relief flooded through her. But she did not show it. 'How long is the trip?'

'About eight hours.'

'Where do we end up?'

'On the island of Andros. Bahamas.'

'And what about a boat from Andros?'

José Luis shrugged. 'There are many people in the Bahamas with boats.'

The pensión had only one toilet, which did not flush properly, alongside of which was a cold water shower, without a nozzle, which did not drain properly; the bed in their room was hard, and they slept in their clothes so they could run for it at a moment's warning; but thank God none of that had stopped them sleeping. The exhaustion of days of tension followed by their relief that they were getting out of Venezuela so quickly laid them both out for eight solid hours.

Morgan woke up with a groggy start; he looked at his watch – seven o'clock. Morning or night? He dropped back on the pillow, collecting himself. Then he heard the knock on the door again. That's what had woken him. He scrambled up. 'Anna?' He snatched up the gun and hurried to the door. He opened it a crack.

A young man stood there. He said something in Spanish. Anna came to the door, blinking. The man spoke again. She interpreted: 'His name is Paco. José Luis sent him.'

'Get the bag.'

They followed him down the stairs. Still half-dazed with sleep. They came out into the dark street.

An old car was waiting down the block. Another man was sitting in the back. Paco motioned Anna into the back seat, Morgan into the front.

The other man's name was Fernando, they learned. They drove in silence down narrow, poorly lit streets, past shops and

115

houses and shacks. Then they were in the country. Heavy tropical foliage flashing by in the headlights.

The car wound into jungle. There were some cleared pastures, cattle. There was a moon. Paco drove fast, a man who enjoyed driving. After twenty minutes, he swung off the dirt road. The trees parted.

Ahead was a long strip of open, grassy earth. They bounced down the rough airstrip, to the end. Paco swung the car around to face the way they had come.

He switched off the headlights. He said something in Spanish. Anna interpreted: 'We wait.'

They did not talk. Within five minutes Morgan heard a drone. He peered, and saw a small shape looming down over the black jungle. Paco switched on his headlights. The beam lit up the airstrip.

The plane came steeply down towards the airfield, then it levelled, and touched down. It came careening down the grass, bouncing and droning. Morgan saw that it was a twin-engine Cessna. It came straight at the car, slowing; then it turned ponderously around.

It came to a stop, its propellers still turning. They all got out of the car. The co-pilot's door opened and a man climbed out onto the wing. Paco turned to Morgan. He held out his hand. '*Dinero, por favor.*'

Morgan went to the car's headlights. He pulled the money out of his pocket. He crouched down with Paco in the headlights and started counting it out.

Fernando had gone to the boot of the car. He hefted out three sacks. He slung one over his shoulder, and ran to the aeroplane with it. He loaded it into a luggage door in the fuselage. He spoke to the co-pilot. The co-pilot shouted something up to the pilot. Fernando ran back to the car. He got another sack. The co-pilot started walking towards the car.

Morgan looked up and saw a hard face glaring down at him in the headlights. He snapped something in Spanish. Paco looked up, clutching the money. He spoke earnestly in Spanish. The man glared then said in a harsh American accent: 'No *way*, *compadre*!'

He turned and strode back towards the plane. Paco hurried after him. Fernando was loading the second sack into the fuselage. Morgan turned to Anna. 'What's the guy loading?'

'Oh God – what do you think? Drugs, of course!'

'*Oh God no!*' He turned furiously for Paco. Anna said: 'The pilot doesn't want to take us.'

'Of course he doesn't!'

He started after Paco. The pilot's door opened and a man climbed out. He dropped to the ground. Fernando was running back to the car for the third sack. The two pilots spoke. Then the pilot came walking slowly through the moonlight towards Morgan and Anna. He stopped in front of them.

'Who the *hell* are you, buddie?'

Morgan said, 'Customers of José Luis. We chartered this plane.'

The pilot glared, then said, 'Jesus . . .' He turned and shouted to Fernando. '*Rápido!*' He beckoned to Paco. 'Come here, pal.'

Paco walked away with him. They stopped out of earshot. They were arguing. Then the American turned abruptly and shouted at them angrily: '*Get in.*'

Anna grabbed Morgan's arm. 'Do we want to do this?'

Morgan clenched his teeth furiously.

'No. But we haven't got much goddam choice! We're here and Paco's got our money! How long does it take to get out of this mess and get another plane? . . .'

He grabbed her elbow and started towards the plane. The co-pilot stopped them at the wing.

'Not so fast, buddie! Let's check you out. Hands above your heads.'

For a furious instant Morgan was going to take him. Knock the man flat, grab Anna, get the hell out of this. But anything could happen. He raised his hands.

The man frisked him, and found the gun.

'I thought so.' He flipped the pistol. 'You get this back at the end of the trip. Now you, lady.'

He frisked Anna. He looked in her bag.

'Okay. Get in.'

Morgan led Anna to the right wing. She clambered up onto it. 'Into the back,' the pilot shouted. She crouched into the aircraft. Morgan followed. He sat down beside her. She looked at him, white-faced.

117

The pilots clambered in and slammed the doors. Neither looked at them. Their faces were grim in the lights of the instrument panel. The pilot wound up the engines, and the propellers screamed. He let go the brake and the plane went lurching down the dark airstrip.

They did not have headphones so they could not hear each other above the engines. Morgan was shaky, furious. *Goddammit he'd been a fool to trust that José Luis bastard!* They were in enough difficulty without the risk of being caught by narcotic agents. Oh Jesus . . . But they wouldn't have got their money back without a fight – and what would have happened to Anna in that?

The dark coast of Venezuela dropped behind. Ahead lay the Caribbean Sea.

The aeroplane droned through the moonlight at ten thousand feet. Morgan peered over the pilot's shoulder, and noted that they were steering 315 degrees. He sat back, urgently trying to visualize the map. He had a good idea of it. From Venezuela to the northern Bahama islands opposite Miami would be about twelve hundred miles, was his educated guess. About halfway was Haiti and the Dominican Republic. The maximum range of this Cessna would be about a thousand miles. Unless it had extra wing-tip fuel tanks. Then its range would only be about thirteen hundred miles. If he were a drug smuggler he would refuel halfway, so he had plenty in case he had to run from the Drug Enforcement Agency planes. That meant Haiti, or one of the nearby Virgin Islands.

He tried to make himself untense, to think what he was going to do when they refuelled.

Because if he were a drug smuggler and he wanted to get rid of unwanted passengers who were witnesses to his crime, that was where he would murder them.

17

About five hours later he felt the plane begin to descend. He sat forward, to look at the instruments. The co-pilot whirled around, and a gun was pointed between Morgan's eyes.

He froze, staring at the man; then sat back slowly, his heart pounding. Anna stared, aghast. The plane was coming down steeply now. Morgan's mind was desperately trying to race. *They were going to be murdered . . .* And he was filled with fury and he wanted to lunge and kill kill kill the bastards before they killed him. He sat there, aghast, his mind fumbling. And oh God there was no chance. If he went for the gun they would both get their heads blown apart. And the pilot would also have a gun . . . If he somehow got at both in time the plane would go screaming down to the ground while they fought . . .

He made himself sit back, rigid, sick fury in his guts. The plane was coming droning down in the moonlight. Down, down it came. Then it levelled, then hit the earth and bounced. It went racing down a dirt airstrip, roaring. Then jungle was looming up ahead. Morgan glimpsed a hut on the edge of the trees. The pilot brought the plane to a roaring, trundling stop.

As he wrenched on the handbrake the co-pilot flung open his door. The pilot twisted in his seat, and another gun was pointing at them.

The co-pilot scrambled out, onto the wing. He crouched in the propeller blast. '*Out!*'

Morgan shouted: '*Why? We won't tell anybody! –*'

'*Get out!*' the pilot roared.

Anna shouted, '*Please – we won't tell the police –*'

The pilot rammed the gun against her head. She jolted back, shocked, the gun hard against her temple. '*Now get out . . .*' Morgan stared, heart pounding; then he heaved himself out of his seat. Shaking. He clambered through the doorway, and the co-pilot jumped down to the ground. He backed off, pointing the gun up at him.

'*Now your girlfriend . . .*'

Morgan crouched on the wing, and held his hand out for Anna. She looked at him, terrified; then came crouching out of the back of the plane. Out onto the wing, her hair flying. The co-pilot motioned them to the ground with the pistol; Anna jumped. Morgan desperately measured the distance to the man, but he was too far. He jumped to the ground.

The co-pilot motioned them towards the forest, thirty yards beyond the plane.

Morgan took Anna's hand. It was trembling. Her face was a mask of fear. He started towards the wing tip. It was unreal. All he knew was that he had to lunge at the man, lunge and swipe and go down fighting. The co-pilot followed, three paces behind. Morgan reached the wing tip. He walked on four paces. *Now* . . .

He wrenched Anna's hand and slung her and in the same movement he sprung wildly on the co-pilot, and he hit him. Swiped him with all his hate and might across the face with a karate chop and the pistol cracked and the man reeled. He crashed sideways against the wing, and Morgan bounded wildly after him and hit him again with all his might and the man crashed backwards, arms outflung – and the propeller got him. And there was a crash and half of him was gone. Gone in a screaming smash of flying flesh and bone – in an instant he was cut in half by the propellers, flesh and blood flying high into the night, and the plane lurched and began to rumble forward and Morgan screamed at Anna, '*Get out of the way! –*'

He threw himself flat and the wing rumbled over him. He looked desperately for Anna. She was running wildly towards the forest. He scrambled frantically for the corpse, feeling the bloody earth for the gun. He found it and jumped up. The plane was swinging its tail towards him. He ran after it, flat out, rasping. The plane swung into the last of its turn, and there was a burst of gun fire from the cockpit, *crack – crack – crack* – and Morgan dropped to his stomach. He held the gun in both hands, aimed, and he fired. The plane skewered. It went trundling slowly away into the moonlight, and Morgan scrambled up and raced after it.

He ran flat out for the right wing. He caught up and he flung himself onto it, belly first. He got the handgrip and swung his legs up and flung open the right-hand door. The pilot was slumped, blood all over his face. Morgan got in frantically. He slammed in the throttle and wrenched on the handbrake.

He sat a moment, rasping, gasping, then he flung open the door again. '*Anna!*'

She was running frantically through the moonlight. Morgan scrambled out and jumped to the ground. '*Get in!*' He ran around the tail and jumped up onto the left wing. Flung open

120

the door. He feverishly pocketed the dead man's pistol, then seized his collar, and heaved.

The torso came out, slopped onto the wing. Morgan seized his trousers and heaved again. And again. The man came out onto the wing, headfirst, and slid off, onto the ground. Morgan jumped down. Rasping. He grabbed the body by the ankles. He started dragging it across the airstrip towards the jungle.

He dragged it and dragged it, ten yards into the trees, then dropped it. He ran back for the other corpse.

It was a hideous sight. The left arm, left shoulder and the back of the head were gone. Morgan grabbed the ankles.

He dumped the two bodies together, then crouched and frantically went through their pockets, looking for money. He stuffed a wad of notes and coins into his pocket, then went scrambling back out of the black jungle. He ran to the plane. Anna was in the co-pilot's seat frantically examining the instruments. Morgan leapt up onto the wing. 'Can you fly this thing?'

She shouted, 'I'm figuring it out!' She shook the checklist. 'It's the same as Horst's but a newer model!'

'I'm going to look for fuel!'

He leapt back to the ground, and looked feverishly along the edge of the jungle for the hut he had seen. It was a hundred yards away. He ran to it, crashing through the undergrowth. It had a padlock. He kicked at the door, and it splintered. He kicked again, with all his might, and it burst open. And, yes, inside were the barrels he had expected. He shook one, and it was full. He shook another drum. Also full. A third – it was empty. He cast desperately around in the gloom, looking for the hand pump and the iron bar. He saw them. He heaved the first barrel over, onto its side, with a thud. He rolled it out of the door.

He rolled it onto the airstrip, panting. Up to the leading edge of the wing. He heaved it upright. He ran back to the hut for the pump and the iron bar.

He inserted the iron bar in the cap of the barrel, and twisted. He unscrewed the cap feverishly. He smelt the fuel, to make sure. He lifted the fuel flap on the wing. He rammed the pump into the barrel and the hose into the wing tank and he started to pump furiously.

He looked feverishly about as he worked. There were no

lights. It took an interminable time to empty the drum. Then there was the gurgling noise. He rolled the barrel out of the way. He leapt up onto the wing. Anna was going down the checklist, shakily touching instruments as she read. 'Hurry!' Morgan shouted. She nodded feverishly, without looking up. Morgan ran back to the hut. He rolled out the second barrel. Back to the plane. He unscrewed it, and began to pump. He emptied it, then rolled the barrel out of the way.

He ran back to the plane, to the luggage compartment, to throw out the drugs. He twisted the handle. It was locked. He cursed and ran to get the keys. He scrambled aboard, and clambered into the pilot's seat, panting. There was blood on the instrument panel. There was a second key on the ring holding the ignition key. He twisted it off the ring feverishly, leaving the ignition key in place. Anna rammed on a headset and nudged him to do the same. He rammed his on. Anna tapped the DME and the chart and shouted over the intercom: 'We've done six hundred and nineteen miles! Did you notice the course?'

'Three one five.' Morgan snatched the chart from her. She thrust a parallel ruler at him. He feverishly laid off course 315 degrees from the northern tip of Venezuela. It passed through Haiti. He measured off six hundred odd miles along course 315 degrees – it took him to western Haiti. So that's where they were. He laid off a new course, for the northern Bahama islands. He rasped, 'About three three zero.'

'Three three zero.' She thrust a checklist at him. 'Quickly go through this!'

'I've got to get rid of the drugs! Rev her up!' He scrambled out of the cockpit. He jumped to the ground and ran to the luggage compartment door.

Anna tested the yoke, back and forth, left and right. She moved the pedals, back and forth. She opened the throttle, watching the rev. counter, then eased it back down.

Morgan rammed the key into the lock and twisted. It did not move. Wrong key! He wanted to bellow. The key must be in the pilot's pocket! He turned desperately for the forest. Then he saw the car lights. They were approaching the airstrip, coming through the forest, but still a hundred yards from the edge. His heart lurched.

He leapt up onto the wing and scrambled into the cockpit. '*Go!*' He pointed. The car lights were flashing through the trees. Anna stared, then crossed herself, and she opened the throttles again.

The engines wound up to a roar. Up, up, the revolutions went. Now the plane was straining. The car lights were closer. She slammed off the handbrake, and the plane lurched forward.

The plane went careening bumpily in the moonlight, gathering speed. Now the car lights were swinging onto the airstrip. Faster and faster the plane went and Morgan felt as if they were being pursued by the hounds of hell; then it was going flat out, the jungle at the end racing towards them, and the car came onto the airstrip. The headlights shone straight at the plane, blindingly. Closer and closer the lights raced, then the plane reached V–R and Anna eased back the yoke, and the nose came up. The car lights raced towards them. Closer and closer – then the plane left the ground with a lurch and the lights flashed by below them. The plane went climbing into the moonlight. Anna let out a quivering sigh.

'God – who were they?'

Up, up, up, the plane climbed; she banked to the left, and kept climbing. The black jungle was dropping away below. Morgan looked back down. The car was at the far end of the airstrip. Anna turned onto course three three zero, and kept climbing. Morgan's shoulders slumped. His mouth was salty dry. '*Bloody well done . . .*'

The plane was still climbing. Anna was ashen, concentrating fiercely; then she untensed her shoulders. She said over the intercom: 'Who the hell were they?'

'Accomplices. Or police. Both crooks. How does the plane feel?'

'She's more tender than Horst's.' She glanced at him. 'So they'll find the bodies. And the drugs.'

'I'm afraid so.' He wasn't going to tell her that the drugs were still aboard. She had enough to worry about flying the aeroplane.

'Oh my God . . .'

'Stop worrying about that now. We've got away. You've done bloody well!'

There was no way he could get at the drugs without putting the plane back on the ground.

18

He was feverishly furious with himself.

The aeroplane was locked on three-three-zero degrees. Here and there were the distant twinkle of ships' lights, the scattered jewels of shore lights on the chains of islands. He had told her to fly at a hundred feet, to keep under the radar of the dozens of stations that would be tracking them across their airspace, but she had been unable to maintain it. It was too dangerous, too nerve-racking. And it was doubtful whether even a hundred feet was low enough to avoid radar over the sea. If they had to go above a hundred they might as well go to ten thousand.

The plane droned through the night. They hardly spoke. The cocoon of the cockpit, the noise of the engines, the vibration. Anna's face was gaunt in the glow of the instruments. She was flying the plane on automatic, trying to push the horror of the night out of her mind, and what lay ahead. They had been through the checklist together, until they knew where everything was. Morgan had flown the plane for an hour, to get the feel of it, so he could take over from her and let her rest. But he felt far from confident. Anna was dreading landing. Though she had not told him that. He had enough to worry about. Standard Approach and Landing Procedure. Yes, but on what, in what wind? In what light? She had never landed on anything other than a proper airfield. Morgan was over the shock now, the terror of almost being murdered; now he only felt the feverish fury with himself for failing to offload the drugs, and murderous hatred. He had never killed a man before and it did not bother him one bit that he had just killed two – and he would furiously murder the next drug bastard who crossed his path.

But please God not today . . .

Oh God, today . . . In a few hours, they had to put this plane

124

down somewhere in the Bahamas. Today, way ahead in that blackness, the bastards were waiting for this plane . . .

If it weren't for the drugs he would have flown the plane straight into America. Arriving in daylight, finding an airfield, and brazening it out. Telling some tale and abandoning the aeroplane. It would have been risky, but private pilots are buzzing around America all the time. But the drugs made that impossible.

So it had to be the Bahamas. The safest place to land a plane loaded with drugs. The Bahamas, however, was exactly where the drug bastards were waiting for this plane . . .

He looked at her. 'Rest,' he said. 'We need you rested.'

'I am resting.'

'Try to sleep. I'll watch her.'

Anna closed her eyes.

Course three-three-zero degrees. Straight across the island of Andros, for the islands of Bimini. That's where he had said they should land. She had been relieved, because it had a conventional airfield. 'Shee-it,' Big King had said, 'the whole fuckin' Caribbean's got more illegal fuckin' airstrips for drug smugglers than Carter's got pills . . .' Indeed the chart had scores of airstrips marked on it in pencil on dozens of islands. But she had been frightened of landing on anything but a conventional airfield. So Morgan had said Bimini, to put her mind at rest. But he dared not land there, or on any other airstrip. He dared not land a stolen smugglers' aeroplane on islands infested with murderous drug smugglers who were gunning for them. And even if they were lucky and landed the plane without being seen, how would they get off any one island, to the next? And to the next after that? He didn't know the islands – nor did Anna. There was only one way to land this plane and get rid of it.

Morgan sat in the glow of the instruments, his mouth dry and salty, and told himself there was nothing to it.

One of the first things they teach you at flying school

Except you never actually *do* it at flying school. Or any other time, if you have your way. Everybody *knows* how to do it, but only the unlucky few have ever had to – not even those shit-hot instructors have ever done it.

He glanced at Anna. She seemed to be asleep at last.

In the hour before dawn he saw the scattered lights of Andros. Where José Luis had said this plane was bound for, where, right now, some murderous bastards were waiting to collect their millions of dollars' worth of drugs.

God, Morgan wanted this next hour to be over.

The pinprick lights grew closer and closer. Then the southern shoreline of Andros was sliding under the aircraft's nose.

A hundred miles or so to the Biminis.

Morgan checked the chart, mentally did the arithmetic again. And he shut those bastards down there out of his mind.

The very first light was coming into the east when he made out the lights of the Bimini islands, dotted south to north in the vast Gulf Stream.

Closer and closer they came. He peered, searching the sea for lights of boats. There were none. He prayed, *Please God no unlit ones, and please God a flat sea* . . .

'Wake up.'

She opened her eyes, startled. She had not been asleep.

He said over the intercom: 'Those are the lights of Bimini ahead. Are you properly awake?'

'Yes? . . .' Her hands went to the yoke.

'She's still on automatic. Now, listen. Those drugs are still aboard. The car came before I could unlock the door and throw them out.'

She looked at him in the glow of the instruments. 'Oh my God . . .'

He said quietly, 'So we daren't put this plane down on any airstrip, Anna. And we daren't fly it to America either. So we're going to put her down very gently on the sea. And sink her. Get rid of her. There's a life raft aboard, life belts. Now, they taught me at flying school how to ditch at sea. Did they teach you?'

She was white-faced.

'Yes, of course, but we never practised –'

'Of course not, nobody does. But can you do it now? If you can't, I can. But you're the better flyer.'

'Oh my God . . .' she breathed.

The coast of Bimini was six miles away to the left, a small sprinkle of lights.

Anna brought the plane down, down, towards the flat dark sea, her knuckles white, her face white, her heart pounding. Only her instruments told her how high she was. Down, further down, she came, then they saw it, black and terrible, rushing up to meet them. She levelled out, her heart pounding. The sea hurtled past below. She looked frantically at the altimeter – she was sixty feet above it. Down further; now fifty. Now forty. Thirty. Now twenty, now fifteen. The black water was hurtling by just beneath them. Lower she came. Now the sea was ten feet below, flashing past. Now six. Now four. Every fibre of her was tensed and screaming. *Three*, and she eased back the yoke and the nose lifted slightly, and she slammed off the engines.

The tail hit first, and there was a lurch that wrenched them forward, then the wheels hit. There was another gut-wrenching jerk and spray flew like stones and there was a blinding crashing jolt that hurled them forwards and there was nothing in the world but the sea flying over them like grapeshot. And the plane ploughed to a blinding stop.

'*Out!*' Morgan rasped.

Anna flung off her seat belt and flung open her door. She scrambled out onto the wing.

The plane floated, half submerged. Morgan frantically unlashed the life raft. He wrenched open the emergency exit, and shoved the life raft through into the sea, and he ripped the cord. There was a bang and the rubber raft mushroomed with a hissing noise.

He scrambled out of his seat, across hers, out onto the wing. The water was rushing in, up to the seats now. Anna heaved the raft up to the wing. He grabbed the painter from her. '*Get in!*'

She got into the raft. Morgan crouched into it, and shoved off with all his might. He snatched up an oar. He punted hard away from the sinking plane.

He paddled twenty yards, then stopped, panting.

The aircraft was settling now. The wings were submerged. Just the tail and the cockpit and propellers were showing. He looked feverishly all around, at the horizon.

There were no boats in sight. Bimini was just a flat blur.

The plane was sinking fast now. Anna had her head in her hand, holding her stomach. Morgan said: '*Bloody well done.*' He picked up the other oar.

19

Scattered along the airfield of Bimini are the twisted fuselages of smugglers' aeroplanes that have not landed too well. The planes bring in the cocaine and heroin and marijuana from South America; in the harbour lie the boats that take it on to Florida, only fifty miles away. And out there, beyond the blue horizon, are the United States Coastguard, the fast cutters with cannon, the helicopters and the spotter aircraft. Sometimes there are shoot-outs, sometimes the smugglers set fire to their boats in mid-Gulf Stream to destroy the evidence before the Coastguard cutter catches up, sometimes pilots ditch their planes and take to their rafts to get away from pursuing aircraft, sometimes the Coastguard make big hauls: but there are just too many boats and aircraft to catch them all.

The sun was well up when Morgan and Anna walked into the town. The air was oily warm. Morgan's chest felt raspy from over-smoking and he felt sweaty, wrung-out, exhausted. And very conspicuous. They walked through the little town in the early morning, carrying the bag, trying to look like two tourists out for an early stroll, desperately looking for an open café to hide in until more people were about. To check into a hotel at this hour would have made them more conspicuous. They walked past the Elizabeth Hotel. Ahead was the harbour. The whole town was quiet, not yet open for breakfast. Then they saw Fred's Eating House, the door open, a black man mopping the entrance.

They sat at a window, which overlooked the waterfront road, and drank beer while Fred mopped the floor and Mrs Fred cooked breakfast. The beer went into his empty gut like food. God, he was tired. And still shaken. Anna put her hand on his. 'Before we do anything more we've got to sleep.'

'We've got to get off this island today.'

'Not before you've slept.'

'You did the flying – you're the one who needs sleep.'

Just then there was the sound of an aeroplane approaching. It was a seaplane. It came roaring low over the harbour, big and white. Then it hit the water and spray flew. It went churning down the harbour. It came to a stop and turned. It came churning towards the shore. On the waterfront was a wired enclosure with a concrete ramp into the sea. Two wheels unfolded under the plane's wings, and disappeared into the water. The seaplane ploughed towards the ramp, then came roaring up it like a huge duck. Chocks were put against its wheels. It cut its engines. The door opened, and passengers started climbing out.

'We'll say we came in on that plane. I'll go and get us a hotel room. Stay here.'

He walked out of the eating house. He headed back down the waterfront, to the Elizabeth Hotel.

It was a small hotel. He checked in, and went upstairs to the room. Its window overlooked the street. The door locks were sound. He looked down the corridor; there was no fire escape. That was a pity. He went downstairs to the foyer. There was a framed nautical chart on the wall showing the Bimini islands and the coast of Florida. He ran his eye down the American coast, looking for ports. Then he left the hotel.

The first passengers were coming along the waterfront. He felt better, with other people about. He walked back to Fred's. Anna smiled at him as he entered. He was not yet used to her having black hair. He picked up his beer and drank it down, down, down.

'Two more beers here, please.'

'See those long boats?' Anna said.

There were five or six, tied to moorings. They were sleek, with high prows. On the sterns of each were at least two, sometimes three, big outboard motors. Anna said. 'Those are the ones smugglers use all over the Caribbean. Called "cigarette boats". They can do seventy miles an hour. Outrun any Coast-guard boat.'

Fred brought the beers. He said, 'You folks up early.'

129

Anna said, 'We've been for a walk.' She added: 'To watch the sunrise.'

Morgan said, 'Beautiful.' He was beginning to feel better, with the beer.

Fred picked up his mop again. 'Didn't see that plane, did you?'

Morgan's beer stopped in front of his mouth.

'What plane?'

'Plane ditched into the sea round about dawn. The boys out lookin' for it now.'

Anna was white-faced.

'Was it a passenger plane?'

'Hell, no. What d'you think it was carryin'?'

Morgan said: 'What boys are out looking for it?'

The black man said, 'Black Cat's boys.'

'Who's Black Cat?'

Fred glanced at them. 'Oh,' he said. 'Okay. You don' know who Black Cat is, Fred ain't the guy to shoot his mouth off.'

Anna stared at him. 'Were there any survivors?'

'Must be, lady, 'cos they found the life raft buried on the beach.'

Morgan took a deep breath.

'But was it Black Cat's plane, or his cargo, or what?'

'Don' ask me, Mister, the boys gonna be askin' plenty questions enough.'

Mrs Fred came out of the kitchen, carrying plates. She put them down in front of them. Morgan felt sick in his guts. He said softly to Anna:

'As soon as we've finished this, I'm taking you to the hotel. Lock yourself in. I'm going straight out to rent us a boat. I don't like the sound of this Black Cat.'

It was too early for many people to be about, but he could not wait. He walked along the harbour. There were several signs offering boats for hire. He saw a black boy fishing on a jetty.

'Who rents boats around here, son?'

The boy pointed at the next jetty. 'Charlie do.'

Morgan walked back to the road, to the next jetty. An old

white man was sitting on a small yacht, drinking tea. 'Good morning, are you Charlie?'

'Yep, sure am.'

'I want to rent a boat. For a few days' fishing. Without crew. What have you got?'

'But I knows where the fish hangs out,' old Charlie said. 'You needs me along.'

Morgan's nerves were stretched tight. 'We want to be alone, we don't care if we don't catch fish. Lie in the sun, drink a little wine. Do a bit of scuba diving. A little nude swimming.'

'Aw, shucks,' old Charlie said, 'I'm used to that. I don't *like* rentin' my boats bare.'

'Then it's no deal.'

Old Charlie said grumpily: 'Okay . . .' He looked at him. 'You ain't figurin' on divin' on that aeroplane crashed this mornin', are yer?'

Morgan's heart missed a beat again. 'What aeroplane?'

'Ditched into the sea this morning, that's all I knows.'

'Were there any survivors?'

'Danged if I know. But the boys is out lookin' for the wreck and they won't take kindly to strangers tryin' to muscle in.'

'What boys?'

Old Charlie smirked. 'Shucks, what boys? What d'yer think was on that plane? Worth a lot of money. An' the boys will be lookin' for it, an' they won't take kindly to you helpin' them. Like, cut your throat.'

'Wherabouts did this plane crash? So I can stay away.'

Old Charlie waved his hand. 'Over east somewheres an' I don't want to know more. I just knows where the fish hangs out.'

'What boats have you got?' He felt feverish.

'You lookin' at it. Or that one.' He pointed.

It was a speedboat with a small cabin and one outboard engine. Morgan didn't trust it to cross the Gulf Stream. The little yacht Charlie was on looked all right, but would be slow.

'Anything faster? Like one of those?' He pointed at the long cigarette boats.

'Those belong to Black Cat an' the boys, an' they ain't in the habit of charterin' to nobody.'

'Who's Black Cat?'

Old Charlie smirked again. 'Black Cat's Mr Big aroun' these islands.'

'Is he black?'

'As the ace of spades.'

'Why's he called Cat?'

'I can take a guess,' old Charlie said. 'Most rental boats are already hired for today, anyways, you gotta book.'

Morgan clambered onto the little boat and examined it quickly. It was a twenty-four-foot sloop, called *Rosemary*. Her rigging looked all right. It had a cabin, a small galley, two bunks, a toilet, the standard layout. It looked a good little boat, but six knots would be top speed. He looked feverishly across the harbour for other people moving about. He saw a boat enter the harbour, mean and sleek. It swung towards the jetty. Three men were in it, all black. It roared towards them, then swung into an arrogant turn, broadside on to the jetty. A tall black man leapt out and came striding up the jetty.

'That's him,' old Charlie said.

He was lean and powerful, and Morgan's blood ran cold. He looked like a cat, face round, his eyes slanted and piercing, his ears unusually pointed. He strode, with a face like thunder. The two men followed, hefting aqualung tanks.

'Come back for air refills,' old Charlie said. 'They madder 'n hell.'

Black Cat strode furiously past, off the jetty, and across the waterfront road, heading for Fred's Eating House. He disappeared inside. Morgan turned back to old Charlie. 'Okay, I'll take it. For three days. Is she ready to go?'

'Hundred bucks per twenty-four hours,' old Charlie said happily. 'Plus a hundred bucks deposit on the rods and gear. Take a couple of hours to crank her up.'

'Two *hours*?'

'Got to change the oil, an' tank her up. An' I guess you'd like ice, and bait.'

'Forget the ice and bait. I want her ready in half an hour.'

'Get the ice an' bait same place as the diesel. Booze an' some cans of food aboard, yer pays at the end for what you takes.'

'One hour – maximum. This is my *holiday*, man!'

'No can do,' Charlie said happily. 'Two hours.'

He wanted to hurry straight back to the hotel, but he dared not walk past Fred's. Black Cat had not yet come out. Morgan turned left, away from Fred's. He walked feverishly along the waterfront, trying to look casual. He took the first road to the right. He walked fast, past old houses and shops. At the end of the block he turned right again. Now he was in a road behind Fred's. He walked for three blocks. Then turned right again, back to the hotel.

He did not look left or right in the foyer. He mounted the stairs, two at a time.

He scratched lightly on the door, then put in the key.

She sat on the bed, her back in the corner, the pistol in her hand, her head hanging. She was deep asleep.

He closed the door and locked it. He looked at his watch. Only twenty minutes had passed since he left Charlie.

He went into the bathroom and turned on the cold shower. He stripped off and stepped under it. He let the water beat down on his head then turned his face into it. He soaped himself, and washed his hair. He dried himself, and he was sweating again. He washed his clothes, and pulled them on wet. He put more black rinse in his hair. He looked at his watch. All that had only taken twenty minutes.

Then there was a loud knock on the door.

He froze. Anna woke up with a start. He held up a warning finger at her. The knock came again, louder. 'This is the manager! Open up!'

'What is it?'

'Open up, man, I wanna talk to ya!'

He knew it wasn't the manager. He cursed himself for answering. He pulled the dead pilot's gun out of his pocket. His hands were shaking. 'Go away, I'm resting!'

'You the folks at Fred's Eatin' House this mornin' early?'

His hammering heart missed a beat. 'No! – go away or I'll call the police!'

'Police? . . .' Contemptuously. 'Listen, man, you the folks were out watchin' the sunrise?'

'No! – we only arrived this morning, so go away!'

Striding footsteps. Then a knocking on the room next door. Morgan whispered feverishly: 'Get ready. Leave some things behind, like a pair of panties.'

133

There was more knocking, further down the corridor. Anna hurried into the bathroom and started collecting her things.

The knocking was further away now. Then he heard a voice: 'Hey, what you doin'?'

There was the sound of argument. Morgan waited, tensely. Then the sound of striding footsteps. They clattered down the stairs.

Morgan turned feverishly to the window.

A young black man came striding out of the hotel. Morgan could not see his face, but it was not Black Cat. The man disappeared around the corner, in the direction of Fred's Eating House.

'Come on!'

Anna emerged from the hotel, turned right, away from the waterfront. Morgan followed, ten paces behind, carrying the bag. The gun was tucked into his waistband, under his shirt. The other gun was in the bag. It felt as if all eyes were watching them. Anna walked up the street, desperately trying to look casual. At the end of the block, she turned left.

It felt better, out of sight of the main road. They walked three blocks down the back street, twenty yards apart. There were plenty of people about, mostly black. Anna came to the road that led down to Fred's. The windows down there seemed to shriek at her. She crossed the road. Out of sight of Fred's.

At the end of the next block she turned left. Down there was the harbour. Morgan looked desperately for Charlie's yacht. It was not there yet. But Black Cat's boat was still there. They walked down towards the waterfront. On the corner was a dress shop. Morgan hissed to her and she glanced back. He nodded at the shop. She turned into it.

Morgan followed her inside. Anna pretended to examine dresses. A black sales girl came to Morgan.

'I'm just looking. Something for my wife's birthday.'

'We have those sundresses . . .'

The girl left him alone after a minute. He could see the jetty through the shop window. He looked at his watch. *Still forty-five minutes to wait . . .*

He pretended to look at dresses. Dress after dress.

'What's your wife's size, sir?'

He turned to the sales girl harassedly. 'Your size.'

'That's ten, sir.'

'May I try these on?' Anna called across the shop.

Just then he saw Black Cat's men hurrying onto the jetty again, carrying four aqualung tanks. Morgan stiffened, his heart knocking with relief. He waited for Black Cat to appear. He did not. The two men got to the end of the jetty, hefted the tanks into the boat. Morgan waited for Black Cat. The two men untied the boat, and his heart sank. The boat surged away. It went roaring across the harbour towards the open sea.

Ten minutes later he saw Charlie's little yacht chugging across the harbour.

'I think I'll have to bring my wife here,' he said loudly so Anna would hear.

Anna emerged from the changing cubicle in a yellow frock. 'I'll take it,' she said.

It seemed a long walk. In the blinding glare of the sun. The whole world watching. A hundred yards away were the windows of Fred's Eating House.

They crossed the street, side by side. They walked onto the jetty. Morgan could feel eyes everywhere. Old Charlie was waiting, wreathed in enamel smiles. The engine was running. 'Hi,' Charlie beamed.

Anna clambered down into the cockpit. 'This is my wife.' They shook hands. 'Go and put the stuff below.'

'Say,' Charlie said cheerfully above the engine noise, 'youse ain't the couple out watchin' the sunrise this mornin', is yer?'

Morgan's heart missed a beat again. 'What?'

Old Charlie said, 'Heard at the fuel jetty the boys is lookin' for a couple who was out watchin' the sunrise. Figure they know somethin' about this plane.'

'No, we only arrived this morning, on the seaplane. Let's go. Where're the charts?'

Old Charlie lifted a seat-cushion and pulled out one old, folded chart. 'The boys is runnin' round town like blue-arsed flies. Boy, is this town gonna jump!'

Morgan snatched the chart and unfolded it. It trembled. 'Were they witnesses to the crash?'

'Witnesses, hell. Black Cat an' the boys figure they were

flyin' the plane. Cos the pilots sure as hell weren't. They been found very dead down south somewheres.'

Morgan felt his stomach contract. He feverishly tried to concentrate on the chart. It only showed the Bimini islands. The coast of Florida was not shown. 'Where're your other charts?'

'Got none. What you need more charts for?'

Morgan turned to the engine controls. 'Throttle, gears. How do I start her? With a crank?'

'Right. Under here.' Charlie started to lift a hatch.

'Never mind. Compass. Knot log. Okay, Charlie, untie her.'

'Whatsa hurry? I better show you the ropes . . .'

'I know the ropes. Untie her please!'

Charlie said, 'You better come back before dark. Or go into South Bimini. There's a storm warnin' out for tonight.'

He didn't care if there was a hurricane coming. 'I will.'

Old Charlie clambered up onto the jetty. Morgan looked back at Fred's. Charlie untied the bowline. Morgan pulled it in. Charlie walked creakily down the jetty, and untied the stern-line. Morgan pulled it in. Charlie shoved against the gunnel. Morgan turned the tiller hard over, and eased open the throttle. He waved to Charlie.

'So long.' The yacht began to throb away from the jetty. 'Stay below,' he called to Anna.

The boat went chugging through the harbour. He looked back. Charlie was watching them, but there was nobody else on the jetty. He turned the tiller, pointed her towards the harbour mouth. He looked back again.

The yacht went chugging between the boats towards the open sea. It looked as if there was only a slight swell out there. Oh God, he dreaded what lay behind him. Those fast boats. He willed the little yacht to go faster. Now he was entering the harbour mouth. He looked at the wind direction.

'Come up and take the helm.'

He pointed the boat into the wind, and Anna took the tiller. He clambered to the mast, unlashed the ties, then started to winch up the mainsail. It went up jerkily, flapping. He cleated the halyard, then hurried to the bows and unleashed the fore-sail. He pulled it up, it flapped noisily. He shouted:

'Steer two-seven-zero.'

She turned onto course. The sails stiffened and the boat surged.

He pulled in the sheets and cleated them. He took over the tiller again.

Two-seven-zero, due west. That was the best he could do without a chart. But that would find Florida.

'Open two of Charlie's beers.'

She went down the hatch. She came back up with two cold cans. She passed him one. He upended it to his salty, bristly mouth, and swallowed.

He looked back at Bimini. It was still large as life. He looked at the knot log. Five knots with both engine and sail.

'About fifteen hours to Florida.' He looked at his watch. It was ten o'clock. 'About two o'clock tomorrow morning we'll get there.'

It felt as if he were trying to shake off the hounds of hell.

20

He awoke with the crashing of sea. He struggled off the bunk, and another wave hit with a thud like cannon. He clung, then grabbed a lifeline out of the locker. He clawed up the hatch.

Anna sat at the tiller, her hair flying, water running off her exhausted face. The sky was an ugly grey. The sea was running in big, ragged swells. Another wave struck and spray flew, and the bows reared up. He clawed his way over to her and sat.

'*How long has it been like this?*'

'*About three hours. It's been coming up steadily.*'

'*Why didn't you wake me? Have you seen any boats?*'

'*Only one sail boat, heading for Bimini.*'

The storm warning would keep most boats in port – it should keep Black Cat there too. He shackled on his lifeline, and hooked it to the rail. The knot log read thirty-seven nautical miles. Halfway to Florida. He looked at his watch. Just after five o'clock. Thirty-seven miles divided by seven hours – they were averaging five knots. He had slept nearly six hours. He said, 'Go below and get some sleep.'

She unclipped her lifeline and clawed across the cockpit. She clambered down the hatch. She was cold and sodden. He shouted, 'Pass me a beer, please.'

The yacht was ploughing up the side of a big running swell. Up, up she ploughed, then the crest hit her with a thud and she shuddered and spray flew; then *down* plunged her bows. She went ploughing, down into the trough on the other side, and the next swell was coming.

Anna clawed up the hatch again, a beer in one hand. He stretched and took it. 'Can you light me a cigarette?'

She disappeared again. He upended the can to his mouth. It tasted like nectar. Anna reappeared, and held out a cigarette to him. He took a deep drag. It tasted like food. The yacht was ploughing up the side of the swell. The crest hit and the spray flew and his cigarette was knocked sideways in his mouth.

It was soaked. He threw it over the side angrily.

He looked astern. There were no boats to be seen.

In the night the big winds came.

They came out of the south-east, whistling louder and harder, and the *Rosemary* lurched and surged, her rigging straining. And the seas ran harder and deeper and faster and the waves crashed harder and louder and the spray flew like grapeshot. The *Rosemary* ploughed up, up the running swells, heeled over, sails straining, and over the crests she went and then *down*, down the other side; then the bows rearing up again, the thud, the spray flying, and then down, *down* she plunged again into the next trough. Morgan sat hunched, his head turned against the flying sea, the tiller wrenching in his hand, trying to hold the course, the bows swinging and rearing and crashing, the compass needle swinging wildly. The cabin hatch slid open and Anna's head appeared. He shouted: '*Stay down!* . . .'

'*I'm coming up to relieve you.*'

She came clutching her way up, and a mass of flying spray hit her. She clung, head down, then she lurched into the cockpit. She snapped her lifeline onto the rail, and crashed down beside him. She grabbed the tiller and shouted: '*Go below* . . .'

Oh, the relief of not hanging onto that tiller any more, and the bliss of slumping his spine and shoulders; and oh just to throw himself down onto that narrow bunk below and let the aches and the cold flood out of him in sleep; he shoved back his head and straightened his spine. No way could he leave her up here alone. '*Only a few hours to go.*'

He clung there, head down against the flying spray, cold to his bones. It was ten o'clock. Only four or five hours before the coast of Florida . . . Yes, and how did he get in to the coast in seas like this? . . . He was too tired to care yet. Just thank God that Black Cat and his boys would not be out in this.

An hour later the Coastguard helicopter appeared.

They did not hear it coming above the crashing of the waves; it came out of the night, a great black shape with winking lights suddenly chopping towards them out of the howling sky. Anna gripped his arm and pointed. The helicopter came chopping angrily closer and closer, and then they could hear the thudding of its engines. A searchlight came on and the machine went chopping over the top of the ploughing *Rosemary*. They were bathed in light. The helicopter went thudding around the port side, and now they could see a man behind the light. He was signalling at them with his hands. Morgan stood and clutched the rigging and forced a smile onto his frozen face and waved his hand energetically. He shouted to Anna: 'Wave! Cheerfully!'

Morgan held up his thumb. The helicopter went chopping past the bows, into another circle. Morgan waved his hand at the sea cavalierly. Then he clawed his way to the hatch. He slid it open, clambered down into the heaving cabin and grabbed a bottle of wine out of Charlie's cold box. He clambered back into the cockpit. He held up the wine bottle to the helicopter in offering. The machine went chopping down the side of them, the co-pilot staring down. Morgan clambered back to Anna, flung his arm around her and planted a big kiss on her cheek. '*Laugh,*' he rasped.

The machine went round their bows for the last time. Then it went chopping away into the blackness.

She looked at him, drenched, her hair flying like rope. He said: 'They just wanted to know if we were all right.'

'But they may send a cutter to look at us.'

'There won't be too many around in weather like this. But we'll change course.'

He took the tiller and swung the bows away from the wind.

The little yacht came around, and he slacked off the mainsheet and the mainsail swung out with a crack, and the knot log needle jerked upwards. He slacked off the foresheet and the foresail billowed. The *Rosemary* surged, ploughing before wind, and suddenly it was almost silent and almost warm, as the yacht ran with the seas, getting the hell away from the US Coastguard.

For two hours they ran before the wind, the little yacht surging up the swells, then over the crests she went and down the other side, *down*, and the swell heaved at her stern and she was almost surfing; then Morgan swung the bows west again, and the wind came back on their beam in all its fury. And the *Rosemary* heeled hard over, her sails filled tight and her rigging twanging, fighting her way across the running seas again, and the spray flew like grapeshot again.

'*Go below*,' he shouted.

At about midnight the really big winds came.

Came howling up the Gulf Stream, and now the seas were great running troughs, spray flying in great lashing sheets and streaks, and now the crests were angry breakers coming crashing down like thunder; and the little boat lurched and shuddered. A wave came crashing over the cockpit, and Morgan felt himself go.

He sprawled and the wave swept his legs up and there was nothing in the world but the crash of salt water in his ears and nostrils and the deck disappearing beneath him, and he went over the side, into the sea. And there was nothing but the terror and the fighting, and then the wrench at his guts as the lifeline stopped him. He broke surface, gasping, being dragged behind the ploughing boat, stunned. The rudder crashed about, free, and the little boat swung into the wind and the sails flapped and crashed about wildly, and Morgan heaved on the lifeline. He heaved himself, hand over hand, back towards the stern, gasping. He reached up wildly and gripped the stern. He clung there, as the bows heaved up into the coming swell. Up, up, up the bows went; then the crest broke and the wave came crashing down. It thundered into the cockpit and over the stern and over Morgan, and wrenched him again, but he clung; then he kicked with all his might, and he swung up one leg. He got

140

it over as the bows crashed over the crest, and he rolled back into the cockpit.

He scrambled up, gasping. The yacht was ploughing into the bottom of the trough now. He seized the end of the mainsail sheet, and frantically tied it round the tiller and lashed it into the midships position. Then he heaved in the mainsail, and lashed the boom to midships. He unclasped his safety line, and scrambled for the mast. The yacht was riding up the next swell now. He made it to the mast as the wave broke over the bows. He clung to the mast with all his might, and tons of sea crashed over him. He frantically uncleated the halyard, and the mainsail came crashing down into the cockpit. He let go the next halyard and the foresail came cascading down onto the deck and he scrambled for the bows. He clutched his way, tooth-clenched. He thrust one sail-tie under the mess of sail. He frantically lashed the bunch to the railing as the bows rode up the next swell. He tied the knot and the wave hit him. Like an avalanche, wrenching, and he clung. It swept away in a crashing rush, and he started to scramble back to the cockpit, and he saw Anna.

He saw her disappear in a mass of crashing water and he bellowed, '*Get back!* –' and the wave rushed over the stern, and he saw her again. She was naked, both arms flung around the boom, and she was lashing the sail down, and he cried '*Thank God* –' He jumped into the cockpit as she finished the knot, and he seized her arm. He looked wildly at the next swell coming at them, and he flung open the hatch and shoved her down it. The next wave hit, and he scrambled into the hatch after her. The wave came crashing down the deck, over him, into the cabin and he slammed the hatch shut above him.

He clung, heaving, braced. She was on the bunk, clinging to the mast, dripping, her hair matted to her head, grinning at him weakly. It was the first time in six years that he had seen her naked. 'You shouldn't have gone there without a lifeline.'

'Hark who's talking. So – bare poles, is it?'

'It's safest.' He lurched to the bunk opposite her, crashed down, and braced. He looked at her, his hair matted, two days' growth of beard on his face, and with all his exhausted heart he wanted to take her in his arms and possess her. There was a thud and the boat shook, and they braced themselves. He said: 'You should put something on.'

'Everything's wet.' She picked up a towel and draped it around her shoulders. She looked at him.

'Oh Jack, Jack, beautiful Jack. The things you've done for me. Now this.' She clung to the mast as the boat ploughed down. She waited till it hit the bottom of the trough. Then said: 'If you want to quit when we get to port, I'll understand perfectly. I mean that.'

'And what'll you do?' The boat was heaving up the next swell.

'I'll carry on alone.'

He said: 'It's nice to just sit and talk, isn't it?' The crest of the swell hit them, and they lurched. 'Well, it beats ditching aeroplanes.'

'You haven't answered me.'

The bows hit the bottom of the trough. He said, 'These people have got no rights over you.'

She clung to the mast. 'You're doing this because you think you love me.'

'I do love you.'

'Yes, I believe you do.

You didn't before?'

He grinned: 'I didn't know those bastard pilots were coming.' The boat hit the crest with another thud. 'Or this bloody storm. I thought it was just going to be a breeze with Big King.'

'So my evidence is questionable?'

'But your verdict is sound.'

Then her exhausted eyes filled with longing. She stood up, and she pushed the mattress down onto the deck between the two bunks. She dropped to her knees onto it, and held out her hand to him.

He held her hand tight, his heart pounding.

'I don't want a reward, Anna.'

'It's a gift! Of love!'

And he came down off the bunk, onto his knees beside her, his heart hammering, and he slid his arms around her bare shoulders, and oh, the blissful feel of her smooth wet nakedness, and they toppled over onto the mattress. And she clutched him and kissed him, her mouth and teeth crushed against his; and oh, the wonderful feeling of her in his arms at last, the cool softness of her, her breasts pressed against his sodden chest,

the wonderful feel and taste of her soft-hard mouth; then she
broke the kiss, her eyes full of tears, and she laughed at him:

'I was going to be beautiful for you.'

And he laughed with her and he kissed her again, devouring
her. The boat heaved and crashed and rolled about them, but
they did not know it in the joy of each other at last.

21

The first pearly light came into the east.

The wind was gone. The *Rosemary* drifted in the early-
morning Gulf Stream, gently rising with the swells, slopping in
the little wafts of breeze. Down in the bottom of the boat Anna
Hapsburg and Jack Morgan lay together, arms entwined about
each other, deep in beautiful sleep. With the sunrise, the big
sleek boat came cruising towards them.

The noise of the engines woke them. Morgan scrambled up,
his heart pounding, every muscle tense, ready to fight, to kill.
He peered through the porthole. And stared. He saw the big,
grey steel hull of a United States Coastguard vessel. Anna was
pulling on her blouse frantically.

'No! Just clutch the towel around you. Embarrass them.
Stand in the hatch and act dumb.'

She clutched the towel to her bosom. She ran her fingers
through her ropey hair and slid back the hatch. The cutter
towered over her, the sunrise behind it. 'Ahoy there,' a voice
called.

'Oh, hi.' She smiled uncertainly.

The officer looked down at her from the bridge. 'Are you all
right?'

Anna stood in the hatch, naked but for the towel clutched
to her breasts. 'Sure. We had a pretty bad time last night. Had
to bare-pole it.'

'Where're you heading?'

Her mind fumbled. 'To Bimini . . .'

'Where you from?'

'Fort Lauderdale.'

'Were you approached by a Coastguard helicopter last night?'

'Why, sure. We tried to tell them we were okay.'

'But you were heading towards Florida at that time.'

Morgan closed his eyes.

'Yes, we got worried about the storm, thought we better turn back. Then it got so bad we had to bare-pole it.'

'Didn't you hear the storm warning on the radio?'

'I guess not. We kind of like to set sail and go.'

The officer muttered something. Then: 'Well, you're in the middle of the shipping lane, lady. If I were you I'd wake up the husband.' He added: 'And listen to the radio next time.'

Anna gushed, contrite. 'We will.'

Morgan whispered: 'Ask them for a bearing for Fort Lauderdale.'

'Say –' Anna called '– can you give us a bearing for Fort Lauderdale? We want to go back now.'

The officer sighed, and went into the bridge-house. He came out a few moments later.

'Two eight five, ma'am.'

'Thank you!'

'Okay, ma'am.' He saluted wearily, and gave an order.

Morgan watched the cutter go, limp with relief. Anna came down the steps, her face wreathed in smiles. Morgan turned, grinning. 'Well done . . .' He put his arms around her.

'I think God's looking after us!'

He squeezed her. 'Let's get the hell out of here.'

It would take Black Cat only one hour to catch up with them in weather like this. He yanked on his trousers. He lifted the hatch, exposed the engine. He inserted the crank, and wound her up. The little engine thudded into life, *doem – doem – doem*. He went up on deck.

Anna came up, and Morgan's heart seemed to turn over like a porpoise. Her hair was hanging in salty tresses, her full lips unpainted, her face drawn from days of strain, and she was beautiful. And the beautiful sunrise, gold and pink and red, fanning out across the eastern sky over the gentle sea and he wanted to laugh and spread his arms and thank the Lord for giving him his true love at last.

And maybe God *was* looking after them.

At eleven o'clock on that beautiful morning the yacht chugged into Leeside Marina outside Fort Lauderdale, Florida. Morgan had a smile all over his face. Oh God, it felt good to be alive, to be with her. At the end of the mooring lane was the jetty marked 'Arrivals'. He nosed the yacht up against it. Anna jumped ashore with the bow-line. Morgan made the stern fast.

They grabbed the bag, locked up the boat. They hurried up the jetty to the office. The concrete seemed to heave under their feet. It felt as if they were home from a long voyage. There was a public telephone. Anna went into it. Morgan went into the office. 'Good morning!' And by God it *was* a beautiful morning! He did the paperwork and paid for three days' mooring. He handed the man the keys and said:

'Tomorrow or the next day a man called Charlie will come and take the boat away.'

He got a fistful of coins from the office. He went outside. Anna was hanging up the telephone. She said: 'A taxi's coming. There's a train in fifty minutes.'

'Good.' He went into the call box. He looked at his watch. In England it was after five pm now. He dialled the code for international calls, then the code for England, then a number in Berkshire.

A faraway female voice said: 'Zenith Flying School.'

He recognized Sarah Makepeace. 'Is the instructor around?'

'Somewhere. Shall I call him?'

'No. Just tell him to be in head office in twenty minutes.'

There was a moment's hesitation. 'Oh, okay . . .'

'Thank you. Goodbye.' He hung up. He turned to Anna happily. 'That's lucky. He could have been out of town.'

'Where's his head office?'

'A contact number. A pub. That was his wife.' A taxi swung into the marina gates. 'Come on.'

They hurried to it. 'Railway station, please.'

Morgan slumped back in the seat. He felt drained and he felt elated. He took her hand. He wanted to take her in his arms. He closed his eyes. And, oh, he was in love! The taxi swung onto the road for Fort Lauderdale. She squeezed his hand and put her mouth to his ear:

'I love you . . .'

He wanted to throw his arms wide to the sky. He whispered:
'And I love you and I love you and I love you.'

They stopped outside the railroad station. Anna stayed in the taxi and Morgan hurried inside, to the public telephones. He lifted the receiver, and listened. Then he made a note of its number. He hurried back to the taxi.

Four minutes later the taxi dropped them outside the Western Union telegraph company. He told the driver to wait.

Anna wrote out a telegram to Charlie, care of Fred's Eating House, Bimini, telling him where his boat was. Morgan asked for the Manhattan yellow pages telephone directory. He looked up Hotels. He selected one and wrote down the address. He dialled it, and booked a room for Mr and Mrs Denton.

'Certainly, Mr Denton. Have a nice day.'

Then he telephoned Thomas Cook's Travel Agency and asked about seat availability on flights from London to New York today. Plenty of space. 'Thank you, have a nice day.' Then he looked up the Brew and Burger restaurant chain. He noted down an address. He looked at his watch. He waited one minute more, then dialled the code for international again, then a pub near Thatcham in Berkshire, England. It rang only twice, and Makepeace said: 'Rose and Crown.'

Morgan said slowly: 'Go outside to a public telephone box and call me in exactly seven minutes at the following number. Got a pencil?'

Recognition dawned on Makepeace. 'Oh . . . Okay.'

Morgan gave him the number of the telephone at the railway station. He hung up.

He grabbed Anna's hand and they hurried back to the taxi.

Seven minutes later he stood at the public telephone at the station. Anna was at the ticket office, buying two first-class sleepers to New York. Morgan looked feverishly at his watch. The train was due in two minutes. *Come on Makepeace!* Anna pointed at her watch. The telephone rang. Morgan snatched it up. 'Hullo?'

'Hullo,' Makepeace said. 'What you doing over there?'

'Listen, ask no questions. I've got a job for you. It's perfectly legal. Lick your pencil.'

'Okay,' Makepiece said obediently.

146

Morgan said slowly: 'Meet me in New York – in the Brew and Burger restaurant, in Times Square, at the corner of Forty-third Street, for breakfast at ten am tomorrow. Got that? And bring a reliable partner. There're plenty of flights, I've checked.'

'How do you spell the place where I meet you?'

'*Brew* as in beer, *Burger* as in hamburger, dammit! And bring two blank passports. Not British.'

Anna said urgently: '*The train's coming in!*'

'In *what* square?' Makepeace said.

'*Times.*'

'As in tick-tock?'

'Bravo. Now if you think you can remember all that –'

'What about money?'

'Bring plenty!'

'You know what I mean . . .' Makepeace whined.

'You'll get paid. Unlike some unfortunate people I know!'

He slammed down the phone.

The train was easing to a halt. They ran for it.

Two minutes later they slumped into chairs in the saloon car, as the train eased forward. They felt elated as if they had just won a long race. Anna looked at him; then blew out her cheeks, and smiled. 'That was all very clever.'

'I had three days to think about it.' He got up happily and went to the bar. There were only three other people in the saloon car. He bought four Budweisers, got two plastic glasses and took them back to their table. He slumped down. He upended a can to his bristly mouth, and swallowed, and swallowed, and it went down into his dry empty gut like a mountain brook. Anna poured a can into a glass, closed her eyes and took a long swallow.

She said: 'They couldn't have tapped that conversation, could they?'

He shook his head. 'They might have been tapping his contact number at the Rose and Crown. Though I doubt that too. But they couldn't have set up a tap on all the public telephones in the area in five minutes.'

He thought, Oh couldn't they? They would figure he'd need the help of somebody like Makepeace. And they knew about

Makepeace. And if they had tapped the Rose and Crown's telephone they would soon find out that the telephone number he had given Makepeace was on Fort Lauderdale railway station. And it wouldn't be long after that before they figured out where they had gone, on which train.

But for the moment he did not care. He had done his best, in the circumstances. There was nothing more he could do right now. It was wonderful just to sit still with her and be in love and drink beer and let the train take them, and know that for almost twenty-four hours there was nothing they could do. They were going to have a long lunch, with all the wine they wanted, and then he was going to take this beautiful, wonderful woman back to their compartment and make love, love, and more love.

Part Four

22

In the morning it was still like that. When he first woke up, before first light, he thought he was in his bunk at the bottom of the ocean in his submarine; then he remembered, and all he knew was the utter joy of her, after so long the dream had truly come true, and the horror of the last few days was unreal. Only this happiness mattered and even what they had to do today did not weigh on him – their luck would hold! The British could not know which of the thousands of banks in the world they were going to – and they were in civilized America and she was perfectly entitled to open her own safety-deposit box – today was going to be plain sailing . . .

Then he woke up properly, and he knew that today their luck could very well run out. If the British were tapping Makepeace's telephones they had had twenty hours to get into gear. And what made every nerve tense up again was what could happen to her and to their wonderful happiness . . . He sat up abruptly. *Positive thinking!* . . . He swung off the upper bunk and slid carefully down to the floor, so as not to waken her.

'Hullo,' she said.

She was sitting in the dark at the window, fully dressed.

He was surprised. 'Hullo . . .' He sat down and held her against him. 'Did you sleep all right?'

'I slept. Just nerves now.'

He held her. 'I love you,' he whispered.

'I love you too, Jack.'

He let her go. 'What are you thinking?'

She sighed, and sat back.

'I've been trying to think how Max would do this.'

He was further surprised.

'And, how would Max do it?'

She looked out of the dark window.

'He was . . . so experienced in wheeling and dealing. Pulling strings. Bullying people. Compared to him we're babes in the wood.' She put her hand over his and turned from the window

151

. . . 'Please, you've done wonders. Through thick and thin, you've got us here. Max couldn't have pulled that off.'

He repeated, 'What would Max have done to solve this problem?'

She shook her head, and sighed again.

'He had so many friends in high places. Used his financial muscle, I suppose. Bribed people. Got the smartest, crookedest lawyers in the business to do his dirty work.' She added: 'Hired the Mafia if necessary.'

Morgan sighed. This was what he had put off talking about. 'Cross the bridges as we come to them.' But at the end of today they might have to cross that bridge. He said:

'Anna, we have to think this through very carefully. What happens after today, if the goods aren't in the New York box?' He paused. 'I've given this a great deal of thought.'

She squeezed his hand. 'And so have I.'

He said: 'And you have three options.' He held up a finger. 'One: You do it legally and hand this whole thing over to a good lawyer. Hear me out . . . Two: You collaborate with the British authorities – trust them, and your lawyer acts as your watchdog.'

Anna closed her eyes. 'Three,' Morgan said: 'You get into Max's box in Switzerland *illegally*. With all the dangers inherent in that . . . Now let's consider the options in detail.'

He lit a cigarette and blew the smoke out hard.

'I'm sure the best option is to get a very good, honest lawyer to handle this for you. To protect your legal rights, which would also protect you physically. He'll take all the necessary legal procedures to get into the box in Switzerland and safeguard the contents –'

She cut in quietly, 'Jack, I have to get a lawyer sometime – to wind up Max's estate, and get the British off my back. But he can't protect me from the KGB. And, for God's sake, how long will it take a lawyer to get into Max's Swiss box? What's involved? Max's will is unsigned. That means I have to inherit under the laws of intestacy. That means waiting for court orders and trustees and God knows what – and all the time the contents of the box are out of *my* control. Where other people can get at them.'

'The box'll be in the Swiss courts' hands, Anna, under lock and key.'

152

'But how many people have access to that *key*? How many clerks who could be bribed? How many *burglars* could be hired? . . .'

'It stays in the bank until it's finally handed to you.'

'But meanwhile the court and all the clerks know the box number – and the British! It'll be a matter of court record, and don't tell me the British and KGB couldn't find out what's written in a court record. But right now only *I* know. And that's why the British and KGB are after me.' She pressed her eyelids. 'And anyway it's highly likely that Max kept this stuff in a box under his *assumed* name – Maxwell Constantine. In which case a lawyer *cannot* get at it for me. And . . .' She sighed. 'I don't trust the lawyer keeping his mouth shut if he's pressured.'

Morgan sat back. He hadn't finished with that option, but he passed on to the next.

'Option Two.' He took a pull on his cigarette. 'Collaborate with the British government, with a lawyer as watchdog.' He added, 'At least that way you keep this information out of the hands of the Russians.' He paused. 'Do you still intend to destroy it when you find it?'

'Yes.'

'How?'

'With my nail scissors. In the bank.'

He said, 'Think about that. If it's so important, should not the competent authorities deal with it, with all their expertise?'

She looked at him, squarely. 'That's what you really want me to do, isn't it?'

He sighed, then said: 'I can't answer you. Because I don't know what's on the microfilm. I only know it's highly important.'

She demanded, 'Do *you* trust the British?'

He sighed again.

'I've thought a hell of a lot about this and I'm still thinking out loud now.' He paused. 'I'm still a Royal Navy man at heart. Trained and steeped in it. I'm used to obeying orders and having my orders obeyed. I used to think the British were the best in the world. For fair play. Justice. And by and large I still do. But only "by and large". In a notoriously bad world. That means that if the stakes are high enough . . .' He shook his head. 'I've seen what they were prepared to do to get to you.

It was undoubtedly kidnap. But that still leaves the question: If this secret is so important, and the Russians want it so badly, I think you should – as a matter of common sense, or patriotism, if you like – you should let the British government handle it, with all their wisdom.'

She said: 'Don't imagine I haven't thought of all that. And I wish I could tell you what this is about, to help me. But I dare not. Not because I don't trust you, but because what you don't know can't be sweated out of you by third degree interrogation.' She looked at him grimly. 'Do you trust the British not to exploit this secret?'

He said: 'They would certainly exploit it.'

'Unfairly?'

'If worthwhile, yes.'

She nodded. 'And do you think my watchdog lawyer could stop them doing that?'

He sighed. 'He may not be able to stop them.'

'Exactly. And do you trust the British not to . . . dispose of me, after I've yielded up the secret. If it's important enough?'

'Your lawyer will protect you from that! If the British try to "dispose" of you, your lawyer will create a terrible scandal. It would topple the government. The British wouldn't risk that.'

'But that wouldn't protect me from the KGB! And the lawyer would only be iron-clad protection against the British *after* I've destroyed the evidence. After *that* I'm harmless – they wouldn't need to dispose of me because they can just deny it all as the ravings of a lunatic. *But*, if they *have* the evidence, and they're exploiting it, and I could ruin everything for them by opening my mouth, do you completely trust the British not to find a way of disposing of me? – lawyer or no lawyer.' She added, 'And dispose of *you*, if they thought you knew.' She looked at him. 'Do you absolutely, one hundred per cent trust them?'

Morgan gave a bitter sigh.

'Exactly,' Anna said. 'So isn't that the complete answer to Option Two?'

Morgan hadn't finished with that one yet, either.

'Option Three.' And, oh Jesus, this was the one he really had not wanted to think about. 'That means we've got to fly to Switzerland and somehow get into that safety-deposit box illegally. Somebody has to impersonate Maxwell Constantine.

And forge that signature.' He added: 'You cannot do it yourself. So who impersonates Max Constantine?'

She pressed her eyelids. 'Exactly.'

He said: 'Perhaps a trustworthy private detective? Or even, maybe, an accomplished forger. But I don't think friend Makepeace can produce such a person, especially not in a hurry. So, where do we look?'

'That's why I'm sitting up in the cold light of dawn, after a deliriously wonderful yesterday, trying to think how Max would have done it.'

Morgan said: 'And *you* would want to accompany that person to the box, wouldn't you? To find the evidence yourself, and destroy it.' He raised his eyebrows. 'That means that if *he* is caught out in his forgery, both of you go to jail.'

'That's a risk I've got to take.'

He said carefully: 'I'm not prepared to let you take that risk.'

She looked at him squarely.

'I love you, Jack. But you will not stop me.'

He said relentlessly: 'But if you find a person to impersonate Max Constantine, would you trust him – if you don't even trust a lawyer?'

'Again, exactly! But if I think enough there must be a solution.'

Morgan sat back. Oh God, he did not want to say this.

'There is a solution. Me. I impersonate Maxwell Constantine.' He added flatly, before she could interrupt: 'I've had a good look at the signature. It wouldn't be hard to forge. It is itself a forgery and therefore has no veteran flourishes.'

She took his hand.

'No. That's exactly why I'm sitting up trying to use my tiny mind. I'm not having you take that risk. I *mean* that.'

Morgan sat back. God, he didn't want that risk, either. He tried to hang on tight to the happiness, to the lovely feelings he had woken up with, he did not want to think any further about what would happen if today went wrong.

'Those are your options, Anna. Before the day's out we may have to decide on one. But we're crossing our bridges before we come to them.' He held a finger out at her. 'Let's get one thing straight in your mind . . . Today you are walking into *your* bank. To open a deposit box which is in *your* name . . .

To get whatever you goddam want out of it. You're in America, the Land of the Free. Not all the Queen's horses can legally stop you. And I consider it very, very unlikely they would have the audacity to try . . .' He paused. 'Now, we're going to walk into that bank this morning bold as brass, with Makepeace to look after us, and he's one of the best karate men the Royal Navy's ever known. I don't think we need him but we're very well prepared . . .' He shook his finger at her: '*Confidence*. That's the attitude today, Anna. We'll reconsider the options when the time comes. Got that?'

She looked at him.

'Got it,' she said.

23

It was 6.15 am when the train pulled into the station in New Jersey, one hour from New York.

It was cold, and they had only summer clothing. Morgan got out at one end of the carriage, Anna at the other. She set off down the long platform, shivering. Morgan followed, carrying the handgrip, feeling very conspicuous in shirtsleeves. There were only a few other people leaving the train. He glanced over his shoulder. There was nobody.

Anna hurried through the ticket hall, out into the early morning. There was a taxi rank. She hurried to the first vehicle. Morgan looked about. Nobody was paying attention. He hurried over to the taxi and climbed in beside her.

'You folks gonna catch your death like that,' the driver said. 'Where to?'

'Somewhere we can get coffee. Then, in an hour's time, come back and drive us to Manhattan.'

'To *where*? . . . I'm sorry, Mister, I don't go interstate.'

Morgan held out a fifty-dollar bill.

'What's on the meter, plus this.'

At nine that morning the taxi dropped them outside Macey's department store in New York, very pleased with his fifty bucks. 'Have a nice day!'

It was bitterly cold. People were hurrying to work, wrapped up. Morgan and Anna hurried into the big store. The sudden warmth inside was a relief.

He said: 'Wig and hairdye. And just enough clothes to look respectable. Meet me back here in forty-five minutes.' He turned and hurried away.

He went to the public telephones. He looked in the yellow pages for multi-storey car parks. He made notes.

Then he went to the floral department. He ordered roses to be delivered to Mr and Mrs Denton at the Royalton Hotel, 44 West 44th Street. He wrote on the card: *Welcome to New York! How about a drink at our old haunt (Pete's Tavern, 3rd Avenue near Union Square) at eleven am?*

He sealed the card in the envelope. 'Will that go immediately?'

'Immediately, sir. Have a nice day.'

'You too.' He hurried away to the men's department.

He bought a cheap raincoat, a navy-blue blazer, three shirts, vests, socks, underpants, a tie, trousers and shoes. It took him twenty-five minutes. He went to the changing rooms and put the new gear on. He looked at himself in the mirror. He was still not used to having black hair. He stuffed his old clothes into his shopping bag. Then he went to the stationery department and bought three identical street maps of Manhattan, a notebook and a bottle of glue.

He went to meet Anna.

He was early. He had to force himself not to pace. He went to the cosmetic counter and took great interest in Helena Rubinstein's fine products. 'Just browsing, for my wife,' he said to the salesgirl. And he thought: *Wife.* That's a lovely word. He looked up and his wife was coming towards him, wan and beautiful and smiling brightly. She wore a fawn raincoat over a blouse and skirt and no-nonsense walking shoes, and she took his breath away. She was as beautiful with black hair as she had been with blonde. He took her arm.

He led her back to the telephones. He pulled out the note he had made in Fort Lauderdale. He dialled. It rang only twice. 'Brew and Burger.'

Morgan handed the receiver to Anna. She said, 'I'm meeting

157

somebody there about now. A tall man with blue eyes, called Douglas. Have you got such a gentleman?'

'I'll have a look . . .'

A minute passed.

'Hullo!' Makepeace shouted.

Anna said slowly: 'I've booked us a room at the Royalton Hotel, forty-four West Forty-fourth street. Mr and Mrs Denton.'

She hung up. Morgan felt limp with relief. Anna said, 'Do you think they could have tapped that call?'

'Possible. If they managed to tap our calls yesterday, they'd know we were meeting at the Brew and Burger. But even if they're following him right now to the Royalton Hotel, they don't know about the flowers.' He looked feverishly at the list he had made of things they had to do.

He got the telephone directory again. He telephoned Thomas Cook and made some airline reservations. Then he telephoned a store that sold medical equipment, and reserved one wheel-chair. Then he called a car-hire firm, and ordered a car, with driver, to fetch them immediately.

Ten minutes later the car arrived outside Macey's. 'Where to, sir?'

'First, somewhere we can get passport photographs taken quickly. Then . . .' He produced one of the maps he had bought. 'To the World Trade Center. From there, to this multi-storeyed car park I've marked on the map. Slowly.' He explained: 'I'm a movie producer. I'm looking for suitable streets to film a car-chase scene.'

Pete's Tavern is an old-fashioned New York bar, with dark ceilings and wooden booths and red-checked tablecloths. They sat where they could see the door. The young man called Spider Webster sat alone in another booth.

'You don't *know*?' Morgan said to Makepeace. 'Did you *look*?'

'I mean,' Makepeace said earnestly, 'I didn't see anybody suspicious.'

'Was there anybody in the hotel foyer?'

'A few people. I left Spider in the foyer. I checked in, and went up to the room. Saw the flowers. Read your message, and left. Nice room,' he added. 'Could have done with a sleep, got none on the plane.'

'Did you leave your bags in the room?'

'*No*, Spider's got the bags, I'm not stupid. When I got the flowers I figured the room was just a dead-letter box.'

'When you left, were the same people in the foyer?'

'Spider says no. We got a taxi straight away.'

'Did anybody follow you out of the hotel and get a taxi?'

'No. But there's another quite big hotel across the street, and taxis were leaving there all the time.'

'Did you watch through the rear window?'

'Of course. But the streets are full of taxis. Told mine to go to Grand Central Station, seen it in the movies. We got out, walked round the station a bit, then got another cab and came here. Got out two blocks away, walked the rest. I did the right *things*. I *thought*,' Makepeace complained, 'this was "perfectly legal"?'

'It is. Did you get the blank passports?'

'Got them.' Makepeace was a tall man with a surprised, triangular face. 'From Danziger. You owe five hundred pounds.'

'*Danziger knows they're for me?*'

'*No*,' Makepeace sighed. 'You owe *me* five hundred nicker. And the rest,' he added.

Morgan said: 'Danziger? I don't trust that man. Did he know you were coming to join me?'

'Of *course* not,' Makepeace said plaintively '– I know about professional secrecy. All he knows is I left London in a hurry and needed two blanks. He had them hand-delivered to me at the airport. I *had* to use Danziger, he's the only guy who can lay his hands on everything in a hurry.'

Morgan sighed grimly. 'You steer clear of Danziger. You'll get a bad reputation. And this guy you've brought, Webster' – he nodded down the bar '– is he safe?'

'Perfectly. Ex-SAS.'

'Why did he leave the SAS?'

'Usual reason. Money.'

'And what's he costing me?'

'Same as me,' Makepeace said. 'Two thousand up front, plus five hundred a day. Plus expenses.'

'Jesus. You don't come cheap, do you?'

'It's okay,' Anna said.

'It's *cheap*,' Makepeace said indignantly. 'That's special rates, for a friend. You should see what Danziger charges.'

'All right.' Morgan sighed. 'Call Webster over.'

Webster came and sat down in the booth with them. He was a shy, smallish young man, with a ferrety face and a crew cut.

Morgan said: 'This morning, we are all going to Anna's bank. Where she has a safety-deposit box. Now, as we leave that bank, it is your job – and mine – to bodyguard her.'

Makepeace said, 'What's she going to take out of the box?'

'Never mind. But it's hers. And it's important.'

Makepeace blinked. 'Who're we bodyguarding her against?'

'Against anybody who tries to rob her.'

'I haven't got a shooter – couldn't take one on the plane.'

'Of course not. I've got one for you.' He carefully slipped the dead pilot's pistol from his pocket. 'Smith and Wesson. Loaded.' He held up a finger: 'But you only use that as a very last resort – otherwise it's unarmed combat. And they won't shoot at us. They'll only try to strong-arm us into a waiting car. We fight them off and run to our own waiting car. Which *you*,' he added, 'are about to rent from Hertz. We drive away like hell, and shake them off.'

Makepeace said worriedly, 'Who are these guys?'

'Never mind. I tell you if and when you need to know.'

Makepeace blinked. 'And where do we drive *to*?'

'I have a route, which I'll outline very carefully. But first let me point out that it is *very* likely that there will be *nobody* waiting to rob us outside that bank. In which case –' he spread his hands – 'we drive away without a care in the world, and your job is probably over, Dougie. If we've been lucky and got what we want from the bank, you fly home to sunny England.'

Makepeace was all rapt attention. He said hoarsely: 'But if you haven't been so lucky?'

This was the bridge they did not want to cross until they got to it. Anna hunched forward, her hands clasped. Morgan said:

'Then your job is only just beginning, Douglas. Then *you*,' he pointed his cigarette at Makepeace, 'probably have to jump on a plane to Paris. Spider stays with Anna and me to ride shotgun.' He paused. 'In Paris there are plenty of small aircraft for hire. You rent us a plane. Anna, Spider and I arrive in Paris the next day. From Washington. We're hoping like hell this won't happen but I booked the seats this morning, in case.' He paused. 'You arrange for somebody to meet us at Paris airport. With a rented car. With a chauffeur's cap on his head, so I can spot him easily. He drives us to the airfield, where you are waiting with the light aircraft. And you fly us to some *private* airstrip in Switzerland. Without, of course, going through immigration control.'

Makepeace was grappling with all this.

'Switzerland?' he complained – 'What do we do in *Switzerland*?'

'But you must work out a good route from Paris airport to this airfield where you're waiting, so the driver can shake off anybody following us. And a system whereby we can change cars to confuse them. That means you'll have to get two more of your SAS pals over from England to help. Maybe three. To drive, and do whatever muscle-work is necessary.'

'Do they come to Switzerland with us?'

'They must be *prepared* to do so.' He held up a finger. 'The same money as you're getting. Not a penny more.'

Makepeace stared at him worriedly.

'*Paris*? . . .' he complained. 'But I don't know Paris. I don't even polly-voo the lingo, hopeless I was at school. Now, *Amsterdam* I know, and they all speak English in Amsterdam – but *Paris*? . . .'

Morgan looked at him, thinking.

'This may be a good idea.' He turned to Anna. 'There's a public telephone outside the toilets. Phone a travel agency. Not Thomas Cook's. See if you can book us on a flight Paris to Amsterdam tomorrow night.'

'Why don't we fly direct to Amsterdam from America?'

'If we're spotted at Washington airport, boarding the flight for Paris, they'll be expecting us to emerge from Paris airport. But we won't emerge. We'll go to the transit lounge, and board the flight to Amsterdam. They won't be expecting us in Amsterdam.'

'What name do I reserve the seats in?'

'The same names as we're putting on the blank passports.

161

Armstrong. Spider's ticket will have to be in his real name, Webster.'

Anna left the booth. Morgan sat quiet a minute, thinking. Then said to Makepeace: 'So you can organize everything in Amsterdam. And, do you know of private airfields in Switzerland?'

Makepeace's brow furrowed.

'Switzerland's easy. All those valleys. I can find out like *that*.' He snapped his fingers. 'Where in Switzerland do you want to go?'

'And,' Morgan said, 'we need a car waiting at that airstrip in Switzerland. And a hotel room reserved.'

'Where?' Makepeace demanded.

'And from the hotel room we go to another bank.'

'An*other* bank? . . .'

Anna came back to the table. She nodded at Morgan.

'*Where* in Switzerland are we going?' Makepeace demanded plaintively '– where's this other bank?'

'You'll be told *when* you need to know it. It may never happen. We'll know this afternoon. But if it does, you've got the same job in Switzerland. Bodyguard us as we leave the bank. And provide a getaway car. Shake off anybody following us. Drive us back to the airfield. And fly us out.'

'Where to?'

'I'll decide that closer to the time. Then,' he ended, 'your job's over. Anna and I are on our own again.' He sighed deeply. 'But, again, it's very likely there will *not* be anybody trying to pounce on us outside the bank in Switzerland, if we have been successful in covering our tracks. And even *if* they spot us at Amsterdam airport, you'll shake them off. Won't you?'

Makepeace shifted unhappily. 'Who *are* these guys?'

'*Won't* you?'

Makepeace's furrowed brow.

'*Sure* I can shake them off. I *know* Amsterdam. And I can figure out a plan for Switzerland. But New York? I've never been here – all these one-way streets. You need a professional getaway driver for New York.'

'Where the hell do I get one? From the Mafia? I don't know a soul in New York, Douglas.'

'Danziger does, he'd arrange it, he's the best in the business.'

Morgan snorted. 'I don't *trust* Danziger! Forget it. Now, that's the plan. Are you in? Or out?'

Makepeace blinked. 'In,' he muttered.

'Spider?'

'In,' Spider said.

Morgan sat back. It was still unreal. 'All right.' He pulled out two folded street maps of New York. 'One for you, one for Spider. You're going to Hertz to rent a car. And Spider's going to Avis to rent another one. They *must* be different colours. Got that?'

'Got it,' Makepeace said unhappily.

'Spider first drives to this address.' He handed him a note. 'And picks up a wheelchair I've ordered. Then he drives to a multi-storeyed car park. I've marked it on the map. He leaves the car in there and then joins us in *your* car. And the four of us spend until two o'clock this afternoon driving carefully along the route I've marked. From the bank, onwards. Over and over. Until you're familiar with the lights and the landmarks. Right?'

'Right,' Makepeace said worriedly.

'And remember they drive on the *right*, here, Makepeace.'

'Right,' Makepeace said miserably. 'On the right.'

24

The twin silver towers of the World Trade Center reared up into the cold, grey November sky, lights twinkling mistily.

On the ground floor stands the Hong Kong & Shanghai Bank, its portals guarded by two big iron lions, imperialistically recumbent. Across the side-road is a post office building, with parking reserved for official vehicles.

It was just after two o'clock when Spider dropped them off, half a block from the bank. Spider drove on, to the official parking area outside the post office.

They walked up the busy sidewalk, Anna and Makepeace in front, Morgan five paces behind them, his shoulders hunched against the cold, his eyes darting. This was it. He might have done a great job so far, but if the British or the Russians knew about Max's banks, they would be watching this one now. And all his hair-raising work would be for nothing. He just prayed that that microfilm was in this deposit box, that tonight they could drink champagne and start living happily ever after . . . They turned the corner, and there were the lions guarding the bank's entrance, thirty yards ahead. Anna walked resolutely, Makepeace gangling beside her. They turned into the portals. Makepeace pushed the door open.

Morgan's eyes swept the street. Nobody seemed to be paying any attention to them. He walked into the bank.

It was a small banking hall, with armchairs, and only about five customers. Anna walked to the enquiries counter. Makepeace sat down in an armchair. He picked up a brochure and pretended to read. He looked over the top of it, through the windows, at the street.

Anna turned from the enquiries counter. She walked through a doorway, to an elevator. Morgan followed her.

They got into the elevator together. Anna pressed the button for the first floor. The doors closed, and the elevator rose. She was pale and tense. He said: 'There's nothing to it. This is your own deposit box.'

The elevator stopped. The doors opened onto a corridor.

Through a door was a large room. A marble counter, with three clerks behind. At the end was a sliding grille. On this side of the counter were armchairs for clients. Morgan sat down. Anna walked to the counter. A clerk came.

'I'd like to see my box please.' She pulled the bunch of keys out of her handbag. 'I'm afraid I've forgotten which it is.'

Morgan saw Anna sign a form. She produced her passport. The clerk went to a cabinet. Produced a card. He compared the form with the card. He returned to the counter and picked up the bunch of keys. He selected one.

'It'll be this one, madam.' He pressed a buzzer. 'Mr Fredericks will look after you.'

The grille slid back and Mr Fredericks appeared. 'This way, madam.'

Morgan sat back. And massaged his thumb across his forehead.

Please God this is it. Please God today this is all over . . .

164

Mr Fredericks led her down an avenue of gleaming boxes. He stopped, inserted a master key and turned it. He motioned Anna to the box door. She inserted her key, and turned it. Mr Fredericks opened the little door. Inside was a metal box with a lid. Anna pulled it out.

'This way, madam.' Mr Fredericks led her on, to cubicles at the end of the avenue of boxes. He opened one. 'The key is on the inside of the door, madam.'

'Thank you.' Anna went in. She closed the door and locked it. She felt shaky. She sat down at the little table.

She opened the lid of the box.

She was looking at a small cloth bag, with a drawstring.

She picked it up, and pulled open the string. And stared.

Her heart sank. The bag was half full of middle-sized, unset diamonds. She buried her finger into them, desperately feeling for a roll of microfilm beneath. There was none. She poured the diamonds out onto the table.

They made a small, glinting heap. She spread them out. Nothing. She looked feverishly into the bag again, as if it might be forced to yield up something more.

It yielded up an envelope.

It was folded, tucked down the side. She pulled it out and ripped it open.

It contained one sheet of paper. She fumbled it out.

It was a carbon copy of a hand-written note of three lines. It was on stationery, headed *Banco Ambrosiana*. It was in a stranger's handwriting, in Italian. *Banco Ambrosiana? God's Banker's bank.*

Anna spoke only a smattering of Italian but she could understand the note. It was a receipt. It read:

Received from Banco Ambrosiana, for and on behalf of P2, the sum of one million dollars, in kind.

It was signed, *M. Hapsburg.*

Anna sat back. And held her head.

No microfilm . . .

She sat there a minute. Then she feverishly scooped up the diamonds, back into the bag. She put the receipt back in the box. She hesitated a moment, then shoved the bag of diamonds into her handbag. She got up and unlocked the door.

'*Mr Fredericks?*'

She followed him back to her slot. She shoved the box back inside, locked the door. She hurried back to the sliding grille.

Morgan got to his feet, expectantly. And his heart sank at the expression on her face.

He sat in the armchair beside her, sick in his guts.

'Anna, the time's come for you to tell me what this microfilm is about. So I know what we're up against.'

'We're up against the British government and the Russians.'

Morgan slapped his knee angrily and stood up. 'So, we go to Switzerland.'

Anna grabbed his hand. She pulled him down beside her.

He sat again. She looked at him.

'No, I'm on my own now.' Morgan sighed angrily, and she continued resolutely: '*Thank* you, darling Jack. For every wonderful thing you've done. But I'm on my own from here on in. I've got Makepeace to help . . .' She squeezed his hand hard. 'I'm not exposing you to risk any further. I'm going to rethink this whole thing, and make my own decisions.'

For a moment he felt relief. 'You mean you're going to hand the whole problem over to the British authorities?'

She began to speak, and out of the corner of his eye Morgan saw the British authorities walk into the room.

He stared. 'I don't believe it . . .' he whispered.

Christopher Carrington, Captain of Submarines, was walking towards them, wreathed in his crooked smile. Behind him came Makepeace, looking very worried.

Morgan got to his feet, glaring, his heart knocking.

'Good afternoon, Jack.' Carrington walked up to them as if pleased with a prank he had played. 'And this –' he gave a little bow – 'is the charming Mrs Hapsburg?'

'*Who the hell are you?*' Anna whispered.

Another little bow. 'Christopher Carrington, Royal Navy, at your service, madam.'

Morgan gripped Anna's arm to silence her, his mind racing. 'How did you know we were here?'

'Oh, you were very good,' Carrington said reassuringly – 'you had us running round the Caribbean for days. No, it was your side-kick here who let you down.' He turned to

Makepeace. 'You'll have to change your contact number, Douglas, if you want to keep it a trade secret. The Rose and Crown is old hat.'

Makepeace looked embarrassed. 'Thank you, sir.'

Morgan hissed: 'You don't call this bastard sir, Makepeace! If you call anybody sir right now it's me!'

'Oh,' Carrington went on, 'you did all the right things, Jack. But as we thought you'd have to call on somebody like Douglas for a spot of help, we had him tapped. And all the others we know about. And with some nifty footwork we got the nearest public phones tapped too, in time to learn about the Brew and Burger. We followed him to the Royalton Hotel, without difficulty. And you would have foxed us there again, with that bunch of flowers. Except Douglas left your note behind in the hotel bedroom.'

'*Jesus*, Makepeace . . .' Morgan seethed.

'And what do you want?' Anna snapped.

Carrington said seriously: 'I would like, please, what you came here today to get.'

'*Well you're not getting it!*'

Morgan rasped softly: 'Get out of our way, Carrington. Or I'll break your neck.'

'Jack,' Carrington said earnestly, 'I am not alone. I have a goodly number of men outside –'

'*Jesus Christ*,' Morgan whispered – 'a senior officer of the Royal Navy, acting on the orders of Her Majesty's government, intends to rob an American citizen in an American bank! –'

'*Jack* –' Carrington interrupted urgently – 'that is exactly what I'm *not* doing! I am *asking* for your cooperation – and Mrs Hapsburg's. That is why they sent me along, as your former commanding officer! To *avoid* trouble, not provoke it. *Jack* – cooperate now, and relieve Mrs Hapsburg of a frightening responsibility – *and* danger, I might add – and the government will forget all this misunderstanding ever happened. Your deception in Trinidad, your breach of duty, this whole silly business. And you and Mrs Hapsburg will live happily ever after. You will even be reinstated in the Navy with full seniority and pension entitlements.' He turned to Anna: 'Mrs Hapsburg, I appeal to you –'

'And if we refuse,' Anna said furiously, 'your men outside will rob us!'

'*No*, madam,' Carrington said earnestly. 'All I have to do –' he pointed at the counter – 'is pick up that telephone. And within minutes the Cousins, the American authorities, will be here to take care of the matter. Officially.'

'*And I*,' Anna flashed, 'have only to go to that same telephone and call the manager of this bank down here! And my lawyer! And the press! –'

Morgan interrupted venomously: 'Bull*shit*, Carrington! The Americans would not *dare* come into this bank and try to do anything "officially". Because they've got no legal *right* to do so! Because Mrs Hapsburg has committed no offence in going to her own deposit box!' His eyes narrowed. 'And Her Majesty's government dare do absolutely *nothing* about my so-called deception in Trinidad! Because firstly, your detention of Mrs Hapsburg was *illegal*. And secondly because officially I took *no* part in the American invasion of Grenada, remember! I was Sergeant Jackson, remember! And Sergeant Jackson is dead and buried in Alaska! Sergeant Jackson doesn't *exist* any more, to be punished! And our venerable Prime Minister has already officially and internationally protested to the American government about their invasion of Grenada, remember! So how can she now admit that she sent her dear and loyal subject, Jack Morgan, to take part in it dressed up as Sergeant Jackson?' He looked at Carrington with contempt, then held his finger up under the man's nose: 'Now get your lily-white arse outside, Carrington, and tell your gorillas to go home. And tell Her Majesty and Ronald Reagan to leave us alone! Or else.'

Carrington studied his pipe. Then put it between his teeth. 'Or else what?'

'Or else, apart from breaking your neck, we'll blow this *shameful* story sky-high!'

Carrington snatched his pipe out of his mouth. '*Jack*,' he implored – 'I am here on a diplo*matic* mission, and my *gorillas*, as you quaintly call them, are not here to rob you, but to *protect* you – as we leave this bank. From the *Russians*, Jack.'

Morgan stared at him. So did Anna. Carrington hurried on with his advantage: 'The KGB –' he pointed in the direction of the street – 'are also waiting outside, Jack.'

Morgan snapped: 'How would they know we're here?'

'I don't know – they haven't taken me into their confidence. Perhaps they knew that this was one of Mr Hapsburg's banks. Or perhaps they've been following *me*.'

'Have you seen them outside?'

'Do you know,' Carrington turned to Anna, 'that a member of the Russian embassy visited your house only hours after your husband was killed?'

'No,' Morgan snapped before Anna could answer. His heart was knocking. 'What makes you think so?'

Carrington looked at Anna significantly. Then at Morgan.

'Fresh tyre marks, on the drive outside the front door. And bloodstains. And fingerprints.' He raised his eyebrows: 'The tyre marks matched exactly the tyres of a Russian vehicle found in town nearby. With a dead Russian in it. His blood group matched that of bloodstains found in Mrs Hapsburg's bathroom. So were his *fingerprints* to be found. And . . .' he raised his eyebrows again, 'Mrs Hapsburg's fingerprints – or what we *believe* to be Mrs Hapsburg's, because they are to be found on things like her hairbrush – were found in the dead Russian's car.'

Anna was staring at him, white-faced. 'I know nothing about all that!'

'I'm sure you don't, dear lady.' Carrington gave a little bow. 'But, of course, our Red friends are rather upset about losing such a promising member of their diplomatic corps. And once the dust settles in Grenada there're bound to be all kinds of investigations. And –' he frowned wearily – '*complaints*. Of course, one dead Russian is neither here nor there – the more the better, some heartless souls may say – but of course, the Americans *do* have this evidence and they must be *seen* to do the right thing if there's an official Russian complaint about their awful dead comrade. They can't have the Russians accusing the American soldiery of doing it, can they? Besides –' he glanced at his pipe – 'the ballistic evidence shows that the poor man was killed with a shot fired from a weapon which is *not* standard US military equipment.' He glanced at Anna. 'It could have been fired from a Smith and Wesson. And I believe your husband had such a weapon? A firearm licence to that effect was found in your house.'

Anna started to protest and Morgan cut in furiously: '*Have you seen Russians waiting outside?*'

Carrington turned to him. 'Yes. We expected nothing less. Nor did you. That's why you got Dougie Makepeace over here. But' – he shook his head – 'you haven't got enough manpower, Jack. So I urge you to accept our safe-conduct. And come with us to a place of safety. Where we can discuss all this sensibly.'

'*Well we're not going!*' Anna snapped.

Morgan squeezed her arm. 'Where's this place of safety?'

'The British consulate.'

'Good. So send your gorillas to sort out the KGB gorillas on our behalf. And Her Majesty's.'

Carrington shook his head patiently. 'We can't attack them unprovoked, old man. And the KGB men are dotted all over the place. There's doubtless more. The Comrades aren't short of muscle.'

'You've got a walkie-talkie radio on you, haven't you?'

'Yes.'

Morgan squeezed Anna's arm to silence her. 'Okay. It's a deal.' He pointed. 'We're going downstairs. And you're going to radio your gorillas, and tell them we're coming out.' He took a breath. 'And all of us here are going to walk out of this bank together. And your gorillas are going to hold off the Comrades. Correct?'

'Correct,' Carrington said earnestly.

'And then *you*,' Morgan jabbed the man's chest, 'are coming with *us* to *our* car. Not to yours – to *ours*. Because *you* –' he jabbed again – 'are going to drive with us to the British consulate. *You* are going to be our hostage for the course of that journey. Is that agreed?'

Carrington's eyes did not flicker.

'Agreed.' He added: 'I come in peace.'

'You'd better be, Carrington. Or you'll go in pieces.' He glared: 'Okay. Now go.'

Carrington turned towards the door.

25

They came out of the bank, into the cold grey afternoon.

Makepeace was walking in front with Carrington; Anna was behind them, then came Morgan. He swept his eyes up and down the street. There were people hurrying in all directions. He saw only one man standing still, studying a street map. A taxi was waiting at the kerb. Further down, a dispatch rider sat on a motorcycle. Further down the block was another stationary taxi. Makepeace and Carrington turned towards the post office. Spider's car was parked there, the engine running. Morgan glanced over his shoulder. Nobody was immediately behind them. 'Fast!'

They lengthened their stride. Ahead now was the corner of Church Street. 'Give that corner a wide berth!'

Makepeace began to steer wide of it. Morgan glanced behind again. He saw two men busily striding up behind him, as if hurrying to catch a train. Two more men were behind them. He shouted '*Watch out* –' and a man charged around the corner. Morgan grabbed Anna's arm, and ran.

He looked wildly over his shoulder and he saw a man racing at Anna. He swung at him, and another man hit Morgan and he went staggering backwards and the man hit him again. In the guts, and he saw another fist swinging at him again and then suddenly the man disappeared, reeling, as one of Carrington's men got him, and Morgan saw Anna being wrenched to her feet. He charged towards her, but Carrington got there first, and he hit her attacker with a karate chop. The man collapsed, and Anna scrambled up wildly, hair awry, and somebody else got Morgan. It was a glancing blow, and Morgan swung on him with all his might, for the guts, and the man crumpled. Morgan looked wildly for Anna and he saw Makepeace running with her across Church Street, Carrington plunging after them. He started to run and somebody tripped him and he sprawled. He started to scramble up and somebody grabbed his arm and wrenched it up behind his back – then suddenly his attacker collapsed, and a Cockney voice rasped *'Run, sir!'*

Morgan scrambled up and ran flat out across Church Street for the car. Anna was scrambling into the front seat and Makepeace was shoving Carrington into the back. The car was already moving, the engine roaring. Morgan flung himself into the back beside Carrington.

'Go!'

He slammed the door as Spider swung the car out. It roared at the intersection and the lights were mercifully green. Suddenly there was the wailing of a police siren. Outside the bank men were racing in different directions, people shouting. Spider roared the car into the intersection and Morgan saw the blue flashing police light midst the traffic a hundred yards away on the left. He looked the other way and saw one of the taxis lurch away from the kerb. Then the intersection was behind them in a jumbled flashing of people and lights and cars. Carrington panted:

'Well done, chaps.' He had a cut over his eye and his hair was awry. *'Now* do you believe me, Jack?'

Morgan rasped at Makepeace, *'Blindfold him.'* He looked out of the rear window.

'I beg your pardon? . . .' Carrington panted indignantly.

'Blindfold him! With his monogrammed handkerchief! And tie his hands behind his back with his tie.'

'Now, listen here –'

Morgan snatched Carrington's handkerchief out of his top pocket. He grabbed him by the back of the neck and shoved his head down. He shoved the handkerchief at Makepeace. *'Do it!'* He twisted and looked back out of the rear window again.

'Now dammit, Jack –'

The car was screaming down the road at fifty miles an hour, with cars swerving and people scattering. He saw the yellow taxi come swinging furiously into the intersection behind, then the police car doing the same from the opposite direction. And he saw them collide. There was a silent crash and the front of both vehicles rose into the air midst flying glass, and they crashed down onto their wheels again. Then another taxi came swerving around them, followed by the dispatch rider on the motorcycle.

'*Faster!*'

The next intersection flashed by, cars and people scattering. Makepeace was tying the knot behind Carrington's head. '*I say –*' Carrington was protesting.

Morgan wrenched the tie off Carrington's neck. 'Wrists!'

'*I say,*' Carrington muffled '*– this is a felony –*'

'You don't say!' Morgan rasped. '*Faster!*' he snapped at Spider.

The car screamed down the block and the lights at the intersection turned red. Spider slammed his hand on the horn and trod harder on the accelerator. Cars began to enter the intersection from the south. Spider swung in ahead of them, the car heeling over and tyres squealing. He straightened out and went roaring up Third Avenue.

'Next right again,' Morgan rasped. He looked back feverishly. The traffic was crossing the intersection in a solid phalanx, but the motorcycle swung in amongst them and came roaring after him.

'Only the motorbike.' Then the taxi appeared, swinging into the intersection against the light. '*Oh Jesus – faster –*' Spider roared up Third Avenue. The lights at the next intersection were green. Spider swung into it, tyres squealing and his horn blasting; the car heeled across the intersection, then levelled off, rocking, and went screaming towards Second Avenue. Morgan looked back. The motorcycle swung out of the intersection into the road behind them. The light ahead was amber and Spider slammed his hand on the horn. The motorcycle was two hundred yards behind them, then the taxi swung into the road behind it. Spider went screaming at the red light, his hand on the horn and he roared straight into the intersection. There was a solid row of cars to their left coming at them, and Spider burst through the other side. Morgan looked back and he saw the motorbike skidding to a stop. '*Good!*' Spider went roaring on towards First Avenue.

'Who are those guys – British or Russian?'

'*We,*' Carrington said, blindfolded, 'did not employ a motorcycle. Jack, this is kidnap –'

'*That's how Mrs Hapsburg felt about it!*'

The car screamed towards the next intersection, and the light was red. Cars were racing north up First Avenue. Ahead was a truck. Spider slammed on his horn and swung out to overtake it. He roared past the side of it, and a man dashed across the road, and Spider swerved inwards and his fender crashed the truck. There was a screech of metal and flying sparks and Spider swung away. He roared past the truck, into the intersection, and swung left, cars wildly swerving out of his way. Morgan looked back. And saw the motorcyclist roaring into the intersection back there.

It started to rain.

Spider swung into the side-street, the car heeling over. Halfway down was the multi-storeyed car park. He slammed on his brakes and swung into the entrance. He rocked to a stop at the barrier. He leant out and snatched the ticket. The automatic boom went up and he roared the car forward. As it disappeared up into the building the motorcyclist came screeching round the corner into the side-street.

The cyclist saw the car disappearing into the building and skidded to a halt. The taxi swung into the street, and braked hard at the car park. The back doors burst open and two men scrambled out. They ran to the exit of the car park, and the taxi roared forward into the entrance and the driver snatched a ticket and went up the ramp into the dark.

Spider swung around the corner, up onto the third level, as the taxi swung onto the first level.

There were cars parked on each side in the gloom. The taxi drove slowly down the avenue, the two Russians peering at the cars. It came to the end; then it roared up the next ramp, to the second level.

Spider drove hard up the ramp and swung onto the fourth level, and there was the other rented car. He slammed on the brakes and Morgan and Anna scrambled out. They ran to the other car. Morgan started the engine. Makepeace was hauling Carrington out, saying 'Sorry, sir . . .' He hustled him towards the second car. Morgan was reversing out. He braked and Makepeace flung open the door and shoved Carrington in. He got in after him. Spider roared the first car into the vacant parking space, scrambled out and flung himself at the back door of the new car. As he slammed the door the taxi was approaching the end of the third level. Morgan roared away towards the exit ramp. '*Heads down everybody!*'

He swung down onto the ramp. The headlights of the taxi were coming up to the fourth level. Morgan's taillights disappeared down. The taxi swung onto the level. It began to proceed slowly down the avenue of cars. Then it braked.

Morgan sped along the third level, then swung down the next ramp. He surged down the second level, then swung down the last ramp. Straight ahead down there was the street, the cashier's kiosk. A Russian was standing just inside the exit, pretending to read a newspaper. 'Keep your heads down!' Morgan stopped at the barrier and held out his ticket and five dollars. The Russian looked at the car, then returned to his newspaper. The boom went up.

Morgan rolled the car down the ramp. Out into the rain. He swung the wheel, and he drove away down the street.

He looked in his rear-view mirror. No Russian was to be seen. Only the motorcycle standing by the kerb.

He slowed at the intersection, then turned left, northwards into First Avenue. 'Keep your heads down.'

He turned at the next intersection. As he went round he looked back. He could not see well through the rain, but nobody was following them. He let out a trembly sigh of relief, and trod on the accelerator.

'Do you mind telling me,' Carrington muffled from the floor, 'where we're going?'

'To dispose of your odious body!'

It was raining hard and getting dark when Morgan turned into Central Park. He drove through the park for half a mile, then he pulled up. There were no cars coming either way.

'Okay, throw him out. Loosen the knot on his wrists but don't undo it.'

Makepeace scrambled out. 'Come on, sir.'

'And don't call him sir!'

Makepeace helped Carrington out. He was still blindfolded. He stood in the teeming rain. Makepeace loosened the knot on his wrists, then got back into the car.

'Cheerio, Carrington,' Morgan shouted. 'And tell Her Majesty to leave Mrs Hapsburg alone!'

He drove off. He looked back in the mirror. He could just make out Carrington wrenching at his bonds.

The road swept through the rainy dusk of Central Park. Morgan's mouth was dry. He said to Anna: 'Well? It's Option Time.' He glanced at her. 'Option One: Do you want a lawyer?'

She did not look at him. 'No, Jack.'

'Option Two: Do you want to talk to the British embassy people? Or get a lawyer who'll talk turkey to them on your behalf? This town's full of good ones.'

She closed her eyes, her nerves tight. She shook her head, then turned to him. 'And I don't want you involved in Option Three, either. I've got Makepeace and Spider.'

He sighed. He swung out of Central Park. 'Makepeace, we're going to drop you soon. Get a taxi to the airport. Anybody who tries to stop you, you smite down. Spider comes with us to Washington, to ride shotgun. You get over to Amsterdam and organize your people to look after us. Then get straight over to Switzerland.'

Makepeace complained: 'I'll need some money up front. Quite a lot,' he added.

Morgan held out his hand to Anna. 'Give me some diamonds.'

She burrowed into the cloth bag. She pulled out five.

'Three's enough.' He held them over his shoulder to Makepeace. 'That's worth a lot of money, Douglas. Amsterdam's the world's diamond centre. Sell them to a reputable dealer. I want an official receipt and a full accounting.'

'Okay . . . But *where* in Switzerland am I going?'

'Anna?' Morgan said.

She put her hand on his knee. 'I don't want you involved.'

'Where in Switzerland, Anna? Makepeace needs to know, now.'

She took an uptight breath. 'Zurich.'

'Zurich?' Makepeace said attentively. 'But *where* in Zurich?'

'Anna, the man needs to know.'

Anna shot him an anguished look. 'Need I tell them now?' 'Yes.'

She said carefully: 'The bank is in Bahnhofstrasse.'

Morgan said, 'In Bahnhofstrasse, Dougie – Got that?'

'Bahnhofstrasse,' Makepeace repeated worriedly. 'But which bank, there may be half a dozen there.'

Morgan said: 'No need to know more yet, Dougie. Check out all the banks in Bahnhofstrasse, and work out all the possible escape routes from there to the airfield.'

Anna put her hand on his knee again. 'Thank you.'

Morgan said to her, 'So, you go off to jolly Zurich while I lie back in the sun somewhere and wait happily for you to call?'

'I don't want you involved in any further *risk*.'

'I *am* involved. Up to my neck.'

She said: 'And emotionally. My emotion will still be there when I come back.'

'If you come back.'

He slumped back in his seat. And for a moment he was almost happy. He had shaken them all off. The whole fucking lot of them, the British and the KGB. The only trick left right now was to drive this car to Washington DC and find a motel, and tomorrow get on that plane without being identified, and oh God, God, just to sit back in that aircraft and know that there was nothing more he could do about it for eight solid hours, nothing but drink beer and sleep, with Spider riding shotgun.

Part Five

26

Vladimir Ustinov never carried out surveillance himself. As Cultural Attaché at the Soviet embassy in Paris it would have been ridiculous if he were recognized hanging around street corners; as a colonel in the KGB, in charge of operations in France, surveillance work was beneath him. But when the Soviet embassy in Washington advised that the Lovebirds had been identified at Dulles airport and were on the wing to Paris, he had gone out to Orly airport to take charge personally. He had posted cars along every route leading away from the airport, put his best people inside the air terminal itself. None of which, he reflected, is as easy to do without being noticed as Moscow would think – because the British were onto this one too, and maybe the French and they would be watching for Russians, after yesterday's débâcle in New York. It wasn't going to be an easy job to deal with the Lovebirds unobserved. And it was not made any easier by not knowing *why*.

All he knew was they were presumed to be lovers, that they were probably in possession of a roll of microfilm: he had to overwhelm them and find it; after the identity of the film had been verified by experts, the Lovebirds were to be disposed of. Very well. But, if the microfilm was not found? Then Vladimir's orders got more difficult. In that event the Lovebirds were to be let go – and then followed again. To the ends of the earth, until they *did* come into possession of the said microfilm.

This was doing things the hard way. If the film was not found on them the first time it would be much easier to extract the information as to its whereabouts by the usual means. But, no. Well, you didn't have to reach the rank of colonel before you were smart enough to figure out why not. Obviously the microfilm was with somebody who would only give it to them personally, and who would want to see them alive and well before doing so.

Like a trustee of some kind. Like a bank? Or a lawyer?

Vladimir did not have a photograph of the male Lovebird.

181

Not even a name for him. Only a description. Presumed to be an American. Height, about six foot. Build, average. Age, from thirty-five to forty-five – he had greying black hair, but that could be dye. Last seen at Dulles airport wearing a navy-blue blazer. And in a wheelchair.

The female Lovebird was better documented. He knew her real name. And he had a photograph of her.

What a beautiful woman. She reminded Vladimir of Sophia Loren, but with blue eyes.

It would be a shame to kill her.

Sergei Suslov also had the photograph of Anna, but he did not think it would be a shame.

Sergei was one of the most promising operatives the KGB had in France, and, unlike most operatives of his intelligence, he enjoyed executing his own 'wet affairs'. Many operatives will ask for a specialist to do that job. But it gave Sergei a sense of professional and physical fulfilment. And now he was excited at the prospect of being allowed to murder one of the most beautiful women he had ever seen. The photograph had been taken in Grenada and she was wearing a slinky evening dress. He looked at it again. Her tawny American good looks, those golden bare shoulders, the line of her breasts and her legs. Sergei could feel already the extraordinary sexual pleasure of her writhing and kicking, the terror of her beautiful eyes, her sensuous mouth contorting into her strangled death-scream – and then the long final joy as her struggles grew weaker and weaker, succumbing to his power. The thought of it gave Sergei an erection.

Whereas all the other KGB operatives at Orly airport that night were stationed in the public part of the building, Sergei Suslov and a female operative called Natasha were stationed within the prohibited area. They were to follow the Lovebirds from the moment of their arrival, through immigration and customs control, into the waiting arms of the KGB beyond. Sergei and Natasha had got into the prohibited area by buying airline tickets, presenting passports, and entering the departure lounge. Upon the announced arrival of the flight from Washington, they had proceeded towards the departure gates, then diverted to the arrival bays. Now they waited, separately, near the arrivals concourse, like passengers waiting for travelling companions to catch up.

About 200 people off the Air France flight had thronged past Sergei before he spotted the wheelchair.

He watched them coming up the passage. The good-looking woman pushing the wheelchair had black hair, but the man in the chair was wearing a navy-blue blazer. Sergei waited until they were level, then he saw her big, almond-shaped, blue eyes, and he was quite sure. He joined the throng of passengers behind them. He lifted his sleeve to his mouth and muttered into the transmitter to Vladimir:

'Both Lovebirds have landed, together.'

He had hardly slept, and he hated being in the wheelchair.

He felt vulnerable, like a paraplegic, when every nerve was tight to leap up and fight and run. *And he felt naked without a gun.* It was a considerable comfort knowing Spider was behind them, but Spider didn't have a gun either – they had had to dump both weapons before going through the security check at Dulles airport. And he bitterly regretted this idea of changing aircraft in Paris to confuse the enemy. Okay, in principle it was a sound idea, but they were tired from days of running and he was by no means sure, having had eight sleepless hours to think about it, that he had fooled anybody with this cumbersome route and disguise. If both the Comrades and Her Majesty were so on-the-ball that they were waiting outside the bank in New York, they were also smart enough to keep nearby airports like Washington's covered, and they weren't likely to be fooled by wheelchairs, and you didn't have to be George Smiley to figure out that maybe Paris was only a decoy point: if he were Georgi Smilovitch he would have Orly airport transit lounge well covered by the simple expedient of buying airline tickets. They would have been better off flying straight from Washington to Amsterdam where they had all Makepeace's boys – right now they had only Spider. And right now he wanted to get rid of this goddam wheelchair.

Ahead, was the sign, 'Transit Passengers'. Anna worked her way out of the throng towards it.

Twenty paces behind, Sergei whispered into his transmitter:

'They're not going through immigration. They're going to get another flight . . .'

Anna wheeled him down the long corridor. Spider was five paces behind her. Twenty paces behind him came Sergei Suslov and Natasha.

Ahead was a women's toilet. Then a men's. Then, beyond, the toilet for paraplegics.

Anna wheeled him to it, pushed the door open, wheeled him inside. She was about to shoot the lock when the door opened again, and Spider came in. Morgan was scrambling out of the wheelchair. *'You shouldn't have followed us in here!'*

'I thought I must follow you everywhere.'

'Go out again! Looking confused! Go back to the men's toilet. Stay five minutes, then meet us in the transit lounge.'

Sergei passed Spider in the corridor. He glanced back. Spider walked back towards the men's toilet. Sergei turned and followed him. Natasha hurried back into the women's toilet. It was empty. She held the door ajar a crack, so she could see down the corridor.

Spider was splashing his face, when Sergei walked in. Sergei glanced around, to ensure the toilet was empty. He passed behind Spider, and he hit him.

Anna was feverishly adjusting her auburn wig. Morgan folded the wheelchair and shoved it inside the lavatory booth. 'Come on.'

He opened the door a crack. There was nobody. They walked out briskly, down the corridor. When they reached the corner of the transit lounge, Morgan glanced back for Spider. He saw only a woman, twenty paces behind them.

There were several dozen people in the lounge. Morgan went to the information desk. Natasha walked up to the desk also. Morgan said: 'I have to pick up two tickets for Mr and Mrs Armstrong, to Amsterdam, and pay for them.'

Up the corridor, Sergei emerged from the men's toilet. He hurried to the paraplegic toilet. He went in and locked the door.

There were not many places where somebody could hide a roll of microfilm. He looked under the wash basin. Behind the lavatory. He felt along all ledges. He examined the wheelchair, turned it upside down. Then, satisfied, he left.

As he walked into the lounge, Natasha was saying in French: 'But my travel agent assured me on the telephone he had made the reservations.'

'Well, no harm done, there are seats available. Will this be cash or credit card?'

Morgan watched the corner for Spider. There were at least half a dozen solitary males in the room who could be agents. 'Where's Spider?' Anna muttered.

Morgan glanced at his watch angrily. Almost fifteen minutes had passed. They were due to board soon. 'I'll go and see. Don't move.'

He walked out of the lounge. He hurried down the corridor to the men's toilet. He opened the door.

'Spider?'

There were two lavatory booths. The door of one was closed. He opened it.

Spider was sitting on the lavatory, slumped sideways against the wall, his head hanging.

Morgan stared, his heart knocking. He lifted Spider's head. His eyes were closed. There was a large contusion behind his ear. Morgan grabbed his pulse. Then put his hand on Spider's heart.

He whispered, '*Oh God . . .*'

He strode feverishly out of the toilet. Down the corridor.

He walked into the transit lounge, towards Anna, trying to smile. She stood up. 'They've called our flight,' she muttered: 'Where's Spider?'

He said shakily: 'He's coming. He'll go straight to the plane.'

There were about thirty people joining the flight. Morgan kept in the middle of them. He held Anna's arm. He shepherded her aboard.

The aircraft was three-quarters full. Anna sat down, and strapped herself in. She whispered: 'Where's Spider?'

Morgan sat down beside her.

'He's dead.'

She stared at him. Aghast.

'Oh God . . . Poor little Spider.' She felt sick. 'So they're here . . . Aboard this aircraft . . .'

'Undoubtedly.'

He took a deep breath that quivered. He whispered:

'Now listen. At Amsterdam airport you and I are likely to be going in separate cars to the airfield – to divide the forces of the enemy. But until we get into those cars you are not to go out of my sight. If you need to go to the toilet, do so before we get off this plane. And I'm coming with you to guard the door.'

She pressed her fingers to her eyes, and nodded.

'Oh, God,' she whispered. 'They're here . . . .'

27

She could feel eyes on her back. She walked down the corridors of Schipol airport, Amsterdam. Morgan strode grimly behind her, carrying their handgrip. And with all his exhausted ferocity he hated the bastards, the goddam British and the Comrades, and oh God he would kill the next bastard who came near them. Kill first and ask questions afterwards. God he wanted this over, and please, please, please, God, Makepeace had everything organized in Zurich. They came out of the customs hall, and the first person he saw amongst the crowds was Makepeace, with a chauffeur's cap on his triangular head.

He whispered to Anna: *'The prick's still here! . . .'*

Makepeace gave him a wink, and turned away, towards a newsagent's shop. Morgan and Anna strode after him. Makepeace strolled into the shop, and picked up a book. Morgan walked up beside him. He snatched another book off the shelves. He glared at the book and whispered furiously: *'What the hell are you doing here? – you're supposed to be in Zurich!'*

'Spot of bother,' Makepeace whispered. 'But everything's okay now. Go to the Hertz car park at the end of this hall. Third car on the left from the door. Somebody will be covering your back. Anna comes with me.'

Morgan shoved the book back on the shelf, and turned away

angrily. He strode out of the shop. Down the hall towards the car-rental desks. Makepeace and Anna were heading in the opposite direction. There were two men following them. Morgan glanced over his shoulder, and he couldn't believe it: *Danziger was following him.*

Danziger gave him a wink.

Danziger? . . . Oh, Christ, Makepeace! . . .

Morgan strode down the hall with a face like thunder. To the side of the car-rental counters was a glass door. Beyond was a car park holding twenty-odd Hertz cars. Morgan strode out into the cold, for the third car. There was a man behind the wheel. He started the engine. Morgan flung open the back door and got in.

'My name is Joop,' the driver said. Danziger opened the other door and got in. Joop surged the car forward.

Morgan glared. 'What the hell are you doing here, Dan?'

Danziger put his hand in his pocket and pulled out a pistol. He flipped it, then handed it to Morgan. 'Standard Smith and Wesson. Loaded. And this.' He handed him a shoulder holster.

'How did you get in on this?'

Danziger smiled. He was a smallish man, with neatly groomed, thinning hair and grey eyes. 'That's not the welcome I expected, sir. I'm your bodyguard. Makepeace sent me an SOS in London this morning. He was having trouble getting manpower.' He added: 'And the brain power. So I dropped everything and came.'

Morgan sat back and seethed. *Oh goddam Makepeace . . .* The car was swinging past the front of the terminal. There were cars parked against the kerb. A red Ford pulled out onto the road ahead of them. 'That's Makepeace,' Danziger said.

'How many people has he got with him?' Morgan snapped.

'Four. Spider, a Dutchman, a guy called Clark and a guy called Stillgoes.'

'Spider's dead in a Paris lavatory. The Comrades got him.'

Danziger raised his eyebrows.

'Pity. He was a handy little soldier. So the Comrades are on the ball.'

Morgan looked through the rear window angrily. There were several cars behind them. 'They were on the plane with us. And they're doubtless behind us right now.'

'Doubtless. And the Brits probably. I spotted a few likely-looking types. Anyway, we'll soon know.'

Makepeace's car was pulling up at traffic lights. Beyond, the road led out of the airport complex, onto the Amsterdam–Rotterdam highway. Morgan could not see Anna in the car. So she was crouched down. He looked back. There were a dozen cars behind. He said: 'How many of your own people are involved in this?'

'Only Clark and Stillgoes. Stillgoes was with Spider in the SAS. I brought him because he happens to know Zurich pretty well. Both good men, sir. Clark's a Yank, used to be in the Green Berets.' He added: 'Spider was one of my boys.'

'*Spider* was?'

'Well, we're all freelance, but I used him quite often. And I've done a few jobs with Clark. Last one was in Lebanon. A banker had been taken hostage by the Muslims, his family got us to spring him out.' He added: 'Done a few jobs with Makepeace too.'

'Yes,' Morgan said tersely, 'I know.'

'Good man, too, Makepeace is. Handy with his karate. But he's a bit short on the brain power, sir. And the contacts. You should have got me over to New York, sir. All the contacts in the world there. I could have sprung you out of the US and nobody would ever know you were in Europe. This,' he waved a finger over his shoulder, 'is a mess.' The lights changed and the car surged forward. 'But we'll straighten it out, sir.'

Morgan sighed, deep and angry. But he had to admit that there was comfort in having Danziger on his side. Danziger was a crook and a killer but he knew his soldiering. Morgan held out a finger at him.

'Danziger. You are not to kill anybody, except as an absolute last resort in defence of Mrs Hapsburg and myself. Do you understand that?'

Danziger smiled. 'You and I got along okay in Special Boats, didn't we, sir?'

'You were a goddam troublemaker, Dan. That's why you left. And I don't like what you do for a living now.'

'Right now I'm looking after you, sir. Don't you like that?'

The car was speeding out of the airport complex. Then came the bridge over the six-lane Amsterdam–Rotterdam highway, cars flashing by below. Ahead, Makepeace accelerated to sixty miles an hour and Joop did the same. There was a fork on the bridge, one leading to Rotterdam, the other to Amsterdam. Makepeace roared towards the centre of the fork, Joop screaming along behind him. Then Makepeace swerved to the right onto the cloverleaf heading down to Amsterdam, and Joop swung to the left. Morgan looked behind. He saw a car go roaring after Makepeace, and another car swerved to the left and followed Joop. Ahead was another cloverleaf. Joop went tearing into it, the car heeling over, tyres squealing. The car behind came tearing after them. Morgan rasped: 'Blue Renault.'

Joop sent his car squealing down the cloverleaf, then they burst onto the highway to Rotterdam. The Renault came screaming down after them.

'How many cars?' Joop asked.

'Only the Renault.'

'Okay . . .' Joop said. He put his foot flat.

The car went roaring down the six-laned highway. Fields were flashing by in the night. Half a mile ahead was another cloverleaf. Joop screamed towards it, then swung onto it with a squeal of tyres. The Renault swung off the highway, after them. Joop roared up the cloverleaf. It ended abruptly at a T-junction. The lights were red; traffic was going in both directions. Joop roared straight through the red light and swung right. A signboard said Amsteleven. The Renault came racing through the red lights too. It swung right, rocking, and came screaming after them.

Anna crouched on the floor of the car as it sped towards Amsterdam. Makepeace asked, 'Still following us?'

Clark looked through the rear window. 'Yeah – both the Datsun and the Ford.'

Makepeace put his foot flat. Looming up was a fork to the right. He raced towards it at eighty miles an hour, then swung into it. The car went heeling onto the road to Utrecht. Open fields flashed past in the headlights. Behind them, the other two cars came round the bend, one behind the other.

'How far behind?'

'Four hundred metres,' Stillgoes said.

189

Ahead was a bridge over a canal. Makepeace roared over it. Into another curve. Ahead was a turnoff. He swung hard into it, tyres screaming. He straightened out and went roaring through the suburbs of Amsteleven.

Joop sent the car hurtling down the black country road, the Renault five hundred yards behind. 'Okay,' Joop said, 'here we go.'

Ahead was a crossroads with tall hedges on all sides. In the road to the left, another car was parked. Joop slammed off his headlights, then swung right at the crossroads, then slammed on his brakes. The car screeched to a halt.

Danziger flung open his door and threw himself out, into the ditch. Morgan flung himself after him. Joop's car roared away. Morgan lay flat, heart pounding. The Renault came round the bend. The headlights swept above them, then it accelerated away after Joop's car.

'*Come on!*'

They scrambled up out of the ditch. They ran flat out back to the crossroads. A man sat behind the wheel of the waiting car. Danziger and Morgan scrambled in. Before the door slammed the car roared away.

Makepeace looked in his rear mirror. The Datsun's headlights came round the bend after him, then the Ford's. Ahead was an intersection. He slammed on the brakes, then swung around the corner. Two hundred yards ahead was a parked car. He slammed on the brakes again, and deliberately put the car into a skid.

He skidded sideways, tyres screeching, to a halt, blocking the road. '*Out!*'

They flung open the doors. The Datsun came screaming around the corner. Anna ran flat out for the car parked down the road, Clark and Stillgoes beside her, Makepeace behind them, his gun out. The Datsun's driver saw the car blocking the road. He stood on the brakes, and swung the wheel. His car went screeching wildly. It hit Makepeace's car. There was a crash of metal and flying glass. Then the Ford came tearing around the corner, on two wheels. There was a mad scream of tyres, and another crash of metal and flying glass. Makepeace flung himself into the waiting car. The others were already in it. It roared away down the dark road.

Morgan's new driver was called Hans. He drove fast down the country roads, turning left and right. Morgan suddenly realized that they seemed to be heading towards the lights of Amsterdam, not away from them. '*Hey – where're we going?*'

'To the Yab Yum,' Hans said.

'Best whore-house in town,' Danziger said.

Morgan was amazed. 'What the hell we going into Amsterdam for? – we're supposed to be going to an airfield!'

'Don't ask me, man,' Hans said, 'I just do as I'm told.'

'I told you, sir,' Danziger said solemnly, 'that you should have got me to organize this job for you.'

'But Christ – we're driving back towards trouble! We've shaken them off now, why aren't we going to this airfield?'

'Makepeace had problems organizing things at short notice.'

'*Oh Jesus Christ!*'

Danziger murmured: 'You get what you pay for.'

'*Shut up Danziger!*'

Morgan hunched back furiously in his seat.

Hans turned the car onto a major road. '*Slower!*' Morgan rasped – 'we don't want the cops chasing us as well!'

Apartments, a canal, a bridge, a major highway flashed past. Hans accelerated hard, then swung the car into a sharp U-turn.

'*Was that legal? For God's sake, we don't want cops!*'

Hans sped down the street. *Slower*, Morgan prayed. He closed his eyes. He felt the car turn left, then left again. He slumped, trying to hang on to his nerves. They seemed to drive for an eternity, turning left and right. Then Hans said: 'Now, just do as I say.'

He suddenly braked to a halt. 'Now get out normally.'

Morgan opened the door. They were in a dark street, with scattered lamplight. In front of them was a building, painted black. A car's headlights appeared at the top of the road and drove towards them. 'Oh Jesus . . .'

'Walk normally.'

They walked to a red door in the black wall. Hans inserted a key and pushed it open. Morgan entered.

Into a luxurious anteroom of red carpet and subdued lighting and Regency furniture and the tinkle of music, and the smell of women. A mature blonde in high heels and a diaphanous black pyjama suit was coming towards them. 'This way.'

They followed her. Morgan could see her naked buttocks through the diaphanous material. He looked over his shoulder. Hans waved and called, 'I work here . . .' The blonde led him hurriedly past a bar with several girls in it.

'Where're Makepeace and Anna?'

She said over her shoulder: 'I don't know anything except I've got to get you out the back.'

There was a door at the end of the corridor. She slammed open locks.

'*Hurry*. If anybody has followed you here, they will not yet be at the back yard. That is our customers' car park. There is a brown Volkswagen, with driver.'

Morgan hurried out into the dark car park, followed by Danziger. He saw the Volkswagen. A girl sat behind the wheel. He flung open the rear door and scrambled in. Danziger got in beside him. '*Go*.'

The car turned left. Then turned right. 'Is this your car?' Morgan asked.

'No, it is rented,' the girl said.

'Where are we going?'

'To Yab Yum.'

'I thought that *was* Yab Yum!'

'No. That was Johan Bik's. Yab Yum's the opposition.'

Oh, Makepeace . . .

The car was driving alongside the Keizersgracht canal now. 'Anybody following us?'

Morgan looked through the rear window. 'No.'

The girl brought the car to a stop alongside a houseboat. 'Here!' she commanded. She pointed at a speedboat tied up to the houseboat. 'Get into that.'

A car's headlights appeared at the end of Keizersgracht.

Morgan jumped onto the houseboat. The speedboat's engine started. Morgan ducked across the houseboat, as the car came driving fast alongside the canal. He scrambled into the speedboat, Danziger after him.

The boat surged away. Its nose came up and water began curling from her bows.

The car roared alongside the canal road, after them.

The boat swung into a tight turn. It heeled, the spray curling high. Then it went speeding back up the canal in the opposite direction.

The car slammed to a halt. It swung into a turn, then roared off down the road again, chasing the speedboat.

The Dutchman opened the throttle and the boat's bows came up higher. Ahead was an intersection of canals. The Dutchman swung the boat right, and it went speeding away into the darkness.

On the other side of the canal the car slammed to another halt. It started turning around again. But the speedboat had disappeared.

28

The speedboat turned into Blauwburgwal canal. A bridge swept by overhead, and they burst out into the broad Singel canal. Elegant old Dutch houses flashed past. Trees, lampposts, parked cars. Then the Dutchman swung the boat up against the stone embankment. Morgan and Danziger scrambled up onto the narrow cobbled street. The boat surged away into the night.

They strode down the patchily lit canal street. Morgan glanced back. Nobody was to be seen. 'Where is it?'

'There.'

A large green lantern hung above an ornate door. Alongside were the words, in polished brass: 'Yab Yum Men's Club'. Danziger hurried up the steps and rammed a key in the door. Morgan hurried inside.

They were in a softly lit hall. To the left was an ornate desk. Beyond it, a marble staircase. The walls and ceiling were dark blue with elegant lamps and chandeliers. There was a man-size Thai statue in glittering gold, and in the corner sat a big beaming

Buddha. And all around were ferns and flowers. To the right a large door opened onto a bar. A tall woman of about forty, in a cocktail dress, emerged. 'Oh, it's you,' she said to Danziger. She held out a hand to Morgan. 'Xaviera,' she said.

'Good evening. Is Anna here yet? Makepeace?'

'Not yet. Will you come into the bar to wait?'

'I don't want to be seen.'

'You are safe here. I don't know what this is about, and I don't want to know. But here you must behave like an ordinary client. My ladies don't talk. Discretion is our business, otherwise half the politicians of Amsterdam would be in trouble. There are no other customers at the moment, Saturday is a quiet night. Just act normally for ten minutes, then I'll take you to your room and nobody will think anything about it.' She turned into the bar.

It was large, ornate mahogany, carved pillars reaching up to the ceiling. There was a lounging area with soft lights and flowers. Another glittering Thai statue, another Buddha. Only three girls sat at the bar. One wore a *cheongsam* split up to her hip, with fishnet stockings and black high heels; the other wore a Victorian dress with a cut-away bodice showing magnificent breasts. The third wore only a scarlet corset, panties, stockings and high heels. They all smiled politely. Morgan went to an empty stool. Xaviera had gone behind the bar. 'What will you have, sir?'

'Beer, please.'

She snapped the cap off an Amstel and gently poured.

'Mind if I drink on duty, sir?' Danziger said.

Morgan shot him a look. 'Go ahead.' He lifted his glass, and swallowed and swallowed. He lowered the glass and closed his eyes. 'Where's goddam Makepeace?'

'Probably arrested for speeding,' Danziger smiled.

Morgan shot him another look. 'How long are you on duty *for*?'

'Until you dismiss me. I'm a hired gun.' He smiled.

It was on the tip of Morgan's tongue to say, 'You're dismissed'. 'And you know what Makepeace has planned from here?'

'He consulted me. I gave him my advice.'

'And that was?'

Danziger smiled. 'That I take overall charge of this operation, sir.'

Morgan snapped: 'Any other advice?'

'Oh, sure. But since Makepeace is my paymaster, I discuss it only with him.' He added: 'The client often gets too emotionally involved to be clear-headed.'

'Jesus, Danziger – *I'm* your paymaster!'

'Not entirely, sir. I'm doing this job for Makepeace at a reduced fee. Because when it's over, Makepeace is going to do a little job for me.'

Morgan glared. 'Makepeace doesn't take contracts, does he?'

'To kill? No. He's too much of a schoolboy at heart for that yet. But he'll learn.'

Jesus. 'Did Spider take contracts?'

'Not that I know of. And I usually know what contracts are on offer, and who takes them up.'

'You don't snap them all up yourself?'

'Sometimes the pitch gets a bit crowded. I like plenty of elbow-room.'

Morgan held a finger out at him.

'Let me make one thing perfectly clear, Dan. Right now you're working for *me*. *I'm* your paymaster. I'm not having any private deals between you and Makepeace cloud the question of who gives the orders around here.' He glared at him: 'Got that?'

Danziger looked him in the eye, with a twitch of a smile.

'Yes, sir. Three bags full, sir.'

Morgan wanted to grab the little bastard by the shirtfront. Except the little bastard would have thrown him across the room. Morgan picked up his beer and drank it. He banged the glass down. 'May I have another, please? And take it up to my room?'

'Certainly.' Xaviera snapped the cap off a bottle. 'Alone?' She added: 'You're paying enough.'

'I'm afraid so.'

Danziger smiled: 'Begging your pardon, sir, but a girl may make it look more authentic.'

'Thanks for the advice, Danziger.' He added grimly. 'You better come up and check there're no Comrades under the bed.'

They followed Xaviera. Danziger went ahead up the stairs. They stopped on the first floor. Xaviera opened a door.

The large window was draped in red velvet and the walls were in regency stripe. There was a triple bed. The room was richly carpeted and split-level. On the upper level was a large, circular, sunken bath. Danziger said:

'Okay, no bogeymen, sir. I'll check upstairs, and the fire escapes, then go back to the bar and watch the stairs.'

Xaviera went to the bath, turned on the taps. Steaming water gushed into the sunken tub. She threw in some suds, and bubbles frothed up. She smiled. 'Anything else?'

'No, thanks. You've been very kind.'

'Mine is the kindest business in the world.'

All he wanted to do was collapse in that bath but he had to ask some questions. 'How do you know Dougie Makepeace?'

'Oh, I know Dougie. But in my business we don't talk.'

'Did you know Dan Danziger?'

'Oh yes. What matters to me is what I *don't* know. I don't harbour criminals but I also don't want to know my clients' business any more than if I were selling him a shirt. But when Dougie asked me to look after you, I checked you out with the police. I have some very good friends there. You are not wanted by the Dutch police. That's good enough for me.'

Morgan stared at her. The *police*? *Oh Jesus, Makepeace* . . .

'And now I leave you to have your nice bath.'

She dropped the lock on the door as she left.

Morgan stood there. He wanted to bellow his fury with Makepeace to the skies.

He ripped off his clothes and slung them into the water.

He had just finished scrubbing himself when there was a knock on the door. 'Who is it?'

'Makepeace.'

He scrambled out of the bath and slung a towel around his waist. He flung open the door. 'Where's Anna?'

'In the dungeon, having a bath.' Makepeace strolled in, and waved his hand. 'Ain't this something?'

'Makepeace,' Morgan sighed furiously. 'Why the *hell* aren't you in Switzerland? And what the *hell* is Danziger doing here? And why the *hell* did you tell this woman my name? She checked with the police!'

'I didn't tell her your name on *purpose*,' Makepeace whined, 'it slipped out . . .'

'"It slipped out" . . .' Morgan groaned furiously. 'Jesus. Do you realize what you've done? You've undone all that hair-raising escape-driving we did from the airport! Because the Dutch police now know we're holed up at the Yab Yum whore-house! And if the British ask them, the Dutch will tell them!' He pointed at the street. 'Carrington's mob are probably out there right now! Waiting patiently to follow us to Zurich!'

Makepeace protested, 'She didn't ask the police *officially*, she only asked a *friend*, it'll never go any further. Anyway,' he muttered sulkily, 'the Comrades don't know.'

'Unless *they*'ve got a contact in the Dutch police! Which they doubtless have.' He glared at him. 'And what are we doing in the heart of Amsterdam? The reason why we came to Holland was to avoid the problem of getting out of Paris because you've got no contacts in France. So we come here, and we're *out* of Amsterdam, and you very efficiently shake off the people following us, and we're in nice open country, and what do you do? – you bring us *into* Amsterdam! Now we may have to shake them off again!'

'But Amsterdam's the best place in the world to shake off a tail,' Makepeace protested '– all these canals and one-way streets! . . . And they may have followed us to the airfield! And besides, as Danziger says, why fly from an airfield, which you can be followed to, when you can fly out by *sea*plane which can land on water anywhere –'

'*Danziger?* . . . So Danziger countermanded me! And what the *fuck* is Danziger doing on this job anyway?'

'But you told me to get more men. And I thought about it –'

'A difficult process!'

'– and I thought: What would have happened in New York if Carrington's boys hadn't been there to back us up against the Comrades? So I concluded that we needed the best professionals –'

'You know I don't trust Danziger! There're plenty of other SAS guys!'

'Because he's the *best*. And you gave me discretion, that's why we chose Amsterdam.'

Morgan took a deep breath.

'As soon as we leave Amsterdam, I want him off the job.'

'He's already gone,' Makepeace said '– and Clark and Still-goes.'

'Gone *already*?'

'I mean,' Makepeace said earnestly, 'they've gone to Switzerland. To set things up for us.'

Morgan stared at him. '*That was your job!*'

'But I haven't had *time*,' Makepeace pleaded.

'*So Danziger knows everything?*'

'*No*,' Makepeace sighed '– even *I* don't know everything. All I know is we're going to a bank somewhere in Bahnhofstrasse, Zurich. All his instructions are, to have a car waiting for you, hidden in the forest where we land, and to check out the entire area of downtown Zurich and work out several escape routes from Bahnhofstrasse. And *that*'s why a seaplane is so good, because there're lakes all around Zurich!' He ended: 'All he knows is that he's to ride shotgun when we leave the bank.'

'Jesus, Makepeace! . . . Danziger would take a contract on his own *mother*.'

'Bullshit,' Makepeace said '– he's got his reputation to maintain. He'd never get another job if he double-crossed a client.'

'If he double-crossed *this* client –' Morgan slapped his chest – 'he wouldn't *need* another job! You know what the Russians would pay for the information that we're going to a bank in Bahnhofstrasse, Zurich? And the Brits! Get onto the telephone! Phone Schipol airport and tell them to come back!'

Makepeace said: 'They haven't gone to Schipol airport – in case the Comrades are still watching it. You think we're stupid? They're driving to Brussels airport.'

'Yes, I think you're stupid! Phone Brussels airport!'

Makepeace said, very sensibly: 'But what's the point, Jack? Danziger already knows about Zurich, even if we do fire him. If he's going to double-cross us, he can do it whether we recall him or not! But he's not going to double-cross us. And we're lucky to have him.'

Morgan sat down on the bed, and held his head. 'Oh, sure, he might have been out of town assassinating some politician . . .' He shook his head in his hands. 'Oh, Makepeace. Why didn't you stay in Special Boats?'

Makepeace stood there sulkily. Morgan held a finger out.

'Danziger told me he's doing this job cheap because you're going to do a job cheap for him. Just remember that *I'm* employing you, not Danziger! Your loyalty is to *me*!'

'Of course,' Makepeace muttered.

Morgan gave an angry sigh. 'Did you sell those diamonds?'

Makepeace pulled out a plastic bag. He threw it on the bed. 'Twenty-four thousand dollars. What's left of it. I paid myself only my upfront money but I paid Danziger and the boys for three days. It's all written down.' He complained: 'I could have got more on the black market, but you wanted an official receipt.'

'All right,' he sighed. 'So we're flying out of Holland by seaplane. Is the pilot to be trusted?'

'Of course, he wants another job after this one.'

'And what's he costing me?'

'Five hundred bucks an hour flying time, fifty bucks an hour standing still. About fifteen thousand dollars.' He added: 'That'll clean out that plastic bag.'

Morgan turned to the handgrip. He found the cloth bag, and pulled out more diamonds. 'Is the black market open on Sundays?'

'Sure.'

Morgan looked in the plastic bag. He examined the receipts, Makepeace's accounting, and counted the money. 'And how do we get out of this whore-house without the Comrades and Brits following us, now that the Dutch police have kindly told them where we are?' He held up a hand. 'No, let me guess. The dungeon of this whore-house is connected to a tunnel, which leads to the sewers of Amsterdam, which open into the sea –'

'*Right*,' Makepeace said belligerently. Then said sulkily: 'You get to the plane by speedboat. Through the canals.'

'They'll be wise to that one now! They'll have both ends of the canal covered by their own boats!'

Makepeace said, wearily: 'Cars come to fetch the girls at the end of their shift. You leave with them. The car drops you off on *another* canal, where your boat's waiting. The Comrades can't be covering *every* canal in Amsterdam. You'll shake them off easy.'

Morgan thought. 'And where's this seaplane going to be?'

Makepeace produced a map of Amsterdam. He tapped a large expanse of water on the north-east edge.

'That's the IJ-meer. An inland sea. It goes for miles. There're forests all along it. It's joined to Amsterdam by canals. You get out to that inland sea in the dark. Down comes the seaplane. Off you go. Schipol airport will see you on radar, but you'll be gone before they can do anything.'

Morgan looked at the map. He sighed.

'Okay, Dougie . . . That's a good plan. Safer than leaving from an ordinary airfield. And where do we land in Switzerland? Got a map?'

Makepeace glowed. 'Sure.' He unfolded one. 'Of course, the beauty of the seaplane is that Switzerland is full of lakes. But, as Danziger pointed out, the Swiss air traffic controllers will see us on their radar, see us disappear down when we land, then see the plane again when it takes off a few minutes later. So the best plan is to *jump*. That way, the plane appears legitimate all the way. It simply flies across Switzerland to Italy as per a filed flight plan and we jump *here*.' He tapped the map. 'Where the car's waiting for us.'

Morgan was staring at him. 'Jump?' he said.

'Yes. With parachutes,' Makepeace added helpfully.

'And what makes you think Mrs Hapsburg is capable of jumping?'

'Hell, there's nothing to it,' Makepeace said – 'I teach ladies to parachute every weekend, it's a popular sport. A couple of hours' instruction and they're up there doing it.'

'And if she refuses?'

'Then we have to land on a lake. But it's a pity. The Swiss air traffic controllers will want to know why.'

Morgan sighed. Oh, Makepeace. It made sense, and the question of Anna jumping was academic because he had other plans for her – but oh Makepeace . . . 'Dougie? Don't you know I hate jumping?'

Makepeace blinked. 'No, sir. You never told me.'

'Hate it,' Morgan sighed.

'But you can still do it, sir,' Makepeace said encouragingly. 'Just one, two, three, *woops* –' he gave a little jump – 'count to ten, then rip her.' He added earnestly: 'The alternative is to land on a lake and attract attention.'

Morgan rubbed his chin.

'And Danziger knows a good place to jump over?'

'Perfect. Deserted. He'll be waiting, with a car.'

Morgan nodded unhappily. 'And the seaplane?'

'It flies straight on to Lake Como, in Italy, as per legitimate flight plan. There it refuels. The pilot files another legitimate flight plan, to the Zurich See, outside Zurich. He lands, and waits for us. We come out of the bank, jump in a boat, rush off to the seaplane, and off we go. We'll be gone before the Comrades can say Jackski Robinovitch.'

Morgan took a worried breath. Then put his hand on Makepeace's shoulder.

'Okay, Dougie. That's a good plan.' He looked at his watch. It was nearly midnight. 'Where's the plane right now?'

'In Copenhagen,' Makepeace said cheerfully. 'I go up to Denmark tomorrow. The pilot's a pal of mine, who flies rich anglers to Scandinavia. We fetch you tomorrow night.'

Morgan sighed. 'Another whole day we're at risk! With the wolves at the door.'

'You're at no risk here. They've got a good bouncer here, a very tough guy called Erik. A hundred per cent reliable. This is a perfect setup for you. Anyway, you need a day's sleep. And so do I.'

Oh, yes, he was right on that one. 'This guy, Erik – does he sleep on the premises?'

'Yes, he's here twenty-four hours. Sleeps upstairs.'

He dropped his hand on Makepeace's shoulder again. 'All right, Dougie.'

'May I ask a question?' Makepeace said, encouraged.

'Yes?'

'Well,' Makepeace said earnestly, 'if this job is legal, why don't we call in the Swiss police to give Mrs Hapsburg protection when she leaves the bank?'

'For two reasons,' Morgan said wearily. 'Firstly, if she asks for police protection, she'll have to explain *why* – tell the Swiss authorities the whole story. And she does not trust the Swiss not to collaborate with the British. She wants *secrecy*, Douglas. Besides we're hoping that the Comrades and the Brits will *not* be waiting outside the bank in Zurich – so calling in the Swiss police would be defeating all our efforts at secrecy, wouldn't it?'

'I see,' Makepeace said. 'Of course. And where do we fly to after we've done the job?'

'I don't know yet. England probably.'

'You better think about it pretty damn quick – the pilot will want to know so he can file a flight plan and appear legitimate. How can you go to England if the Brits are after you?'

'I'll get a lawyer. *Then* I'll demand official police protection.'

Makepeace shook his head. 'I wish I knew what all this was about,' he said, 'then I could be more help. And the second reason? – why you can't go to the Swiss police for protection?'

Morgan sighed tensely. 'That's all.'

But of course, there was a second reason. And the thought of it made his nerves cringe. It could blow everything up in his face and send him to a Swiss jail for a very long time. Because the day after tomorrow he had to walk into a Swiss bank and impersonate Max Hapsburg, alias Maxwell Constantine, and forge one or other of his signatures.

But there was no need for Makepeace to know that.

Xaviera led him down the sweeping staircase. There was a tinkle of laughter from the bar. She led him round the bottom of the staircase. 'Do you see a door here?'

'No.'

She smiled. 'Our customers who want this particular service like to feel dramatic.' She pressed a button, and a section of panelling opened, to reveal a stone staircase. An ornate gas lamp flickered on the wall.

She led the way down. At the bottom was a stout door, with a grille. She held up a big iron key. 'Most important.' She inserted it. The door swung open. She pointed imperiously: *'Get in there!'*

He looked at her, astonished. Her face broke into a pleasant smile. 'Come in.'

The dungeon's walls and floor were stone, flickering in artificial gaslight. On one side was a cell, iron bars from floor to ceiling. On the other was a medieval rack, and a whipping post. And all around, from the stone walls, hung manacles, collars, chains, black leather whips, corsets and masks. In the centre stood a double bed, glistening with red satin sheets. Next to it was a small table with a candle and a bottle of wine.

'There's a very nice bathroom through there, which Anna is using right now. You're perfectly safe here. Our clients only use this place by appointment. So we can get an expert in.' She explained: 'None of my girls do it, you see.'

Morgan smiled, exhausted. 'These clients really enjoy pain?'

'Agh, it's mostly in the mind. We try not to hurt anybody. Their wives won't play with them, you see.'

'I see.'

'In the morning, you'll find a kitchen upstairs. Help yourself. Including the bar. Sleep well.' She handed him the key.

Morgan sat a long moment on the bed, then heaved himself up. Before he collapsed asleep. Tomorrow he had to perfect Max's signatures – but he could not bear to think about it tonight. And he could not bear to think about the deception he was going to commit on Anna. He picked up the bottle of wine, and walked to the bathroom.

He opened the door, onto billowing steam and the fragrance of soap. Anna lay in the swirling suds of a whirlpool bath, her head back, hair sodden. She opened her eyes, and smiled.

29

They had not even made love. He had wanted to, desperately: to cling to her, maybe for the last time. Too tense, too exhausted, they had both just fallen asleep.

He was suddenly awake at six o'clock that Sunday morning, his nerves cringing for more sleep. Today was the day he was leaving her, tricking her. And tomorrow he was going to perpetrate a deception that she would probably find unforgivable. He lay beside her in the pitch blackness, and with all his heart he longed to take her in his arms, feel her softness and smoothness, to calm himself, to claim her. He lay there a minute, trying to clear his mind, get the tension out of his body. Then he swung out of bed.

He went into the bathroom and turned on the shower. He let the cold water beat down on his head for a full minute. Then he rubbed himself dry. He looked at his hands. They were trembly. He went back into the dungeon and got dressed. He picked up their bag. He unlocked the dungeon door, and climbed the steps.

He emerged into the ornate, silent hall. The concealed lights were burning amongst the ferns, setting the Thai statue aglow. He found the kitchen door, behind the reception desk. He was not hungry but he made himself eat some cold chicken. Then he went into the bar.

He sat down on a stool, under a light. He opened the bag. He took out all Max's keys and put them in his pocket. He took out all Max's passports. The photographs of himself he had had taken in New York, the bottle of glue, the notebook. Then he saw something in the bag he had not noticed before. It was a paper packet.

Printed on the paper was *Farmacia Lopez, Garrucha*. He opened the packet, and pulled out the contents. He was looking at a little box of condoms.

He was astonished. Anna had bought condoms in Garrucha when she bought clothes and hairdye? . . .

He smiled briefly. Well, well, well. He returned the box and the packet to the bag.

He opened his penknife. He carefully, very carefully prised the photographs off all three of Max's passports.

Then he carefully pasted glue on the back of three of his own photographs. He carefully pasted one into each of Max's passports.

He looked at them.

His photographs lacked the official embossment on the corner, but they would pass brisk scrutiny. Jack Morgan was now both Max Hapsburg and Maxwell Constantine.

But which was he to be on the fateful day? Tomorrow.

In which name was the deposit box?

That question made his stomach turn over. He thought he knew, but the doubt made him feel feverish. He could telephone the bank with some ruse, to try to find out – but it was very risky. And he would only have one chance. He had to be able to do both signatures in case he got a last-minute clue as to which name the box was in, but once he had started the impersonation he could not switch. And if he used the wrong name, if there was no box in that name, suspicion would fall on him like a ton of bricks. Honest men do not walk into strange banks trying to gain access to non-existent boxes. Questions, attempted fraud, police. And it would be all over.

He dragged his hands down his face. *One step at a time.*

He picked up Maxwell Constantine's passport.

It was more likely that Max had put the microfilm in a box under Maxwell Constantine's name.

He opened his notebook.

He studied the signature. It had no flourishes: it was made by a man who was not accustomed to using the name.

He picked up his pen. He carefully, slowly, began.

That day seemed unreal. The beautiful whore-house completely silent; the Thai statue and Buddha staring at him out of the gloom; his nerves tight, the cramped frustration of torturing out the same picture of lines over and over and over again. That's how he came to think of it – a picture, like a cartoonist's sketch. And as a cartoonist can draw the same face over and over again, so became his forgeries. He could close his eyes and visualize each millimetre of every letter, each curl and twirl.

It was after eleven o'clock when he finally threw down the pen. His shoulders ached, his hand ached. If he pushed his tendons through the same motions once more he would scream. He heaved himself off the stool, and walked behind the bar. He got a beer out of the refrigerator, and poured it. He took three deep swallows.

He went back to his stool. He lit a cigarette and inhaled it deeply. He stared into the gloom.

This time tomorrow it would all be about to begin . . . This time the day after tomorrow he could be sitting in a Swiss prison. Or in a Russian safe house. Or lying on a mortuary slab.

This time tonight he would be saying goodbye to Anna. Maybe forever.

He dragged his hands down his face. *Now cut that out. Cut the melodrama, and think positively . . .*

It was going to be all right! He would sleep this afternoon, and he would sleep on the plane and tomorrow his hand would be steady. He had those two signatures off pat. Only a handwriting expert would catch him out. And he would have Makepeace and the boys riding shotgun for him as he left the bank. What were the chances of being overwhelmed with those guys looking after him? He had all the advantages – even if the Comrades somehow managed to follow him to Zurich, they would not know which bank he was heading for, nor when.

All the advantages are on our side. And how big a fight dare they start in broad daylight outside a Swiss bank?

He squeezed his eyes with his fingertips.

The answer was, A very big fight. We saw that in New York. And the Swiss police are my problem too. If they arrive on the scene I will have a lot of explaining to do about forging a dead man's signature – and the British won't come forward to help me . . .

He took another big swallow of beer. *By the time the Swiss police arrive you'll be miles away. Airborne.*

Flying to where? . . .

He drew deeply on his cigarette.

To England. Fuck 'em. Say what you like about the British, about the likes of Christopher Carrington and Brink-Fucking-Ford, but when it comes to the protection of the law that's the only place I really know and trust. Say fuck 'em all and fly back to England and get the best lawyer and then walk into Carrington's office and tell them to get the Comrades off my back or I'll blow your whole story sky-high and sue Her Majesty to Kingdom Come . . . And Anna and I are going to get married and live happily ever after . . .

He pulled on his cigarette.

And if you screw up at the bank? . . . If you try the wrong name and they blow the whistle on you? . . . Or you screw up the signature? . . . And what about destroying Anna's trust? . . . He stubbed his cigarette out. *Think positively! And remember that what you're doing is right!*

Yes, *right.* He had to keep reminding himself of that, when the risks loomed huge and terrible. Yes, he was taking these risks for Anna, because he loved her and because there was no stopping her and if he didn't take the risks she would take them alone – but *yes*, he was also doing all this because he believed he was doing the right thing, the *responsible* thing, as one of Her Majesty's former officers: *He simply could not allow Anna*

Hapsburg to blunder headstrong into the world of Intelligence and destroy a body of information which was of vital importance to the Western world. Information so important that the British and Americans and the Russians were all desperately after it, the French government blackmailed by it. He simply did not trust Anna's judgement. Anna Hapsburg was a very intelligent woman, of very high principle, politically wise beyond her years – but Anna Hapsburg also had her beautiful head in the idealist's clouds, and she was desperately emotionally involved with this one and it somehow involved her beloved Holy Roman Church. 'I'll burn in hell first!' And she believed in hell. No – Jack Morgan, RN Compulsorily Retired, may not be an officer and a gentleman any more, he may hate the Navy's guts and the underhand contraventions of the Dirty Tricks Act by Her Majesty's government, and he certainly didn't trust the bastards not to pull the plug on Anna if they had to, but underneath all his outrage he was still a Royal Navy man who had spent the best years of his life shadowing bastard Russian submarines – and No Way could he let Anna destroy vital evidence until he had brought his own judgement to bear. Maybe he would agree with her – but it was much more likely to be something that the British government *needed* to thwart those slave-driving bastards in the Kremlin. He did not really know when this decision had crept up on him in the terrible hurly-burly of this last week, because he had been prepared to let her destroy it in New York: but now he knew loud and clear what he was doing was right. And that sustained his uptight nerves at twelve o'clock on a Sunday morning in an empty whore-house in Amsterdam without enough sleep, about to parachute into Switzerland and risk the wrath of the law and the trust of the love of his life . . . He did not know how he was going to win back that all-important trust, and if he let himself worry about that now his nerves would crack . . .

He took another gulp of beer. *Cross the bridges as they come.* Just think about your beautiful wife whom you're doing all this for. Oh, yes, *wife.* Isn't that a pretty word? My wife in the beautiful house I'm going to buy her one day, the roses climbing over the door. And she'll come to sea with me, we'll sail the seven oceans and we'll trade in the islands and we'll drink wine under the stars and every day will be a honeymoon, I'm the

207

happiest man in the whole wide world – just thank God for my beautiful wife lying asleep down there in that ridiculous dungeon . . . There was a pad of feet behind him, his wife slid her arms around his neck.

'Hullo.'

He turned and held her tight. She was still warm from the bed, clad in the Bimini sunfrock with nothing on underneath. And, oh, the beautiful feel of her.

'What have you been doing?' she said.

'Planning our wonderful. life. And practising forgery.'

She looked at the notebook. She picked it up and examined the columns of signatures closely.

'They're very good,' she said. 'Very, very good.'

'A dazzling career in crime wasted.'

'I couldn't tell these from the real thing.' Then she turned to him. 'Are you truly sure you're prepared to do this?'

He felt his nerves stretched.

'Who else can do it? It's too late to change horses now.'

She sat down on a bar stool. Morgan sighed. This was it – he was about to start tricking her. He picked up the notebook and said:

'But which name am I going to use? What exactly did the note say in Max's book?'

She said: 'Just the initials of the bank, plus the number of the box.' She went on: 'I've been thinking about how we may find out which name. With a phone call to the bank –'

'Yes, I've thought of that too. But first tell me exactly what Max's note said.'

'I told you.'

Oh Jesus. It was a clumsy attempt and she had probably seen through it. 'Anna, I now need to know the bank and the box number. You've been right to keep it from me in case something happened to me, but now I *need* to know.'

'Why can't it wait until tomorrow?'

'Because I need to know all my facts now, to generate self-confidence!'

She put her hand on his arm. 'I'm sorry.' She stood up, and paced across the floor. She sighed. 'It's not that I don't trust you, please.'

'For Christ's sake, Anna!'

208

She stopped. And held up her hand. 'All right. You need to know now.' She turned. 'The note read: UBS 7224 Bahnhof-strasse, Z. The Z stands for Zurich.'

He gave an inward sigh of relief. He repeated carefully: 'Seven two two four. And UBS stands for?'

'Union Bank of Switzerland. It's a world-famous bank. Bahn-hofstrasse is its headquarters.'

Morgan sat back.

'All right. Now, tell me about your clever phone call to the bank.'

She turned again, and paced. She said:

'It's more likely that Max used the name Constantine for the box. So you telephone the bank and say your name is Max *Hapsburg*. You want to know when your rental of your box expires. And they look up their records, and say: "Mr Hapsburg, your rental is paid up until, say, January." You then know the box is in the name of Hapsburg. *Or* they say, "Mr Hapsburg, we have no record of you having a box here." In which case you say, "Oh? – this *is* the Swiss *Credit* Bank, isn't it?" They say, "No sir, it's the *Union* Bank." You say, "Sorry, silly me, phoned the wrong outfit." And you then know the box is in the name of Constantine.'

Morgan got up and began to pace too.

'Yes, I've got to try something like that.' He shook his head. 'But there are serious risks involved . . .' He paced. 'Firstly, the man on the phone may say, "What's your box number, Mr Hapsburg?" If I say "Seven two two four" he may come back to the telephone and say, "I'm sorry, Mr Hapsburg, that box belongs to somebody else." I then know the box is in the name of Constantine. But when I go into the bank later and say "My name is Maxwell *Constantine*, please give me box seven two two four," the man will think, "That's a coincidence, only this morning a Mr Hapsburg asked about this same box . . ." And his suspicions are immediately aroused. Wouldn't yours be? And so he looks at my signature very very carefully. And at my phoney Constantine passport – with my unembossed photograph . . .' He turned to her. 'He'd blow the whistle for the police.'

'Oh God . . .' She sat on a bar stool. She thought. 'But you could say on the telephone, "Sorry, I can't remember my number, I haven't got my key on me – it's in my wife's hand-bag."'

He shook his head. 'I doubt whether a smart bank would discuss a client's safety-deposit box with somebody who doesn't even know the number – unless they knew that client's voice. Which is another problem. I may find myself speaking to somebody who *knew* Max Hapsburg. Remembers him. In which case I'll be in big difficulties.' He raised his eyebrows. 'If the box *is* in the name of Hapsburg and I find myself speaking on the phone to somebody who knows Max – that's it.'

She said: 'Of course – I wouldn't dream of letting you go into the bank. Mission Impossible. Back to square one.'

Morgan went behind the bar. And oh God he hoped that was what happened tomorrow – Mission Impossible. Then it would have to be Option One, the lawyer. He uncapped two bottles of beer. He poured them, and handed her a glass. She said:

'You're going to tell me something else. What is it?'

He sighed tensely. This was the biggest part of the trick he was playing on her. He walked back and sat down beside her. He took her hand. He said:

'Last night, Makepeace, Danziger and I made a change of plan. Now, I don't want you to argue about it. We're both tired, and it cannot be changed now. And it is this: Tonight Makepeace and I and the others are flying down to Zurich, to case the joint and work out an escape route. We're flying by seaplane.' He paused. 'You are not coming with us tonight. Assuming everything seems safe, the seaplane will come back and fetch you tomorrow night. And we go to the bank together the next day.'

She was astonished.

'Why are you leaving me here in the first instance?'

'Because it's safest. We've got to see the lie of the goddam land. You'll be in the way. And you can't look after yourself in a fight.'

'And if there is a fight tomorrow while you're reconnoitring?' she demanded.

'Then we run for it. Run away and think again.'

She looked at him angrily. Then she slid off the stool.

'No *way*!' she said. 'And if they kill you?' She held up a hand

210

to silence him. 'This is my responsibility, Jack! And I'm going to be there to take my share of the risk!'

His nerves were going. 'Bullshit, Anna! This is no time for standing on quixotic principle. There is no risk tomorrow because they're *un*likely to tackle us until we come *out* of the bank with the goods in our possession. Tomorrow we will *not* be going into the bank at all. Only reconnoitring the area around it.'

'If there's no risk, there's no reason why I shouldn't come!'

He held out an angry finger. 'Anna, you have entrusted the planning of this whole operation to me –'

'I've been in on every stage! Consulted! I'm coming.'

He calmed himself. He played his trump card: 'Do you know how to parachute?'

She stared at him. 'No. What are you talking about?'

He demanded, 'Would you like to start learning tonight?'

She stared angrily. 'No.'

Morgan nodded grimly. 'But that's how the boys and I are entering Switzerland, Anna. To avoid being seen on radar. And *you* can't parachute.' He added, 'And even if you could, I don't want the woman I love leaping out into thin air over mountains in the dark.'

'Nor do I want the man I love doing that!'

'I'm a trained parachutist, Anna. And parachuting in is the only sure way of entering Switzerland undetected.' He ended grimly: 'And that's the way it's going to be.'

'And so how the hell do *I* get into Switzerland?'

He sighed theatrically. 'The pilot will land on the Zurich See with you, with a perfectly legitimate flight plan. Officially you'll be co-pilot, with false papers to prove it. But the immigration people don't check crew. You'll come ashore without problem. We pick you up, go to the bank and do the job.'

'So, why don't we all go in together that way *tomorrow*?'

'Because we can smuggle *one* person in that way, as crew, but not *five* of us, Anna.'

She thrust both elbows on the bar and held her head.

'*Oh* . . .' she breathed angrily. Then she cried, 'Why wasn't I consulted? Why am I presented with a *fait accompli*? Everything's slipped out of my control!'

'Makepeace and Danziger presented *me* with that *fait accompli* last night. But it's the best plan. And that's what you're paying these professionals for. And it's too late to change.'

She took a furious breath, then straightened up.

'Okay. So bloody be it! Yes, it is the best plan, I can see that!' She breathed. '*But* . . .' she looked at him squarely down the length of the bar: 'Do you swear to me, on all that's holy, that you're not going into that bank tomorrow to open that box without me? You know the bank and the box number now!'

He made himself look astonished. And oh God he did not care any more that he was lying, all he wanted was for all this to be over and live with her happily ever after.

'Anna? Are you saying that you don't trust me?'

She cried, 'This is *my* problem, *my* responsibility, *my* decision! It's *intensely* important to me and *highly* secret! And now everything has slipped out of my control! –'

'You had to get people to handle it for you. Could you have handled it by yourself?'

'That's why I trusted you!'

'Am I a man of honour or am I not?'

She cried, 'You persuaded me to tell you the name of the bank and the box number knowing full well that I wasn't coming with you tonight!'

'Because I knew you would kick up a fuss just like you're doing now. And I need to know those details, woman, because *tomorrow* I'm going to telephone the bank, *just* like you suggested, to try to find out what bloody name the box is in. I don't want to leave these uncertainties to the last minute! I need self-confidence, Anna – I'm not an experienced forger!' He glared at her, and she glared back. 'Now. Do you trust me or not?'

She said slowly: 'Do you swear to God that you're not going into the Union Bank of Switzerland tomorrow to open box seven double-two four?'

'*Answer* me, Anna.'

'You answer *me*, Jack!'

And, oh God, he did not care any more about what oaths he broke. He said:

'I swear it.'

'To God?' she demanded angrily.

'Yes, to God!'

She glared at him. He got up and walked down the bar, and put his arms around her.

30

The dungeon was pitch black. He awoke, with a start, at his lowest ebb; and all he wanted to do was get her up and hurry her out of this place and run, run away with her to somewhere safe and forget all this ever happened. There was another knock on the door and he realized what had woken him. 'Yes?'

'Your car will be here in fifteen minutes.'

He scrambled out of bed. He grabbed his trousers containing the box keys and hurried into the bathroom. He slammed on the shower.

When he came out, she was sitting on the bed, fully clothed. She said quietly: 'I'm coming.' She stood up.

He was astonished.

'No you're not. The plane's coming back for you tomorrow.'

'And I'm flying into Switzerland as crew?'

'Correct.'

'Then I can fly as crew tonight. You jump, I'll stay with the plane all the way, as crew.'

'You agreed this morning! —'

'And I've been awake all afternoon rethinking it. There's no reason why I shouldn't come. Flying back here for me will cost a bomb. It's the same plan, only easier. And cheaper.' She added, 'And I'm paying for it.'

Morgan seethed. 'Anna, you've entrusted the planning to me. And it's going to be the way I say! Jesus — there're too many cooks for this broth. Me, Makepeace, now Danziger, now you!' He sat angrily and pulled on his shoes.

'It's my broth! And I'm the paymaster.'

'Anna, I'm not having you in Zurich until I've seen the lie of the land.'

'I'm coming,' she said quietly. She turned for the door. Morgan

213

bounded off the bed at her, and grabbed her arm. He pulled her back to the bed and firmly pushed her down onto it. She tried to scramble up and he firmly pushed her down again. He snatched up his jacket and turned for the door. He snatched the big key out of the lock. Anna bounded up and grabbed the door. He shoved out his hand to push her away, and she grabbed his arm, and the next moment he was rolling through the air. In one movement she had caught him off balance and dropped her shoulder and rolled him over her back, onto the floor.

He hit the stone tiles with a thud. He looked up at her, absolutely amazed. He said, 'How did you do that?'

She stood over him, hair awry.

'Oh Jack, are you all right?' She dropped to her knees beside him to help him up. 'Oh, I'm sorry! Are you hurt?'

Morgan clambered to his feet.

'When did you learn judo?'

'I'm sorry, I just did it naturally –'

'Nonsense, you did it expertly.'

'I learned it at university.' She tried to dust him off.

'Any other accomplishments I don't know about? Alligator-wrestling, maybe? Sword-swallowing?'

'Jack, I'm coming.'

Morgan closed his eyes. Then realized what to do.

'All right,' he sighed. He waved his hand at the bathroom. 'Go'n get your things.'

She turned and hurried across the dungeon.

Morgan strode through the door, and slammed it behind him. He rammed the key in the lock and turned it. He leant against it.

'Hey!' Anna pounded on the door. 'Hey – open it, you bastard!'

'Anna?' he said. 'I love you.'

He turned and bounded the stone steps, two at a time.

'*Jack, you bastard!* . . .'

Morgan emerged through the door under the stairs. There were bangs from below. He closed the door shakily behind him.

Xaviera was the same height as Anna. Under a raincoat, she could have been of a similar figure. She wore a headscarf.

'Pity we can't dress you up as a whore,' she said, 'but we don't go in for bull-dykes here.'

The bar was in half-darkness; there were three girls, in overcoats, waiting to go home. Jesus, he didn't like all these people knowing. Xaviera went to the front door and looked out through the spy hole. 'Do these girls know who we are?' he whispered.

'They don't even know Anna's still downstairs. They just think you're a sado-masochist who's had enough for the day. The only one who knows is Erik.'

'They're not coming in the same car with us, are they?'

'No. Another car.'

Morgan turned to Erik. He was a big man in his mid-forties, tough and neat in a dinner jacket. Morgan led him aside. He handed him the key. 'Anna's a bit upset. In about an hour will you take her a nice bottle of wine?'

'Certainly, sir.'

Morgan said, 'She's very worried and wants to come with me. I've persuaded her against it, but she may change her mind. Will you see she doesn't leave the house, under any circumstances?'

'Certainly. I keep the keys to all outside doors, anyway.'

'Good. Be kind to her, Erik.' He slipped two hundred and fifty dollars into his hand. 'You get the other half when we come back for her.'

Xaviera was looking through the spy hole again.

'Here it is.' She unlocked the door. 'Come.'

Morgan hurried down the front steps beside her, his eye sweeping the dark canal. There were many parked cars in the shadows.

Their driver was Joop who had first driven him last night. He drove off down the canal street. Morgan looked through the windows. All was still. Then a car reversed out of the shadows on the other side of the canal.

'Here we go . . .' he muttered. And he felt exhausted again. And furious with Makepeace again for shooting his mouth off to Xaviera. And sick about leaving Anna like that.

Their car was approaching the end of the block. He looked back again, and he saw something else: a motorboat was cruising down the canal. He sat back angrily. 'Have you seen the boat?'

'*Ja*,' Joop said.

'Well that's the first job – lose the boat. Go where it can't follow us. Then lose that car. Where's the canal we pick up our boat?'

'On the other side of town.'

He thought shakily: So the Dutch police have tipped off the British. And some nice bent Dutch copper has probably tipped off the Comrades as well . . . But there was one consolation: the Dutch police had not raided the Yab Yum. Which meant that the British were definitely playing a waiting game, to see where they went. Which meant that they had not cracked the Swiss code of banking secrecy.

Joop turned down a narrow street towards the Royal Palace. And the boat was lost. As easy as that.

Morgan looked back. The car following them turned onto the bridge. It was a Citroën.

Joop swung right out of Mozes en Aaronstraat, in the Damrak, at normal speed. The Citroën turned after them. Joop turned right again, into Duitersteeg. '*Hou vas!*' he said, and he trod on the accelerator.

The car roared up the short one-way street. Ahead was Kalver Straat. Parked on the corner was an old Renault, its engine running. Joop swung right into Kalver. The Citroën was just turning into Duitersteeg. The Renault pulled away and swung into Duitersteeg, towards the Citroën. The Citroën slammed on its brakes, its horn blasting.

'Bloody well done! Whose plan was that?'

Joop was driving fast down Kalver. 'Dan Danziger.'

Morgan looked back. Nobody was following them. The streets were quiet, at eleven o'clock on a Sunday night.

He sat back, with a tense sigh of relief. And tried to put Anna out of his mind.

Joop drove fast across Amsterdam, turning left and right, and right again and left again. Street signs, canals, bridges, lights sped past. Morgan kept looking back, but nobody was following them. Ahead now was the wide Amstel canal. Joop drove along the left bank, then turned into a narrow street. A canal ran alongside it, with houseboats and barges moored.

'Your boat is at the end.'

Morgan gripped Xaviera's hand. 'Thank you. Look after Anna.'

'Erik won't let her out of his sight.'

'She's very upset. Almost irrational. Be kind to her.'

Joop stopped the car. 'Out.'

Morgan scrambled out of the car. A speedboat was moored to the embankment, a man behind the wheel. Morgan clambered down into the boat. The man slipped the mooring line, and shoved off. The boat surged away.

It turned left into the Muidergracht. There was a bridge. The Dutchman opened the throttles, and the bows came up.

Ahead was the harbour. The boat sped down the dark canal. Now they were in dockland, big warehouses, barges, cranes. Behind them were the lights of central Amsterdam, the IJ haven, the railway terminus. The boat swung into the Mond, and the harbour opened out. They sped through the locks. And ahead lay the IJ-meer, big and black, and the Dutchman opened up the throttles wide.

Morgan felt limp with relief. 'Thank you! What's your name?'

'No names, no comebacks,' the man grinned.

The boat sped over the black inland sea, the bows smack-smacking. Way ahead to the east was a sprinkling of shore lights.

For fifteen minutes the boat smacked out into the blackness, without any lights. Then the Dutchman slowed the engines to idle. The boat settled, gently putt-putting. There were no lights of other boats. The Dutchman produced a torch from under the seat.

He pointed to the north-east. 'That's where he'll come from.'

The Grummond twin-engined seaplane came roaring low out of the night, no lights on. The Dutchman flashed his torch.

The floats hit the water and spray flew up. The Dutchman eased open the throttles on the boat.

The seaplane went churning across the dark sea, the radio angrily rasping at it; then it turned around, spluttering. The boat swung out and went churning around the back of it. The boat eased into the blast of the propellers. Morgan grabbed the float. He clambered onto it, clutching the strut. Makepeace had the door open. Morgan flung his bag up, then clambered up.

'Where's Mrs Hapsburg?' Makepeace shouted.

'She's not coming.'

The Dutchman was already churning away. Morgan clambered into a rear seat and the pilot eased out the throttle and the seaplane surged forward. Morgan pulled on the headset and heard Schipol control rasping: '*Repeat – where are you? –*'

The seaplane went roaring across the sea, faster and faster, the spray flying, then the pilot eased back the yoke. And up she came, and the lights of Amsterdam began to unfold. The pilot pressed his radio button and said:

'Terribly sorry about that, Schipol. I had a spot of engine trouble and just had to put down, but I'm all right now. This is seaplane Alpha Victory Zulu three four two proceeding to Lake Como, Italy, as per my filed flight plan . . .'

A few minutes later, an air traffic control officer at Schipol airport was taking his hourly break. He went down to a public telephone. He dialled the home number of a policeman.

'I think I have your man. It's the only aircraft that has made an unauthorized landing and take-off tonight. I'll give you the flight plan he filed in Copenhagen . . .'

Forty minutes later the Dutch policeman was sitting in his car alongside a dark canal, talking to Vladimir Ustinov and a cultural officer of the Russian embassy.

'The flight plan gives the destination as Lake Como in Italy. They're flying a Grummond Twin, which means they can only cruise at about a hundred knots, so they'll get there just after sunrise. You have ample time to alert your people in Italy. Meanwhile, as a policeman I can telephone the Italian police at Lake Como and tell them I'm very interested in where the people on this plane go. And tell them to ask the Italian air traffic control for the details of further flight plans this aircraft files . . .'

31

The pilot's name was Ole Eriksen. He had a round, creased face and a scraggly blond beard.

The lights of Amsterdam slipped by below. Makepeace handed Morgan a can of beer, then clambered out of the co-pilot's seat and came back to him. 'Why didn't you bring Mrs Hapsburg?'

Morgan took a long swallow of the beer. He hardly tasted it. 'Too dangerous. We saw what happened in New York.'

'But, I thought she had to get into her safety-deposit box?'

Morgan's nerves were tight. 'She's given me a Power of Attorney to open it. It's perfectly legal.' He did not know whether Makepeace believed that and he did not care.

'I see,' Makepeace said. 'So, after you've been to the bank, where do we go?'

'Back to Amsterdam to fetch Anna.'

Makepeace shook his head. 'And then? Still to England?'

Morgan sighed. It depended on what was in that goddam box. He could not bear to think about what he was going to do with that. 'I hope so.'

'You *hope* so? You better think about it pretty damn quick. Danziger is not going to like flying back to Amsterdam to fetch Anna. He's planned a direct flight from Zurich to Ireland.'

Morgan's anger flared. 'Ireland, huh?'

Makepeace said earnestly, 'He's got a safe place for the seaplane to land, a safe house for you to hole up in. From Ireland to England there're no immigration formalities. Perfect.'

'So you've spoken to him since last night?'

'He called me in Copenhagen. To check everything was All Systems Go.'

'And what did he say?'

'He told me about Ireland. And that everything is A-okay his end. Cars, boats, escape route, everything.'

'Was the telephone line secure?'

'Sure. It was pay-phone to pay-phone.'

Morgan sighed.

'Okay, Dougie. Thank you. But there's something else I'll thank you to remember. *I'm* the paymaster, not Danziger. So, you hired Dan, and he seems to have taken over the planning. So far he's done well. But *don't* tell me Danziger is not going to like this or that change of plan. I'll fly to goddam Timbuktu if I like! I call the shots around here, Douglas. Understood?'

Makepeace glowered. 'Understood,' he muttered. 'But it's going to be no simple matter picking up Mrs Hapsburg, we can't keep dropping out of the sky like tonight, they'll be wise to us – it'll take *planning*. *That's* what this whole operation has lacked so far. Everything's off the cuff.'

'Everything's *happened* off the cuff! So tell the pilot and start planning.'

'I wish I knew what all this was about,' Makepeace grumbled '– then I could plan better.' He added: 'Personally, I don't think you should go to England, if the heat's still on. Maybe you should lie low for a bit.'

'Like where?'

Makepeace said, 'Like my farm in France. I mean *your* farm, now. It's nice there, up in the mountains. Not a soul would know you're there. No neighbours. Forest.'

'That's no good. I own the place, that must be known to the French authorities.'

'Is it? Registered in your name already?'

'I gave the title deeds and our contract to a solicitor in London, and told him to fix it all up.'

'There you are!' Makepeace said. 'So it's still registered in my brother-in-law's name.'

'Your brother-in-law? I bought the bloody place from you!'

'Yes, but *I* bought it from my brother-in-law. But I never actually registered it in my name because I was broke. I only did that when I sold it to you, so that legally I could sell it . . . So the French are still working this lot out. It takes *years* in France. *I* haven't yet had any papers from the Frogs, you know – transfer taxes and all that crap.'

Morgan sat back.

'Makepeace? You sell property to a friend, which doesn't yet legally belong to you? . . .'

'It *did* legally belong to me! It just takes *time*.'

Morgan rubbed his brow. He didn't care. Oh, to lie low for a bit, and not be on the move. 'No, I can't hide any more. I've got to face the bastards down, and get it over. They've got no right to hound us.'

Makepeace frowned. 'And the Comrades. What'll you tell them?' He shook his head. 'I wish I knew what all this was about,' he said.

It was a long night. The seaplane droned along at ten thousand feet, the lights of Europe sliding slowly by. Down there, in the string of air traffic control towers, their blip showed on radar screens all the way: when they passed off one screen, they reappeared on the next. At each stage the pilot reported to the air traffic controllers, who confirmed their permitted altitude and flight path.

Morgan slumped in the back seat, trying to rest. Trying not to think about it any more.

The lights of France slid by below. Then, way ahead, the Alps began to loom, big and black and white. It was almost four o'clock in the morning when Ole Eriksen said over the radio: 'Geneva Control, this is Alpha Victory Zulu three four two, heading one seven zero for Como, Italy . . .'

In Geneva, the air traffic controller acknowledged the transmission and watched the little blip on his screen.

The mountains droned by, gleaming silvery white and black, sprinklings of lights here and there, black ragged patches of lakes.

Morgan sat with his parachute on, eyes closed, not daring to look at that terrifying beauty below. Then Makepeace shook his knee. 'Okay, get ready, off we go . . .'

Morgan shoved out of his seat before he lost his nerve. Makepeace slid open the door, and the icy night blasted in. He put one foot out on the wing. Ole Eriksen held up a hand, looking at his chart. Makepeace waited. Morgan's heart was knocking. Ole dropped his hand, and Makepeace got out onto the wing. For an instant he clung, facing the propellers, then he jumped backwards, and he disappeared into the blackness.

Morgan scrambled to the door, his heart pounding. Before

he could funk it, he climbed out into the roaring blast. He clung a moment, eyes closed, terrified, then he launched himself.

And there was nothing in the world but the purest terror of falling backwards through nothingness, blackness hurtling about him, the numbers stuttering blindly in his head – then he ripped the cord and there was a wrench, and suddenly he was floating.

Floating through the freezing night sky at a rushing rate. The deafening silence of space. He prayed *Thank You God*, and he looked frantically for Makepeace. He was over there, below him, his canopy bulbous. Morgan gripped his strings and pulled, and his parachute veered across the sky. The landscape was easing up towards him, patches of white amongst blackness of trees. A snowy road. A car moving along with only parking lights on. Closer and closer came the black and white earth. Faster and faster. Then it was rushing up towards him. He bent his knees. The earth hurtled towards him, and he hit it with a bone-jarring crash and he rolled.

He rolled over once in a mass of snow, half-winded. He unclasped the harness and scrambled up and ran at his parachute, stumbling, rasping. He grabbed it, hand over hand, bundled it up roughly. He turned and started for the road.

He scrambled down onto it, and ran for the car. Makepeace was already there. Danziger grabbed the parachute from Morgan.

'So, no Mrs Hapsburg?' he demanded. 'Now look here, sir – you can't just spring these surprises on us –'

'Tough, Dan! I'm the paymaster around here!'

Morgan strode to the car door. Stillgoes slung the parachutes in the boot. They all got into the car. Danziger did not put on any lights. He started driving fast down the forest road. 'Everything all right?' Morgan demanded from the back seat.

Danziger's anger seemed to have gone. 'Everything's perfect, sir. I've got us rooms in a nice motel. I've got us a perfect escape route. What we'll do now, sir, before the city wakes up, is drive into town and go over the general area – a familiarization tour. Then we'll go to the motel and go over the plan in detail.' He added: 'You'll have to tell us the name of the bank, now, sir.'

'Yes,' Morgan said.

Danziger said: 'I've studied the surrounds of all the banks in Bahnhofstrasse, sir, and the escape route is basically the same for all of them – only a few preliminary streets are different.'

'What time do you reckon we'll start the job?'

'A couple of hours for the briefing. About ten o'clock this morning. Of course, we can only start the job *after* the seaplane has arrived safely, in case the pilot hits a snag and doesn't show up. We'd look silly sitting on the lake.'

'Yes.'

'But he'll be in Zurich about nine o'clock.' Danziger waited, then: 'Well, sir? What's the name of the bank?'

Morgan said: 'I'll tell you when we get into the city for the familiarization tour. We may be ambushed by a carload of Comrades round the next corner – in which case, the less you guys know the better.'

'Quite right, sir,' Danziger said.

VOLUME II

Part Six

32

The Zurich See curves away out of sight down a valley in wooded mountains. At one end of this lake is the pretty city of Zurich, and along the shores are suburbs and parks, yacht clubs and bathing beaches. In the summer the lake is gay with sails: but in November it is grey and empty. Danziger pointed at the large-scale map he had taped to the motel-room wall.

'As you saw this morning, the old, central part of Zurich is actually a triangular island. Bahnhofstrasse runs down the middle of the island, from the railway station –' he pointed – 'down to the lake. And your Union Bank of Switzerland is almost bang in the middle of Bahnhofstrasse.

'Now, this triangular island is bounded on one side by the Limmat river, about a hundred metres wide, and on the other side by this little river, Schanzengrabe, which is really more like a canal. Shallow. Both the river and the canal flow into the Zurich See.' He pointed. 'There are small boats moored all along this little canal. There're nine bridges across it. Some are one-way, one is only for pedestrians. And *this* canal, sir, is the escape route I have chosen.'

Morgan watched him with increasing relief. The man was a professional. And he liked the look of Clark and Stillgoes. Danziger went on:

'We have rented a powerful speedboat, and moored it under this *pedestrian* bridge, on the canal. Clark waits in the boat. I repeat, it is the *pedestrian* bridge, and it leads off a little plaza, which is also for pedestrians only. From the Union Bank to this bridge is about six hundred yards.' He paused. 'If we're being chased, we drive flat out from the bank by this series of one-way streets,' he traced his finger – 'Into the pedestrian plaza, and *onto* the pedestrian bridge. We abandon the car *on* the bridge. We jump into our boat, and *away* we go at top speed. *Straight* down the canal, and out into the Zurich See. A total distance, by canal, of about a thousand yards.' He paused and looked at them. 'Whoever's following us by car will first have to cross the pedestrian bridge – and our car will be blocking that – and then go down all kinds of one-way streets. They'll lose sight of us in seconds.' He spread his hands. 'And within half a mile on the See is our seaplane. With a perfectly legal flight plan. Its engines will be already turning, because we'll have warned the pilot by radio. We board the aircraft and off we go.'

Danziger picked up a walkie-talkie telephone-radio.

'We will each have one of these. You, sir,' he said to Morgan, '. . . when you're ready to leave the bank, you telephone Makepeace from the *bank*'s telephone. He'll be waiting here –' he tapped a map – 'in the Carlton Pub, sitting near the public telephone.' He handed Morgan a slip of paper, with the number written on it. 'Makepeace then signals to me – I'll be outside, near the corner of Bahnhofstrasse, in the car, keeping watch. Stillgoes will be nearby, in a strategic position. Stillgoes and Makepeace walk towards the bank and I radio you to emerge. I drive to the bank's door. You dash for it, and off we go. To the pedestrian bridge. We jump into the boat.' He looked at them with a little smile. 'Simple.'

Morgan said: 'Have you got a contingency plan? – in case the seaplane won't start, for example.'

Danziger held up a finger. 'Good question, sir. Yes, we have rented two other cars, and parked one on each side of the lake. Here,' he pointed at the map. 'And here. The ignition keys are taped under the drivers' armrests. Before we go to the bank, we'll drive past these cars, to identify them. So, if it becomes impossible to get to the seaplane, we scream across the lake to one or other of these cars.'

'And then go where, if that happens?'

Danziger cocked his eyebrows. 'That's up to you, sir. Underground, if you like. I've made provision for that possibility, which I'll explain in a moment. But you see, sir, you've sprung a change of plan on us today. We were going to fly you safe and sound to Ireland. Now you want us to return to Amsterdam and fetch Mrs Hapsburg. Okay, you're the paymaster, but I'm not a thought reader, sir.'

'Get on with the contingency plan, Dan!'

'However,' Danziger said, 'in case we need to go underground, I have a safe house for us, and I had the forethought to bring a number of blank passports with me. If you want them, there will naturally be an extra charge, sir.But with a fake passport you could fly out of Switzerland by ordinary airline. Or by train. We could all come with you, if you like. Or you're on your own to worry about Mrs Hapsburg.' He shrugged. 'But whatever you decide, I strongly recommend that you prepare yourself for the contingency plan by buying one of these passports. Have you got photographs?'

'Yes. How much?'

'Of course,' Danziger said, 'I gave Dougie an insider's price when he brought those two blanks for you to New York. These will be a little more expensive. Five hundred pounds each.'

Morgan said slowly, 'Dougie told you those first two passports were for me?'

'Yes? . . .'

'I *didn't*!' Makepeace blurted angrily – 'I only told you *after* I'd called you to Amsterdam!'

Danziger said smoothly, 'Oh yes, so you did.'

'And what was the insider's price?' Morgan said slowly.

Danziger glanced at Makepeace. Makepeace was blushing, mortified. He muttered: 'A hundred and fifty quid each.'

'But I paid you *two* hundred and fifty quid each, Dougie . . .'

Makepeace glowered at the floor. 'A man's entitled to a little profit, isn't he? It was still cheap.'

Morgan sat back. He said to Danziger:

'Done. Two passports, please. But for the second one I only pay insider's price.'

Danziger smiled. 'Fair enough, sir. Between old shipmates. But shouldn't you take two more, for emergencies?'

'At insider's price, yes.'

'You drive a hard bargain, sir.'

'But your irrepressible generosity towards old shipmates compels you to accept.' There was a ripple of laughter.

Danziger smiled: 'I assure you, sir, that my concern is only for the efficient execution of a mission. We want you in and out of this job quickly and successfully.'

Morgan nodded. 'Thank you all, gentlemen.'

Danziger said, 'Thank you, sir . . . There remains the question of funds. Dougie has paid us for three days. There's at least another day's work, plus, of course, other expenses – our air tickets, this motel, meals, the rented cars, et cetera.'

Morgan heaved himself up. His nerves were tight.

'I've got the cash on me. Draw up your accounts.' He sighed tensely. 'Meanwhile I've got to make a phone call now.' And, oh God, he did not want to be going into that bank today impersonating a dead man. 'Then we'll go through the whole plan again, step by step.' He added, to reassure himself as much as anybody: 'But there's one point I want to make.' He looked at them. 'We're not going to let our guard down for a moment, but we have *every* reason to expect that this is going to go like clockwork . . . We have done an *excellent* job at covering our tracks getting here. Thanks to you all. Of course, we must expect the *un*expected, but we have *every* reason to have self-confidence. High morale.'

Danziger said, 'Hear-hear, sir . . .'

Morgan's hands felt clammy. He unlocked his bedroom door.

The telephone directory was still open. He checked the number again. Then he sat down on the bed, while his nerve was still up, and dialled.

A Swiss voice said, 'Union Bank of Switzerland.'

Morgan said in English, 'Safety-deposit department, please.'

He waited, eyes closed, heart knocking. Oh God, if this didn't work he should call the whole thing off and send the boys home. 'Box Department, good morning.'

Morgan swallowed. 'Good morning. My name is Max Hapsburg. I'm a client of yours. I want to put a lot of new stuff in my box today, but I'm not sure it's big enough. Can you tell me the dimensions of my box, please?'

'What is your number, Mr Hapsburg?'

'I'm sorry, I haven't got my keys on me, they're in my wife's handbag . . .'

The man said, 'I'm sorry, but we cannot discuss a client's box on the telephone without proper identification. If you come in, we can change your box for any size you need.'

Morgan closed his eyes.

'Of course. Thank you. Goodbye.'

He put down the telephone. And held his head in both hands.

Oh God . . . He still did not know the name under which the box was registered.

33

Bahnhofstrasse is pretty, tree-lined street, with tramlines. It has good-looking shops and hotels and restaurants and banks. The Union Bank of Switzerland, one of the mightiest in the world, straddles a whole block, like a monument to Swiss banking respectability. The street on one end of the block is for pedestrians only, with a big, modern sculpture at the entrance but a car can squeeze around it. On the other side of the block is the Carlton Pub.

It was just after twelve o'clock that morning when Danziger walked into the pub. Morgan was already there. Danziger went to the other end of the bar, and slowly scratched his face with his left hand. Using his left hand meant that he had seen nobody suspicious during his final reconnaissance.

Morgan said to the barmaid: 'A double cognac, please.' His voice felt husky.

Danziger raised his eyebrows. The barmaid poured the liquor and Morgan picked up the glass. It trembled slightly. He took a big mouthful. It almost made him retch. He controlled it, and hunched over the bar, trying to steady himself.

Self-confidence and high morale . . .

The seaplane had landed two hours ago. Morgan had spent an hour practising the signature again. Then they had left the motel, identified their two rented cars parked on either side of the lake; then driven into the city. Morgan had gone straight to the bar. The others had separated, each doing their final reconnaissance.

Now Makepeace came into the bar. He went to an empty stool. He stroked his eyebrow with his left hand.

Morgan took a deep breath.

This was it, then . . . It was hard to grasp that he was actually about to do it: he did not even know which name to use. If he screwed that up, it wouldn't be the Comrades or Carrington who hauled him away, it would be the Swiss police. He took another swallow of cognac. He did not taste it. He looked at his hand – he could not register whether it was trembling or not. Then he quaffed back the cognac in one big swallow. He banged down the glass, and walked out of the bar.

It felt as if the eyes of the entire world were upon him. He hardly felt the cold. He walked briskly up the sidewalk. Unreal. Trying to look like a man with honest business on his mind. He turned the corner into Bahnhofstrasse. And there, ahead, were the bank doors, and everything was real all right. He glanced across the road and saw Stillgoes strolling past the shops. There were no parked cars. There were plenty of people, but they all seemed to be moving. He took a deep breath and turned into the big doors of the bank.

To the left, a commissionaire sat at a desk: straight ahead, the banking hall. To his right was a waiting area with armchairs. Elevators. A marble staircase leading down. Morgan said to the commissionaire: 'Safety-deposit department, please.'

The commissionaire pointed at the stairs.

Morgan's ears felt blocked, as if he were descending from a high altitude. Yet his footsteps sounded loud. Down the stairs. Round a bend. To the bottom. A red carpet, a glass door. The doors slid open automatically. Beyond was more red carpet, armchairs, desks, a marble counter, vases of roses. To the right, a grille guarding the portal to the deposit boxes beyond. Morgan walked up to the counter. His throat felt thick and his legs felt shaky.

A clerk with receding hair came up to the counter. '*Bitte, mein Herr?*'

Morgan cleared his throat. He tried to smile. His voice sounded loud: 'I'd like to go to my box, please.'

'Yes, sir.' The clerk produced a book of forms. 'Your number, please?'

'Seven two four.'

The clerk scribbled the number on the form. 'Your name, sir?'

His stomach contracted. The dreaded question.

'Constantine . . . Maxwell Constantine.'

He expected a siren to start wailing. The clerk printed the name. He murmured: 'Your passport, sir?'

Morgan pulled out Max Constantine's passport. He pressed it on the counter so it would not tremble. The clerk pushed the book of forms at him. 'Fill in the counterfoil, please, sir, and sign.'

Morgan took out his ballpoint pen. This was really it. He pressed his arm hard on the counter.

He bent over the form. He printed Constantine's name on the counterfoil. The box number. He pressed the pen hard, trying to stop his hand trembling. The last item, the signature. The blank space shrieked at him. His ears blocked. What he was about to do could land him in a Swiss jail for a long, long time. He took a deep breath, and held it. Then, before he could hesitate, he scribbled the signature.

His ears were ringing. He shoved the form over the counter.

The clerk had the passport open. He glanced at Morgan, comparing him with the photograph. He looked at the form, then at the signature in the passport. He said:

'One moment, sir.'

He turned away. Morgan stood, staring at the man's back. It was unreal. The next few moments decided it all. And then, suddenly, he felt almost calm. He had done it. Done his best. If all was lost, so be it. The clerk was bent over a pile of cards. He pored over one, and the passport and the form.

He straightened up. He said something in German to the clerk at the next desk. He walked back to Morgan.

He reached below the counter and pressed a button.

The iron grille slid open, and Morgan jerked. A dapper man in a suit was striding officiously towards him.

The clerk ripped the form from the counterfoil. He handed it to the dapper man and said:

'Take Mr Constantine to his box, please.'

He was walking on air. He felt laughy with relief. He followed the dapper man through the grille. He had to work at it to keep a grin off his face. He wanted to do a little skip. Through a vault with red carpet, the walls gleaming with the tiers of silvery boxes from floor to ceiling. Through an arch into another big room. More vaults led off. Red carpet all the way, the walls gleaming with boxes. Into another vault. A spiral staircase leading down to more vaults.

The dapper man stopped at box 7224. He inserted his own key and turned it. 'Now your key, please, sir.'

Morgan pulled out the bunch of keys. 'I forget which one it is.'

'It will be this one, sir.'

Morgan inserted it shakily, and turned it. The man opened the little door. Inside was a metal box about two inches in depth. He handed it to Morgan. 'This way, sir.'

Morgan clutched it. He could hardly believe he had it. The man led the way into another room. There were rows of tables, divided by partitions.

Morgan said huskily: 'Haven't you got private rooms?'

'Cabins? Yes, sir. Follow me.'

He led into a corridor. It had doors down each side. Above each shone a light, some green, some red. He went to the nearest door showing a green light, and opened it. The cabin had a desk and a chair.

'When you are finished, press the bell, sir.'

'Thank you.' Morgan closed the door behind him. And locked it. He leant against it, and closed his eyes. He was trembling with relief.

'Thank You, God . . .' he whispered.

He pulled out the chair, and sat down at the desk. He lit a trembly cigarette.

He lifted the lid off the box.

He was looking at a small metal cylinder, a tape-recorder cassette, and an envelope.

He picked up the cylinder slowly. He unscrewed the cap. He looked inside. Then he tipped the contents out, into his hand.

So this was it. This was what everybody was after, the British, the KGB.

It looked like a small roll of camera film. He felt helpless. How do you develop microfilm? Who could he trust to do the job? Could you do it in an ordinary darkroom, with the ordinary equipment?

He picked up the envelope, and opened it.

Inside were some papers, and some film negatives. He glanced at the papers. One was a photocopy of a banker's letter. The other document was an airline waybill. He held the strips of film negatives up to the light. Black-and-white negatives. Indistinct, of people, not documents.

He picked up the cassette.

Handwritten on the label was: *Klaus Barbie, 1982.*

Morgan stared. Klaus Barbie, the Butcher of Lyons!

On that tape, he was sure, was a verbal explanation of what was on the microfilm . . .

Of course it was! What would you do if you were Klaus Barbie? – what does any blackmailer do? He *tells* his victim what he's got against him – he doesn't show the original, he shows a copy! But Barbie could not make a copy of the microfilm so he summarizes his evidence verbally, on this tape!

Morgan felt feverish. If he could play that tape, he would know what this whole business was about. Know what they were up against, what to do about it. And he was not going to leave the security of this building until he had listened to that tape . . . He rang the bell.

A few moments later there was a knock on the door. He opened it. 'Yes, sir?' the dapper clerk said.

'I want to dictate some notes onto a tape. You haven't a portable tape-recorder, have you?'

'No sir. But we could hire you a stenographer.'

'Where's the nearest shop I could buy a tape-recorder?'

'Jemboli, sir. A department store, a few blocks away.'

'Jemboli. Thank you. May I use your telephone?'

The man led him back to the room which contained the desks. Morgan was clutching the deposit box. 'The telephone directory, sir.' The man pointed, and walked away.

'Thank you.' Morgan pulled out Danziger's note of the public telephone in the Carlton Pub. He dialled it feverishly.

It rang twice: 'Hullo!' Makepeace said breathlessly.

Morgan said carefully: 'I'm not ready to leave yet. Now listen. A few blocks away is a store called Jemboli. Go there, and buy a portable tape-recorder. The type that can play one tape and record it onto another cassette. Get a couple of blank tapes. Plus good batteries. And it must have an earpiece, so I can listen without anybody else hearing. Got that?'

A stunned silence. 'A tape-recorder? What kind?'

'Any goddam kind! And then bring it into the bank. Down to the safety-deposit department. They'll be expecting you. Tell them it's for Mr Constantine.'

'*Constantine?*' Makepeace whispered.

'Correct. And then you have to stay *in* the bank in case the Comrades jump you. Sit upstairs in the foyer. Danziger must take your place by the telephone.'

Makepeace said worriedly, 'He's not going to like this.'

'*Fuck Danziger! Do as you're told!*'

He hung up. The dapper man strutted back to him. Morgan said, 'My assistant will come shortly with a tape-recorder. Would you bring it to my cabin?'

'Certainly, sir.'

At that moment another clerk walked into the room. He was leading another client to the corridor of cabins. The client was Sergei Suslov.

Morgan paid no attention to him. He was trying to think what to do with the microfilm after he had listened to the tape. Then suddenly he knew. At least it was the first step. He said to the clerk: 'I think I need to rent a new box – a bigger one.'

'You have to go to the front desk for that, sir.'

The man led him through the vaults, back into the front room. The clerk behind the counter came forward. Morgan said huskily, 'I've decided my box is too small. I'd like to rent a bigger one, please. In fact, I'd like to make it a numbered account. Is that possible?'

'Yes, sir. It is more expensive. But it means that henceforth you will be known to us only by your number. Your signature will be your *number*, written in words. Instead of your name, you write out your number, in words, and we compare your writing with the word-numbers on your original application form – and *that* is your signature. It means that nobody could forge your normal signature and get to the box.'

'I see. Yes, I'll have one of those, please.'

Fifteen minutes later he was back in his cabin. With his new, bigger box, and his new keys.

Now he was the only person in the world who knew where the microfilm was.

He picked up the banker's letter and read it hurriedly.

It was a photocopy of a letter from the Vatican Bank, signed by two officers with Italian names. Dated September 1st, 1981. It was addressed to Banco Ambrosiana, Andino, Peru, and to Ambrosiana Group Banco Commercial, Nicaragua. Morgan's pulse fluttered. Banco Ambrosiana? God's Banker's bank. The letter read:

> Gentlemen:
> This is to confirm that we directly or indirectly control the following companies:
> Manic SA Luxembourg
> Astolfine SA Panama
> Nordeurop Establishment, Liechtenstein
> UTC United Trading Corporation, Panama
> Erin SA Panama
> Bellatrix SA Panama
> Belrosa SA Panama
> Starfield SA Panama
>
> We also confirm our awareness of their indebtedness towards yourself as of June 10, 1981, as per attached statement of accounts.

The attached statements showed an indebtedness by the Vatican Bank to the South American banks of 907 million dollars.

Morgan frowned. So? God's Banker owned Banco Ambrosiana, and his bank evidently had partnerships in other banks in Peru and Nicaragua. So, the companies listed in the letter had borrowed money from the Peruvian and Nicaraguan banks, and as the Vatican Bank owned or controlled the companies, it owed the money to those banks. So? On the face of it, nothing remarkable about that. 907 million was an awful lot of money, but not to the Vatican Bank. Anna had told him that God's Banker and the Vatican Bank did some business together, and this simply confirmed it.

But what was this letter doing in Max Hapsburg's deposit box?

Morgan snatched up the airline waybill, and speed-read it.

It was a carbon copy. It was simply a contract note specifying that this airline, called Meteor Air, was going to deliver sixteen crates of bulldozer hydraulic lifts from Malta to Bellatrix SA, in Panama. The delivery date was June 17th, 1982.

Morgan tried to concentrate. Bellatrix was one of the companies mentioned in the letter, owned by the Vatican Bank. So? So, okay, Bellatrix dealt in bulldozer parts, and it had bought sixteen pieces in Malta, and Meteor Air was going to deliver them to Panama. So what? The only thing that was possibly significant was the delivery date, three days before Anna's birthday last year, the day before God's Banker was murdered.

Then he realized something else. This was a *carbon* copy of the waybill, which is given to the consignee: when his goods arrive at their destination, he presents this copy to identify himself and his goods, takes delivery and the waybill is receipted. But there was no receipt on this. It appeared, therefore, that these sixteen crates of bulldozer parts had never been delivered.

So?

But, again, what was this doing in Max Hapsburg's box?

He feverishly picked up the first strip of film negatives, and held it up to the light again.

People. Groups standing, looking at the camera. Male and female, but he could not identify faces. A tractor in this one. This one looked like a picnic, a bottle of something being flourished. More party scenes . . . He snatched up the second strip. And frowned.

These were more indistinct. Taken indoors. A window – a bedroom. Two people lying on the bed? Embracing? In this one, they were sitting up. One person was definitely female. Breasts. She appeared to be naked. Clothes on the floor? He glanced at the other frames hurriedly. All he could make out was bodies. Pornographic pictures? Blackmail? . . .

There was a knock on the door. 'Your tape-recorder has arrived, sir.'

Morgan scrambled up and unlocked the door. 'Thank you!'

He relocked the door. Sat down and examined the machine.

He inserted the Klaus Barbie cassette. He put a blank tape into the other side. The earpiece in his ear. He took a piece of paper from the rack. He switched the recorder on, and listened intently.

There was a hissing noise: then a guttural voice began, in French:

'My name is Klaus Barbie.

'I was an officer in the SS during the Third Reich. At the end of the war I returned to Germany openly and despite spurious allegations that I was wanted by the French and American governments as a so-called war criminal, I was employed by the CIC, a department of the American occupying army which hunted down communist spies in post-war Germany. In 1951, this employment ended, and the Americans arranged and paid for the passage of myself and my family to South America, providing me with all travel documents. This surely proves that the allegations that I am a war criminal are groundless.

'During my employment by the American army authorities in Germany, I came into possession of certain evidence which is most important to the Western world. It was a file compiled by the KGB, as it is now called, and it was stolen from them during the Second World War by a German spy within the KGB, and brought to Berlin. I took this file with me to South America and subsequently had a microfilm made of it, because it was so bulky, and destroyed the file itself. When the film is developed it will reproduce, in actual size, photographs of all the original KGB documents. How I came into possession of this file is not important, as the film proves its own authenticity.

'I am now about to summarize, on this tape-recorder, the evidence contained in that film, because it's too lengthy for me to write.'

Morgan was exultant. He was right! . . . He heard the rustle of notes. Then the voice continued:

'The story begins in the year 1931, in Moscow, under Joseph Stalin . . .'

34

It was the depths of winter in Russia. The wind had encased the trees with ice, so it looked as though they were made of glass. Deep in the white forest outside Moscow was a *dacha*, a holiday house. Smoke curled out of the chimney and lights twinkled in the windows. It looked cosy. But it was surrounded by a high security fence, and inside it was little more than a classroom.

One wall was a blackboard, at which stood the teacher. He

was dressed as a Jesuit priest. There was only one pupil, a youth of sixteen. He was being intensively tutored in the advanced tenets of Catholicism. He was being taught in the English language, and his accent was American. He answered to the name of Pieter Gunter.

The lesson ends, and another instructor enters, also in Jesuit robes. He tutors Pieter in advanced Marxist theory. When that lesson ends, other priests take over. They are all experts in their subjects: Latin, modern European languages, the science of espionage. They work long hours with the boy. Each tutor leaves the house dressed as a civilian, and drives to another isolated house.

There are half a dozen such houses in the countryside around Moscow. In each there is only one student. None of these students knows of the others. Each is characterized by his very high intelligence, they are being tutored in the same subjects, but each in a different European language. They are fluent and their accents perfect.

They are all doing exceptionally well in their studies. They are almost ready to be sent out into the Western world, to join Catholic seminaries.

Klaus Barbie paused. He forgot to switch the machine off. He muttered to himself, then shuffled some papers. Morgan waited, pent, staggered by the enormity of the idea. Barbie gave a cough, then continued:

'It had been, and was to continue to be, a long process, and it would be decades before the Kremlin's investment began to pay dividend. But it was worth it . . . For the Roman Catholic Church is the biggest, richest, most powerful and influential institution in the world, with more adherents than the entire population of Europe and America combined: and one day the Kremlin may have the prize of archbishops and cardinals as their agents, and, one day, the Vatican itself in their pocket. One day one of their protégés may be Pope . . '

Barbie paused, then added: 'I repeat, not one of the students knew of the existence of the others.'

Morgan snapped the machine off. And held his head.

What was he going to do about this? . . .

He could not think straight. But thank God he had taken

this out of Anna's hands! But what was he going to do with it?
If this was true, if the Pope was a communist agent, he had to
be got rid of! And the rest of his kind in the Church. But by
whom? By Jack Morgan? How? By shooting him in Saint
Peter's Square again? . . .

Morgan held his fingertips to his eyelids.

God's Banker hanging from Blackfriars Bridge in London.

Murdered because he knew about the Barbie microfilm?

Oh, this was too big for Jack Morgan. This needed the might
of Great Britain to handle. The expertise, the manpower.

'I'd rather die like God's Banker.'

Yes, and if he handed this over to the British he would lose
Anna Hapsburg forever. She would never trust him again. He
would have cheated her, broken solemn oaths. Destroyed her
love, destroyed himself over something she would rather die
for than divulge. Yes, and that's what would happen to her, if
he didn't – she would die like God's Banker too. And that's
what would happen to him, also . . .

He dragged his hands through his hair.

And who were 'They'?

Who killed God's Banker?

*How could he trust the British after they had tried to kidnap
Anna Hapsburg?*

He pressed his fingertips hard to his eyelids and tried to put
fear out of his mind and concentrate.

Klaus Barbie's gravelly voice continued:

'I proceed now to list the assumed names of the youths
who were infiltrated into the Catholic Church over the years.
Thereafter I will list the coded passwords assigned to each.'

Morgan waited impatiently. There was a rustle of papers,
then Barbie read out:

'1931. Antonio Perrelli, joined the seminary in Rome.

'Juan Santiago, joined in Madrid.

'Clive James Watson, joined the seminary in London.

'Pieter Gunter, joined the seminary in Portland, Oregon . . .'

Morgan listened, eyes closed. The voice rasped on. And on.
The names meant nothing to Morgan.

'The class of 1934:

'Angelo José Hevilla, to Barcelona; Roger Benjamin Whitfield to Plymouth . . .'

He could hardly bear to listen. He pressed the forward button and advanced the tape. He hit the play button again.

'Michael Otto Oetz, to Switzerland . . .'

He hit the advance button again, then pressed play again. Barbie said:

'. . . because the Allied forces were advancing on Germany and our agent within the KGB was unable to continue his work. But what we know for a fact is that between 1931 and 1945 a total of eighteen young Russian agents were planted in the Catholic Church.'

Barbie paused, but left the tape running. Morgan waited, numbed. *Eighteen*. Desperately trying to think what to do, trying not to think about what was going to happen outside this bank . . . Barbie began again, but in a new tone now, that of a man delivering a prepared speech:

'And now we come to 1945 . . .' He paused dramatically. 'The year of crossroad for all mankind . . . The year the decadence of the West began . . . The beginning of the end for world justice and decency . . . The year the West made a fatal error that will ultimately lead to its downfall and repression under the communist yoke and whip.' He paused. 'I am not referring here to the defeat of Germany but to what the *Allies failed* to defeat, and in so doing abysmally failed the whole of mankind . . .' He paused again; then continued bitterly: 'The Allies, to defeat Germany, had aligned themselves with Russia, with the greatest forces of evil the world had ever seen, and, knowing this, failed to annihilate their evil partner when there was no more use for him – to scotch the snake, to kill the evil python in its nest! History will forever condemn the Allies for this terrible weakness, this sheer *criminal* dereliction of duty to mankind. For, as the Allies advanced on war-ravaged Germany from the south, the Russian army was racing down from the north, spreading east and west as hard as it could in order to seize forever as much of Europe as it could to expand her evil empire. Russia's intentions were well known and it was known to German Intelligence that there was urgent debate in the highest corridors of Allied power about whether, after Germany had fallen, the Allies should not turn their cannon on the

Russians and drive them back whence they came, even march on to Moscow and liberate the whole vast Soviet empire from the communist yoke.' He paused dramatically. 'But no, they did not! . . . They were war weary and gutless, and' – a sneer came into his voice – '*it would have been electorally unpopular . . .*' He snorted bitterly. 'So, the deafening sounds of war subside, and Russia stands head and shoulders the greatest winner! She has wrested from Europe, *forever*, Poland, East Germany, Czechoslovakia, Hungary, and the other "eastern bloc" countries. *Even Berlin is divided . . .*' He snorted again. 'For the Russians do *not* have to face an electorate back home – by definition, there is no democratic nonsense in Russia! They immediately imposed puppet communist regimes and their rod of iron . . . They made a giant leap forward in their overall strategy of global domination. And the West took their first big step backwards, into decline, moral decadence, and eventual servitude . . .'

Barbie paused again: then cried: '*And they knew it . . . How gutless can a generation be, to sign the death warrants of future generations, for the sake of a little temporary peace and quiet? . . .*'

He took a deep breath for dramatic effect. Then went on scornfully:

'And they soon began further steps backward, opening further corridors for Russian advance – they began to dismantle their colonial empires with *cowardly* haste. Laudable though it may be to create democracy where people are ready for it, it cannot be denied that the West recklessly *abandoned* their responsibilities, towards their colonialists, towards the native peoples they governed, *and towards the world . . .* by hastily handing huge tracts of the earth over to primitive people, to hastily elected, immature, local self-seekers, thereby creating tribal fighting and oppression, warlordism, corruption, mismanagement and abysmal poverty and starvation, ripe for Russian subversion and takeover. In short, the Russians did not need to resort to arms any more to achieve their goal of ruling the world, because the West was handing it to them on a plate . . .

'What a *feast*, for Russia, the next forty years were to prove . . .'

Barbie paused. Morgan waited, his nerves stretched. Barbie shuffled papers. When he continued it was in his storyteller's voice again:

'And so we come to the year 1978, and our scene moves to Rome . . . The old Pope, Paul VI, is dead. The cardinals are arriving from all over the world, to elect a new pope. And one of them, of course, is Pieter Gunter, the brilliant cardinal from America who is now the Papal Secretary of State . . .'

Morgan slammed off the machine.

He recognized the name now. *Cardinal Pieter Gunter!* 'The Henry Kissinger of the Vatican.' The man on the cover of *Time*. *The Man Behind the Throne*, they called him . . . *Oh God no* . . .

Morgan sat there sick in his guts. Trying to think. Then he slammed the machine on again.

'. . . who in many countries is a household name. Academically he is renowned for his erudite books on Christianity, comparative religion, morality, ethics and his stance on nuclear disarmament. Long before he became Papal Secretary of State he was a voice to be reckoned with by the powers that be, a man who could arouse a huge groundswell of public opinion: as Vatican Secretary of State he walks the corridors of international power, a clever advocate of moderation, of peace in a world of superpower confrontation. As a priest he is a remarkably charismatic holy man, as an intellect he is a giant, as a politician he is consummate, as a man he is loved by all who know him, for his warmth, his wit, his charm. When the cardinals gathered in Rome in 1978 to elect a successor to Paul VI, he was widely tipped by the press to be the next Pope . . .' Barbie paused. 'And he *is*, of course, one of the Russian agents who was infiltrated into the Roman Catholic Church as a youth.

'But Cardinal Pieter Gunter was *not* elected Pope in 1978. To the world's surprise, Cardinal Albino *Luciani* was elected, and became Pope John Paul I. And what happened to Pope John Paul I?' Barbie snorted. 'He *died* after only thirty-three days . . .'

Barbie paused, then laughed shortly. He said rhetorically: 'He *died*? . . . Yet he was in perfect health! . . . He "*died*"? . . . And yet the Vatican permitted no autopsy to be performed!

246

. . . He "*died*", they say? . . . I say to you, *Pope John Paul I was murdered* . . .'

Morgan held his head, sick in his guts. Barbie continued theatrically:

'So all the cardinals had to come back to Rome to elect yet another new Pope! And *again* it was widely thought that Cardinal Pieter Gunter would be elected. But again he was not. Instead Cardinal Karol Wojtyla from Poland was elected and became Pope John Paul II . . .' He paused again; then said slowly: 'And within fifteen months, they try to murder him *too* . . . Within fifteen *months* a Turk called Agca tried to shoot the Pope in Saint Peter's Square . . .' Barbie snorted again. Then said slowly: 'We *know* "They" are the Russians . . . We *know* that Agca was hired by the KGB, through the Bulgarian airline officials, to kill Pope John Paul II – he has admitted that. So we know, *irresistibly*, that it was also the *Russians* who murdered Pope John Paul I . . . And why? . . .

'*Why* was Pope Paul I murdered after only thirty-three days? . . . *Why* was Pope John Paul II shot only fifteen months later? . . .' He paused dramatically, then said emphatically, 'The answers are irresistible! . . . *Because Russia wants their man Pieter Gunter sitting on the papal throne* . . .'

Barbie let that hang. Then he ended, softly: 'And he is waiting in the wings . . .'

Morgan felt wrung out. The tape turned slowly. He thought the man had finished.

What was he going to do about this? . . .

He tried fiercely to concentrate. Some new pieces of the jigsaw seemed to be nearer fitting.

Anna knew that the Russians had infiltrated her beloved Catholic Church – because Max had told her in a drunken row. She knew that the Secretary of State was a KGB agent. Knew that John Paul I was murdered. *Yet she claimed she was going to destroy the evidence* . . .

He did not believe her. She intended doing something about it . . .

And she knew that God's Banker had been murdered whilst trying to get his hands on this evidence that Max had – '*I'd*

247

rather die like God's Banker'. Max's passport proved that he had gone to London that very day. To make a deal with God's Banker about this evidence?

And what was God's Banker going to do with it?

Blackmail the Vatican? But for what? Simply for money, like most blackmailers do? Or for something else as well? – like a political advantage.

A political advantage for whom? Against whom?

Morgan hunched over, trying to think. And then he remembered something else: the condoms which she had bought in Garrucha. And he knew for certain that she had not intended destroying the evidence. She had dissembled. If she had found the microfilm in New York she would have put it in a condom and hidden it in her vagina, walked out of the bank and disappeared, to do whatever she intended. And that's what she would have done today if he had not tricked her . . .

Suddenly Klaus Barbie's voice came on again:

'Pieter Gunter is waiting in the wings. And it will not be long before there is another attempt on Pope John Paul's life, because now is the time the Russians sorely need to have a pope in their pocket.

'For Pope John Paul's sermonizing on Human Rights is very much *not* to their liking. True, they can exploit some of this in oppressed, under-developed countries in Latin America, but his message has also penetrated their eastern bloc countries where not only is there a revival of religious interest but now *worker* unrest, taking the form of trade unions. This, of course, is *anathema* to the Kremlin. In Poland, which is ardently Catholic, the charismatic trade union leader, Lech Walesa, has founded Solidarity – and the rot has spread to other satellite states. Russia intends to tolerate *no* such democratic nonsense in her Workers' Paradises! Martial Law has been declared in Poland and the Russian army stands ready to "restore order", as it did in Hungary and Czechoslovakia. And Russia has other troubles: her invasion of Afghanistan has soured into an expensive Vietnam situation; her frontiers with China are forever hostile; the communist economy is stagnant as ever, with food shortages; and now the West, NATO, is not only re-arming but is going to accept American missiles, pointed at Russia! In short, with the resurgence of America under President Reagan, Russia is losing her military superiority in Europe . . .' He paused. 'Now is a *very* important time for Russia to have a pope in their pocket . . .'

Morgan hunched over the desk, his head in his hand. Klaus Barbie let the point hang; then he ended:

'And what a wonderful pope Pieter Gunter would be! . . .

'Whereas Pope John Paul is a star, Pope Pieter Gunter would be a superstar! Whereas Pope John Paul came from the backwaters of Poland, Pieter Gunter will come to the papal throne with all the sophistication of a lifetime in America behind him! Whereas hardly anybody had ever heard of Karol Wojtyla, Pieter Gunter is a household name already! Whereas Pope John Paul is little more than a priest when it comes to politics, Pieter Gunter is a sparkling expert who is used to dining with kings! And while Pope John Paul is busy jetting around the world like a rock'n' roll tour, Pieter Gunter is back home in the Vatican, in the role of Carmalengo, deputy Pope, running the whole vast empire, daily widening his powerbase. Pope John Paul is indeed popular, and it is true that crowds have been known to burst out into the song "He's got the whole world, in his hand . . ." But compared to Pieter Gunter he is an amateur star: Pieter Gunter is the real thing, and that song would truly become his signature tune . . .'

There was a pause; then Barbie ended:

'I repeat: "The *whole* world, in his hand . . ."'

Morgan snapped the tape-recorder off. He slumped back in his chair.

What was he going to do about this? . . .

There was a knock on the door. He snapped around.'Who is it?'

'I've got an urgent message for you, sir.'

A message could only be from Makepeace and it could only mean trouble! Morgan scrambled up and unlocked the door.

Sergei Suslov shoved his way into the cabin

Morgan was knocked backwards against the desk. Sergei held a canister up, the nozzle pointed at him.

'This is a nerve gas, which instantly knocks you out. There is no defence against it.'

Morgan was staring at the man, shocked. Sergei went on quietly: 'You will not dare to shout because you are impersonating Mr Max Hapsburg and have fraudulently opened his box. That is a serious criminal offence. And believe me I am an expert at unarmed combat. Now, I am going to take the contents of Mr Hapsburg's box. And, you are going to tell me where Anna Hapsburg is.'

Morgan's mind was desperately trying to race. *The plane – somehow they had tracked the seaplane to Zurich. But how did they know which bank?* He said shakily: 'Who double-crossed me? . . .'

Sergei jerked the canister. 'I can knock you unconscious in one squirt. And then kill you with one blow.'

And if they had tracked the seaplane, they had it covered right now – they were waiting at the seaplane . . . He desperately tried to stall for time. 'Who do you think you're kidding, Boris? You daren't kill me inside a bank. Not until you know whether I've got what you want –'

'*Where is Mrs Hapsburg?*'

Morgan was still pressed back against the desk. The canister two feet from his face. His mind fumbling with the basic rule they taught him at combat school: Never stand so close to your man that he can reach you. Sergei had to break the rule because the cabin was so small. Morgan said shakily: 'I'll make a deal. You can have the box. But Mrs Hapsburg you leave alone . . .' and he began to turn to the box behind him, and he lashed around.

One hand lashed the canister aside and his other fist swung with all his might at the Russian's stomach. Sergei crashed back against the door, and Morgan hit him again. Sergei's hand came swooping down in a wild chop and Morgan saw stars and he hit him with his elbow with all his frantic might in the solar plexus. Sergei crashed into the corner, and Morgan hit him again. His fist crashed down on his head like a club, Sergei tried to scramble up and Morgan clubbed him again wildly with his other fist, and again, and again with his other fist, and again and again. He wildly clubbed him twice more, after the man slumped unconscious, bloody.

Morgan staggered back against the wall, heaving, gasping. The man's face was blotched in blood and contusions. Morgan looked for the canister, rasping. He snatched it up off the floor.

He turned feverishly to the desk. He snatched both cassettes out of the recorder and stuffed them in his pocket. Plus the envelope of documents and film negatives. He shoved the microfilm back in the box.

He grabbed Sergei's collar and heaved him away from the door, panting. He opened the door a crack. The corridor was empty. The cabin opposite had a green light shining. He scrambled over the Russian's body, dashed across the corridor and opened the door. Back to his cabin. He grabbed Sergei by the collar, and heaved him out into the corridor. Across it, into the cabin opposite. He dumped him. He pulled out the canister of nerve gas, thrust it under the Russian's nose. He held his breath, and squeezed the plunger. Then he scrambled back into the corridor and closed the door.

He dashed back into his own cabin. He shakily smoothed his hair, straightened his tie. He snatched up the box and the tape-recorder.

He strode shakily down the corridor, holding the canister of nerve gas in one hand. He went around the corner. The clerk came towards him. 'Finished, sir?'

'Yes, thank you.'

The clerk led him back through the red-carpeted rooms. They came to his new slot. The clerk inserted his key. 'Now your key, sir.'

Morgan inserted it. It trembled in his hand. He slid the box into the little vault.

The door swung closed. The keys turned.

'Thank you.'

Morgan took a deep breath. His knuckles smarting, his head throbbing where the Russian had hit him. He touched the gun under his arm. He started walking fast out of the vaults. To face the world.

35

It all seemed unreal. And terribly real.

He came up the last stairs. His legs still shaky. There was the

251

foyer. Makepeace sitting in an armchair. He stood up. Morgan walked over to him.

'A Comrade tried to roll me in the vaults.'

Makepeace was wide-eyed. 'In the *vaults*? . . .'

'They must have tracked the seaplane from Lake Como to here – they've got friends in air traffic control.'

'But we weren't on that plane – how did they know which bank?'

'They knew the flight plan was to the Zurich See. So they had all roads into town covered. They spotted us on our way in. And that means that they've got the seaplane covered right now. They're probably aboard the bloody thing.'

'Oh Lord . . .' Makepeace whispered.

'So we've got to use the cars.' He took a breath that quivered. 'And there's another change of plan . . . You get back to Amsterdam as fast as possible, and look after Anna –'

'What about you?'

'This job is far from over. I've got to go somewhere else. And you've got to get Anna to a safe place and stay with her until I join you.'

'*Where* are you going?' Makepeace whispered.

'You needn't know that. But I need to know where you've taken Anna. Is that place of mine in France safe?'

'But,' Makepeace protested – 'why don't you come with me to fetch Anna –'

'Because I've got to go somewhere else and I'm not taking her because it's too dangerous! And the fucking Comrades don't know where she is right now and I'm scared they'll follow me to her. So you go alone. Now, is my place in France *safe*? Can you think of anywhere better?'

'No,' Makepeace said worriedly, '– but Danziger would.'

'I don't want Danziger to know a thing about this! Once we're out of here he's off the job!'

'Okay,' Makepeace muttered '– A safe house somewhere? I'll think about it . . .'

'You can't *think* about it – I've got to know *now*.'

'Then it's the farm, or we stay in the Yab Yum in Amsterdam. The farm's much better –'

'Then get her there, by hook or by crook, and don't leave till I get there!'

'What'll I tell her?'

Morgan held up a shaky finger. 'You tell her that we did *not* get into the bank today. Got that? – did *not*. But the Comrades tried to roll us during our reconnaissance, and we ran away to think again. Tell her I've gone straight to the farm to await her there. I went separately, to divide the forces of the enemy. Got that?'

Makepeace blinked. 'Got it.'

Morgan pulled out one of the blank passports Danziger had sold him. 'Tell her to use that.' He took a shaky breath. 'Okay . . . Let's get out of here.'

He turned to the client's telephone beside the armchairs. He dialled the Carlton Pub. He prayed it wasn't engaged.

'Hullo?' Danziger said immediately.

'Have you seen any Comrades?'

Danziger said calmly, 'Stillgoes reports three suspicious characters window-shopping but nothing conclusive.'

'It's conclusive. But it's Go.'

'Roger, Go. About sixty seconds.'

Morgan replaced the receiver shakily. He put the tape-recorder amongst the flowers, and abandoned it. He needed both hands free.

And suddenly, now that it was about to happen, he was calmer. Reckless, uptight-calm. This was what he had bargained for and now he had to be furiously calm to fight for his life. They stood back from the glass doors, five paces away. It was snowing. People were hurrying in both directions. Morgan was counting the seconds. *Forty-three, forty-four* . . . The elevator doors opened and a woman stepped out. She walked towards the glass doors and stopped when she saw the snow. *Sixty-one* – and Danziger's car came into sight.

'*Go!*'

They both strode for the glass doors. Morgan pulled the can of nerve gas out of his pocket. Danziger's car slammed to a halt. Morgan and Makepeace came bursting out of the bank. They ran across the sidewalk, dodging and side-stepping people, and the Russians came charging at them.

Came charging from across the street, four men running flat out, barging through people. Stillgoes was running flat out at them. Another car was roaring down the street. Morgan bounded at Danziger's car, and the first man lunged at him and Morgan swung on him with the canister and squirted, and the man sprawled. The other car screeched to a halt. Morgan flung open the back door and another man bounded at him, and Stillgoes knocked him flying. Two men leapt out of the other car and Makepeace hit the first and he whirled like a ballet dancer and his foot caught the next man in the chest. Somebody seized Morgan by the collar and slung him. He went reeling backwards across the pavement, and the man bounded after him and hit him and Morgan sprawled. The man bounded at him and seized him in an armlock and wrenched him towards the car, and Makepeace did another of his ballet numbers. He bounded and kicked, and the man crashed on top of Morgan. Stillgoes grabbed Morgan's arm and wrenched him up and ran him towards Danziger's car. He shoved him in and flung himself after him.

Danziger roared the car away from the kerb and the door jerked shut and Makepeace flung himself at the roofrack. They were thirty yards down the street when the Russian car lurched away from the kerb after them. Morgan looked wildly through the rear window and all he could see was Makepeace's belly flattened against the glass. Danziger swung the car left at the monument, tyres squealing and people scattering, and the car jumped the pavement and the centrifugal force sent Makepeace's legs flying out into midair and he clung with all his might to the roofrack. Danziger straightened the car out and roared across the pedestrian pavement, down into the one-way street, his hand on the horn. Morgan grabbed Makepeace's belt through the window and clung fiercely.

The car went roaring down Pelikanstrasse, horn blaring, cars scattering. A hundred yards behind came the Russian car, leaping onto the pavement at the monument, and now there was the wail of a police car. It swung around the corner of the bank, at the monument. Danziger roared into the intersection of Pelikan Platz, and swung left with a scream of tyres. The Russians' car roared down the one-way street, and the police car came screaming up behind it and the Russian swung out and the police swerved and the co-driver rasped into the transmitter:

'They're doing a hundred kilometres approaching Pelikan Platz, trying to beat us off –'

The Russian swung in front of them again and then went roaring left into the intersection. The police car swung behind, then came up on their side, siren screaming. The Russian swung back in front of him, and there was a crash of metal and the police car swerved and the Russian trod flat on the accelerator again.

Two hundred yards ahead Danziger was roaring across Peterstrasse, people scattering. Ahead was the intersection with Barengasse and the lights were red and Danziger leant on the horn and hunched over the wheel. A truck was entering the intersection, and Danziger rammed his foot flat and he swung right into the intersection, in front of the truck, tyres squealing. And a hundred yards ahead was the park with the pedestrian bridge over the canal.

Morgan clung onto Makepeace and looked back wildly through the rear window. *'They haven't come round the bend yet!'* Danziger drove at the kerb and the car leapt onto the paved park. People were scattering, yelling. Danziger drove for the canal, then slammed on the brakes, and the car screeched to a halt on the bridge.

Morgan let go of Makepeace and scrambled out. He looked wildly back, and he saw the Russian car roaring towards the park but there was no police car. Morgan raced down the steps to the canal, the others bounding behind him. There was the speedboat, engine spluttering. They leapt into the boat. Clark let go of the bank and opened the throttle, and the boat surged out from under the bridge.

It went roaring down the open canal. Morgan looked back and he saw the Russian car screech to a halt at the bridge. Four men burst out and ran to the railings. Two vaulted down onto the footpath, and started running flat out after them. But the boat was already a hundred yards away. The other Russians were frantically pushing Danziger's car out of the way. Clark sent the boat roaring under the next bridge. Now they could no longer see the Russians. They raced under two more bridges, the water flying off the bows, then they were in the last stretch of the canal. Back at the Barengasse the Russians had pushed Danziger's car off the bridge. They piled back into their car and roared across the bridge. They swung left into the narrow street alongside the canal. And now there was the wail of more police cars.

But in the boat they did not hear it above the outboard motor. Ahead was the last bridge, the Quaibrucke. Clark swept underneath it and there was the open Zurich See, the rowboats moored. Clark swept between them, scattering ducks, and he opened the throttle wide.

Morgan looked back. He could not see the Russian car. He peered forward into flying snow. The lake disappeared into greyness. There were no other boats. His heart was still pumping hard. He put his hand on Danziger's shoulder and shouted: 'We have to go for the cars! The Comrades will be waiting at the plane – they must have tracked it here! How else would they know?' Danziger looked at him, his face screwed up against the wind. 'Did you radio the pilot we were coming?'

'Yes.'

'What did he say?'

'Just "Roger".'

'That could have been anybody! So go for the cars!'

Danziger put his hands to Clark's ear and shouted the instruction.

Morgan looked back at Zurich. He could hardly make out the buildings in the snow. He could see no boats following them. He looked forwards, into the flying snow. There were no boats. But there must be a Russian boat waiting somewhere. They sped down the See flat out, and now Zurich was gone in snow and lowering dusk, only a hazy twinkle of lights now.

Clark swung the boat west, and slowed down. They cruised towards the dusky shore, guns ready, peering. Clark reduced the throttle: the boat puttered up against the shore.

Morgan scrambled out, into the icy water, and held the boat. The others scrambled out and clambered onto the bank. Morgan scrambled back into the boat.

'Hey –' Danziger hissed '– where the fuck you going?'

Morgan held a finger out to Makepeace in warning, then he opened the throttle and swung the wheel and the boat surged away. 'Hey! –' Danziger shouted. Morgan opened the throttle wide. The boat went roaring out into the dark, snowy lake. He shouted into the wind:

'*Just keep helping me now, God! . . .*'

36

From Berne you take the train to Brig, way up there in the mountains. At Brig you change to the little electric train that winds up, up into the Alps, through great rock gorges, through Swiss hamlets clinging to the mountainsides; and up, up further, until at last you see the Matterhorn gleaming high and mighty into the sky, the very top of the Alps. At the foot of the Matterhorn is the ski resort of Zermatt. And from Zermatt you take a series of cable cars and tee-bar tows up to the Theodulpass. And there you are, standing on the very knife edge of Switzerland, beside the Matterhorn, and below you is Italy, the ski resort of Cervinia nestling down there, and the Alps stretching away below you, going on and on, all the way to the horizon.

It was three years since Morgan had been there, but he remembered it all clearly.

The train from Berne was half full. Many of the passengers were skiers. Morgan sat in the midst of them, his mind's eye feverishly following that route: the electric train, Zermatt, the cable cars. He was sure he had not been followed from the shore of the Zurich See to Berne. But his eyes darted every time somebody moved, every muscle suddenly tensed to jump up and fight.

And all you do is ski down from the Theodulpass, with all the other skiers, and there you are in Italy, in Cervinia. No passport control when you leave Switzerland, no passport control in Cervinia. And from there you take a bus to the next railway town. And you take a train to Rome . . .

The connecting door slid open with a bang, and Morgan jerked and turned. Then slumped his shoulders. It was a stewardess with a trolley.

And by God he needed a drink . . .

He bought two bottles of beer. Then two small bottles of wine as well.

He ripped open a beer, and swallowed and swallowed and swallowed.

He sat, feeling the balm of the beer, letting the efficient Swiss train take him, looking at the lights flashing past, watching the reflections of the passengers in the window.

And when you get to Rome, then what? . . .

He did not know.

He did not know what he was going to do about this. Whether he *could* do anything. He only knew he could not leave a KGB man as Secretary of State for the Vatican, stalking the corridors of power, plotting the death of the Pope, manipulating eight hundred million Catholics and heads of state for his Moscow masters. He only knew that he could decide nothing and do nothing until he had some local knowledge, knew the lie of the land, physically *saw* it. Local knowledge. Then maybe, just maybe, his options would become clearer. Then he could try to make a plan – go to his rock farm in France and think it all through. Have *time* to think. *Planning* – that's what this whole thing had lacked so far. This was the first opportunity he had had to sit still and *think*, for Christ's sake. He did not give a damn that he had deceived Anna, Anna was Makepeace's problem right now – *stop even thinking about Anna, she is as safe as you can make her.* . . .

He tipped the second can of beer to his mouth and drank it down, down, to stop himself thinking about Anna.

He slumped back trying to feel the balm of it. *You cannot think any more until you have local knowledge.*

And when you have it? What? Go and tell the Pope that his Secretary of State is a KGB man waiting to murder him? Let him sort it out, set his own house in order? But how do you get to see the Pope? Without letting anybody else in the Vatican know why. This must be for the Pope's ears only – otherwise the cat will be out of the bag. And, would the Pope believe him? He might say it was just an old Nazi plot to discredit the Church. And if the Pope did investigate it, who would he entrust? – would that man be trustworthy? Or might he also be a KGB man, recruited by the Secretary of State himself? Maybe the Pope *himself* was under their control now.

Oh Jesus. *Just take one day at a time. Right now all you worry about is getting there.*

He unscrewed the cap off a bottle of wine and took a swallow.

But one thing was sure – the Comrades now knew that he had that microfilm, and they would be in Rome in force. And pretty damn soon the British would know about his little bunfight outside the Union Bank of Switzerland, and they would be in Rome too. Both the bastards gunning for him.

Just take one day at a time.

Think of Anna . . . Thank God he hadn't brought her today.

He took another swallow of wine. Don't think about Anna either. You've done the only bloody thing you could! Where else could she go to be safe? England? . . . No way. Not with Her Majesty's secret services so shameless that they try to heist her inside the Hong Kong & Shanghai bank in New York – what would they do if they found her in England?

Oh, Jesus, the whole business shocked him to the marrow! *Shocked him! The Vatican, the KGB, his own British! . . .*

Oh, God, he was a babe in the woods . . .

Now cut that out. You've done well. You've done marvellously! You've beaten the sons of bitches off in New York and Amsterdam and Zurich! Now all you worry about is getting to Rome. Right now Anna is Makepeace's problem, that's why you've got Makepeace. . . .

It was eight o'clock when the electric train pulled into Zermatt, the ski resort nestling below the Matterhorn.

He waited till all passengers had left his coach. When he got down onto the platform, nobody was lingering. He walked into the main street.

The snow crunched underfoot. It was cold. The street was pretty and alpine, the shops twinkling, and the bars looked cosy. There were quite a lot of people about, their faces ruddy. There were horse-drawn cabs with bells, and small electric-powered taxis, for no cars are allowed in Zermatt. He walked fast, hoping to find a ski shop still open. But they were all closed. The Matterhorn was hidden in cloud. He came to the Platz. There was the hotel he remembered, the Monte Rosa. He walked in.

It is a lovely hotel, with low-beamed ceilings and panelled

walls. He had not stayed here on his holiday in Zermatt, but he had used the bar.

He got a room, in the name of Jefferson, and paid. He walked into the bar.

It was cosy. He sat down at the mahogany bar and ordered a whisky. He took a big sip. It burned, tasting good. And he suddenly felt better, in a respectable public place. They wouldn't dare roll him in here.

The bar was half-full. There was a group of well-scrubbed, middle-aged Americans, talking earnestly. He wondered why Americans talk so goddam loudly. He heard 'related experiences' and 're-evaluations' and 'participated realization' and 'grown-up responses', and he wondered why Americans love abstract nouns so much. And then he realized they were talking about Swiss *wines*. He thought, Amazing people . . . But they were somehow reassuring. And he envied them. Next week they would return to their nice mortgaged homes in Hartford, Connecticut, and Boysie, Idaho, and nobody would try to kill them. The only thing they might die of prematurely was terminal sincerity. He wished he was like that. Just then another one walked into the bar.

She was about thirty-five, and pretty, in a bruised sort of way. Her coat had snow on it. She wore a tweed skirt and fur boots. She glanced around, and then made for the empty stools near Morgan. She flashed him a smile as she sat down. 'Hi.'

'Good evening.'

'A bourbon on the rocks, please,' she said to the barmaid. 'Gee, it's cold outside,' she said to Morgan.

'Very.'

'How's the skiing been?'

Now come on, he thought. This was either the easiest pick-up of his life, or she was a Comrade sent to pick him up. 'Poor today. Have you just arrived?'

'Yes. Isn't that electric train something else?'

In case I noticed you on the train? Or was she for real, just suffering from chronic friendliness? 'Delightful. Should do it in daylight. You touring Switzerland?'

'Uh-huh. Just another American tourist.'

You don't say. But American accents are the easiest to imitate. Hers was a drawl. How much baggage did she have?

260

If she was a Comrade who had followed him from Berne she wouldn't have baggage. She said: 'What's the restaurant like in this hotel?'

Now he was almost sure. 'Very good.'

'Great, then I guess I'll eat in. It's cold out.'

He said: 'You didn't bring ski clothes all the way from America, did you?'

'No, I'm going to buy gear tomorrow.'

Like I am. And he thought, Oh Jesus. But there were scores of people checking into hotels, going to buy or rent ski gear tomorrow. 'What part of America are you from?'

'Texas.'

That accent was phoney. If God had intended Texans to ski He'd have made bullshit white. He said:

'Tell you what. I'm dining in, too. Would you care to join me?'

She gave him a pleasant, bruised smile. 'What a good idea.'

He thought, And I haven't even asked your name. But maybe she was just a lonely all-American tourist, big enough to look after herself over dinner with a fellow guest in a respectable hotel. He felt brutal saying it: 'And afterwards, perhaps we can retire to my room and there make polite, and hopefully efficient, use of each other's bodies.'

There was a silence.

'Perhaps,' she said, 'the subject may come up, more indirectly, after dinner.'

He smiled at her, embarrassed. And he did not know what to think. Except that he wished he'd had the guts to try that one in the past. But she had not knocked him back, and that was enough. He drank down his whisky. He did not even taste it.

'I must shave and freshen up. I'll meet you here in . . . twenty minutes?'

'Fine,' she said, a little frostily.

He walked out of the bar. He followed the signs to the ski locker room. It was empty. He let himself out of the door, into a lane.

He was uptight again. He walked away from the Platz. He turned left and then right down back streets. He looked back. Nobody was following him. He took the next street, to the

261

modern Zermatterhof Hotel, and went in the ski locker door. He went up to the foyer.

He took a single room in the name of Johnson. He paid. If he could have done so he would have left town, but there are no cars in Zermatt, and the train had stopped running.

He went up to this room. Oh God, God, he hoped he was wrong. He hoped he had only spoiled a nice American lady's evening.

He sat on the bed. He touched his pistol under his arm. Then dragged his hands down his face.

If she was a Comrade she would have telephoned her controller from Brig, where they changed trains for Zermatt. And reinforcements would be on the way right now. And there was no way he could get out of town till the morning.

He dared not go down to the restaurant. He picked up the bedside telephone angrily. He ordered a bottle of wine, steak, eggs and chips.

He sat there, waiting for it.

And, oh, just to pick up the telephone again and call the Yab Yum in Amsterdam and speak to Anna, and tell her he loved her . . .

Good God, was he mad? . . . Taking on the KGB and MI6 and the Vatican itself? . . .

He pressed his fingertips to his eyes. *How was he going to get to the Pope?*

37

The night was a turmoil of frightening, shallow dreams. But when he awoke, before first light, unrested, he was almost calm. He would shoot any Russian bastard who came near him. If the bitch was a Comrade, there would be a dozen of them in town by daylight, covering the railway station, the cable cars. If the bitch was a Comrade he was cornered in the Alps and he had only one thing going for him – they had to take him alive, to find out where the microfilm was. And they couldn't do that easily if he kept in the midst of people. And he would shoot and run and go down fighting. He swung out of bed, and telephoned room service for a large pot of coffee. Then he chain-smoked grimly, waiting for the shops to open.

At eight-thirty he left the hotel via the ski locker room. It was a grey day, snowing lightly. He took the back streets. He went into the first shop selling ski gear.

He bought ski trousers, an anorak, goggles, a woollen cap, gloves and a small rucksack. He put them on in the store. He bought a tube of 'Sudden Tan' lotion and rubbed it well into his face in the changing cubicle. He looked in the mirror. The tan looked real. He bought a can of Nivea cream, and smeared the white ointment on his lips. He pulled his cap down low, put his goggles on his forehead. He stuffed his other clothes into the rucksack. He kept his gun in the shoulder holster, under the anorak.

Two doors away was a rental shop. He selected a pair of ski boots. He chose short skis, a hundred and seventy centimetres, to give him easier control. He rented them all for one week, and paid.

He left the store. He lowered his goggles over his eyes. There were plenty of people about now. He shouldered the skis, and set off down the sidestreets, heading for the cable-car station on the slopes.

There were hundreds of skiers trudging up to the cable car. He looked up the mountain. The slopes disappeared into cloud. He tramped up into the bleak station.

There were scores of people. He swept his eyes over them. He did not spot the woman. He looked at the notice board. And gave a sigh of relief. All the ski runs were open despite the cloud. He joined the queue, and bought a one-day ticket.

He clomped up the steps, to the cable-car platform. He went through the door, into the clamour of the cars bumping into each other. And he saw her.

She was leaning against the wall, holding skis, studying a map of the slopes. She was wearing a silver-grey ski suit. Morgan strode past her. She did not look up. He hurried to the cars. There were half a dozen people ahead of him. Each car was for four people. The first four skiers got into the front car, the next couple into the one behind. They slammed the door, and the dispatcher went to lock them in, but Morgan hurriedly rammed his skis into the slot, re-opened the door and scrambled in. They looked peeved. But no way was he going to get into an empty car and give her the chance to ride with him alone. He slammed the door, and the dispatcher locked it.

The car jerked forward. It began to ascend. He looked back.

She was not standing at the wall any longer. He looked at the car behind. There were two people in it. He could not make out faces.

It takes about ten minutes to the first way-station of Furri, up a beautiful yawning canyon, the ski runs twisting down it – but Morgan saw none of it. His nerves were tight. He was sure now she was one of them.

The station loomed up, perched on a crag, its black mouth engorging cable cars. He got ready. The car entered the mouth, swinging. As the dispatcher unlocked the door, he scrambled out. He snatched his skis and strode away. The next car was approaching the mouth. He rounded the corner, and he ran. He could go three ways, to the cafeteria, to the snow, to the next cable-car platform. He clattered up the steps, dodging people.

There were about a hundred people waiting at the platform. A car was just coming in. It was capable of carrying a hundred and twenty people. He made his way into the midst of the crowd.

The car came rocking in. Its gate opened and the passengers began to board. Morgan was amongst the first. He walked to the far corner. He turned and watched.

The car filled up about him. There were still people arriving on the platform. And there she came.

She was hurrying up the steps. The last people were boarding. There was still space. She hurried aboard.

Morgan turned his back and closed his eyes.

Again he did not notice the beauty, the breathtaking chasms. He studied his ski map feverishly. Trying to remember what the different runs looked like, what hills and forks there were to lose her on. There was an '*Aaah*' and he looked up. And there was the Matterhorn.

They had passed through the cloud layer. The great sharp peak reared up, steep and savage, black and white. And there was the knife edge between the mighty Matterhorn and the Klein Matterhorn, the Theodulpass in the saddle, the border of Switzerland and Italy.

Please God she doesn't follow me over it. Please God I don't have to kill her . . .

The car came to rest ponderously at the Trochenersteg platform. The big doors slid open, the skiers started filing out. She had to be amongst the first to leave because she was standing at the door. She walked out, without a backward glance. Morgan hung back. She disappeared off the platform. But he knew what she was doing: standing around the corner, pretending to study her ski plan, waiting for him to emerge. As the last person in front of him stepped out onto the platform, Morgan turned and walked back into the car. The new passengers started coming aboard.

Morgan leant against the far window, and watched the door. She did not reappear.

The door slid shut. The car began to move.

He took a big, tense breath. He had lost her. But there was a snag. He had to come back here, to get up to Theodulpass. If she was a Comrade, she would still be waiting.

38

The cable car clanged to a halt back at the Furri station. Morgan was the first out. He strode through the complex. He saw the arrow pointing to the Schwarzsee cable car. He followed it. A car was loading. He squeezed on board. The doors slid shut behind him.

The car swung out into midair, and began the ascent to the Schwarzsee station. He looked at his ski map feverishly.

There was no way she could be there. No ski runs from Trochenersteg joined up with ski runs to Schwarzsee. He still had to go back to Trochenersteg, where he had lost her. But he would arrive from a different direction, on a different cable-car system, on a different platform.

He strode off the platform at Schwarzsee, clattered down the steps, out onto the snow.

He threw his skis down, dug in his poles. He kicked the ice off his boots, and stepped into the skis, and the bindings snapped on. He shuffled his feet, testing himself. He pulled on his gloves. It was two years since he had done this. He dug in the poles, and shoved off, down the slope.

He kept his skis twelve inches apart. He gathered speed. He bent and stretched his knees, getting the feel of the snow again. Then he dug in one pole and swung his weight. He skidded sideways to a stop. He shoved off down the slope again. He dug in the other pole, and swung into a halt in the other direction, and he sprawled.

'*Shit!*'

He clambered up, angrily. *He had not had his fucking mountain shoulder forward!* He shoved straight off again.

He tried it again. And remembered to turn his mountain shoulder forward. He got it right.

It was over an hour since he had lost her.

The cable car rocked into the Trochenersteg station. He kept in the middle of the disembarking passengers. He tramped through the complex, looking for the silver-grey ski suit. He followed the signs, and emerged onto the snow. He glanced around. There were dozens of people. He did not spot her. He put on his skis.

A few hundred yards below was the tee-bar that would tow him up to the knife edge of the Alps, the Theodulpass. He shoved off and skied down to it.

There was a short queue. She was not in it.

He shared a tee-bar with a dentist from Vienna who said that the beer, wine, food, service, weather, accommodation and skiing was better and cheaper in Austria.

The top of the tow loomed up; at the right moment, he let go. He swung out of the way, and came to a stop. He began to edge up to the very top of the Theodulpass, feverishly.

He came to the top, panting, his legs aching. There below

him was Italy. Snow-clad peaks and valleys stretching on and on, all the way to the horizon. And nestling down there was the Italian ski resort of Cervinia.

There were many people on the slopes, skiing to Cervinia. None seemed to be wearing a silver-grey ski suit.

He dug in his poles and shoved himself off the top.

He skied fast, avoiding the tricky bits, his eyes sweeping the slopes for silver-grey ski gear. He stopped only once, around a hillock, to rest his legs. He edged off the *piste*, and up the hillock for ten yards, and waited. People coming around the bend would not see him unless they looked back. He waited five minutes, and many people flashed past but nobody looked around at him.

He shoved off again.

He passed the cable-car station halfway down the mountain, skiing fast, but avoiding trouble. On the easy bits he looked back over his shoulder. There were plenty of people behind him.

He skied to the lower cable-car station, and swung to a halt. There was not a policeman in sight. He took off his skis, and shouldered them.

He set off down the snowy road, into the resort, trying not to appear in a hurry.

It was not as pretty as Zermatt. There were many cars. He headed towards the square where the buses wait. Before the square he turned left. Halfway down the street was a bar. He went in. It was almost empty.

He ordered a cappuccino. He watched the window. Nobody came in.

He ordered another cappuccino. While the barman prepared it, Morgan went into the toilet.

He locked the door. He pulled his jacket, trousers and shoes out of the rucksack. He took off his ski gear and put on his ordinary clothes. His shoulder holster. He stuffed his ski gear into the haversack. He kept his ski cap on. He picked up the rucksack and walked back to the bar. He pushed a fifty-franc note across to the barman. 'Can I leave my skis here for a couple of days?'

The barman took the banknote. 'Okay, sir.'

'Thank you. Somebody will come to fetch them.'

He paid for his coffees in Swiss money, and left. He made his way by sidestreets, down towards the square.

He was told that the next bus left in forty minutes, to Valtourneche. He bought a ticket, and left the square. He stopped at a souvenir shop and bought a pair of sunglasses, an envelope, and stamps. He went back to the bar.

He ordered coffee, and sat in a corner where he could watch the door. He wrote a letter to the shop in Zermatt from which he had rented the skis and boots. He explained he had hurt himself and told them where the gear was.

Then he sat and drank the coffee, waiting for the minutes to pass. Trying to maintain the reckless calm.

He left the bar after twenty-five minutes. He stopped at a money-changer and converted a thousand dollars into Italian lira. He posted the letter.

The bus was waiting, its engine rumbling.

He sat at the very back. About a dozen people got on after him. None paid any attention to him.

It was a long five minutes' waiting. More people came aboard. Then the door closed with a hiss. And Morgan closed his eyes in relief.

The bus moved off.

A hundred yards down the road he saw her.

He slumped low in his seat. She was walking hurriedly, towards the square. The bus rumbled past her.

Part Seven

39

It was early morning when his train pulled into Orvieto, south of Florence. It was cold and misty. He asked at the ticket office where the bus station was. It was still dark when he got there but the café was open. He caught the next bus to Rome.

It was just after ten o'clock that November morning when he arrived in the suburbs of Rome. He walked a few blocks, until he saw a taxi. He told the driver to take him to the Colosseum.

From here he knew his way to the centre of the city. He walked up the hill, alongside the Esquilino park, to Via Merulana. He stopped at a store selling electrical goods. He bought the cheapest portable tape-recorder. Then he came to the cathedral of Santa María: a few blocks to the right was the railway station. He turned away from it. The railway station was one of the places they would be looking for him.

He found a room in a place called Pensione Umberto. He paid for four days' lodging. His room was on the third floor. It had a telephone.

He locked the door and lay down on the bed. He screwed his eyes up, then looked at the ceiling.

Rome . . . So, he had made it here. Against tremendous odds. And now what? . . .

He ran his hand across his eyes. God, was he mad? . . .

He swung off the bed, and sat up. *Get the calm back* . . .

Local knowledge, that's the first step. See the lie of the land. Determine the possible. Get a map of Vatican City. Brief himself. And get some kind of disguise.

And listen again to the Klaus Barbie tape. Make notes of the names of every Russian boy who had been planted in the Catholic Church and their passwords.

And get those strips of film negatives developed. If they were indeed pornographic, and he could see who was in them, it could tell him a lot. But how do you get pornographic photographs developed? Take them to your friendly Kodak dealer? To a

271

sleazy Italian chemist? What if he makes a few copies and uses them for blackmail too? Everything could blow up then.

Trace Meteor Air. How? Telephone air traffic control in Malta? The airport manager? The Chamber of Commerce?

First things first. He pulled the Barbie cassette out of his bag. He inserted it into the tape-recorder and pushed the rewind button.

'I repeat: "The *whole* world in his hand" . . .'

Morgan smacked the machine off, and lay back on the bed.

How did this tape of Klaus Barbie end up in Max Hapsburg's secret deposit box? . . .

He had turned that question over and over in his mind all the way from Zurich.

'*I'd rather die like God's Banker.*'

Deduction: When she and Max had their drunken row, he had thrown God's Banker's murder at her, as proof that he had the microfilm which would show down her beloved Catholic Church.

Fact: This row had taken place on her birthday, 20th June 1982, two days *after* God's Banker was found hanging.

Fact: Max's forged passport, in the name of Maxwell Constantine, showed that he had flown from New York to London on the eighteenth.

Deduction: Max Hapsburg and God's Banker had both flown to London to do business together about the microfilm.

Deduction: God's Banker, who was bankrupt, intended using the microfilm to blackmail the Vatican.

Deduction: He was murdered to stop him getting it.

Question: What was Max Hapsburg going to get out of it? Money? But he had plenty. Was there some other purpose?

Question: Who murdered God's Banker? The Russians, to protect their secret weapon in the Vatican? Or some persons in the Vatican itself? – to protect the Vatican.

Morgan dragged his hands down his face. Did those two questions matter? Wasn't the only important question: How to get rid of the communist agents in the Church? How does one get to see the Pope?

He swung his legs off the bed and sat up. He picked up the

telephone book. He began to search through it. The pages rattled in his hand. He dialled a number.

'*Informazioni turistichi*,' a female voice said.

'May I please speak to someone who speaks English?'

'Can I help you?'

'I'm a tourist from England. I am in the theatre there, I'm a make-up artist and I would like to meet some people in Rome who do the same work, to compare techniques. Can you suggest how I start?'

'Hold the line please, sir.'

Morgan waited. A minute later the woman came back.

'I suggest you try the Teatro Romano. Here is their number . . .'

Five minutes later he was speaking to a Dutchman called Hugo de Vries.

'Sure,' Hugo said. 'Always a pleasure to meet other people in the game. What company do you work for?'

'The Royal Shakespeare. Stratford-upon-Avon.'

'Nothing but the best, huh? Good, come by the theatre at five o'clock tonight, we'll be making up the actors then, I'll give you a tour.'

Morgan said: 'Is it possible for us to meet now?'

'Sure, why not? We can have lunch in the canteen. I'm on the second door, back. Just ask for Hugo if you get lost . . .'

He was a skinny man, six foot four. His room looked like a run-down hair salon. Plastic heads everywhere. A long mirror bordered with light bulbs. A long table covered in cosmetics. Shelves of wigs. A workbench with a half-finished wig on it.

'The finest lace. Flesh-coloured. I stitch each hair on by hand. Real human hair. Once it's glued on, you need a magnifying glass to see it's a wig.' He went to an old refrigerator and got out two beers. 'But you're not into wigs yourself?'

'No,' Morgan said. 'But I'm interested in everything.' He added, for something quick to say: 'How do you get the wig off?'

Hugo looked at him. 'With acetone. What do you use?'

'Acetone, too,' Morgan said hastily. 'I just wondered if you had something special.'

Hugo smiled at him.

'What do you actually do in theatre?'

Oh God, he was too tired to act. He looked at Hugo wearily.

'Look, I'm sorry. I'm not really in theatre. That was just a ploy, to get to talk to you.' Hugo stared at him. 'You see, I'm doing some detective work. I need to be in disguise.' He looked at him squarely. 'Would you make me up, for a fee? Wig, moustache, et cetera?'

'Detective work, huh?'

Morgan sighed. 'Look, I can go to a hairdresser and get a wig. I can go to a novelty shop and buy a moustache. But I want it to stand up to close scrutiny.'

'What are you detecting?'

'Does it matter?'

'Yes, it does matter. Are you a legitimate private detective? Show me your identification.'

Morgan shook his head wearily. 'No, I'm not a certificated detective. But that's what I'm doing. It concerns my wife.'

'Your wife?'

'Okay, my girlfriend. She's the same as a wife.'

'And what's she up to?'

'What do you think? I want to follow her and find out. She's on holiday in Rome. She thinks I'm back home.'

Hugo turned away. A long pause.

'You assure me this is legal?'

'Absolutely legal.'

'You're not going to rob a bank, or something?'

Morgan smiled, despite himself. 'No.'

Pause. 'Do I get my wig and moustache back afterwards?'

'If you want. But I would prefer to buy them off you.'

Another pause. Then:

'If I get my wig back it's one hundred pounds. If you keep the wig, three hundred pounds. And that's cheap.'

Relief. 'Fine,' Morgan said. 'But I'll have to pay you in dollars.'

'Okay. What size head are you?'

'I don't know.'

'About fifty-eight. Have you got the money?'

Morgan pulled out a wad of notes. He counted out four hundred and fifty dollars.

'Okay,' Hugo said. 'You bring the wig back, you get back

274

three hundred dollars.' He was all business suddenly. 'Sit.'

Morgan hesitated, then decided to try it.

'Something else you may be able to help me with? Do you have any way of developing pornographic pictures? With complete confidentiality.'

Hugo blinked. 'Pornographic? Of whom?'

'My girlfriend, I think. I've only got the negatives.'

'You think? Who took them?'

'I don't know. I found them amongst her things, after she left. That's why I followed her here.'

Hugo leant on the chair. 'No I don't. And I'm liking this less and less. You assure me what you're doing is legal?'

'I do. Okay, forget it.' He sat down before the man changed his mind.

Hugo stood behind him, and put his hands on his shoulders with some misgiving. He looked at him in the mirror.

'If I make you an Italian, I'll have to do a lot of cosmetic work. But your complexion is easy for a brunette. What do you want?'

'Not Italian. I don't want to worry about cosmetics.'

'How about a wavy chestnut hairstyle?'

'Good.'

'Ten years older? A touch of grey?'

'Good.'

'Okay ... .' Hugo said.

He set to work.

40

It was a strange feeling, and a comforting one. He felt *incognito*.

He walked into a department store. He bought an umbrella and a raincoat. He watched the salesman closely, and the man did not appear to look at the wig or moustache.

He left the store, and walked until he saw a taxi.

'*Vaticano, prego.*'

It was almost two o'clock. He settled into the back seat, and closed his eyes.

It was raining. The taxi crossed the Ponte Umberto and turned left along the Tiber. And then there, to the right, was the Via della Conciliazione, sweeping up to the crescent of colonnades, the open arms of Saint Peter's Square. And Morgan felt his primitive Catholic heart turn over.

He looked up at the statues of the saints looming up against the rainy skyline, the mighty dome arching up above the crypt of Saint Peter himself, and he felt the age-old Catholic awe of coming to the holy of holies, the very heart of the Roman Church; and he loved it, and feared it, and he knew that he was a Catholic in his marrow. And he knew with absolute certainty that he was doing the right thing, and more than anything he wanted the right thing to happen for the Church.

There were tourists huddled under umbrellas around guides. Morgan told the taxi-driver to turn into the sidestreets on the edge of the Vatican City. He told him to stop when he saw a bookstore.

There were hardly any people on the streets, because of the rain. He hurried into the store.

He examined all the guide books on the Vatican City. He chose the one with the longest text, and he bought a large pictorial map.

Down a sidestreet he found a bar. It was a cosy place, chianti bottles hanging from the ceiling. He sat at a table in the corner and ordered spaghetti and a bottle of red wine. He opened his map and the guide book.

It was an excellent pictorial map, like an aerial photograph.

It was clear that the Pope's palace was connected by a series of rooftops to the southern wall of Saint Peter's cathedral. From the map, it seemed possible to lower oneself by rope from the rooftop of the cathedral, onto a rooftop below, and make one's way by connecting roofs to the papal palace.

Sure, a good burglar could do it. And Morgan had been trained for this sort of thing. But doubtless this possibility had not escaped the attention of the bright boys responsible for Vatican security. That palace rooftop was surely bristling with alarm devices. Sure, a nutter had managed to get into Buckingham Palace, sit on Her Majesty's bed and have a midnight chat with her. But he bet nobody could pull off the same trick now.

Another possibility: the Gate of Saint Anne was the business entrance into the Vatican City itself. Every day hundreds of cars and thousands of people who worked in the Vatican City passed through those gates. There were sentries and one had to have a pass. But surely it would be possible to get a pass somehow, get through the gate, and thence to the papal front door. Disguised as a priest, for example. Better still, disguised as a monsignor – purple bib and purple socks. Most people don't challenge monsignors.

All right . . . Doubtless it could be done. But, a lot of homework. A monsignor visiting Rome from where? He would have to have a perfect story. What's his reason for needing an audience with His Holiness? How would such a priest go about it? Write a letter? Telephone for an appointment? How many officials would he have to bluff his way through? If he said it was a matter of life and death, for the Pope's ears only? . . .

By the time he had finished the wine he had learned one important fact from the guide book: the Pope himself sometimes heard confession from the public. This was only at Easter on a regular basis, but there were other times. One could enquire at the Vatican Information Bureau, about what other functions he officiated at. One applied at the Prefecture for permits to attend a mass audience the Pope gave to visitors.

When the Pope heard confession he would have an opportunity to speak to him . . .

And say what? 'I've got to see you in private, to tell you something very important. To save the Church . . .'?

Morgan lit a cigarette, and blew out smoke.

It was a very long shot. He would have a very short time to convince the man, before he was politely told to go away. Dismissed as a nutter.

But it was worth thinking about. Though it meant waiting until Easter. Almost six months hence.

And then he thought of something else: Does the Secretary of State, Cardinal Pieter Gunter, also hear confession from the public? . . .

If Cardinal Gunter heard confession, he would get a very

different reception. Because all he would have to say were the passwords . . .

Morgan pulled out the list he had made that morning. 'The elk is not only a Siberian creature.' Those were Pieter Gunter's passwords.

He sat back, thinking.

Go into the confessional, say those words, tell the man you want to see him privately. *He would not dare refuse.* Even if he had found God since being planted in the Church he would not dare refuse for fear I blow the whistle on him. He would have to find out what I want . . .

Suddenly somebody was standing at the table. Morgan jerked. It was the waiter. Asking him if he wanted anything before the kitchen closed.

Morgan folded his map, and paid his bill.

He hunched into his raincoat. Okay, this was what he had come to Rome for. He would soon find out if his disguise was effective.

He tried to look like a tourist, his guide book in hand. He walked under the curving colonnades. Then, on the right, was the flight of stone steps leading up into the Prefecture. Two Swiss guards, in their medieval uniforms, stood at the top, armed with lances. Morgan ascended the wide steps.

'I wish to apply to the Prefecture for a permit.'

The officer waved him through, and pointed at another staircase. Morgan passed the guards' room. He wondered if there was a cell in there, for people like him. The staircase was baronial. Stone balustrade. A coat of arms. Grey stone walls. Two security guards in dark uniforms on the first floor. 'Permit, please . . .'

They waved him through another door. A small office, marble floors, a desk. A grey-haired priest was bent over documents. '*Avanti.*' There was no friendliness in the voice.

'May I have a permit to visit the tombs, please?'

'It'll have to be for tomorrow.' It was an Australian accent.

'Thank you.' Morgan took a breath. 'Tell me, is it possible to get a permit to visit the Secretariat of State?'

The priest looked at him. 'No. Why?'

'You see,' Morgan said, 'I'm making a study of the Church, to write a book. This is my first visit to the Vatican, I'm just feeling my way, getting the atmosphere. I've come all the way from Australia for this . . .'

'Where in Australia?'

'Sydney.' He had been there once and stayed with friends in Double Bay. 'Belleview Road.'

'You don't sound Australian.'

'I'm not yet. Will be in a few years. I've immigrated.'

The priest nodded. 'It would be a great country if they could get rid of the corruption.'

'*Right*. How long have you been over here?' Keep the man talking.

The priest sat back. 'So you want to write a book on the Church? You a Catholic?'

'I suppose you would call me a lapsed Catholic. Who is finding his way back to the Church.'

'What brought this on?'

He said, almost truthfully: 'It's something I've been wanting to do for a long time. And lacked the courage, maybe.'

'"Oh Lord, make me good, but not yet"?'

Morgan smiled. 'Saint Augustine. Yes.' And it was almost true. He went on, while the iron was warm: 'I wonder if you would be so kind as to refer me to . . . anybody who could point me in the right direction on certain aspects.'

'Of?'

'I'm after general atmosphere at this stage, while I'm in Rome. How the modern Vatican works. Day-to-day. The protocol, the colour, the ceremony . . . In particular, I'm interested in the political role of the Church.'

'Well, we're an open book. The Procurators of the various religious orders may be prepared to give you some time. There're two English-speaking seminaries, British and American, where students study for the priesthood – somebody there may think it fun to help you.' He added: 'To help bring a sheep back into the fold.'

'Where are they?'

'Ask the Information Bureau. Which,' he added, 'this office is not.'

'I see. Thank you. One more thing. When does the Pope next

celebrate mass, publicly? When the public can take communion from him.'

'Christmas week.'

Christmas! That was only six weeks away!

'Does he also personally hear confession from the public then?'

'Yes.'

He almost blurted it: 'How does one know which confessional box he's in?'

'You'll have to keep your eyes open. You and the thousands of other people who think it would be nice to say your confession to the Pope himself. That is hardly the attitude to adopt to confession.'

'"Nice" is not my attitude,' Morgan said.

'Good,' he said unsmilingly.

'It would have a special spiritual significance for me.' He added, 'Can you tell me, do senior cardinals, like the Secretary of State, hear confession from the public, too?'

'All priests perform religious duties. But Secretaries of State usually have more pressing things to do.'

'How can I find out details like that?'

'Not from this office, I'm afraid. Try the Procurators.'

Morgan knew he was pushing his luck. 'But would you be so kind . . . if I telephoned you, would you tell me whether the Pope has scheduled a public mass and confession before Christmas?'

'I'm afraid not. If you want a friend in court, you'll have to look elsewhere.'

Morgan put on his most charming smile. 'Not even to bring an errant sheep back into the fold?'

The Australian almost smiled for the first time.

'Ah, you think you've got me there. Yes, saving souls is still my business even if I'm a pen-pusher. But if you're serious about your soul, there're better people for the job than me.' He sloughed over that one. 'All right, I'll say goodbye now.' He lowered his head over his papers.

It had stopped raining, but it was freezing after the warm Prefecture. He pulled up his collar and walked briskly up the wide stone steps into the portico of the basilica.

There were many tourists, wet and discommoded, huddled around guides. He walked through the great bronze doors, into Saint Peter's.

He intended going straight to the southern side of the great cathedral, to the elevator which takes tourists up onto the rooftop. But he just had to stop for a moment, and look at the majesty of the holy place.

The majesty of it. He stood, taking it in, feeling. And, oh yes, he knew he was a Catholic, in his bones, that this was the very heart of Christianity, the supreme temple. And with all his heart he wanted to do the right thing by this place and all it stood for. And, oh God, he wanted to pray for that.

But he did not have time. He turned, and strode through the vast cathedral, to the elevator.

He paid, and rode up to the top with half a dozen tourists. He walked out, onto the red-tile rooftop.

The dome rising up; and all around lay Rome, misty in the grey afternoon.

He walked to the front, to the statues of Christ and the apostles: and looked down onto Saint Peter's Square. The tiny people down there. He wondered which of them were looking for him. He looked to the left. The papal palace . . .

He studied it. Five storeys high, built around a courtyard. Brown stucco in colour, a red-tile roof. He knew from his map which were the windows of the Pope's apartment – the top right-hand corner. The second-last window was the one he appeared at to give his blessing to the masses. Three floors below was the apartment of the Secretary of State, Cardinal Pieter Gunter.

The rooftop. Part of it, the northern side, was flat.

Morgan walked slowly past the row of saints. To the corner, closest to the palace. He ran his eye slowly along the connecting rooftop. Then looked at his map.

Yes, the roof of the palace was connected to the rooftops of the *Loggias*, from there to the Court of the Pappagalli, and from there, by other roofs, to the very wall of Saint Peter's, where he now stood. He could lower himself by rope down onto the rooftop below. And with a bit of courage, make it all the way to the Pope's rooftop.

All right. It could be done. That's all he wanted to know.

He rode down in the elevator. Back into the mighty cathedral.

He went to the holy-water stoup. It was held by two marble cherubims bigger than himself. He dipped his finger in the water, and crossed himself. Then he walked down the vast, marble-floored nave, towards the Confessio. The very heart of the temple, the sunken tomb of Saint Peter himself.

Morgan walked slowly towards it, feeling the majesty of the holy place. Between the great twisted pillars of the baldachin canopy he could see the throne of Saint Peter at the very apex of the apse. The light of the stained-glass windows glowing down upon it, like the Holy Spirit. Morgan stood beside the tomb, in the flickering lamplights, and he looked up at the mighty dome above him, reaching up, up, the mosaics depicting Paradise aglow in the light coming in from the windows up there: and inscribed around the base the holy words, in Latin: *'Thou art Peter, and upon this rock I build my church, and the gates of Hades shall not prevail against it.'*

He turned away. He walked into the southern pier of the nave. He began to count the confessional boxes.

They were heavy, elaborately carved kiosks. On one side, behind a stable door, sat the priest-confessor: on the other side the penitent knelt and whispered his confession. There were eight such boxes in the first pier of the apse, and each had a notice over the door indicating the language which the priest spoke: Italian, English, French, Dutch, German.

Morgan walked down the side of the nave, counting all the way back to the entrance; then down the other side of the nave, back to the northern pier.

He counted over twenty-four confessional boxes in all.

He walked away, towards the black, bronze statue of Saint Peter. He looked at it. The toe of the statue's foot was worn away, from people kissing it. He reached out and touched the toe, and then crossed himself again. But he was not thinking about Saint Peter.

In which confessional would Pope John Paul sit on that day in Christmas week?

He walked slowly back up the centre of the nave.

In Christmas week this vast nave would be chock-a-block with pews. If he were sitting here, in the approximate centre, how many confessional boxes would he see?

Only about four. And would he recognize the Pope from that distance? In the gloom?

What robes would he be wearing?

He had to find out these details. Or he wouldn't stand a chance.

He walked slowly back towards Saint Peter's sunken tomb, trying to evaluate the best place from which he could keep watch on the maximum number of confessionals. From here, six. From here, eight.

From here, almost in front of the sunken tomb of Saint Peter, twelve.

Okay . . . He had reduced the odds significantly. But they were still long.

Which entrance does the Pope enter by? . . . That would narrow the odds again.

Does he sneak in by a side entrance, and go to any confessional? Or does he come down the centre of the nave, with fanfare? And what language would he hear confession in? . . . If he knew that he would narrow the odds further.

But it was still hit or miss.

It was raining again. He put up his umbrella. He walked back across Saint Peter's Square. Down the back streets, to a public telephone. He dialled the Tourist Bureau again.

'I'm a journalist from England, visiting Rome. Can you please give me the address of the Press Club?'

41

Press clubs are similar the world over: the members are hard-bitten, hard-drinking, hard-working (or so they say), hard-talking, and friendly. And evidently, in Rome, hard of hearing. There was a babble of voices, in half a dozen languages, pressmen loudly arguing, telling stories, complaining, laughing. Nobody challenged him when he walked in, but he had an alibi ready. He found a place at the bar and ordered a beer.

'Excuse me,' he said to the man next to him. 'Do you know Cyril Wilkinson?'

'Who?'

'Cy Wilkinson. He's a BBC man, told me to meet him here.'

'Can't rely on the BBC,' the man said jovially.

'I hope I haven't missed him, he's only in Rome for one day. He was going to introduce me to some Vatican-watchers.'

'Plenty of them around here.'

'But I'm not a member, he was going to sign me in.'

'I'll sign you in if he doesn't show. Why you want to meet Vatican-watchers?'

'I'm trying to write a book.'

'Nice man,' Tony Watson said. 'A really *nice* man.'

'Superstar,' Whacker Ball growled. 'Thinks he's a superstar.'

'Have you met him?' Morgan said to Tony.

'I've been to his press conferences. And you can *see* his charm. You can feel his presence across a crowded room.'

'Some en*chanted* evening,' Whacker crooned.

'And when he speaks, he's so good. *Clever* is the only word. He commands attention. And charming. Have you read his book, *Letters to the Mighty*?'

Morgan shook his head. 'But I will.'

'He is an excellent Secretary of State. In fact, with Pope John Paul running around the world so much he virtually runs the whole Church as Carmalengo – sort of deputy Pope.'

Morgan said, 'Does a man like that ever actually hear confession? – from the public?'

Tony shrugged. 'I don't know. The Pope sometimes does.'

'Yes,' Morgan said. 'When he does, is it known which confession box he's going to use?'

'No. Otherwise there'd be a queue a mile long.'

'Which is another thing,' Whacker complained. 'Why does the Pope do it so seldom? What happened to the good old days when the apostles were approachable by all? Fishermen and carpenters. Nowadays, if you want to see God's vicar you have got to be an ambassador at least.' He turned to Morgan. 'Do you know what his papal jet tours cost last year? Over a hundred and thirty *million* dollars. Meanwhile people are starving in Africa.'

'He's reaching the masses,' Tony said, 'spreading Christianity.'

'Pity he doesn't spread a little more largesse. I, you may gather,' Whacker said to Morgan, 'am a Protestant.'

'Fact or fiction?' Whacker growled.

Tony had gone. Whacker was a heavy, jowly man with grey hair and a whisky tan.

'Fiction. But my facts must be accurate.'

'A book . . .' Whacker complained. 'Isn't a newspaperman alive who doesn't want to write a book. But can we? No, it's bloody lawyers and housewives who can't even spell who write the books and make the money, while we professional wordsmiths who feed them all the stories every day just get cirrhosis of the liver and several divorces. All right . . . So you've come to Rome to sniff out a story. What's your hero's problem?'

It felt good to be amongst almost-normal people, not hiding. 'He has to get to see the Pope privately.'

'Tricky. If not impossible. What's his job?'

'He's a private detective.'

'And why's he got to see the Pope?'

'Because the Pope is about to be murdered.'

'Ah. And why doesn't he tell the police? Or his ambassador?'

'Because they'll say he's a nutter.'

'Uphill struggle all the way, huh? Conflict, that's what stories are made of.' Whacker hunched aggressively over his glass. 'Which is another thing that annoys me. Somebody wants to see his Pope. To discuss some very important moral issue, say. Like starvation. Or to have his soul saved. Can he? No. The apostles went out and spoke to everybody, against the slings and arrows of outrageous fortune. But the Pope? Oh no, he's royalty. If you want to see the Pope you've got to have an ambassador recommending you in triplicate, your application is scrutinized right the way to the top. If you're just a nice private detective, forget it.'

'What would happen if he wrote the Pope a letter saying he had vital secret information, for the Pope's ears only?'

'What happens if you write a letter to the Queen of England? She wouldn't even see it. Every day Buckingham Palace and the papal palace receive tons of mail from nutcases.' Whacker shook his head. 'Your man's letter to the Pope would be filtered through half a dozen officials. It would probably be chucked in the waste-paper basket. Anyway, it wouldn't be secret any more.'

Morgan sat back. 'Are there any *un*official channels?'

'Of course. Your detective could do what Clint Eastwood would, and shin up the drainpipe. Or pretend he's come to repair the television.' He shrugged. 'Unofficial? Sure. But you've got to be pretty official to use them.'

'Meaning?'

Whacker sighed irritably. 'Meaning that the Vatican, just like any government, has its information network, its spies. Particularly in Rome. Rome is full of diplomats. There're parties which diplomats attend for the principal reason of picking up titbits of information. Rome is full of rumours and gossip the Vatican needs to hear. Now, your detective could somehow wangle an invitation to one of these parties, and somehow send an unofficial message to the Pope.'

'Does the Pope attend any of these parties?'

'Occasionally. But he's pretty hard to get close enough to whisper in his holy ear.'

'Could I wangle an invitation to such a party?'

'You'd have to be very lucky in pulling your strings. And patient.'

Morgan sighed. 'What about the Secretary of State? My man also wants to see him.'

Whacker shook his head. 'Same problem. Even if you somehow get an official pass to enter the Vatican you still would not get past the reception area of the Secretariat. Unless, again, you have an introduction from somebody like an ambassador.'

'But he'd get as far as the reception area?'

'Yes.'

Morgan thought: And I hand the receptionist a letter addressed to Cardinal Gunter, marked personal, and written inside is simply *The elk is not only a Siberian creature . . . Meet me at so-and-so*. Would the cardinal get it? Or would it be opened by a secretary? And the secret would be out.

'Of course,' Whacker went on, 'your detective would find it easier to meet the Secretary of State *outside* Vatican City.

Because, being a somewhat lesser mortal, the Secretary can have a more informal private life. Go out to restaurants, for example. Play golf. Without fanfare and a host of security men.'

Morgan looked at him. 'Does Cardinal Gunter play golf?'

'Yes.'

'Which club does he play at?'

'He's a member of the Appia Antia Country Club.'

Morgan felt elated. 'How often does he play?'

'I've no idea, I'm not a golfer.' He added: 'Bill Fletcher's a member. He's a stringer for the *Guardian*. Look his number up in the book.'

'Thanks.' Morgan made a note. He felt he was getting somewhere at last. 'Which restaurant have you seen the Secretary of State dining in?'

Whacker sighed. 'I've seen him at Borodini's. That's a famous joint. But he gets around a lot, I'm told.'

Morgan said: 'The Calvi affair – God's Banker, who was found hanging from Blackfriars Bridge. Do you think it was suicide?'

'Is this for this book of yours?'

'Maybe I can work it in.' He stood up. 'Another scotch?'

He went to the bar and came back with a double whisky, and a beer for himself. Whacker growled:

'Who commits suicide like that? When he's got a gun – a clean way out. Besides, he wasn't desperate enough. His bank may have been bankrupt but he himself was a multi-millionaire – he'd been robbing his own banks for years.'

'Why did he go to London, do you think?'

'You better talk to Mike Milano. He's an Italian–American journalist. He really dug into the Calvi affair, covered the inquest in London, the prosecution of Calvi in Italy, the lot. Thinking of writing a book himself.' He pointed at Morgan's notebook. '"Miguel Milano, *Il Figaro* newspaper".'

Morgan made a scrawled note. 'Thanks.'

'Don't say thanks every time, it makes me nervous.'

'Sorry.'

'Or sorry.'

'Okay.' Morgan grinned. It was a relief to smile.

Whacker said, 'Of course, the Vatican's got a spy network.

Maybe your detective could get to the Pope through one of them.'

Morgan looked at him. 'Do you know any of them?'

'A good spy doesn't admit it, you know. But yes, I've heard of one in particular.' He sighed. 'I'll make a phone call. She better tell you herself, it's her story. How do you fancy a pizza, around the corner?'

It was a *trattoria* called Mamma Mía near the Press Club. It had candles in chianti bottles and the waiters sometimes burst into song.

Renata was a pretty German woman of about thirty-five, with long brown hair and a sallow face, without make-up. She moved with difficulty, with a walking stick. She said:

'Anyway, the doctors don't know what to do with me. And that's how I met him. He's a masseur. At the Sacred Heart hospital.'

Whacker rumbled: 'That's a Church-run hospital.'

Renata said: 'He's famous, as a masseur. Supposed to have almost a healing power. The diplomats go to him. Including Pope John Paul. All this is no secret. His name's Benetti.'

Morgan made a note. Renata went on:

'I went to him, for my illness. The Nigerian ambassador arranged it.'

'Nigerian?'

'I worked for Save the Children and other affiliated organizations. I travelled a lot. I knew a lot of embassy people here in Rome, particularly from black countries. The black embassy people go to Benetti a lot, you know how they love a hint of magic.'

'And this Benetti is part of the Vatican information network?'

She said, 'He hears a lot of gossip. He goes to ambassadors' homes, to do massage. He's invited to their parties. A lot of big industrialists go to him too. He knows all the big-wigs, either as patients or socially. And he reports to the Pope.' She added: 'He's been around a long time.'

'How do you know he reports to the Pope?'

'Rumours,' Whacker growled. 'This town is full of rumours.'

'But it's true.' She nibbled a piece of pizza. She had no appetite. 'Once my organization needed a new engine for a

288

helicopter, in Chad. That was during Gaddaffi's invasion of Chad. It had to come from America. It was forbidden to supply it, because of America's embargo of trade with Libya. We were helpless. I mentioned it to Benetti while he was massaging me. He said, No problem. The next day the engine arrived from America, in transit to Chad. Customs, papers, everything legal.'

'That wasn't the Pope's handiwork,' Whacker rumbled.

'In *one* day? It was the Pope himself who picked up a telephone to the White House.' She turned to Morgan. 'Once, I needed a visa to Angola very urgently. You know what these communist countries are like. Two weeks to wait, minimum. I phoned Benetti. I had a visa in one hour.'

'The Pope doesn't issue visas to Angola,' Whacker complained.

'But *one hour*?' She turned to him irritably: 'And I'll tell you something else, Whacker. I haven't told you before because you're such a pain in the ass!'

'If you had an ass like mine,' Whacker said, 'you wouldn't find anybody to massage you.'

Renata sat back with a sigh. 'All right, forget it.'

'What?' Morgan and Whacker said simultaneously.

She shook her head.

'I was only pulling your leg,' Whacker said apologetically. 'This man is trying to write a book.'

'My legs are the problem.' She smiled bitterly. 'And they used to be good legs.' She turned to Morgan. 'Benetti is a very spiritual man. Intense. And . . .' She sighed, ready to be disbelieved. 'He told me he had asked the Pope to pray for me. But it didn't do me any good.'

There was a silence. Whacker staring at his wine glass.

She said, 'But maybe that's my fault. I'm a non-believer.' She paused. 'No, not a non-believer, really. I just don't believe in German priests ardently praying for victory over British soldiers who have British priests ardently praying for victory over German soldiers.' She frowned at him, with liquid eyes. 'What nonsense. Go out to Central Africa and see the starving children. Little things with legs like sticks, who have never done anybody any harm. And all you pray for is *rain*. Not bread. Not medicine and donations . . .' She spread her hands to the ceiling. 'Just water from the skies, to make the crops grow, grass to feed the goats. Nothing complicated.' She snapped her fingers. 'God could do it like *that*.'

She waited. Morgan nodded. She sat back.

'Well,' she said, 'in comparison to ugly Africa, what an unimportant matter is Renata Schuman's pretty legs . . .'

It was almost midnight when Morgan and Renata rode up in the elevator to her apartment. He followed her slowly down the corridor, to her door.

'Thank you, Renata. You've been very kind to help me.'

She leant on her stick. 'Will you not come in for a nightcap?'

He had drunk more than enough, but if she hadn't asked him he had intended inviting her to dinner tomorrow because he wanted to meet Benetti. 'You're not too tired?'

She inserted the key. 'The nights are long these days.' He followed her in. She said: 'Will you get the drinks?' She pointed with her stick at the bar. 'I'll have cognac.'

It was a pleasant apartment, decorated with African artefacts. She eased herself onto one of the bar stools. She said: 'I like bars. When I'm sitting on a bar stool I look normal.' Her stick clattered to the floor. She smiled at him: 'And now tell me what further help you want from me?'

He liked her. She was perspicacious. And he was too tired to play it softly-softly.

'About Benetti, the masseur? Would it be possible to meet him?'

'You or your detective?'

'Me.'

She smiled. 'If you have a muscular problem.'

He said, 'I do. My back.'

'How boring. Tell him you've got sciatica. It's hard to detect and harder to treat.'

'That's what I've got.'

'Apart from your terrible case of sciatica, why do you actually want to meet the man?'

He smiled. 'To get authentic detail. Hemingway said, "Never write about things you haven't experienced."' He added: 'Does Benetti report only to the Pope, or to the Secretary of State as well?'

290

'I suppose that would depend on the nature of the information. What's your story actually about?'

Morgan smiled shyly. 'My hero believes there's a plot to murder the Pope.'

'I see . . .' She rested her chin on her laced knuckles. 'Do you know how true your story may be?'

He was ready to believe almost anything now. 'There's a plot against the Pope?'

Renata said dramatically: 'Against the *last* Pope. Pope John Paul I reigned for only thirty-three days, then he was murdered.'

Morgan looked at her. Klaus Barbie had claimed that too.

'What makes you say that?'

Renata said flatly:

'There was an outcry from the Italian press about the suspicious way the Vatican behaved.' She held up a finger: 'Why did the Vatican forbid an autopsy to find out why the newly elected Pope died? In Italy, like in every civilized country, there must be a Certificate of Death, certifying the *cause* of death. To ensure there's no foul play. Usually the family doctor, who attended the man through his last illness, can certify that. Then he can be legally buried, and his estate distributed to his heirs. But if a *healthy* man dies – even if he's a beggar on the street – there *must be an autopsy*. That's the law.' She raised her eyebrows. 'But the Vatican is a law unto itself. Legally the Vatican is an independent sovereign state. The Italian police could do nothing.' She snorted. 'There were other suspicious circumstances. There were lies. I forget them now. But the Vatican had him immediately embalmed. And he was a healthy man! The Italian press was up in arms. But they got no answers. Now, *why*?'

If what she said was true, he thought he knew why. 'And if I were to go back through the Italian press files, I'll find all this written up?'

'Of course.' She pointed at his nose. 'You write a book about *that*, Jack Armstrong! . . . Can you read Italian?'

'No.'

'Well I can. I'll go to the public library and dig out their newspaper files.' She took a breath of determination. 'And I'll see if I can arrange for you to have an appointment with

Benetti.' She added: 'I'll have to tell him – or imply – that we are close. Lovers. If that's all right.'

'Of course. This is very kind of you, Renata.'

'I want to help you with that book . . .' Then she smiled. 'On the other hand, psychiatrists would say it's because I'm a cripple. The lonely girl eager to ingratiate herself with the tall handsome stranger.'

He was on his guard. 'You shouldn't be lonely. You're a very attractive woman.'

'Ah, yes. The mirror tells me that too. But many do not like to take out an attractive woman with a walking stick. Even though I do not take the stick to bed.' She smiled.

He did not know what to say to that.

'Have you a way of finding out whether the Secretary of State ever hears confession? And if so, where and when?'

She thought.

'I don't. But I'll try.' She smiled. 'You want to whisper something in the Secretary of State's ear?'

'My hero does. I need authentic detail.' He went on: 'You said you know the Nigerian ambassador. Do you ever get invited to any embassy parties?'

'Yes. I don't always go, I don't like standing.'

'Round Christmas, aren't there a lot of embassy parties?'

She smiled. 'You want me to take you as my escort?'

Morgan was embarrassed. 'If you'd be so kind.' He added: 'Does the Secretary of State attend these parties?'

'He's usually invited, but often sends a representative. I may be able to find out if he's coming, on the grapevine.'

God, he might be lucky. 'If I telephone you, say, twice a week in December, will you tell me what parties you're invited to?'

She said: 'You're going away?'

'Yes. But not for a day or two. And I'll be back.'

She nodded sadly. 'Yes, you can telephone me.' She paused. 'And I shall start work on those newspaper cuttings for you. I have an engagement tomorrow night. Would you like to call me day after tomorrow? And see what progress I have made. And come around for a drink?'

'Thank you, yes.'

She sighed. 'All the interesting people are always going away somewhere.' She glanced at him. 'When you come back to

Rome you may stay here, if you wish.' She added: 'I have a spare room.'

He did not want to accept that. 'That's very kind of you.'

She glanced away, embarrassed. 'In fact, you may stay tonight if you wish. It is late and it is raining.'

He mentally closed his eyes. He would sleep with her if he had to, to keep her on his side, but with all his heart he wanted to be true to Anna. 'That's very kind, but I must make an early start in the morning.'

'Where are you staying?'

He said, without thinking: 'A place called Pensione Umberto.'

'I think I have seen it.' She sighed. 'Will you not have one more for the road, as the English say?'

'I really must be going.'

She sighed again. She bent, and picked up her stick.

He followed her to the door. She turned and faced him. She stretched, and kissed his cheek. '*Au revoir.*'

'*Au revoir.*' He kissed her cheek. And she slid her arms around his neck.

She held him a moment. Then turned for the door. She slid back the latch.

'Good night,' she smiled.

'Good night, Renata,' he said.

When he got down to the street he realized something and he was annoyed with himself: he could not go back to his pensione wearing this bloody wig and moustache. They wouldn't recognize him. Or if they did they would be very suspicious. He had the acetone and cotton wool which the Dutchman had given him but he needed a washbasin to remove the disguise. And even if he did manage to remove it in a dark alleyway, tomorrow morning he could not walk out of the pensione wearing the disguise. So he would have to don it in the street again.

He sighed angrily. He set off through the rain.

Looking for a taxi, to take him to another hotel.

It was after one o'clock when he checked into the Excelsior.

He locked his bedroom door. He went into the bathroom, soaked the cotton wool with acetone, then dabbed it across his lip and hairline.

293

A minute later he had both moustache and wig off. He washed his face.

He went into the bedroom. He collapsed on the bed. And stared up at the ceiling.

So far he had four possibilities for getting to His Eminence, Cardinal Gunter, Secretary of State.

One: the golf club.

Two: embassy parties.

Three: the confessional. If His Eminence was not too exalted for such chores.

Four: Benetti, the masseur.

Morgan pressed his hands to his face.

Each possibility had its snags, but instinctively Benetti was the option he liked least. In principle, it was the easiest if it worked. Simply give Benetti a letter to deliver to the Secretary of State personally. The cardinal reads the passwords, and obeys the orders to meet at the appointed time and place . . .

That was the perfect scenario. But there were big snags. It meant trusting Benetti. Morgan was by no means sure that Benetti was as important, as close to the papal throne as Renata thought. Benetti might read the letter – and he would surely identify the passwords as passwords. He would know that something remarkable was up. And, potentially, the cat would be halfway out of the bag. Then anything could happen.

He lay on the bed, trying to think.

But even if Benetti did read the letter and smelt a rat, what was *likely* to happen? If he were indeed accustomed to reporting directly to popes and Vatican heads, would he be likely to interfere? And even if he did make himself a busybody, would not the Secretary of State, with his massive authority, be able to bluff it out and put the masseur off the scent? The Secretary of State did not want his secret exposed.

Morgan sighed. There were so many imponderables . . .

He swung off the bed.

Now cut that out. You've done bloody marvellously in one day. Just take one day at a time.

He took off his clothes. He ripped back the bedcovers; then he hesitated.

He lowered himself to his knees. He leant his elbows on the bed, and prayed.

42

He slept deeply, as if his body had shut down on him in protest. At seven o'clock that Thursday morning he was dressed, pacing restlessly about his room, waiting for Rome to wake up. Tensely phrasing and rephrasing what he was going to say. Rethinking contingencies, what he should say If. The sun came up, and it was going to be a fine, dry autumn day. A perfect day for golf. Which he dearly wished he did not have to play. At nine o'clock he telephoned the Tourist Bureau.

'Good morning, I am a film producer from England, and I want to buy some clerical robes for a film I am making. Can you give me the name of some fast tailors?'

Five minutes later he had the addresses and telephone numbers of two firms, plus the name of a costumier. But he was wary of using a costumier – he would have to leave an address, and if he failed to return the costume the police would be informed. He telephoned the first tailor. But nobody there spoke either English or French. He was luckier with the second. He told the clerk he was a visiting priest and needed a new clerical suit, off the peg – jacket, trousers, bib and collar. Size thirty-eight long, in English measurements. Yes, Father, he was respectfully informed, they had most sizes in stock.

Morgan hung up, relieved. He felt like a criminal, telling these lies.

The next call was no easier to make. He sat on the bed, rethinking what he had to say. Then he dialled the Vatican Press Office.

'Good morning,' he said, 'I'm calling international – may I please talk to someone who speaks English? . . .'

There was a click, then a brisk, female, American voice said, 'Information Desk.'

Morgan said, 'Hullo, I'm calling from the *Yorkshire Evening Post*, in England, can you hear me?'

'Yes.'

'I hear you very indistinctly, do you mind if I hang up and call again?'

'Go ahead.'

He hung up, a little shakily. He waited a minute, then dialled again.

'That's better,' he said. 'Sorry about that. Look, my name is Paul Davidson, I'm calling from the *Yorkshire Evening Post*, and I'm flying out to Rome tomorrow to write a piece about the Vatican. What I'm hoping, if you'll be so kind, is that I can take you to lunch, to talk a little shop?'

'I see.' Weary hesitation of a high-powered press officer dealing with a country-bumpkin pressman. 'I'm very booked up for the foreseeable future, Mr Davidson, but perhaps we can discuss this by telephone? What shop do you want to talk?'

'A drink, lunch, dinner, anything, the *Post* would be delighted. Well, first of all we're interested in the Pope himself, and the Secretariat of State, I believe it's called. You know, Vatican policy, particularly in Africa, where there're intense social and economic problems, the Church's civilizing role, et cetera.' Nervous pause. 'Would it be possible for me to get an interview with Cardinal Gunter, the Secretary of State?'

Weary unhesitation. 'I think it highly unlikely, Mr Davidson, he is a very busy man. Anyway, you'd have to apply to the Secretariat.'

'Oh, dear. And that takes time, I suppose?'

'A long time.' She added: 'Of course, as an accredited newsman, you could attend any press conference he chooses to hold, but none are scheduled for the moment.'

'Oh. And the Pope? I was also hoping for an interview with His Holiness.'

'I see.' He could almost see her smile. 'Well, the same problem, I'm afraid. But even harder. But do apply.'

'Well,' Morgan the newshound from Yorkshire said earnestly, 'Is the Pope in residence at the moment?'

'He is.'

'And the Secretary of State?'

'He is too. But next Monday he goes abroad.'

'For how long?' Morgan demanded.

'It's not officially known, Mr Davidson. Affairs of state sometimes take longer than expected, you know.'

Morgan wasn't sure whether his heart sank or lifted.

'But when is he expected back? The *Yorkshire Evening Post* would hate to pay for me to come to Rome twice.'

'I understand,' the lady smiled, 'I used to work for a newspaper too. I'm afraid nothing is definite. But watch the *Osservatorie Romano*, the official Vatican newspaper. You've heard of that, of course, in Yorkshire? It reports such things as the movements of important Vatican officials.'

'Oh. Yes, of course.' He hesitated, then blurted: 'We hear that the Secretary of State is a keen golfer, madam?'

'That is true.'

'Can you tell me when and where he plays?' He gushed: 'The *Yorkshire Post* would love a few photographs . . .'

'I'm afraid,' the lady said, 'the private engagements of His Eminence are private.'

'I understand,' Morgan said hastily. 'Of course I wouldn't make a nuisance of myself. But can you please tell me when he's playing?'

'I'm afraid not, Mr Davidson. Only his personal secretary would know, and he wouldn't tell you either.'

'I see . . .' He went on hastily, before the woman politely told him to get lost: 'One detail you might be able to give my readers: When does the Secretary of State hear confession, from the public? And celebrate mass?'

A moment's silence. 'I've no idea, Mr Davidson. If the Secretary of State wishes to perform that duty it would be on an *ad hoc* basis, something he would arrange with the priest of the particular church in which he wished to do it.'

Morgan's heart sank. 'I see. But he does do it, sometimes?'

'I dare say he does, but those movements of his are not under the auspices of this office.'

He was pushing his luck: 'Who could tell me?'

The lady got impatient. 'Nobody. It's something he may or may not wish to do, from time to time.'

'I see. I'm sorry. One last question.' He reformulated it hastily: 'All priests have a confessor, don't they? Somebody to whom they say their confessions?'

'True.'

Morgan hurried on: 'Can you by any chance tell me who the confessor of the Secretary of State is? . . .'

An astonished silence.

'I have no idea. May I ask the purpose of that question?'

Morgan said hastily: 'Well, for example, if it's a village priest somewhere it would be excellent local colour.'

The lady said frostily, 'I understand. But I'm afraid nobody would know except somebody very close to His Eminence. Confession, as you doubtless know, is a very personal matter.'

'I know . . .' Morgan said apologetically. He ended, before he was cut off: 'Well, madam, the *Yorkshire Evening Post* is very grateful. And, please? . . . will you have a drink with me when I come to Rome?'

'Call me,' the lady said with polite relief, 'and see how I'm fixed . . .'

Morgan hung up. Feeling drained and elated. He had done that very well. And learned that the Secretary of State was out of town as from Monday. And, oh, that felt like the best news he had heard for a long time – he could hardly do anything before Monday.

He sighed and tried his luck again: he telephoned the *Guardian*'s office, and asked for Bill Fletcher.

'I was given your name by Whacker Ball as being a keen golfer. I'm a visitor, and I wondered if you knew somebody who would give me a game?'

Bill Fletcher could not play that week but he referred him to Brian Kelly, another newspaperman. Kelly could not make it either, but he put Morgan onto Kevin Munro of Associated Press.

'Sure,' Kevin said, 'how about one o'clock tomorrow?'

'Not today? It's such a lovely day, may be raining tomorrow.'

'No can do today, mate.'

Morgan sighed inwardly. 'Tomorrow is fine. Thanks. By the way, can I rent some clubs somewhere?'

'I'll lend you a set. Just buy a ball or two.'

'Excellent.' He added quickly, 'If I get to the club before you? –'

'Just say you're my guest and make yourself at home . . .'

He then telephoned the reception desk of the hotel and asked for the address of a sports store and a shop that sold religious books in the English language.

Then he made the most important call of all. He did not

expect it to work, but if by some fluke it did it would save him a lot of trouble. He mentally rehearsed his lines for the last time, then he dialled the Vatican Secretariat of State.

'Good morning! I am calling from England to speak to the personal secretary of Cardinal Gunter, please! My name is Anderson, Reverend Michael Anderson.'

'One moment, please, Reverend . . .'

There was a click, then a voice said, '*Prego*?'

Morgan said, 'Is that the personal secretary to Cardinal Gunter?'

'It is he. Father Ryan speaking, good morning.'

Morgan said, 'Praise the Lord, I've been trying for days to telephone you from Africa! I'm calling you from England now, Father, I am Reverend Michael Anderson of the Church of England, my parish is in Zambia.'

'Oh yes?' Father Ryan said politely.

'Father, I am flying to Rome today in the hopes of getting an appointment to see Cardinal Gunter. I have something very, *very* important to tell him. Now, how do I go about getting that appointment?'

'Well,' Father Ryan said, 'I would not come to Rome yet, Reverend –'

'I've already come from Zambia, expressly for this purpose, that's why I was trying so desperately to call you from there.'

'You should write a letter –' Father Ryan began.

'There isn't time for that because I've got to get back urgently.'

'– setting out what you need to see the Secretary of State about, Reverend. And that letter should actually come to us from your bishop, or even higher authority, and he should actually refer the matter to the British ambassador to the Holy See, here in Rome, asking him to take it up with this office.'

'There simply isn't *time*. If I don't see him in the next two days it will be too late to save the situation.'

'What situation?'

'It's far too sensitive to discuss, I'm afraid, Father. But it concerns the Holy Roman Church. Would it be possible for me to have a quick word with Cardinal Gunter now, on the telephone?'

'I'm afraid not. I'm afraid an appointment in the next few

days would be equally impossible. The cardinal is extremely heavily committed since he goes away next week.'

'For how long, please?'

'For some weeks. Now I suggest, Reverend, if you're determined to come to Rome, that you take this matter up with the British ambassador to the Holy See.'

Morgan said wearily, 'Very well. May I call you again when I get to Rome? And may I ask that you mention this matter to Cardinal Gunter? Maybe he'll see me.'

'You may telephone me, certainly, Reverend Anderson, but I doubt I'll have anything different to tell you.'

Morgan said goodbye with weary politeness.

He thought, Bloody bureaucrats – All the way from fucking Zambia and he doesn't bend the rules. But it was as he had expected.

He left the hotel. He took a taxi to the sports shop the receptionist had recommended. He bought four golf balls, all-purpose walking shoes, a showerproof tracksuit and a small hold-all.

He went to the bookshop. He bought two copies of *Letters to the Mighty* by Pieter Gunter.

Then he took a taxi to the Vatican again.

First he walked around the entire perimeter of Vatican City, studying the walls and entrances, looking for possible ways to get in. He did not think he would ever do it that way, but the possibility was something he should know about. He saw a few places where it would be possible, with daring and the right equipment, and he marked them on his map. He returned to the point he had started at, Saint Anne's Gate.

It was noon. On the other side of the road is a bar. He got a table near the door. He ordered a beer. He unfolded his map, opened his guide book, and watched the gate.

It is the business entrance to Vatican City. Ornate pillars, in high brown walls, crested iron-work. The map told him that immediately beyond were the barracks of the Swiss guards. Beyond that, the papal palace, where both the Pope and Cardinal Gunter had their private apartments. Beyond that, a miscellany of impressive buildings, joined to each other, containing a confusing array of art galleries, museums, chapels, lesser palaces, and

Vatican government departments. Beyond that, over a hundred acres of sculptured gardens and more official buildings. All neatly numbered on his map, and indexed. But, infuriatingly, the Secretariat of State was not identified on the map. Where Father Ryan, the arch-bureaucrat, festered.

Cars and people were coming and going through the gate all the time. Two Swiss guards in medieval uniforms stopped them, and examined permits.

Or, stopped most of them. Morgan watched. A number of people were not stopped by the guards. Mostly they were priests, who strode through with busy authority, or they were women in civilian clothes. Some were smartly dressed, looking like senior secretaries, but the others looked like housemaids.

All cars were stopped

But that wasn't true either.

Morgan saw an elongated limousine swing into the gates and go through without stopping, with a wave from the Swiss guard. Morgan presumed it was an official Vatican vehicle. He noted the number plate. But the next limousine was not stopped either, and it had different plates. Neither car had anything on it indicating that it belonged to one of the embassies. The next car was the same.

Morgan ordered spaghetti and a bottle of wine, and watched the gate.

Where did these limousines come from? Could he hire one?

Dress as a priest. Hire a limousine with chauffeur. Drive through the gates unchallenged. Tell the chauffeur to take him to the Secretariat of State. Enter with all the authority of a priest who knows where he's going.

Then what? Reverend Anderson from Zambia, come to plead his cause in person with Father Ryan? And say what?

Urgent, urgent, urgent, got to catch a plane back to Zambia. Terrible problems. Just five minutes with His Eminence please. In the name of pity and all that's holy . . .

And if that failed, leave a copy of the cardinal's book for his autograph, with the passwords written on the fly-leaf?

Morgan rubbed his chin.

It could work. But the snags were serious. The cardinal might not even be there when he arrived. If he was turned away, he would have drawn attention to himself. His face remembered.

And he would have alerted Cardinal Gunter. And he might be in trouble for breaking Vatican security.

Morgan sat, watching the gate, thinking it through.

Finally he got up. He went to look for a public telephone. To call the Tourist Bureau again, to ask where he could rent a limousine.

A taxi dropped him outside the premises of Alberto Andreotti, tailor. Morgan walked in.

A priest was being fitted by a tailor at one end. A grey-haired clerk with a tape measure around his neck looked up. Morgan said: 'I telephoned this morning about buying a clerical suit?'

'Ah, yes.' He glanced at Morgan's clothes. 'This is for you?'

'Yes, I'm visiting Rome on holiday.'

The priest at the other end of the shop called, in an American accent, 'Lucky for some.'

Morgan smiled: 'No rest for the wicked, huh?'

'No, *sir.*'

'Well, don't let the lesson be wasted on you, brother.'

The clerk said, 'I'm sorry, Father, but I must ask you for some identification.'

Morgan frowned at him. 'What on earth for?'

'You see, Father, only priests are allowed to buy such suits. Your passport must say what you are.'

Morgan closed his eyes in exasperation. Then he remembered the blank passports he had bought from Danziger. 'I haven't got it on me. Can I bring it in later?'

'What the heck, Alberto,' the American called, 'I'll guarantee the man, he looks overworked enough to be a priest.'

Ten minutes later Morgan was looking at himself in the mirror. White clerical collar, black bib, black suit, black shoes. The Reverend Michael Anderson, from Zambia.

He stuffed his other clothes into the hold-all along with the tracksuit and golf gear. He paid and left the shop, with a brotherly wave to the American.

He took a taxi to the Grand Hotel. He checked in, and paid. He said to the clerk:

'I'm going out soon. I'm expecting an important message to be left for me. If I telephone you, will you be sure to read it to me?'

'Certainly, Father, please.'

He took the elevator up to the room. The bell-boy refused a tip. 'Only a pleasure, Father.'

Morgan rang room service. He ordered a double scotch.

It came immediately. He sat on the bed, drinking the whisky tastelessly, rethinking it through for the last time. Were the chances of success worth the risks?

But it was now or never. Tomorrow was Friday and the Secretary of State left Rome on Monday. If he didn't try the trick today it would be a long time before he could try it again. *Fuck it – yes.* He swallowed back the whisky in one go. He went to his bag, and pulled out a copy of *Letters to the Mighty* by Cardinal Pieter Gunter.

He opened the book at the title page. He presumed that was where authors autographed their books. He took out his pen. His hand was shaky again.

He scrawled casually over the title: *The elk is not only a Siberian creature.*

Well, the cardinal could hardly miss that.

Then he tore a page out of his notebook. He wrote neatly:

> Reverend M. Anderson,
> Room 212, Grand Hotel, Rome.

He put the note in the title page, and closed the book.

He sighed tensely. And picked up the telephone again. He dialled one of the firms that rented limousines.

He ordered a car, with chauffeur, to fetch the Reverend Anderson from the Grand Hotel immediately.

43

The driver spoke French. Morgan said:

'The Swiss guards know me at Saint Anne's Gate, so don't stop, just drive through, because I'm already late for my appointment.'

'Yes, Father.'

The limousine sped across Rome.

Morgan sat in the back, desperately trying to get calm. Telling himself that compared to going into the Union Bank of Switzerland, this was a piece of cake . . . But, oh God, he could not make it. This was what all the effort had been for, and it could all blow up in his face now, everything undone. And then anything could happen. And God, he wanted this whole business over.

The limousine was whisking up the Via della Conciliazione now, and Morgan felt his stomach contract. Up towards the crescent arms of Saint Peter's. The limousine swung right, and there, beyond the colonnades, was the Saint Anne's Gate. Morgan took a deep breath, and crossed himself.

'Please help me, now, God . . .'

The limousine slowed as it approached the gate.

There were people coming and going. Another car was ahead of them, stopped. The limousine's speed dropped more. The car ahead moved through the gate.

Morgan rolled down his window. The limousine drove towards the Swiss guards. The Swiss guard watched, expecting the car to stop. 'Just go,' Morgan snapped. He leant towards the window to show his clerical collar and he held up a slip of paper. *'I'm terribly late.'* And the limousine drove past, into Vatican City.

Morgan sat back, his heart pounding. He looked back through the tinted window. The guard was staring after them. Morgan closed his eyes. He whispered ardently: 'Thank you, God . . .'

The limousine pulled to a stop in the parking bay. There were hundreds of other parked cars.

Morgan got out of the car. Without looking left or right he set off across the compound hurriedly, towards the doorway the driver had indicated.

There were people going busily in all directions, mostly priests. Morgan strode through them, trying to look like a man of God who knew exactly what he was doing. He strode into the big, yellow-stucco building clutching *Letters to the Mighty*.

He glanced about him, his heart knocking. There were signs in Italian. A priest was striding down the corridor. Morgan smiled shakily at him: 'The Secretariat of State, please, brother? . . .'

He mounted the wide stone stairs. Passing people on the way. He came to the landing.

There were big, ornate, double doors. He walked in.

Into an office, consisting of a short counter with two desks behind it. A young priest was studiously typing. He looked up with a busy smile.

'Father Ryan?' Morgan said.

The young man said, with an Italian accent: 'Nobody as exalted as that. Who must I say is calling?'

'Reverend Anderson, Church of England, Zambia, please.'

The young man made a brisk note, and picked up the telephone. He pressed a button and waited. He began to speak rapidly in Italian. He paused, and listened. Morgan turned away, and prayed feverishly: *Please God, we've done so well* . . .

The clerk hung up the telephone. 'He is coming, Father.'

'Thank you.'

Morgan waited the longest minute. Trying to calm himself. *For God's sake, this is a piece of cake compared to the Union Bank of Switzerland* . . .

The door opened, and in walked Father Ryan, in a bustle of black cassock.

The man was annoyed. 'Reverend Anderson, what are you doing here?'

Charm was the tactic. 'Father Ryan, thank you for seeing me –'

'How did you get here, Reverend?'

'By plane –'

'I mean how did you get into Vatican City? Did you get a pass?'

Morgan looked nonplussed. 'Pass? I had no idea I needed one, I just drove in. I'm awfully sorry.'

'It's highly irregular. The guards didn't stop you?'

Morgan looked mystified. 'I didn't even look at them. I was in the back seat.'

Father Ryan shook his head. 'Very lax of them. Now, then, Reverend, I'm very sorry that you've come all this way, but as I said on the telephone –'

305

'Father,' Morgan pleaded with all his charm, 'it is desperately, *desperately* urgent that I see Cardinal Gunter for just one minute, to give him some information of vital importance –'

Father Ryan interrupted. 'I'm afraid he's not even here now, he's left his office for the day. And tomorrow and Saturday he's absolutely fully committed. But if you tell me what this is about, I'll mention it to him when he's got a moment to listen.'

Morgan shook his head. 'It's too sensitive, it's for his ears only.'

'Well, then, if you write a letter –'

'But will he be the only one to read it?'

'I'm afraid not. You can imagine how much mail passes through this office.'

'*Father*,' Morgan pleaded '– just two minutes of his time, tomorrow, or Saturday, or Sunday, anywhere you like –'

Father Ryan said, 'Impossible. So I suggest you take it up with the British authorities. I may be able to short-circuit that by phoning the British ambassador for you.'

Morgan sighed. 'No. Thank you, I'll do it.' He looked at the book, *Letters to the Mighty*, then made a snap decision. No, it was too risky to leave the passwords lying around. And the man might not even see it until he came back from his trip. Morgan had to say the words to his face. He said stiffly:

'Well, at least I've tried to do my duty. As a man of God . . .' He held out his hand. 'Goodbye.'

Father Ryan said earnestly, 'Reverend, if you tell me what this is about I give you my word it will be treated with confidentiality.'

'Thank you, but no.' Morgan shook his head, a man depressed by the folly of the world. 'Goodbye. I have to get back to Zambia.' He turned away.

Father Ryan hesitated. 'Reverend?'

Morgan stopped. The priest sighed. 'Look, where are you staying? I'll mention this to Cardinal Gunter when I see him later tonight. Maybe he'll squeeze you in, as you've come all the way from Zambia.'

Morgan beamed. 'Oh, thank you!' He pulled the slip of paper

out of the book. 'God bless you, Father! I'll wait in the hotel for your call!'

'*Dominus tecum*,' Father Ryan smiled.

He ordered two bottles of beer sent up to his room in the Grand Hotel.

He paced about, excited. He had done it! *He had done it.* He had played that so well! Exactly right – made the man feel a shit for turning him away. *You're a genius, Morgan!* . . .

It was seven o'clock when the telephone rang. He snatched it up. 'Hullo!'

'Reverend?' Father Ryan said. 'I have good news for you . . .'

Oh yes! 'Oh, excellent!'

Father Ryan said, 'Because you've come all the way from Zambia, Cardinal Gunter has arranged that you see Archbishop Lorenzo at noon tomorrow.'

Morgan's heart sank. 'Who?'

'Archbishop Lorenzo is Cardinal Gunter's deputy. But I'm afraid the appointment must be brief – ten, fifteen minutes maximum.'

Morgan stared across the room. 'Can't I possibly see the cardinal?'

'Definitely not. Seeing Archbishop Lorenzo in these circumstances is extraordinary enough, Reverend. And this time I will arrange a pass to be waiting for you at the Prefecture.'

Morgan held his head. So near and yet so far!

'Thank you, Father Ryan. And please convey my compliments to Cardinal Gunter. I will be there at noon tomorrow.'

They said their goodbyes.

Morgan collapsed back on the bed. He wanted to bellow his frustration to the sky.

'*SHIT* . . .'

44

He pulled off his priest's suit angrily, and had a shower. He got dressed in his civilian clothes. He put on his shoulder holster and packed everything into the hold-all. He left the hotel. He went back to the Excelsior, where he had stayed the previous night. Maybe this move was an unnecessary precaution, but there was no point in taking the risk of staying at the address he had given Father Ryan.

He ordered dinner and wine sent up to his room. He hardly tasted any of it, and got into bed.

Before switching out his light, he telephoned the Grand Hotel, and asked if there were any messages for Reverend Anderson. There were none.

He lay in the dark, thinking of Anna.

At nine o'clock the next morning he telephoned the Grand Hotel and asked for messages for Reverend Anderson. Again there were none. He telephoned *Il Figaro* newspaper: again Mike Milano was not available. He then telephoned the Vatican and left a polite message: Reverend Anderson regretted he was unable to keep his noon appointment with Archbishop Lorenzo as he had to fly back to Zambia very urgently. He would be in touch again.

He then telephoned the Maltese consulate. He said to the girl who answered:

'I'm trying to trace a shipment of goods I ordered flown from Malta to Panama last year by a company called Meteor Air. Have you got a Malta telephone directory?'

'Yes, sir.'

'May I come and look at it?'

'I'll look it up for you, sir. How do you spell it?'

He told her. He heard her leafing through the book.

'I'm sorry, sir, no Meteors here.'

'Can you give me the numbers of some Maltese freight agents, so I can ask about this airline?'

A few minutes later he had the numbers of three freight agents in Malta.

The first two had never heard of Meteor Air. The third man said: 'Yes, small outfit, sometimes comes this way.'

'Have you a telephone number or address for them, please?'

'No. But they used to operate out of Marseilles, I think. You can telephone our agents there. Ask for Louis, say George referred you, here's the number . . .'

Three minutes later he was speaking to Louis Laval in Marseilles.

'Ah, yes,' Louis said in French, 'Alex Wallen, Meteor Air. I have a number. How is George?'

'Sends you his best wishes.'

'Tell him to send me some business. Here is the number . . .'

Morgan thanked him and hung up. He sat on the bed, feeling very lucky.

He rehearsed it. Then he dialled the number in France.

'Yes,' a gruff voice said, 'I am Monsieur Wallen.'

Morgan spoke in French. 'Monsieur Wallen, I'm calling on behalf of Bellatrix SA, Panama.'

Silence. Then: 'Indeed?'

'Monsieur Wallen, we had a contract last year for you to deliver some goods to us from Malta, you remember?'

Silence. 'No, I don't. But continue.'

'I have the waybill here, I can give you the number. It was for sixteen crates of bulldozer equipment.'

'Indeed?'

'And we would like to do the same again. Fifteen crates this time. Can you do it? But it must be prompt.'

Silence. 'Who are you?'

Morgan said, 'Jacques Viljoen.'

'You don't sound French, Monsieur Viljoen.'

'I'm not. Only my ancestors.'

'And where are you?'

'In Genoa. Monsieur Wallen, all we want to know —'

'And what I want to know is, is this consignment all arranged this time, Monsieur Viljoen, or are there going to be . . . disappointments?'

So he was right!

'No, we think it is all arranged this time.'

'You think? Have the experts seen it yet?'

Morgan hesitated. 'Which experts?'

'The quality-control experts. I don't want that going on in my warehouse. I run a legitimate airline.'

Oh so! 'Yes, that's been done.'

'And the funds, Monsieur Viljoen?'

Morgan hesitated again. 'We believe the funds are all available.'

'You believe? Has Sanchez paid Henri yet?'

Morgan's mind raced. 'Which Henry? There are two . . .'

'There is only one Hank.'

Morgan fumbled. 'Oh, Hank. Well, I'm told the bank transfers are going through. I'm not handling the money side myself. I thought maybe you meant Henry the lawyer.'

Pause. 'Monsieur Viljoen, who exactly do you work for?'

'I'm an associate of Max Hapsburg.' He added: 'He's dead now.'

'I would probably be sorry to hear that if I knew who Max Hapsburg was.'

'He was involved in the last transaction. It's fallen to me to arrange this one.'

Another silence. Then:

'I'll speak to Hank myself.'

Morgan said hurriedly. 'You've got his new number, have you?'

Surprise: 'His new number?'

'I believe it's new. What number do you have?'

There was a long silence. Then the telephone went click, as Alex Wallen of Meteor Air hung up.

Morgan slammed down the telephone.

Goddammit he had blown it! He should have arranged to meet Wallen instead of trying to get Hank's number so artlessly! If he only knew who this Hank was! And Sanchez. If he only had got a telephone number!

He got up, exasperated, and paced across the room.

But one thing was clear. That waybill was not about a legitimate cargo of bulldozer parts.

Quality-control experts?

For what? For drugs? The famous 'French Connection'? . . .

But Bellatrix was the importer, and Bellatrix was controlled by the Vatican. He simply could not believe that the Vatican was involved in drugs . . .

He looked at his watch angrily. It was time to play goddam golf!

It was a cold, sunny day. It was nearly eleven when his taxi drove through the gates of the Appia Antia Golf Club.

There were only a few cars parked. Morgan mounted the steps, into the club house.

There was a hall with a large lounge beyond. Morgan walked through it. Out onto the verandah.

Below him the greens and fairways stretched away.

A few people were playing, small figures far away. Morgan swept his eyes along the fairways. There were clumps of trees sprinkled alongside various parts. From this distance he could not be sure how good they would be as hiding places. He would have to walk the course.

He retraced his steps to the entrance. He went into the club secretary's office. A female clerk came forward. Morgan said, in English, 'May I see the club secretary, please?'

The girl led him to a door. She opened it, and smiled him through. A well-groomed elderly Italian looked up from his papers. Morgan said: 'Good morning. Do you speak English?'

'A little,' the Italian smiled back.

'I am a guest today of one of your members. I wonder if I may ask a favour?' He unzipped his bag and pulled out *Letters to the Mighty*. This copy did not have the passwords written on it. 'I believe Cardinal Gunter is also a member?'

'He is, sir.'

'This is one of his books. I'm an admirer of his. If I left the book with you, do you think he might autograph it next time he comes?'

'I think that could be arranged. He is a most agreeable man.'

'Thank you very much.' Morgan added: 'How frequently does he play? When should I come back for the book?'

'He usually plays on Wednesday and Saturday afternoons. But I haven't seen him this week. Maybe he's away.' He held up his finger. 'One moment.' He went into the general office. He came back with a ledger.

'He is playing in the tournament commencing seventh of December. Will you still be in Rome then?'

'Yes. He's not booked to play before?'

The secretary flicked over pages shaking his head 'No , , ,'

'Well, I'll telephone you and see if you've had any luck. One last question: I'm a member of the Plymouth Country Club, but I haven't got my card with me. Do you have reciprocal visiting-member rights with Plymouth?'

'Yes, sir,' the secretary said. 'But anybody can play here if they pay a green fee of forty thousand lire.'

Morgan looked at him. 'Anybody? If they pay twenty pounds?'

'Yes, sir. Subject to space.'

Jesus, Morgan thought – so all my clever deception with Kevin Munro is unnecessary. And I still have to make a fool of myself playing golf with the man. This is getting local knowledge the hard way. But he felt elated. He had found out Cardinal Gunter's movements.

He left the secretary's office and made his way through the club house. He stopped at the public telephones. He dialled *Il Figaro* newspaper and asked for Miguel Milano.

'Good morning, Mr Milano! My name is Jack Armstrong. I'm a friend of Whacker Ball and he told me you are very knowledgeable on the Roberto Calvi affair, God's Banker . . .'

One minute later he continued on his way with a spring in his step. He might not be much good at golf but he had the gift of the gab! He followed the signs down to the changing rooms.

They were empty. Rows of lockers. Shower booths. A door opening onto the first green.

He changed into his tracksuit and new walking shoes.

There was a driver's club lying on the bench. Morgan picked it up unhappily.

He gripped the club in both hands and took up his stance.

He squared his shoulders, and wriggled his feet, trying to get the feel of the thing again. He addressed the imaginary ball, frowning in concentration. He took a swing.

There was a crash of glass, as his club smashed the overhead light.

He leant on the club, eyes closed. He whispered, '*I'm doing this for the Church, God. So please give me a hand. Or how about some rain . . .?*'

He found a broom and swept up the glass. He still had an hour and a half to wait. He set off on the fairways, to walk quickly around the course before Kevin Munro arrived.

And maybe God did give him a hand. By the time he got back to the club house, it was starting to rain. And there was something else to be relieved about: there were a good number

312

of ancient ruins and aqueducts sprinkled along the golf course, and thickets of trees. He hurried back into the changing rooms. He hastily drew a sketch of the fairways, marking in the hiding places he had seen.

Then he dressed in his ordinary clothes again. He hurried up to the bar.

Kevin Munro was a good-natured man in his forties. 'What bad luck this rain is,' he said. 'But the beer's all right.'

And there was more good luck. Over lunch Morgan said: 'Well, my day wasn't wasted. I'm a fan of Cardinal Gunter's, so I brought a copy of his book along. And the club secretary is going to ask him to autograph it for me. But the secretary says he's out of town and doesn't know when he'll be back.'

'Well, when I get back to my desk, I'll phone the Vatican press officer. He's a friend of mine, he'll tell me. Give me a call later today.'

'*Thank* you,' Morgan said.

And there was more good luck:

When Kevin Munro drove him back to Rome, Morgan called Renata from a public telephone. She said:

'*Good* news. I have an appointment for you with Benetti for six o'clock tonight! The only thing is you must lead him to believe that you are really in love with me. Okay? And I have spent the day in the library. I have a great deal to tell you tonight! . . .'

Morgan hung up and looked for a taxi, feeling that he had had a good day. He had missed out on Meteor Air but the rain had saved him from golf. He was doubtful if he could trust Benetti, even if he was cooperative. Which was even more doubtful. But it was all potentially useful local knowledge, and it had come his way easily.

He told the taxi-driver to take him to *Il Figaro* newspaper.

45

Miguel Milano was much less approachable in the flesh than he had been on the telephone. He was a sharp-faced, bearded Italian-American in his mid-thirties, with an abrupt manner.

'I'm afraid I can only give you fifteen minutes, Mr Armstrong. And let me say at the outset that there *are* no experts on God's Banker. You would need to be a team of detectives and accountants rolled into one. What do you want to know?'

Morgan said, 'You reported on the inquest in London after he was found hanging from Blackfriars Bridge?'

'Yes.'

'Was he murdered?'

'Yes.'

'Not suicide?'

'He was *suicided*. Meaning murder made to look like suicide.'

Morgan said, 'Who murdered him?'

Miguel said flatly: 'The Vatican.'

Morgan stared. 'The *Vatican*? Not the Russians?'

'What has Russia to do with this?'

Morgan sighed inwardly. Maybe this man wasn't going to be so useful after all. 'Can you prove that the Vatican murdered him?'

'If I could I wouldn't be sitting here today, I would be suicided too. "The Italian Solution" it's called.'

Morgan sat forward. 'Why do you suspect the Vatican?'

Miguel got up and went to a cabinet. He pulled out a file six inches thick. He slapped it on the desk. He pulled out two more files and slapped them down.

'There're the newspaper reports plus the inquest in England, plus Calvi's trial in Italy before he was murdered. You can't expect me to summarize very much in fifteen minutes.'

Morgan said hastily, 'Let me be more specific. Firstly, why did God's Banker run to England?'

Miguel sat down again. 'To get his hands on some documents. With which to blackmail the Vatican.'

Morgan felt his pulse trip in exultation. 'What documents?'

'If I knew that I'd solve the whole mystery.'

'Who was he going to get these documents *from*?'

'From somebody in the P2.'

Morgan blinked. 'What's P2?'

'A secret society.'

Morgan frowned. 'Does the name Max Hapsburg mean anything to you?'

'Sure. He's an economist of sorts. From the Caribbean.'

'Right. Was *he* a member of this P2?' Morgan demanded.

Miguel said, 'I wouldn't know. There're about two thousand members of P2 and only the Grand Master knows who they all are – they aren't even all known to each other. What has Hapsburg got to do with this?'

'Can you tell me more about P2?'

Miguel sighed. He said, by rote:

'P2 is a lodge of the Freemasons. Its declared purpose is to defend the world against communism. Ultra-right-wing. Its members are top army officers, top industrialists, top civil servants, top bankers, professionals, world-wide. They are, or try to be, a sort of government within governments. If Italy elected a communist government tomorrow, for example, P2 would mount a coup immediately and take over the country. P2 bank-rolls right-wing régimes, in South America particularly, does arms deals for them, espionage, pressurizing other governments through their international network, gets them bank loans, trade deals, et cetera. They call themselves "Defenders of the Free World". In practice they are also making fortunes for themselves by highly illegal transactions.'

'Bank loans? To governments?'

'One of their chores. Most of the repressive governments in South America, for example, are bankrupt. They've got massive loans outstanding. They constantly need more loans to cover the old ones.' He added, 'And to buy more arms, et cetera.'

Morgan took a deep breath. Oh boy . . .

'Is it known who the Grand Master of P2 is?'

'A man called Gelli. Italian who's taken on Argentinian citizenship. One of the most powerful men in the world. A king-maker. A master blackmailer on the international scale. That's how P2 gets its power.'

'By *black*mail?'

Miguel said wearily: 'Anybody who joins P2 has to present the Grand Master with two pieces of evidence. One must be damaging to the applicant himself, to ensure his loyalty. The other evidence must be damaging to another important person whom P2 wants to join the club – so that the Grand Master can pressurize that person into joining. And then that person must

315

bring along evidence against some other powerful person. And so on.'

Evidence . . . 'Gelli is literally a king-maker?'

Miguel said, 'For example. Perón was overthrown as President of Argentina, and fled to Spain. Years later he returned to Argentina as President. Who arranged that?' He answered himself: 'When Perón returned, he publicly knelt at the feet of Gelli.'

Morgan sat back. 'Good God.'

'Gelli's been in blackmail all his life. During the war he spied for the highest bidder. After the war he specialized in smuggling Nazi war criminals to South America. He charged forty per cent of what they were worth. And most were worth a fortune in looted treasure.' He glanced at his watch. 'After that, Gelli went to South America himself. Ingratiated himself with the right-wing military people and Nazis down there. Joined the Masons to help himself along. Then he formed P2, a brotherhood within the brotherhood.'

Smuggling Nazi war criminals? 'Klaus Barbie? "The Butcher of Lyons",' Morgan said. 'Did Gelli smuggle him to South America?'

Miguel said irritably, 'What's Klaus Barbie got to do with this? Barbie worked for American Intelligence in Germany after the war, tracking down communists. That had been part of his job under Hitler. Barbie was a wanted Nazi war criminal but the Americans sheltered him because he was useful. When that ended, the *Americans* gave him a new identity, a fake passport, and smuggled him to South America. And when he got to Bolivia, he continued to supply the CIA with information.' He added, 'He also worked for the military régime and he ran a murder squad protecting the cocaine trade for officers in the Bolivian government. He knew Gelli, sure, but it was the Americans who smuggled him out of Germany.' Miguel glanced at his watch significantly.

Morgan said hastily, 'Why haven't the French prosecuted him yet?'

'Because Barbie knows too much. I don't know what but I hear on the grapevine that he threatens to start a smear campaign at his trial, maybe against the heroes of the French

Resistance during the war, who knows? I thought you wanted to know about God's Banker?'

'I do. One more question, please . . .' He marshalled his thoughts. 'God's Banker fled to England to get hold of some documents to blackmail the Vatican? Blackmail them for *what*?'

Miguel said bluntly, 'For money.'

Morgan rubbed his chin. 'But *just* money? You've told me that P2 is into high-powered politics. King-making. Et cetera. Was there something *else* that God's Banker was after, perhaps?'

Miguel smacked the pile of files. 'I simply haven't got time to explain it to you in detail. But God's Banker was a financial adviser to the Vatican Bank. In addition, he was laundering money for the Mafia, was paymaster to the P2, was smuggling money illegally out of Italy for favoured clients, and was stealing money for himself from his *own* bank. To do all this he set up ghost companies in such places as Liechtenstein and Panama and the Bahamas, in collaboration with the Vatican Bank – in fact, the Vatican Bank partly *owned* Banco Ambrosiana. And these ghost companies borrowed money from overseas banks, to do such things as arms deals for South American military régimes. And to buy Vatican assets as part of schemes to get money out of Italy. For example, a ghost company in Panama buys some shares the Vatican owns in an Italian industry. To pay for them the Panama company borrows money from another ghost company owned by Banco Ambrosiana. This company has borrowed money from, say, a British bank. Banco Ambrosiana pays the money to the Vatican Bank for the shares. Because the Vatican Bank is not subject to Italian banking laws it can transfer money out of the country easily. The Vatican hands over the Italian shares to the Panama ghost company – but because the Vatican is a partner in the ghost company it still owns the shares. Meanwhile the Vatican pays the money into God's Banker's private Swiss bank account, less a commission. And everybody is happy. The Vatican is happy because it's still got its shares plus a fat commission on the fraudulent deal, and God's Banker's happy because he's just stolen the purchase price which he's indirectly borrowed from the British bank.' Miguel waved his hand in disgust. 'And the international banks were queuing up to lend money to God's Banker and his ghost companies. Why? Because he was involved with the Vatican Bank – and because Bishop Marcinkus, the president of the Vatican Bank, was on the board of directors of these companies.'

Morgan was astounded. 'Good Lord . . . I'm a babe in the woods . . .'

'But don't imagine that Bishop Marcinkus is.'

Morgan shook his head. 'And how did the arms deals work?'

Miguel said impatiently: 'Same way. The P2 generals in South America need arms. Arms cost money. The generals are bankrupt. So Gelli and the P2 generals lean on God's Banker for money. So one of his ghost companies in Panama buys the arms, with money borrowed from a bank owned by Banco Ambrosiana, who in turn borrows the money from a British bank. The British bank happily lends the money because God's Banker and Bishop Marcinkus are on the board of directors. The arms arrive in Panama, and the ghost company ships them to Bolivia or Peru or wherever. Simple. Disgusting, but simple.'

'So the Vatican *knew* that it was assisting the buying of arms for repressive military régimes?'

'The Vatican *Bank* knew. So what do you think? The *previous* Pope was going to fire Bishop Marcinkus and all the top brass at the Vatican Bank, for this very sort of thing, but *this* Pope re-confirmed them all in their positions.'

Morgan frowned. 'But do you think this Pope is . . . dishonest?'

'Naive. I only know it's very wrong to keep such people running the Church's bank. Or any bank.'

Morgan rubbed his hand over his face.

'So how did the whole thing blow up?'

Miguel said: 'Finally, Banco Ambrosiana was in trouble, with over a thousand *million* dollars missing from its vaults from all his thefts and crooked deals, and the Bank of Italy inspectors were chasing them.' He flicked open the big file and rifled through it impatiently. He pulled out a letter. He said:

'The ghost company in Panama that did most of the arms deals was called Bellatrix.'

Morgan stared at him. *Bellatrix?*

Miguel went on: 'Bellatrix and the other ghost companies borrowed over nine hundred *million* dollars from a bank in

318

Peru, which was partly owned by God's Banker. When God's Banker got into financial trouble, his co-directors in Peru demanded to know who actually *owned* Bellatrix, who therefore actually *owed* them the nine hundred million. So what happens? A miracle!' He leaned forward. 'The Vatican Bank, at God's Banker's request, wrote this letter,' he held up a photocopy, 'to the Peruvian bank, acknowledging that the *Vatican Bank* owned Bellatrix – the company that was buying all the arms – and acknowledging that the Vatican Bank therefore owed the nine hundred million dollars!'

He tossed Morgan the letter. Morgan stared at it. It was the very same letter which he had found in Max's deposit box in Zurich! The letter which was in his pocket right now . . . *So the Meteor Air waybill was in respect of a shipment of arms from Malta to Panama! . . .* Miguel went on:

'So the Peruvian bank directors heaved a sigh of relief. The Holy Roman Church itself was the guarantor for the loan to Bellatrix. But – aha!' Miguel held up a finger. 'There was one little snag . . . It was another letter which God's Banker formally wrote to the Vatican Bank –' He pulled it out of the file – 'dated four days *before*! And in it he says if the Vatican Bank will admit that they are the owners of Bellatrix and responsible for the debt, this "would entail *no liabilities* for the Vatican Bank"!'

Morgan stared at the letter.

'Good God . . . So God's Banker made a secret deal with the Vatican Bank letting them off the hook provided they bluffed the Peruvian bankers? That's fraud.'

'Exactly,' Miguel said with disgust. 'It was a plot to defraud the South American banks into *not* chasing their debt. Thereby gaining time.'

Morgan sat back. Stunned. *And now he knew what God's Banker wanted the microfilm for . . .*

'But,' he said, 'if the Vatican Bank owns Bellatrix, surely they can be legally forced to pay?'

Miguel shook his head with a scornful leer.

'Not yet, they haven't. No, *sir*. The Vatican Bank is piously claiming that they were only the nominees, that they knew nothing about what these ghost companies really *did*, oh dear me no, that their letter to the Peruvian bankers was only a "letter of patronage", a sort of character reference for God's Banker who they had believed was such an honest man, et cetera, et cetera . . .' Miguel glared, then leant across the desk. '*That* is what God's so-called Banker ran to London for . . . to try to get his hands on some documents which would *force* the Vatican Bank to pay up! Blackmail them into paying up over nine hundred million dollars . . . And then some more.'

Morgan stared. Of course. With the microfilm God's Banker could have blackmailed the Vatican to Kingdom Come. He sat back. This was what his Church's bank was involved in? . . . Arms. Fraud. He was appalled. . . .

But thank God that Miguel was wrong in thinking that it was the Vatican who murdered God's Banker to stop him blackmailing them – Morgan knew it was the Russians, to protect their secret weapon in the Vatican. And he was sure there was some further vital point that he was missing. Miguel did not know what the blackmail documents were, but Morgan did, and it was political dynamite. He repeated:

'But was God's Banker going to blackmail the Vatican *only* for money? You've told me that P2 is into high-powered right-wing politics. Wasn't there something *else* P2 and God's Banker were after from the Vatican? Some political purpose.'

'Money to support some right-wing régime. For arms probably. Who for, what for, I don't know.'

'And you've no idea what the documents were?'

Miguel said flatly: 'If I knew that, I wouldn't be sitting here now. I would be "suicided" too.' He slapped both hands on the desk and stood up. He said: 'Be careful you don't write too good a book, Mr Armstrong. Or you may find the Italian Solution applied to you . . .'

46

He had an hour before his appointment with Benetti, the masseur. He went from *Il Figaro*'s premises to the nearest café, ordered coffee, and feverishly made notes of everything that Miguel Milano had told him. He felt drained when he finished.

He sat, staring out into the rainy dusk. And he was sick in his heart about what he had learned about his Holy Roman Church in the last few days. But thank God he knew that Miguel was wrong on one point: the Vatican was *not* guilty of murder.

He went to the public telephone and called Kevin Munro.

'Bad news about your autograph, I'm afraid. The Secretary of State is out of town until third December . . .'

Morgan returned to his table. And what he felt was relief.

Thank God. Thank God the man was going away and there was nothing he could do about him for four whole weeks . . . Tomorrow all he had to do was buy a small car, and this time the next day he would be with Anna. The next four weeks felt like a holiday. . . .

He went into the toilet. He took off his shoulder holster and buried it in his bag. Then he left the café. He got a taxi to the Sacred Heart Hospital.

Benetti's rooms were in the basement. The walls were white tiles. Benetti was a smallish, muscular man, his arms covered in curly black hair. He had heavy eyebrows and a lined face and penetrating, kind, brown eyes. He spoke poor English but good French.

'Take your clothes off, wrap that towel around you and lie down on the table.'

He left the room. Morgan got undressed and lay down. He waited, telling himself he was not going to commit himself to any course of action now, he was simply making contact with a man who could be useful. But he felt like a fraud. Benetti came back.

'Where does it hurt?'

'Here.' Morgan touched his lumbar region. 'Particularly in the mornings.'

'Lie flat.' Benetti gripped his back in powerful hands and began to massage. He worked for a few minutes in silence, then said:

'So you are Renata's friend.'

'Yes.'

Benetti massaged. 'A lovely woman.'

'She is. She tells me you have been very kind to her.'

321

'I have prayed for her.'

'Do you think she'll ever get better?'

Benetti massaged. 'What does she think?'

'She seems to feel it is hopeless. Do you know what's wrong with her?'

'I know what has happened, I do not know the cure.'

'Will she get worse?'

'I don't know.' Benetti hesitated. 'You are very fond of her?'

'Very.'

'I mean in an amorous way?'

'Yes.'

'Are you a Catholic?'

'Yes.'

Benetti sighed. 'It is a pity she does not have much faith. Perhaps you can give her some.'

'She tells me you have asked the Pope to pray for her.'

'That is true.'

Morgan had to try it. 'Perhaps if she were to meet the Pope she would change her attitude. He might inspire her.'

Benetti pressed hard on his back. 'Does that hurt?'

'A little.'

Benetti worked on. 'Is that your idea, or hers? That she meet the Pope.'

'Mine. It might change her negative attitude.'

Benetti worked. 'It might.'

Morgan waited; then asked: 'Do you think that could be arranged?'

'It is possible. The Pope knows about her case.'

Morgan's hopes soared. 'Oh, I think it might work wonders. Psychologically at least.' He hesitated. 'And if I were present too, maybe I could support her psychologically afterwards, keep her optimistic.'

Benetti worked across the lumbar region. Morgan flinched. Benetti said: 'But *she* must want to see His Holiness, she must *want* faith, otherwise there is negativeness.'

'*Exactly*,' Morgan said. 'I will work on that.' He hesitated from pushing his luck, but he had to: 'Have you any idea when this could be arranged?'

Benetti shook his head. 'The request must first come from *her*. Then we shall see.'

Morgan lay there, elated. If this worked . . . Benetti flicked his shoulder. 'I think you will be more comfortable for a while.'

Morgan sat up. He felt good.

'Thank you very much indeed. If I need to see you again . . .?'

'Ask Renata to arrange it. I am busy but it can be done.'

'*Thank* you. What do I owe you, please?'

'Put some money in the poor box.'

'Good. And . . . I have a small favour to ask you? I want to buy Cardinal Gunter's book, *Letters to the Mighty*. Renata says you sometimes see him. If I were to bring the book here one day, could you possibly pass it on to him for his autograph? Do you think he would mind?'

Benetti shrugged. 'I shouldn't think so.'

'Well, thank you so very much.'

He came out into the cold rain, feeling elated. He hurried up the street into the nearest café. He went straight to the toilet. He unzipped his bag, pulled out his shoulder holster and put it on. He went back to the bar. He ordered a beer and drank it down, down, down, and it tasted marvellous. He had had a good day! He now had two extra strings to his bow, potentially. If he failed to see Cardinal Gunter at the golf club, the passwords could be sent to him through Benetti. And if all else failed he might get to see the Pope through Renata, and tell him to put his house in order, take it from there. The depression that Miguel Milano had left him with was gone. He had learned some terrible things about his Church today, but he had made progress. And Miguel Milano might be wrong in his interpretation of events.

He bought a bottle of good cognac for Renata, and took a taxi to her apartment. She opened the door and said dramatically:

'Have I got some facts for you! Pope John Paul I was definitely murdered . . .'

47

He did not want to believe it – all this business about the murder of Pope John Paul I was a red herring. And he was almost prepared to believe anything again. He sat behind the bar with a bottle of beer, his nerves stretched again, his notebook open: Renata sat opposite, photocopies of newspaper cuttings and pages of notes in front of her. She read from them:

'On the 26th August, 1978, Cardinal Albino Luciani, a small, popular, gentle man, was elected Pope John Paul I. He was sixty-five years old and in good health. He neither drank nor smoked. His only health problem was *low* blood pressure, for which his personal doctor gave him medicine which he took twice a day.' Renata tapped the cuttings. '*Low* blood pressure is *guaranteed* not to give you a heart attack.'

Morgan made a scribbled note. Renata read on:

'Thirty-three days later, he retired to bed at nine-thirty pm, as usual. His medicine was at his bedside.' She tapped the cuttings again: 'The Italian press knows these details, because his housekeeper and his personal secretary told them. At four-thirty am his housekeeper brought him coffee as usual. Her name is Sister Vicenza. She had been his housekeeper for twenty years. She knocked and called "Good morning, Holy Father" . . . She left the coffee outside his door. Fifteen minutes later she noticed the coffee still untouched. She knocked again. Finally she opened the door.' Renata looked up. 'She found him sitting up in bed. The light on. His spectacles on. In his hand were a bunch of hand-written notes. He had a grimace of pain on his face. He was dead.'

Morgan was making notes furiously. Renata went on:

'She immediately woke up the papal household. Commotion. Crying. They sent for the Secretary of State, who lives two floors below the Pope's apartment.' She added: 'Not the present Secretary of State, nor his predecessor, who was called Casaroli, but the one before that, Cardinal Villot . . .' She looked at Morgan. 'What happens next *proves* that the Pope was murdered, and that the Secretary of State was either part of the conspiracy to murder him, or decided to destroy the evidence to avoid a scandal . . .'

Morgan waited. Renata ran her finger down her notes.

'The Secretary of State felt the Pope's pulse. Then he picked up the Pope's medicine, *and put it in his pocket*! He then took the papers from the Pope's hand, and shoved *them* into his pocket too! Then he found the Pope's will in his desk and pocketed that as well. Then he took the Pope's spectacles and slippers.' Renata looked up and said slowly: '*None* of those things was ever seen again.'

Morgan began to ask a question, but Renata held up a hand: 'The Secretary of State *then imposed a vow of silence on the papal household*! They were not to tell anybody the Pope was dead until he said so. He returned to his own quarters and began to make phone calls. It was now five am.' She held up a finger. 'He telephoned the undertakers, the Signoracci brothers, who are the official papal embalmers! And he sent a car to fetch them immediately.' She raised her eyebrows at Morgan. 'He then ordered that there would be *no* autopsy! And that the body would be embalmed immediately.' She glared at him. '*Why* no autopsy? . . . *Why* the rush to have him embalmed? . . .'

Morgan sighed.

Renata snorted, and reverted to her notes. 'The Vatican doctor examined the Pope's body at about six am. He had never examined the Pope before, not being his personal doctor. He diagnosed the cause of death as a heart attack. And the time of death as about eleven pm the previous evening.' She banged the bar: 'It is *impossible* to diagnose a heart attack without an autopsy! And even more impossible to give the time of death! That's a fact! The press asked numerous doctors . . .'

Morgan sighed. 'And then?'

'At six am the Pope's body was transferred to the Clementina Hall. He was dressed in papal robes, and put on public view for twelve hours. At six o'clock that night the actual embalming began.' She said slowly: 'The Secretary of State ordered that the body was *not* to be drained of blood! . . . Not *one* drop of blood was to be taken! . . .'

Morgan looked at her. She leant across the bar at him:

'*Why*? Embalming involves draining all the blood and then pumping the veins full of embalming fluid! All previous popes had been embalmed in the normal way! *Why* did the Secretary forbid the draining of blood? . . .' She leant forward again: 'Because even *one* drop of blood would have been enough for any pathologist to tell whether the Pope had been *poisoned* or not! . . .' She spread her arms angrily. 'And how *dare* they embalm *anybody*, let alone the head of the Holy Roman Church, *without first determining the cause of death!* . . .' She glared at him. 'That is strictly forbidden in any civilized country! There must be a proper explanation of death before a body is buried – to prevent murders going undetected! So why did the Vatican do it? *Why?*'

Morgan sat back, and rubbed his forehead. He felt sick in his guts. He started to ask a question, but Renata continued:

'And then the Vatican proceeded to tell *lie* after *lie* . . . Rumours of murder were flying around Rome within hours, and the press were demanding answers.' She began to tick them off on her fingers. 'Lie number one: the Vatican said that the Pope was holding a book called *The Imitation of Christ* in his hands when he was found dead. *Lie*. The papal staff said it was a sheaf of papers! The papers that disappeared into the Secretary of State's pocket!'

'Is it known what those papers were?'

'Wait . . . Lie number two . . . The Vatican claimed the Pope was in bad health, on the point of death, and that he died of an overdose of his medicine . . .' She smiled at him: '*Lie* . . . The press asked his two personal physicians, Dr Da Ros who had looked after him for twenty years, and Dr Rama, a heart specialist, who had been treating him for his low blood pressure for five years. Both said he was in *excellent* health.' She glared at him: '*Neither* of those two doctors were consulted by the Vatican before they buried the man! And the Vatican doctor, who had never examined the Pope in his life, did not sign even a death certificate!'

Morgan leant his elbow on the bar, and held his forehead.

'Three.' Renata held up the fingers. 'The Vatican piously claimed that it was illegal under Apostolic Law for an autopsy to be performed on a pope.' She smiled maliciously: '*Lie*. An autopsy was performed on Pope Pius VIII!'

She went on grimly: 'The Pope's body lay in state for a few days, with Swiss guards on twenty-four-hour guard. Meanwhile, the Italian press were demanding answers. *Then* . . . the day before the Pope was to be buried, something bizarre happened. At seven pm the gates of Saint Peter's were closed, as usual. At about seven forty-five, however, a group of pilgrims from the Pope's birthplace arrived to pay their last respects. They had got special permission. They were taken into Saint Peter's by a side door. They had just gathered around the coffin, when suddenly in walked a number of Vatican officials and doctors. The pilgrims were told to leave immediately! The four Swiss guards were also told to leave! Then large screens were erected around the Pope's body and a medical examination began! It lasted an hour and a half.' She looked up at Morgan and paused dramatically. 'The Vatican Press Office told Italian reporters, off the record, that the examination was only to check on the preservation of the body. They said the examination was carried out by . . .' she consulted her notes, 'by Professor Gerin and the Signoracci brothers, the embalmers, and that some more embalming fluid was injected. *After* the burial, however, the Vatican made an *official* announcement, that the examination had lasted only *twenty* minutes, and that the body was found to be in order.' She leant forward: 'The press then spoke to Professor Gerin and to the Signoracci brothers. *None of them had been present at the examination!*'

Morgan frowned incredulously. She appealed softly:

'Why the lies? Why say the examination only lasted twenty minutes when it lasted ninety minutes? Why say the embalmers and the professor made the examination when they weren't even there? *Why?*' She leant forward again. 'Obviously, because it was not an embalming procedure but an *autopsy* that was performed! Obviously there was pressure from some Vatican officials to answer the worrisome questions! And *if* that autopsy proved that the Pope was *not* murdered, the Vatican would surely have announced it loud and clear, to put a stop to the speculation that was flying around Rome like a snow storm. But, *no*. So? So obviously that little autopsy showed that the Pope *had* been murdered. So they lied, about how long it took, about the purpose, about who was present . . .'

Morgan sighed grimly. He said: 'What were the papers that the Pope was holding when he died?'

'His personal staff came forward when all the Vatican lies piled up, and told the press the *truth . . . The papers were notes of people he was going to fire from their jobs in the Vatican!*' She raised her eyebrows. 'And those papers were never seen again! They disappeared into the Secretary of State's pocket, along with the bottle of medicine that obviously contained the poison.'

Morgan took a weary breath.

Renata collected her notes and put them in the folder of press cuttings. Morgan said, 'What was the name of the Secretary of State at the time?'

'Cardinal Villot,' she said. She spelt it. 'He's dead now.'

Morgan pulled out the list of names and passwords he had extracted from Klaus Barbie's tape. He held it where she could not see it and ran his eye down the list. Villot's name did not appear. He put the paper away.

'And it's not known who the Vatican officials were whom the Pope was going to fire?'

'I don't remember the rumours, but maybe I could find out.' Renata pushed the folder across the bar to him. 'Write a good book,' she said earnestly.

He had not intended staying for dinner, but she pleaded that she had prepared a stew. 'It's *ready . . .*'

She had gone to a great deal of trouble. The best wine, candles and flowers. They went through her facts again all through the delicious meal, until Morgan's nerves were fraying. Over the coffee and cognac, he moved on to the subject of Benetti.

'He is very concerned about you. He feels you have insufficient faith.'

'Which is an understatement,' she smiled.

Morgan said carefully: 'I asked him if the Pope would agree to see you, as he knows about you. In the hopes of changing your negative attitude. He thought it might be possible to arrange. But *you* must request the meeting, and want it.'

She smiled. 'Me seeing the Pope would not change anything. You mean *you* want me to see the Pope, to help you?'

Morgan felt awkward. 'Yes,' he admitted. 'But it may indeed help you too.' He added uncomfortably: 'I suggested to Benetti that I be with you when you met the Pope.'

She smiled. 'So you want me to trick the Pope into giving us a private audience?'

Morgan nodded. 'Yes.'

She sat back, thinking.

'Yes, I would like to meet him, too. I'm sure he is a good man.' She shrugged. 'Okay. Why not? I'll try. When are you going away?'

Morgan concealed his elation. 'Tomorrow. I'll be back in December.'

'So long?' She sighed. 'All right. Please telephone me when you are coming back. And I will take up the matter with Benetti.'

'Thank you,' Morgan said sincerely.

'On one condition. That you write a good book. And give me an autographed copy.' She smiled, embarrassed. 'Why must you go away so long? You haven't got a wife hidden away, have you?'

'No. I really have urgent things to do.'

She said: 'And please stay here when you come back. Save your money.'

He'd worry about that when the time came. 'That's very kind.'

It was after eleven o'clock before he could leave with reasonable politeness. She said, disappointed: 'So early? We have all this excellent cognac you brought.'

'I've got to make some international calls from my hotel.'

'Make them from here! You can pay me.'

'No, they're calling me. And they'll be lengthy.'

'The Pensione Umberto has phones in the rooms?'

'Yes.'

She sighed sadly, a woman who could hardly say more.

She picked up her stick, and walked beside him to the door. She undid the latch, then she faced him. She smiled shyly; then she stepped up against him.

He kissed her awkwardly; then her arms slid around him, and she crushed her mouth against his and gave a little moan. She clutched him tight, then suddenly she froze. She

329

let go abruptly, and she backed off. She whispered, wide-eyed:

'Why are you wearing a gun? . . .'

He was taken aback. His mind fumbled.

'I always do . . .'

'Why?' She stared.

He said, 'I travel to a lot of dangerous places . . .'

She blinked. Then forced a nervous smile. She looked away. 'I see. Yes, of course . . .'

She turned to the door, and opened it, agitated.

'Well, good night . . .'

'Good night, Renata,' he said.

He was furious with himself for letting her near enough to feel the gun. *Goddammit, he should have foreseen that might happen – he should have left it in the bag! He had blown it! – Blown an excellent ally by frightening her! What would she think of a man with a gun who wants to get to see the Pope? And now he dare not go back to Benetti either! . . .*

He walked furiously through the rain back to the Excelsior Hotel. He took off the moustache and wig and threw himself on the bed, and stared up at the ceiling.

He felt wrung out. He had to force himself to calm down.

Maybe it wasn't so bad about the gun.

He would go and see her tomorrow and explain it away. Win her confidence back. She was so obviously smitten, it shouldn't be bad. He felt bad about using her but he needed her help. And he needed Benetti – he had to explore all possibilities of reaching the Pope and the Secretary of State . . .

At nine o'clock the next morning Morgan began his last day in Rome for four weeks. First he telephoned the Vatican Press Office again.

'Sorry to trouble you but this is the *Yorkshire Evening Post*. Could you please tell me the date Cardinal Pieter Gunter was first brought into the Vatican from America?'

'Please call me back in ten minutes,' the voice said.

Next Morgan telephoned Miguel Milano at *Il Figaro*.

'So sorry to bother you again, but I wonder if you can answer one more question. It's worth a bottle of whisky.'

'It better be a short question.'

Morgan said: 'When Pope John Paul I died suddenly after only thirty-three days, I believe there were rumours about murder?'

'And then some.'

'And I believe the dead Pope was found holding papers, which disappeared, never seen again. And the rumour is that those papers contained a list of Vatican people he intended to fire?'

'Yes. His personal secretary told the press that.'

'Now my question is: *who* was he going to fire?'

'You're looking for a motive for murder?'

'Yes.'

'You don't have to look far. I reckon God's Banker had him murdered. Or his pals in P2. Because it was common knowledge by that stage that Pope John Paul I was going to fire Bishop Marcinkus, the head of the Vatican Bank, the very next day, because the Pope detested the Vatican Bank's connection with God's Banker. The Pope was going to sweep the Vatican Bank clean. And if Bishop Marcinkus was swept out, P2 and God's Banker would lose all their invaluable banking tricks. So they had the Pope bumped off. But don't quote me.'

Morgan frowned. 'And so Bishop Marcinkus was never fired?'

'Nope. Bishop Marcinkus is now *Arch*bishop Marcinkus in fact, still president of the Vatican Bank. Confirmed by the next Pope. Makes you wonder, doesn't it?'

'Wonder what? Are you saying –'

'No, the present Pope had nothing to do with the murder – he was in Poland. But the fact that he confirmed Marcinkus in his post, even *promoted* him, when there was such a scandal, makes you wonder about the present Pope's judgement. His wisdom. Now, look, I really must go. And that's two bottles of whisky, pal . . .'

Morgan thanked him profusely. He sat back on the bed. If Miguel was right, it meant that Jack Morgan could hardly rely on Pope John Paul II to set his house in order and get rid of

Cardinal Pieter Gunter – a pope who was so unwise as to confirm Marcinkus as head of the Vatican Bank despite the scandal of God's Banker could hardly be relied upon to investigate communist agents in his Church. But Morgan knew that Miguel Milano was wrong about who murdered the last Pope. If he was murdered it was also done by the Russians, as Klaus Barbie said – the same people who then tried to murder his successor a year later, the present Pope, John Paul II, in Saint Peter's Square, to get their protégé, Cardinal Gunter, on the papal throne, and put the whole Holy Roman Church in their Kremlin pocket.

He put that aside and rehearsed again what he was going to say to Renata. He picked up the telephone and dialled.

The telephone rang and rang.

He hung up feverishly. He had to get on the road.

He waited five minutes, then tried again. Still no reply. He telephoned the Vatican Press Office again. The lady said:

'Cardinal Gunter left America to take up his first position in the Secretariat of State in March 1981.'

Morgan looked at his notes. Pope John Paul was murdered, or died, on 28th September 1978, over eighteen months earlier. So Cardinal Pieter Gunter was not in Rome then.

He tried Renata's telephone number again. Still no reply.

He left the hotel and bought two bottles of scotch whisky. He took them to the hotel receptionist and arranged for them to be delivered to Miguel Milano. He paid his hotel bill, and went up to his room.

He still had to go back to the Pensione Umberto, to collect the rest of his things: the tape-recorder, clothes, the ski gear. He did not want to abandon them and draw attention to Mr John Armstrong.

He tried Renata's number once more, without success. He could not bear to wait any longer. He would call her later. He took off his wig and moustache, and he slipped out of the Excelsior Hotel, and hailed a taxi to take him to the Pensione Umberto.

As the taxi came around the corner, Morgan saw a police car parked outside the pensione, and his heart missed a beat. 'Drive on!' He waved his hand.

The driver looked nonplussed. 'Umberto . . .'

'*Drive.*'

The driver accelerated. They drove past the pensione. A policeman appeared in the doorway and looked up and down the street.

Morgan sat back, his mind fumbling. *Renata.* He had told her he was staying at the Pensione Umberto – she had telephoned the police and told them that an Englishman with a gun called John Armstrong was trying to get to see the Pope . . .

'Where to?' the driver said.

Morgan feverishly pulled out a note he had made of a second-hand car dealer. 'Here . . .'

Part Eight

48

A forestry road winds through the snowy mountains. Then a track leads off down into a little valley: you come out of the forest, into a rocky orchard that extends down to a river. Near the bottom is the old farmhouse. It has high walls around it, forming a courtyard, with a big double door. The walls are half a metre thick, made of stone and clay, whitewashed. The courtyard is cobbled and there are tumble-down cowsheds and chicken coops. The house is double-storeyed with a tower in one corner, holding the water tanks. The windows that look onto the orchard have bars on them. The only other door onto the outside is the kitchen door. There are walnut trees outside the kitchen, and a stream runs between them, on its way down to the little river at the bottom of the valley. The river is crystal clear, tumbling over stones, and trees grow along its banks, and there is a little waterfall, with a rocky pool where it would be lovely to swim in the summer. In the summer, the front of the house would be in deep shade. But now it was November, and most of the trees were bare, and the river was icy cold, and there was snow on the old red-tiled roof, and smoke was curling up the chimneys.

It was almost dusk when Morgan came winding down the track in the car he had bought.

Driving from Rome had given him his first opportunity to worry about what Anna's reaction was going to be to his tricking her in Amsterdam: locking her in that whore-house dungeon, his breach of trust. He pushed it out of his mind, with the fortitude of a man who knew he had done the right thing. She would be breathing bitter fire when she first saw him, but he would weather it. And he still had to trick her yet again, when he returned to Rome in December: but he could not bear to worry about that yet. All he could think about now was getting her trust and love back. Then he came out of the forest, at the top of the orchard, and he stopped the car; and he was so relieved to see the smoke coming out of the chimneys, to know that they had arrived safely, his worry went out of his mind. He was grinning. It was a wonderful feeling to be coming back to her. And oh, the house looked so cosy and safe. He gave a long blast on the horn because he did not want his head blown off by Makepeace. He bellowed: '*It's me! Hold your fire!*' He let the car roll down the slope, towards the house.

Then suddenly the big double door burst open, and Anna came out, breathing fire.

She came running up the snowy track, slipping and sliding and a tearful laugh all over her beautiful face. Morgan slammed on the brakes and scrambled out of the car.

He started running down the track towards her, grinning, slipping and sliding. They ran into each other's arms.

'*Oh thank God,*' she gasped – '*oh thank God . . .*'

Makepeace was up in the water tower, keeping a lookout for a while in case Morgan had been followed.

They sat by the fire in the bedroom, with a bottle of wine. Her whole demeanour was different now. She said:

'All right, so you tricked me for my own good. I can accept that, with reservations. Though locking me up in a whore-house dungeon was adding insult to injury. But I can accept even that, just, because it was all you could do in the peculiar circumstances . . .' She looked at him steadily. 'But I beg you, for *our* sake, not to lie to me now, Jack. And you *are* lying to me. It hasn't taken you a week to get here from Zurich. You've been to Rome. And you *did* go into the Union Bank of Switzerland, and get the box. Makepeace told me.'

He said incredulously, 'Makepeace told you? . . .'

'He started by giving me your version. But I've been in his company for three solid days driving down here. That gave me time to ask a lot of questions, a lot of time for him to contradict himself. I know he bought you a tape-recorder and took it into the bank. I know you were attacked by a Russian in the vaults.' She waited.

Morgan stood up. Oh to have this all over with. He paced away across the room.

'Yes, I've lied to you. Yes, I've been to Rome.'

She sighed grimly. 'What did you need a tape-recorder for?'

'There is a tape made by Klaus Barbie, purporting to be a

338

summary of what's on the microfilm. I've got the tape here. And I bought a recorder, you can listen to it.'

He expected her to be astonished that Klaus Barbie had anything to do with this. She only said, 'And where's the microfilm?'

He had decided to tell her that there was no microfilm, to disentangle her from this mess. But he hesitated from lying any more. 'Why aren't you surprised about Klaus Barbie being involved?'

She said: 'Max told me everything. And please don't tell me that no microfilm exists. Because I saw it.'

He was astonished. 'When?'

'On my birthday, last year. When Max had his drunken outburst.'

'Well,' he demanded, 'what *has* Klaus Barbie got to do with this? And God's Banker? And how did the microfilm get from Barbie to Max?' He jabbed a finger at her. 'You didn't tell me you knew all this. You misled me.'

'Yes.' She held out her hand: 'Give the microfilm to me, please.'

He walked back to the bed and sat down.

'What is this, Anna? You're cross-examining me cold-bloodedly.'

'I feel far from cold-blooded, believe me. I feel hot-blooded.' She looked at him, then shook her head. 'Oh darling Jack . . . you are either a most honest babe in the woods of espionage, or you are still working for the British. You tricked me, in Switzerland. Was it only to save my skin? Or was it also to stop me destroying the microfilm so you could find out what it was about, so that *you* could decide what to do about it? And maybe give it to the British to sort out?'

He was angry that she was right. 'If I were still working for the British, why am I here?'

'Because you are still deciding what to do about it perhaps?'

'Not because I love you perhaps?'

'Yes, that too.'

'Well, I wish you'd look more convinced about that!' He breathed bitterly. 'The microfilm is still in the vaults of the Union Bank of Switzerland. Because it was too dangerous to bring it out, with Russians waiting outside. I'd already been

339

attacked inside. It is in a new box, a numbered account, so nobody can forge my signature.'

She nodded slowly. Unsurprised. 'And you're not going to tell me the number? Because what I don't know can't be extracted from me?'

'Correct. I'll get it out when we need it.'

She breathed.

'All right. That's what I would have done, too.'

He said, 'I thought you would have destroyed it?'

She got up. She began to pace across the bedroom. 'And? Have you got any plan figured out yet?'

'Not yet.'

She did not believe him. She sat down on the bed.

'Was there anything else in the box?'

He said, 'An envelope containing a banker's letter, and an airline waybill.' He pulled out the envelope and extracted the banker's letter.

She read it carefully, expressionlessly. Then put it aside.

He handed her the waybill. She studied it. She made no comment.

'Do those mean anything to you?' he said.

'Anything else?' she said.

'Do the names Sanchez, and Hank mean anything to you?'

'No. Was there anything else?'

He pulled out the film negatives. 'I think some of these are pornographic.'

She took them. She held them up to the firelight.

She studied them grimly, her face set.

'Do they mean anything to you?' Morgan said.

'Are there any more?' She looked in the envelope.

'No. Can you identify anybody?'

'No. But yes, they look pornographic,' she said flatly. She looked at the film again. Then put them back in the envelope carefully.

'Now, please tell me what happened in Rome?'

First he played the Klaus Barbie tape. She listened grimly, her head in her hands. She made no comment. Then he told her about Rome.

He did not tell her about going to the golf club, nor how

he tried to see the Secretary of State disguised as Reverend Anderson from Zambia. He wanted her to believe that he had no plan yet. He told her about Whacker Ball and Renata, what information she had dug up about the death of Pope John Paul I, but he did not tell her about the police waiting at Pensione Umberto, lest that alarm her. He consulted his notes and told her everything that Miguel Milano had told him: about God's Banker and his crooked deals with the Vatican Bank, the ghost companies they set up together, about Bellatrix and the arms it supplied to the military régimes of South America; he told her about the masonic lodge called P2 of which God's Banker was the paymaster, how God's Banker was robbing his own banks, the deep financial crisis he got into, about the Vatican Bank's 'comfort letter' in respect of Bellatrix and their subsequent denial that they were responsible for Bellatrix's debts: he told her Milano's theory that God's Banker fled to London to try to get his hands on certain documents from somebody in P2 with which to blackmail the Vatican into paying so that P2 could get arms.

Anna sat on the bed, listening expressionlessly. She said:

'So this Miguel Milano thinks that the Vatican had God's Banker murdered, to stop him blackmailing them?'

'Yes. But he's wrong. Obviously the Russians murdered him. To stop him getting the microfilm and exposing their secret weapon in the Vatican.'

'Did Miguel have any theories about what weapons were needed, and for whom?'

'No.' He looked at her. 'Do you know? You haven't told me everything that Max told you.'

She started to get up, but he put a hand on hers. He said: 'If Miguel's theory is correct, Max must have been a member of P2, because God's Banker was going to get the evidence from a P2 member. Was he?'

She got up and paced away. 'Yes.'

'But P2 is fascist! Fiercely anti-communist. And Max was hand in glove with the communist government of Grenada.'

She sighed bitterly.

'That's where he was so damn clever. He was hand in glove with everybody. He was pals with Somoza of Nicaragua and pals with the Sandinista guerrillas. Pals with both Castro and

341

Washington DC. That was his value to P2 – his assignment was to infiltrate the communists in the region.'

Morgan sat back on the bed.

'I see. And? How did he get the microfilm from Klaus Barbie?'

She said: 'Barbie wanted to join P2. Max did business in Bolivia, and they knew each other. Barbie approached Max and wanted to join P2, for protection, because the French were after him, and he offered the microfilm to prove how valuable he could be.' She snorted softly. 'And Max hung onto it. And tried to use it for his purposes.'

'And that purpose was? Was it in fact for arms?'

She got up and paced away. He said: 'Why're you reluctant to tell me, Anna?'

She said tensely: 'What am I going to do about this, Jack?'

He said: 'I thought you wanted to destroy the microfilm as a scurrilous lie?'

She cried impatiently: 'I didn't *want* to believe it. Even though I suspected it was true. And now –' she jabbed her finger at the tape-recorder – 'I *know* it's true. It all fits . . .' She sighed angrily: 'I was never going to destroy it if it was true, Jack.'

'What would you have done?'

She put her hands to her face. 'Oh darling Jack . . . you don't know how grateful I am for all you've done to help me . . .' She dropped her hands. 'I didn't know what I was going to do. Get hold of the microfilm and verify it somehow. Then . . . Somehow I was going to see the Pope about it. Maybe I was going to hire somebody to help me.' She appealed: 'But what am I going to do *now*?'

And oh God he hated to trick her again, but he had to.

'We're not going to do anything for the time being. The heat's on us, Anna. We're going to lie low in these mountains until after Christmas.'

For a moment intense relief flickered across her face. Then she appealed: 'For God's sake, there are communists in the top ranks of the Holy Roman Church! What are we going to do after Christmas?' Her eyes were suddenly glistening. 'And please don't suggest that we hand the problem over to the British! . . .'

He snorted. 'You still have a lingering suspicion that I'm working for the British?' He smiled mirthlessly: '*The Spy Who Loved Me*?'

She stood, nerves tight. 'And don't imagine that I can ever go and live in Britain after this.'

He said emphatically, 'We *will*. We'll face them down once this is over.'

She looked at him, then cried:

'Oh – *I'm* the spy, don't you see? . . .' She thumped her breast: '*I'm a trained Russian spy! . . . And I can never run to England . . .*'

He was astonished. She glared at him, then cried:

'*Because it wasn't the Russians who murdered God's Banker – or the Vatican! It was the bloody British! And they'll do the same to me!*'

He stared at her, absolutely astonished.

She cried: 'You're blind, Jack – and your friend Miguel Milano! The answer's staring you in the face and you don't see it! Think! You ask what weapons God's Banker and the P2 wanted the money for! For which country! *Think!* What was going on when God's Banker was hanged from Blackfriars Bridge on the 18th of June 1982?' She jabbed a finger at him: 'You were *there*, Jack! *The Falklands War!* Between Britain and Argentina!'

'Jesus Christ . . .' Morgan said.

'*Think*. Mr Gelli, the Grand Master of P2, was an Argentinian subject! And he was supplying arms to fascist countries with money provided by God's Banker. And now Argentina is at war with Great Britain, and losing, and she desperately needs more arms. But God's Banker is bankrupt . . .' She jabbed her finger at Morgan again: '*That*'s what P2 wanted out of the deal. Money for arms, so Argentina could win the Falklands War! So P2 was going to give God's Banker the microfilm with which to blackmail the Vatican into paying up on that "comfort letter". And God's Banker rushed to London to get it from Max.' She glared, then cried: 'It was *exocet missiles* that Max was going to buy with the money . . .' She pointed at the envelope. 'That airline waybill is for sixteen crates of exocet missiles, not bulldozer parts!'

'Jesus Christ . . .' Morgan whispered. She cried:

'And the British murdered God's Banker to stop the Argentinians getting any! And the very next day Galtieri, the military president of Argentina, fell! *And the war was lost . . .*'

She looked at him, her chest heaving.

'The *British* murdered God's Banker and made it look like suicide! *And that's what they'll do to me . . .*'

49

The night was unreal. Makepeace knocked on the door and asked them if they wanted any supper, but they didn't. He said the coast was clear, and went to bed. Morgan and Anna lay close together in the glow of the fire and the unrealness of the snowy night. She was calm again now, drained.

'I never actually joined the Party at university. But I was a communist all right. I still am a socialist, but an older, wiser, moderate one now. But in those days I was young and starry-eyed.' She snorted wearily. 'I believed in the spontaneous creative vigour that would emerge from the masses if they were unshackled from the yoke of international capitalism. I wanted to see the means of production nationalized, instead of the profits of sweated labour going to Wall Street. I considered the workers of the Third World were getting a raw deal and I wanted to see oppressive, undemocratic governments got rid of. As I still do. *Including* oppressive communist governments.'

He waited. She went on: 'And of course I was reading Marx and Lenin and Mao Tse-tung for my political science degree – along with Adam Smith and Jeremy Bentham and John Stuart Mill. I was awfully knowledgeable, if not particularly wise.' She sighed. 'Then . . . I never told you this, but at the end of my second year I visited Russia.'

He was surprised. 'No.'

She smiled wearily. 'Nor did my parents know. They thought I was spending the summer holidays touring Europe. And when I met you two years later I didn't think it would be smart to tell one of Her Majesty's nuclear submarine commanders,

344

whom I fell in love with at first sight.' She sighed bitterly. 'Anyway, that's where they recruited me.'

He could hardly believe this. She went on:

'A girlfriend called Cynthia and I went. It was supposed to be one of those cultural student tours, arranged by Intourist. And that's how it started – art galleries, ballet, theatre, universities. The Russian students assigned to Cynthia and me as guides made a great fuss of us. We met Russian students who invited us to parties. No real politics at first. Then we went on to the heavier stuff. Touring factories. Collective farms. They were excellent, the ones we saw. Rosy-cheeked Russian girls singing as they worked, stalwart Russian lads in love with their tractors. Tables groaning with food, jolly sing-a-longs in the evening, vodka flowing like water.' She smiled bleakly. 'We really had a splendid time. And everything so cheap. And the Russian boys who were squiring us around were most charming.' She breathed: 'I got very fond of one.' She paused, wearily. 'His name was Ivan, of course. He had just graduated. He was going to join the diplomatic corps.' She sighed wearily. 'We had an affair . . . It got pretty intense. He wanted me to stay in Russia, and marry him, et cetera.'

Morgan was amazed. 'Did you consider it?'

She shook her head. 'Even though I was young and starry-eyed, I was old enough to know that so far it was only a sweet holiday romance.' She went on flatly: 'In the last week, they began to put the pressure on me.'

'How?'

She ran her hand over her head.

'We were invited to various student functions. Much talk of international peace and brotherhood, freedom from hunger and want. All good heady stuff. Then, came the soft-soap: Would I join the International Brotherhood of Students? And contribute articles for their newsletter? Yes, I would. Wonderful, sign here please.' She took a breath. 'Then came the punchline: Would I like to come back at Christmas, as a guest of the Soviet People, to attend a short but intensive course in "Comparative Philosophy", to be held in the Urals?' She looked at Morgan. '*Would* I? A free trip to Russia, plus a university course – in my subject. What an enrichment of my student life! Of course I accepted.'

Morgan lay back. Oh Jesus. 'So what happened?'

'The next day I left for England. With a tear in my eye for Ivan. And a lump in my throat for Russia. Back to dear old Exeter University. But the next month what happens? A phone call from Ivan! From *London*. He had indeed joined the diplomatic service. And posted to London!' She clasped her hands coquettishly. 'Oh, joy. How romantic. My handsome Russian has shown up! That weekend he came down to Exeter by train. And most weekends after that. A couple of times I went to London, and stayed in his quarters. All very romantic . . .'

Morgan did not particularly want to know the details. 'Did you ever send any articles to the International Brotherhood of Students?'

She snorted bitterly. 'A few. But only extracts of essays I had already written for my own professors, I was busy and I only did it to keep my end up.' She took a weary breath. 'Then, towards the end of November, my ardour for Ivan-the-Terrible began to cool. I began to find him boring. Repetitive. And I began to resent his constant assumption that I was a full-blooded, dedicated communist. His "Us against Them" attitude. I was beginning to mature, as a student of political science. Things weren't so black and white as they had seemed. I was turning into a moderate socialist. I found I wasn't even looking forward to going back to Russia. But I felt I should – it was too interesting an experience to miss.' She sighed. 'So, anyway, at the beginning of December I broke it off with Ivan. I told him I was sorry but I didn't love him after all. That I had met somebody else – which I hadn't.'

'How did he take it?'

'Apparently, very badly. He plagued me with anguished telephone calls. Flowers. Impassioned letters.' She shook her head. 'Finally he gave up, swearing eternal love.'

Morgan waited.

'And . . . so Christmas came. And off I went to Russia. Rather unenthusiastically. I arrived in Moscow, transplaned to the Urals. Met, and taken up to the so-called university building. Very pretty setting, but it was like a small military barracks. Fenced. Dormitories. Mess hall. Not that I minded any of that, except there was no bloody *bar*. What I objected to was the course.'

Morgan smiled.

'There were about thirty students. Both sexes. All nationalities, mostly black, but they all came from different parts of the British Commonwealth.' She turned to him. 'But they were all there to study so-called *Intelligence Techniques*. I was the only sucker who thought we were going to be studying Comparative Philosophy!'

Morgan smiled. 'Go on.'

'I soon found out. The first lecture: Surveillance. Second: Coding. Third: Communications . . . At lunchtime, I went to the boss and said, Hey, what's all this crap for? Are you training me to be a spy? He said it was just basic survival instruction for friends of the Soviet Union – the philosophy lectures would start soon. He cautioned me not to cause trouble for myself.' She looked at Morgan. '"*Survival!*" *Trouble!* I began to get scared then.'

Morgan nodded.

She said: 'Bloody scared. What had I let myself in for? What would the authorities do back in Britain if they found out? Or America? But there was nothing I could do. There were military guards and we were miles from anywhere, in the depths of winter. And I worried what they might do if I kicked up a fuss. Nobody knew I was in Russia. So . . . I just had to grin and bear it. And attend the lectures.' She sighed bitterly. 'But I must admit they were quite interesting. I even did quite well in the tests. Especially in self-defence.' She smiled wanly: 'As you saw in Amsterdam.'

He smiled. 'What were the other students like?'

'All red-hot communists. Going to be spies and freedom fighters. We were under strict orders not to discuss our personal histories. But our dedication to the glorious revolution was taken for granted.'

'What was discipline like?'

'Strict. And *hard work*. Breakfast at six-thirty. First lecture at seven. Last lecture at eight pm. Lights out at ten.'

'What else did they teach you?'

She waved a hand. 'Later, let me tell the tale . . . So, at the end of three weeks I emerged from the Urals, a fully fledged little spy. I flew back to London, furious, but very relieved to be out. And who should be waiting for me at Heathrow airport?

347

Ivan-the-Terrible. With flowers and a car, to drive me back to Exeter.' She snorted. 'I was terrified of him now. Maybe he was part of the plot. I said "No thank you, Ivan," and I headed for the buses. He followed me, protesting love. Finally, I yelled "Leave me alone!" and I ran.'

'Of course he was part of the plot. Did you ever see him again?'

She held up a silencing hand. 'I lay low at Exeter for a month. I never went out except in a group. Ivan phoned several times but I refused to speak to him.' She rubbed her brow. 'I received several letters from the International Brotherhood begging for more pieces, but I destroyed them. Boy, was I scared. They hadn't spent all that money on me for nothing, they'd want me to start spying soon, I was sure. But they didn't contact me.' She paused. 'After a while I grew more confident that I had put them off.' She took a weary breath. 'What I didn't realize was that I was a "sleeper". Somebody they keep on ice, until they need him.'

He said grimly: 'And? When was that?'

She took a sip of her wine.

'I wrote my BA finals. Went home to Grenada for the summer holidays. Then I returned to university and started my Honours year. Still nothing happened. Then . . . I met you.'

She turned her head to him. '"Ninety glorious days," we called it.' She smiled sadly. 'How many times did we make love in those ninety days, I wonder? Lord, how did we ever pass our exams? And I wonder why I didn't get pregnant, with all that loving?'

His eyes burnt. 'You told me you'd gone on the pill.'

She smiled sadly, and turned back to the fire. 'Another little lie. I didn't want worry to spoil anything. And I was so in love I *longed* to be pregnant by you.'

He put his hand on hers. 'Well, maybe you are now.'

She sat up. She ran her hands through her hair.

'So, we did pass our exams. And we went to Grenada to introduce you to my parents, then you went back to sea for four terrible months. And I began to prepare for our wonderful wedding.'

Morgan waited. Then said: 'But there was Max.'

'There was *always* Max. Since I was a teenager. We were

348

never lovers. But he was always hanging around. Always waiting to marry me. And yes, he really put the pressure on me now. And there was pressure from my family and friends to think again – they said I hardly knew you. And yes, there were times when I was assailed by doubts . . .' She ran her fingers through her hair. 'But oh God, that isn't why I didn't marry you, Jack . . .'

He waited. She pressed her fingertips to her eyelids; then lowered her hands. She said:

'One day, about two weeks before our wedding, I was sitting on the beach. Alone. When a man came along. A white man. He walked up to me. He smiled, and he pulled a photo album out of his bag. He handed it to me. I thought he was a beach photographer. He said: "Remember your friends." And he walked away.'

She stared at the fire a long moment. Morgan waited

'I was astonished. I opened the album.' She paused. She went on flatly: 'It contained dozens of photographs, of me in Russia. Unmistakably Russia, the Kremlin in the background, et cetera. With Ivan. And . . .' She paused again. 'Dozens and *dozens* of photographs of me in bed with him.' She glared at the fire. 'Taken in my hotel room in Moscow. And in his quarters in London.' She clenched her fist. 'The bastards must have had cameras hidden all over those rooms, to get the best angles.' She pointed at the envelope he had found in Max's deposit box. 'Those are some of them.'

Morgan stared. 'Those are you?'

She said flatly: 'Me. The rejects. Ones they couldn't use because they're too indistinct, I suppose.'

Morgan was amazed. 'Oh, God . . .' He squeezed her hand.

She said: 'Which was another reason why I was rather anxious to get to that deposit box. I wasn't sure they were in there, but nobody likes pictures like that of themselves doing the rounds of Whitehall.'

'But how did they come to be in Max's box?'

'I'm not sure, but I'll come to that.' She took a big, bitter breath. 'And there were photocopies of my application to join the International Brotherhood, translated, showing that I signed a pledge to further the cause of international communism. And photocopies of my enrolment at the spy-school.

Classroom photographs of me. Under the picture of Lenin. Learning to use equipment. Learning self-defence. Plus my instructor's report on me. *Oh* so favourable! Plus extracts from my essays that I had sent the International Brotherhood – distorted, taken out of context . . .'

She turned to him. Her eyes smouldering.

'*That*'s why I didn't marry you, Jack Morgan! . . . *Couldn't* marry you! . . . Because they were telling me that they had the goods on me to make me spy on my future husband! . . . On the second-in-command of one of Her Majesty's nuclear submarines! . . . And if I refused they would denounce me! And *ruin* you . . .' She cried: '*That's why I couldn't marry you, Jack* . . .'

She threw herself back on the bed. She held her face.

That night seemed unreal. The complete silence of the snowy mountains, the candlelight. Morgan fetched more wine from the kitchen. They lay deep in the double bed, and the rest of the story came out.

And that's why she married Max. To cut herself off from Jack Morgan completely, so no harm could be done to him. Distance herself from him completely, to destroy the power of the blackmailer over him. And, yes, to protect herself too, from having to lead a double life. She could not be blackmailed into divulging anything about Max, he had no official secrets to exchange.

'Did you ever tell Max?'

'Of course! That was the only way to destroy the power of the blackmailer – make a clean breast, have nothing to hide. But I could not have done that with you. If I had told you that I was supposed to be a Russian spy, you would either have had to confess it to the Navy and thereby ruin your career because the Navy would never trust a senior officer with an ex-spy for a wife. Or you'd have had to cover it up and be blackmailed . . .'

Morgan lay beside her in the firelight and saw it all: the fear, the heartbreak. She felt frantic. She had to be alone to think, and she was frightened of being alone, in case the messenger came back. She drove. Morgan saw the sun on the turquoise waters, the palms, the white beaches, the heavy tropical foliage, the car driving round and round the beautiful island, parked at the lonely beaches; starting again, driving on.

'The human body finally protects itself from the exhaustion of indecision – it finally just shuts down. I used to fall into exhausted sleep the moment I went to bed. But I only slept a few hours and then I was wide awake again, in the dark . . .'

It took five awful days and nights to know what she had to do. And, oh, the heartbreak once she truly knew it.

On the sixth day she got up before dawn, and drove through the fragrant darkness to her favourite beach. She walked along the dark sands. Then she knelt down and she prayed. Finally she returned to the car, she watched the sun rise, the tears running down her face. When the sun was well up she drove into Saint George's, to the post office. And she wrote out the telegram to Morgan telling him that she was marrying Max. She walked back to her car, and her heart broke, and she dropped her head and she wept, and wept.

Later that morning, she drove to Max's house. He was surprised – he had not seen her for days. She walked into the dining room, and asked the servant to leave. She stood at the table, and she told him she would marry him the following day in Las Vegas.

'When did you tell Max about the Russians?'

She said flatly, 'I intended telling him only after I had married him. But that would have been deceitful. When we got to Las Vegas, I broke down and told him. That night. In bed.' She took a deep breath. 'It was our first night in bed together, remember. We were getting married in the morning. I was numb.' She sighed. 'I told him about my first tourist visit to Russia, the fun, the International Brotherhood, Ivan. My trip back to Russia. The spy-school. How furious I was . . .'

Morgan waited. She stared at the fire.

'But I didn't tell him everything.' She snorted bitterly. 'I was weak. I did not tell him about the Russian messenger coming to me on the beach. About his album of pornographic photographs, my essays. I did not tell him that was why I could not marry you . . .' She shook her head. 'I deceived him. I told it as a confession of something I had done long ago when I was a starry-eyed student.' She snorted softly. 'I simply said that

351

after a lot of soul searching I realized that I did not love you after all. That you were only a flash in the pan.' She clenched her fist. 'I *lied* to him. Even when I was trying not to deceive him, I lied to him! . . .'

With all his battered heart Morgan did not blame her. 'What did he say?'

'Oh, poor Max. Big, rich, powerful, insecure Max . . . He was so in love with me. He was extremely jealous of me, but he knew I'd slept with you of course, and maybe he presumed others. But a *Russian* . . .? And me a trained spy? Yet he laughed – he tried to take it as the silly confession I had made it sound. He said nothing would ever happen. And when I became worried that he was not taking it seriously . . .' She closed her eyes. 'He got down on his knees. And begged me not to worry, not to let it stop me marrying him . . . And I was so grateful. And he wept.'

Morgan lay there, eyes closed. Anna went on flatly:

'We got married finally. In one of those ghastly, twenty-four-hour wedding chapels.' She breathed out. 'Max took my story very well. Until the honeymoon was over.'

Morgan sighed. Oh, what a mess.

'Of course, I should never have married him. He was dear to me, but I could not love him. I should have disappeared and fought my own battles.' She snorted at herself. 'I kept a smile on my face, but my heart was breaking. For you. I tried hard to make it up to him, because I felt so guilty. But you can't fool people about these things. He's a jealous man anyway, and he became obsessively jealous because he knew I didn't love him, no matter how hard I tried and pretended. He figured out for himself that I hadn't married you because of that spy nonsense. He began to drink and then he would taunt me with it. "My spy" he called me . . . I just had to ride it out because I *was* to blame. I threw myself into social work. I helped run clinics and libraries and I taught school. Church work. First Aid classes, domestic classes. I did organization work with the New Jewel Movement before they came to power. Anything to keep myself busy and forget my unhappy home. Always with a smile. I insisted that we have a religious marriage ceremony. I hoped that would reassure him. But it didn't . . . I began to turn more and more to religion. And he taunted me with that

352

when he was drunk. "Confessing your sins". Oh God . . .' She massaged her forehead. 'One of the worst things is that you lose *respect*. I had so much respect for him – he was on numerous government committees, under the old government, and he was very clever at business. But it's hard to hang on to respect when there's bad behaviour. But I felt guilty because I was responsible for his insecurity.'

'How did he react to you joining left-wing politics?'

'Oh, he always knew I was left-wing. I didn't get involved as a politician, only office work. The old Cary government was so corrupt, they needed clearing out, Max knew that and Max is a survivor, he saw the writing on the wall – he began to sell up and move his money out. And when the old government was overthrown and Maurice Bishop came to power, Max was in with them too. He wanted to stay in Grenada . . .' She sighed. 'But then, something happened . . .'

She sighed. She went on flatly: 'Max was a moderating influence on the revolutionary government. He was very opposed to the build-up of Russian influence. Then one day two Russian embassy officials came to his office. They told him to cool it, or else.' She pressed her fingers to her eyes. 'They said they had the goods on me – "very embarrassing evidence" . . . Max came storming home. He demanded to know what it was about. And . . . I told him about the album.'

'Oh God . . .'

She said, 'You can imagine. Not only was he insanely jealous, he was outraged, mortified that photographs of me . . . "fucking" were "doing the rounds". And absolutely outraged that he was being blackmailed, his political position compromised.' She sighed wearily. 'He went storming to the Russian embassy, demanded to see the ambassador. Demanded that their blackmail cease. The ambassador denied it, of course. But with a wolfish smile. Max hit the bastard. He came storming home again. And . . .' She shook her head. 'That was when I began to fight back. I felt as guilty as hell, but I had to fight back, for my sanity.' She took a deep breath, 'And it was because the Russians had the goods on me that he changed his stance against the bastards. He had to hold his tongue. To save me and himself from disgrace. What I did not know at the time was that it compromised his position with P2 – I did not know he was a member at that stage.' She sighed, bitterly. 'Anyway, this was when the real cat and dog life began. Like that shark hoax. Then, when you came back, he went berserk . . . You know the rest. He got rid of you off the island, then got you dismissed from the Navy. About this time Klaus Barbie entered the picture – trying to join P2. At the same time, God's Banker was getting into deep hot water financially. Then came the Falklands War and Argentina needed exocet missiles and P2 sent Max with Barbie's microfilm to God's Banker so he could blackmail the Vatican into paying up. And the British got to hear about it and nipped that in the bud, and won the war.'

Morgan rubbed his hair. 'And how did these pornographic negatives get into Max's box?'

'I don't know for sure. Most of these revelations from Max came out in furious outbursts. Often drunken. I know he tried to bribe the Russians, for the pornographic negatives. But when he came into possession of the microfilm from Barbie, he had something to fight back with. So he tried to make a deal, the microfilm for all the pornographic negatives. They jumped at the opportunity. They gave him some negatives gratuitously, to encourage him. These, I think.' She nodded at the envelope. 'He waved them at me in one of his outbursts. But he realized they must have copies, so he backed off. Then he found another use for the microfilm – exocet missiles, with Vatican money.'

'Did you know the negatives were in the box?'

'I thought they might be. They disappeared from our house. I searched high and low.'

'Why didn't he destroy them?'

'To keep a hold over me, I think.'

Morgan dragged his hands down his face. He felt he had supped full of horrors. She looked at him and her eyes glistened. 'And I've dragged you into this horrifying business.'

He turned and took her in his arms. She went on resolutely: 'I don't want you to do any more. I'll handle the rest on my own. I've ruined my own life, and yours, and Max's. This much I've got to do.'

He held her tight. He whispered: 'We're not doing anything until after Christmas.' He rocked her. 'We're going to *rest*. Then we'll figure out what we're going to do.'

She closed her eyes. Oh, to rest . . . Oh, to do nothing until

Christmas, just be with him, alone in this lovely house, an end to running until after Christmas. And then?

'You must give me the microfilm after Christmas.'

'Yes.'

'Have you really not got a plan yet?'

He shook his head, 'No.'

She knew he was lying and she knew he was doing it for her, to stop her trying to handle this herself, and she loved him for it: he was an honest man, a babe in the woods of big, bad politics that Max used to hunt in, but an honourable man, and for the moment it didn't matter that he was lying to her for her sake. She would get the microfilm from him, but, oh God, all she wanted right now was to rest with him, in his arms, her true love, for the little time they had left together; because she knew the world was a cruel place that was not going to hesitate to destroy her, and it would not care afterwards that it was not necessary.

'Please believe that the only reason I didn't leave Max and come to you after he got you dismissed from the Navy was because he threatened to have you extradited.'

He held her tight. 'I figured that out for myself. But now I've come to you. I'm *back* . . . We're together at last, alone in our lovely house in the mountains and nobody knows.' He squeezed her. 'Isn't this a good old house to have our honeymoon in?'

She held him tight and stifled a sob. 'It's a lovely house. I want to stay forever . . .'

50

Makepeace had got an FN rifle and an old Sterling machine gun from a contact of Danziger's in Amsterdam. 'Danziger doesn't know where we are, does he?' Morgan demanded

'No,' Makepeace sighed. 'Relax.'

'Where is he now?' They were alone.

'In Marseilles, I think. That's where a lot of the boys hang out. He and I have a job together soon, in Spain.'

'Doing what?'

'Never mind,' Makepeace said loftily, 'you have no need to know. Know what I mean?'

'You be careful of that guy.'

'The job,' Makepeace said sanctimoniously, 'is actually for the Spanish government. Against the Basque terrorists.'

Morgan smiled. 'For somebody who has no need to know, I already know quite a lot. Know what I mean?'

Makepeace offered to stay on as bodyguard, for a hundred pounds a day, until the Spanish job came around, but Morgan wanted to be alone with Anna, to forget about the whole awful business, until December. Makepeace dropped his price to fifty pounds, then to nothing, just his food and booze, but Morgan still did not want him. 'I'm sure we're safe here, Dougie. But I want you to come back for a few days at the beginning of December. You must phone me once a week at a public telephone in the village.' He produced a slip of paper. 'This is the number. I noted it down when I passed through the village.'

'What must I come back for?'

'To look after Anna. I have to go away for a few days. I'll tell you when to come, on the telephone. And I want you to bring me two things. Most important. One is a top-quality miniature tape-recorder. The kind I can hide in my pocket and stick the microphone through a button-hole on my jacket.'

Makepeace nodded. 'I know the type.'

'The other thing is a canister of nerve gas. The stuff that you squirt in your assailant's face. Knocks him out.'

'Okay.'

Morgan paced, thinking.

'In your line of business, does the name Hank or Henri mean anything? An arms dealer. And the name Sanchez?'

'No. What kind of arms dealer?'

'Okay,' Morgan said. 'I've got a job for you in Marseilles. Flat fee, three hundred pounds, plus reasonable expenses. No success, no pay. In Marseilles there's a small airline called Meteor Air run by a man called Alex Wallen. He knows who Hank is. I simply want you to find out from him Hank's full name, address and telephone number. And Sanchez's if possible. But Hank is the important one. He is probably an American, with a nickname like that. Sanchez is probably Argentinian.'

Makepeace blinked. 'And how do I find this out from Wallen?'

'Meteor Air air-freights arms for mercenaries. You pose as a mercenary. You tell him you want to contact Hank to make a big purchase, which Meteor Air is going to freight.'

'And if he won't tell me? These guys can be suspicious of strangers.'

'Pester him. Follow any clues. Ask discreetly round the underworld. But if you still don't succeed, work him over.'

'Work him over? How badly? Break an arm?'

'*No*, Makepeace. I have no compunction about working over somebody who traffics in death, but surely you can make a man talk without mutilating him?'

'Supposing he's got heavies? Can I take Danziger along?'

'*No*. And nobody must know you're working for me!'

Makepeace blinked. 'What kind of arms am I supposed to be after? There're all kind of specialists in that game. If you want tanks it's no good going to a pisspot hand-grenade man.'

Morgan said, 'Except as a last resort, you refuse to discuss it with Wallen – you say you'll only deal with Hank. But you must *not* meet Hank. All I want is his details. But it's exocet missiles you're supposed to be after.'

Makepeace stared. '*Exocet missiles*? . . . Jesus Christ.'

'And that's all you need to know.' He sighed. 'And I want to know Danziger's contact number.'

Makepeace was taken aback. 'What for? I thought you didn't trust him.'

'In case I need him.'

'Okay. But exocet *missiles*? . . .'

'And you're not to mention *any* of this to Anna. I just want to have a nice time until you come back.'

They had a lovely time, those long cold weeks of November after Makepeace had gone.

It was a lovely old house. The floors were stone and the beams were hand-hewn. They slept in the downstairs bedroom, on an old four-poster bed. In the mornings he always woke up before first light, suddenly, as if he had heard something, and he lay, tense, listening for footsteps, a turning door handle: but there was always nothing; and then there was only the joy, of her. He lay deep beside her feeling her warm, soft loveliness

357

against him, her smooth back and her long smooth legs spooned against his, and he held her breasts and kissed her back and her golden hair. He lay there a while, rejoicing in her and trying to go back to sleep; but then he could not lie still any longer. He got up and pulled on his tracksuit and went through the cold house to the kitchen. He always took the gun. He stoked up the embers in the hearth, and put the kettle on and made coffee. Then he stoked up the boiler for the bathroom. When the sun came up he went out to look for footprints in the snow.

He took the FN rifle. First he walked slowly round the outer walls, inspecting the snow. It would have been very easy to see if anybody had been around. Then he walked up the track, into the forest, until he could no longer see the house; then he did a big three-sixty. He walked in a circle all the way around his land, through the forest, down to the river, looking for footprints; then along the riverbank, and up alongside the scraggy orchards, back to the point where he had begun. But he never saw any footprints except his own, and hers.

Then he went back to the house, bolted the big doors. He made a pot of coffee, and took it to the bedroom. She was always awake. In the early days she was already dressed, in case he had found footprints; but after the first week she began to relax more.

'Nothing.'

He stoked up the fire, then stripped off and climbed back into bed. And, oh, the warmth of her, the sheer joy of her in his arms.

It was lovely being in the big warm bed together, talking, the snow outside, icicles hanging from the eaves, the fire crackling. This is what he had dreamed about for many years: they had been apart for five long years, and they had run and fought their way half around the world, and now at last they were truly together.

'I want to stay here forever,' she said.

He did not want to think about what he had to do in December, about the terrible thing he might have to do in Rome. He tried to push it out of his mind and just live for today, and for her. He knew she was doing the same. And mostly he succeeded. They did not talk about the microfilm

358

again; they were on their honeymoon and it seemed that if they did not talk about what they had to do, the problem would just go away, be put right simply, and they would be forgotten. He did not yet know how he was going to trick her, what excuse he was going to make for leaving her, and right now he did not want to think about it. For the moment he had stopped running, and he just wanted to rest, in her arms. It was lovely to have nothing to do, to stay in bed as long as they liked.

Finally, they got up and had a bath. They could see the fire blazing in the bedroom. He fetched beers and they sank into the hot iron tub together. Squashed up together side by side, slippery, her long blonde hair piled on top of her head, drinking beer, washing each other's backs. They laughed a lot. They had the same sense of humour. And nonsense was hilarious. He was a scream, apparently. When he told her a story she started to giggle before he got to the funny bits, just in anticipation, and when he got to the punchline she laughed as if it were the funniest thing she had heard. It is lovely to be in love with somebody who thinks you're a laugh-a-minute.

Long hot baths with beer and your own true love is a lovely way to start the day. When the water began to grow cold, she heaved herself up, gleaming, satiny, and they dashed back to the fire. The towels were warm. They rubbed themselves dry in front of the fire, then scrambled into their tracksuits, and they went to have breakfast. And the warmth of the kitchen, the snow in the courtyard and the ice on the windows, and the delicious smell of porridge and fried eggs and sausages. It tasted like the best food he had ever eaten. They opened a bottle of wine, and settled down to another lovely day of doing nothing, and they talked about the things they were going to do one day. She said:

'Start by building a beautiful sunken bath in mosaic tiles with jacuzzi pumps built in, so we can have sexy whirlpool baths. Hanging plants all around. And maybe a bar in the corner. We could buy our own generator for electricity. And we should build fireplaces in the other bedrooms. Get a bricklayer. We can work with him.'

'And a fountain in the courtyard. And vines?'

'Yes . . . We don't need a swimming pool because we've got

359

that beautiful pool at the waterfall. And we'll get two horses, and go riding out over these hills.' She smiled at him, 'Oh, let's stay forever, Jack . . .'

It was a wonderful thought, and usually he did believe that one day this would be their summer home. He did believe, now, that it was the British who murdered God's Banker, and he shared her belief that therefore they would also get rid of her, and him, if they thought it necessary; but as an Englishman he simply did not believe that it would be impossible to make a deal with his own British government, with the help of a good lawyer, say to them, 'The job is done, the communists have been cleaned out of the Vatican and the microfilm is destroyed, so leave us alone now, guarantee our safety and we swear we'll keep our mouths shut, but if you keep harassing us we'll tell the press this whole shameful story and sue you to the highest court in the land . . .' As a Royal Navy man brought up to believe that the British were the best, he simply did not believe that a British lawyer could not pull that trick off with his own British government: but all that was in the future and right now he did not want to think about it. And sometimes she believed it too: in her happiness she believed in the lovely, remote world they were living in, that the big bad world beyond would forget about them and let them live happily ever after once she had done her duty. She looked at Morgan and she loved him with all her heart, and she knew he was a babe in the woods compared to her but with all her heart she trusted him to do what he considered right, even if it was in fact the wrong thing to do. In her saner moments, she knew that all this was but a dream that would never be allowed to come true, but for *now* it was true. It was a wonderful thought, that they could stay here, and do these things to make their lovely home lovelier.

He said, 'I've got a living to make. We'll have to go back and tackle that first.'

She looked at the fire, thinking how best to put it. Then she said carefully, 'I want to put my arms around you when I say this. But I say it soberly, with my heart in my hand: and it is this . . . I have enough money for both of us. There is no urgency for you to go back to work.'

He smiled. 'Thank you, but I couldn't do that.'

'But what is money? We've seen that! And this is *your* land – what's wrong with you working it? We can plant wonderful fruit trees here!'

He smiled. It was a pretty thought. And, it could be done, one day. And sometimes he believed they would do it now, this winter, after Christmas.

November went like that. They were wonderful days. Every morning he went to look for footprints in the snow. Every day he grew more confident that they were safe here.

Then it was the beginning of December, and it was time to go back to Rome. That day he went to the village. He bought provisions, then he made a telephone call to the secretary of the Appia Antia Golf Club. Then he received Makepeace's call. When he returned to the farm he poured two glasses of wine and told her the lie. And he swore to God it was the last lie he would ever tell her. He said:

'Makepeace is arriving tomorrow. I'm going to fetch him at the railway station in Chambery. Then, the next day, all three of us are driving to Switzerland, to get the microfilm. Then we're going to Rome, to sort this out, with Makepeace riding shotgun.'

Her heart was sinking.

'I thought we weren't going to do anything until after Christmas. We haven't even discussed any plan.'

He pushed her glass towards her. 'I've got a plan.'

'Then why didn't you tell me?'

'Today I phoned Renata. She told me she has found a watertight way of getting us to see the Pope.' He forced a smile. 'This solves all our problems.'

She stared. 'The Pope . . .? How?'

'She couldn't tell me on the telephone. But it's through Benetti, the masseur. All she said was "guaranteed".' He smiled at her. 'This is terribly lucky.'

She sat back in her chair.

'Lucky . . .? It is *marvellous*!' She waved her hand; 'All we do is tell the Pope the story. Play him the Klaus Barbie tape, show him the microfilm, and tell him to get on with it – set his house in order.'

He wanted to thank God for helping him deceive her. 'Except we've got to monitor the situation somehow – we've got to be

361

sure that he *does* clean his house out, not whitewash the situation.'

'The Pope wouldn't do that! KGB agents in his hierarchy?' She spread her arms. 'Oh, this is wonderful news! You've done it, Jack! . . .' Her eyes were suddenly shining with relief.

'Renata's done it.'

'But you found Renata!'

'It's almost all over . . .' Morgan smiled.

And oh God, God, he wished it were true; and the past three weeks were like a dream.

The next day Morgan went to meet Makepeace. But not at the station in Chambery; he met him in the local village, for Makepeace had his own car. Makepeace handed him a sheet of paper and said:

'Here's your man, Hank. Henry Wilcox. There's his company, Worldarms Limited, in Lyons. His telephone number. Legitimate arms dealer, apparently, you've got to have end-user certificates and all that jazz before he'll supply even a hand-grenade, let alone an exocet missile.'

Morgan didn't believe that. 'Well done, Dougie. Did you have to use any strong-arm?'

'Nope. First I made a few enquiries amongst the boys in Marseilles. Somebody came up with the name Hank Wilcox. Took a train up to Lyons and checked out his address. A pretty big show. A warehouse, surrounded by security fence. Guards, dogs, the works. Legitimate. Then I went back to Marseilles, and checked out Meteor Air. A one-man band. One plane. The boss was flying it so I spoke to his wife or girlfriend, who was running the shop. Quite a looker, she was. French, but spoke English. Told her I wanted to freight some cargo, could I have some prices? She said it depends on size and weight, and asked what kind of cargo. I said it was coming from Worldarms – did she know them? Yes, she did. Would there be any difficulty air-freighting that kind of cargo? No there wouldn't, provided the documentation was "watertight". She said the export licence was the big thing, you can't get that without the "end-user certificate". So I said I was going to be dealing with Hank Wilcox, he would know all these regulations, wouldn't he? Oh yes, Hank knew everything.' Makepeace shrugged airily. 'So I was sure we were talking about the same chap. Thank you, madam, I'll be back when I've done my shopping. Orry-wa, Monsewer. And here I am. Easiest three hundred nicker I've ever earned.'

'Well done, Dougie! Now forget I ever asked you to do that.'

'Mum's the word. You don't really want an exocet missile do you?'

'No. What do you know about "end-user certificates"?'

'You know, sir,' Makepeace said, surprised.

'Yes, but I'm not up-to-date.'

'Simple,' Makepeace said. 'The arms manufacturers are only allowed to sell to approved customers. That means, to a *government*, who is approved by the manufacturer's government. So if Aerospatiele, who manufacture exocets here in France, want to sell exocets to, say, Italy, the Italian government must issue a certificate stating *it* wants the missiles for their own use, not for resale to somebody else – like Gaddaffi. The French government says okay, that's in order, and it then issues an export licence to Aerospatiele to ship the missiles to Italy. No end-user certificate, no export licence, no exocet missiles.'

'But those certificates can be bought. Or forged. Do you know anything about that?'

'No,' Makepeace said, 'but Danziger would.'

'Forget Danziger! He doesn't know about this, does he?'

Makepeace said, 'He's the guy who came up with Hank Wilcox's name.'

'But he doesn't know you were asking on my behalf!'

'*No*,' Makepeace sighed, 'relax.'

'And Sanchez? Did you find out anything about him?'

'No,' Makepeace said. 'I asked around. But thought I shouldn't press my luck with Mamsell Goldilocks.'

'Pity,' Morgan said. 'But you did the right thing.'

Makepeace handed over the miniature tape-recorder and the canister of nerve gas, and Morgan handed over Anna's passports, and gave him his instructions.

'I'm not looking forward to this,' Makepeace grumbled. 'I wish you'd warned me she wouldn't know you were leaving.'

'Just don't let her out of your sight. And tell her I love her.'

'She's going to be crazy about you,' Makepeace said morbidly

'– you should have seen her in Amsterdam, gave me a terrible time . . .'

Makepeace waited an hour before driving out to the farm, as instructed. By that time Morgan was well on the way. But not to Rome, yet. To Lyons.

Part Nine

51

He had telephoned Hank Wilcox to make sure he was available. 'To discuss very big business.' It was noon when Morgan drove into Lyons, a gracious old city, divided by its rivers. By coincidence, he drove past the Mont Luc Prison, where forty years ago Klaus Barbie had tortured and murdered his prisoners, heroes of the French Resistance, where today Klaus Barbie was imprisoned awaiting trial for his war crimes, and it gave Morgan a brief malicious pleasure to think of the bastard languishing somewhere up there behind those grey walls. *Poetic justice.* He drove on down town, and checked into a hotel. He telephoned Worldarms again.

'Why sure, Mr Blackstone,' Hank Wilcox said, 'but wouldn't you rather come round to my premises – only a pleasure to show you the shop! *Then* we can go back to your hotel for lunch. Except lunch is on me . . .'

Morgan wondered if he was barking up the wrong tree. Hank Wilcox sounded so wholesome.

The security guard said, 'Monsieur Blackstone? – *Oui*, monsieur!' and waved the taxi through. There was a closed-circuit television eye above the entrance to the warehouse, but the steel doors opened promptly. A pretty French girl, flanked by a smiling security guard, admitted him. 'Mr Blackstone, this way, *s'il vous plait.*'

She led him into a reception room. The walls were lined with antique rifles and pistols, the armchairs were leather. There was a bar. On a low table were glossy brochures of Worldarms' fine products, in half a dozen languages, including Arabic. 'What is your pleasure, Monsieur Blackstone?'

'Beer, please.'

He picked up the first glossy brochure. It had a picture of seven different modern rifles, fanned out like a poker hand, and the banner-line read, in Western-style lettering:

THE UNBEATABLE ROYAL FLUSH!
All available for immediate licensed delivery!
Only from Worldarms, Lyons, France!
The Ace: AK 47 KALASHNIKOV. CAL 7.62mm X39.
'The winner! The most popular service rifle ever manufactured! More in service throughout the world than all other rifles combined! Available with both fixed and folding stocks and all accessories . . .'
The King: AUG STEYR. CAL 5.56mm.
'The most advanced all-purpose light-calibre military shoulder-arm in this world . . .'
The Queen: M16 COLT CAL 5.56mm.
'The World Sales Leader . . .'

'*Why, hullo!* . . .' Hank Wilcox said, beaming, with his hand held out, 'is everybody looking after you? . . .'

He was a neat, fresh-faced man of about forty with a college-boy haircut, as American as apple-pie. He wore a floral shirt with a matching tie under a sporty check suit. 'This,' he waved a hand down the warehouse, 'is the biggest armoury in Western Europe. Only guy who comes close is Machine Gun Sam in Manchester – Interarms Limited, my competition. Four hundred thousand weapons here, enough for twenty-odd British divisions. Our annual turnover is well over a hundred million dollars.'

The rifles gleamed in avenues, rack upon rack, like a supermarket.

'There's a complete firing range in the basement. Upstairs we keep our heavier stuff, bombs, explosives, and so forth. The really heavy gear we can only show in our catalogue – tanks, fighter planes, battleships. We usually only act as brokers for such big stuff of course, but I can get you anything, provided you can produce your end-user certificate.'

'Where do you get your Kalashnikovs? They're made in Russia, aren't they?'

'Sure. But they got the factories, they gotta sell. All aboveboard, I assure you. For example I've made an offer to the Iraqi government, for stuff they've captured off the Iranians recently. And most of us in this game have made offers to the

British government for stuff captured in the Falklands War, some excellent Westinghouse radar, and some top-notch German surface-to-air missiles.'

'And you sell to anyone?'

'Sure, if the French government approves the end-user certificate and issues an export licence. It's the government's decision. And the government may *not* approve . . . Like they didn't approve of Idi Amin in Uganda. Machine Gun Sam told him the British government would turn him down so Idi sent his plane to fetch me to Uganda to discuss an army shopping list. I went, and I told him what he needed, but I said, "Idi, I'll sure try but I don't think the French government is likely to issue an export licence in your case." And I was right. Most African countries are non-starters nowadays. Same with Fidel.'

'You've met Fidel Castro?'

'Sure. Nice guy. But same problem. So Fidel gets his gear direct from Russia. Nuts, isn't it? He still gets his guns anyway, so why can't we have the business?'

'Nuts,' Morgan agreed. 'How is business generally?'

'Booming,' Hank said. 'If you'll pardon the pun. We have a saying in this business: I'm not sure what weapons will be used in World War Three, but I know what will be used in the Fourth World War – stones and clubs! Aha-ha-ha! Einstein said that.' Morgan laughed too. 'But you've got to be quick in this game. The moment a war starts, the hardware merchants are there, flogging everything from Band-Aids to A-bombs, to both sides.' He slapped his hands together. 'And on that note, what can I do for you, sir?'

'Exocet missiles,' Morgan said quietly. He raised his eyebrows: 'Lunch at my hotel?'

He locked his bedroom door. He slipped his hand into his pocket and switched on the tape-recorder. He waved Hank Wilcox to the armchair. Hank said:

'Exocets, huh? They're tricky. Who're you buying for?'

Morgan paced across the room. 'I'm both buying and selling, Hank. I don't want them for my private collection, do I? Call me the middle-man.'

Hank watched him. 'What about your end-user certificate?'

'That's where you come in, Hank.' He turned to him. 'I'm

offering you a cut on the deal. A very respectable cut on the mark-up. On twenty missiles, that's a lot of money. For jam.'

Hank slowly got up. He began to pace too.

'What makes you think I do that kind of business, Mr Blackstone?'

Morgan said, 'Our mutual friend, Roberto Calvi. God's Banker.'

Hank's eyes widened. 'But Robbie's dead.'

'Very. The players change but the game goes on. But I worked with Roberto on the last transaction.'

Hank frowned at him. 'And who're you working with now?'

'Bellatrix,' Morgan said. 'Still Bellatrix, Panama.'

'But I thought it was defunct now!'

'Oh, it exists, Hank, it exists.'

Hank thought. 'And the destination is?'

Morgan took a break. 'The same destination as last time.'

Hank stared at him.

'Now wait a minute, sir. That deal is already done! Have you been muscling in on Sanchez?'

Morgan's heart missed a beat. He turned, with a frown. 'Sanchez?'

Hank stared; then a malicious smile crossed his face.

'You're fulla shit, Mr Blackstone! Whoever you are! I don't know what you're talking about! I don't do your kind of business, I play it by the book! Good day! I'm going!'

He turned to the door. Morgan pulled out the Meteor Air waybill and thrust it at the man. 'You did that bit of business!'

Hank stared at it. 'My name's not on that document! Goodbye!'

Morgan grabbed his collar, and slung him. Hank reeled across the room and sprawled on the bed. He lay there an instant, shocked. He whispered:

'I'm calling the police . . .'

Morgan stood over him. 'I don't think so, Hank. They'll be very interested to learn that you conspired to export exocet missiles illegally to Argentina during the Falklands War!'

'I deny it! You can't prove a thing!' He started to scramble up and Morgan shoved his hand on his chest and the man collapsed again.

'You'll lose your licence, Hank! That nice warehouse of yours can be closed down by Mr Mitterrand!'

'You're fulla shit!' Hank started to get up again and Morgan shoved him down again.

'*Who's Sanchez?*'

Hank blinked. 'I don't know who you're talking about!'

'You said you've concluded a new deal for exocets with Sanchez! Who's Sanchez?'

'Go to hell! –' He scrambled up.

Morgan swiped him across the face and the man collapsed again. Morgan bounded at him and grabbed his arm. He wrenched it up behind his back. Hank gasped, his face pressed to the bed. Morgan whispered:

'All I want to know is who Sanchez is, Hank, and you'll live happily ever after as a happy little Death Merchant.'

Hank's face was contorted with pain. 'I'll scream . . .' he warned.

Morgan jerked the arm once, then said, 'Get up, Hank.'

Hank gasped and clambered up, his arm still twisted behind his back. He crouched, Morgan behind him. 'One scream and your arm goes. Now, into the bathroom, please.'

Hank staggered round the bed, gasping. Morgan walked behind him, gripping his arm. He walked him into the bathroom. 'Put the plug in the wash basin, Hank.'

'What? –'

'Do it!' He jerked the arm.

Hank gasped in agony, and fumbled the plug into the basin.

'Now turn on the tap.' Morgan jerked the arm. Hank gasped and fumbled the tap open.

The water swirled in. It crept up to the top.

'Turn it off.'

Hank turned it off, whimpering.

Morgan put his other hand tight on Hank's neck.

'Now this can be very unpleasant, Hank. I'm going to stick your head in the water, over and over, until you tell me.' And he jerked Hank's arm up and he thrust his head down, into the water.

Hank twisted and gurgled and writhed, and Morgan held him furiously. Hank tried to punch with his free arm, and Morgan held him, tooth-clenched. He held him under for thirty seconds, then he wrenched his head up. 'Okay, Hank?'

371

Hank crouched over the basin, his face contorted, his head dripping, eyes screwed up. He gasped:

'*Captain . . . Juan . . . Sanchez . . . de Bourbon.*'

Morgan rasped: 'From Argentina?'

Hank gasped, 'Yes . . .'

Jesus, Morgan thought. 'Army or Navy, Hank?'

'*Navy . . .*' Hank gasped.

'Where is he now?'

'*I don't . . . know . . .*'

Morgan shoved his head back in the water. Hank writhed and struggled. Morgan held him under for twenty seconds, then wrenched him up. 'Where is he, Hank?'

Hank's contorted face was terrified.

'*Argentina . . . Naval Aviation . . . Sub-commission . . . in Paris . . .*'

'Attached to the Argentinian embassy?'

'Yes . . .' Hank spluttered.

Jesus! 'So it's official business, is it?'

'*Yes . . . All official . . .*'

'Except under-the-table? Black-market exocets?'

Hank gasped, '*All official . . .*'

'Bullshit, Hank! The French government refused to give an official export licence for exocets for Argentina during the Falklands War, so why would they do so now? Who're you getting the missiles from?'

'*Aerospatiele . . . the legal manufacturers . . .*'

Morgan jerked him. 'Who have you bribed to give you a false end-user certificate?'

'*Nobody . . .*'

Morgan rasped, 'I'll give you a minute to think about that, Hank,' and he rammed his head back under the water. He held him there for thirty seconds, then wrenched him up.

'That was only half a minute, Hank! Want more time to think?'

Hank spluttered: '*Please . . . The Sudan . . . Ministry of Defence . . .*'

Morgan snorted. 'Sudan, huh? The same guy who gave the false end-user certificate last time?'

'*Yes . . .*'

'And the exocets were going to leave France by air, ostensibly bound for the Sudan? But in Malta the plane has a little breakdown, so the cargo changes planes to Meteor Air, which heads for Panama? Then the pilot has a rush of blood to the head and turns for Argentina?'

Hank gasped, *'Yes.'*

'Jesus Christ,' Morgan said. 'And tell me, Hank: since that little deal fell through for want of quick funds, because God's Banker had that nasty accident on Blackfriars Bridge, and now that the Falklands War is over, why does Captain Sanchez want more exocet missiles?'

'I truly wouldn't know . . . Not my business . . .'

'I'll give you another minute to think about that, Hank! . . .' Morgan rammed his head under again.

He counted to forty this time. He wrenched Hank up. 'Well?'

He was buckling, his spluttering head hanging, his contorted face panic-stricken. He gasped:

'To invade . . . the Falklands . . . again . . .'

Morgan was amazed. Jesus Christ, again!

'When?' He wrenched the arm.

'As soon as . . . they get them . . .'

'And that will be?'

Hank gasped: *'When the money . . . arrives . . .'*

'And who's supplying the money? Argentina is still broke!'

'I don't . . . know . . .' Hank cried.

'Think about it, Hank!' Morgan shoved his head under again. He counted to twenty, and yanked him up. 'Well?'

Hank's gasping head hung. *'Russia . . .'* he gasped. *'Indirectly . . .'*

Through his fury Morgan was amazed. He had not thought of this one.

'Why Russia, Hank?'

Hank's head hung, his chest heaving. He was finished. He went into a shuddering cough. Then he gasped:

'To make . . . Margaret Thatcher . . . go back to war. And she'll lose this time . . . And that'll force . . . an election in Britain . . . And the Labour Party . . . will get in . . . And they'll dismantle . . . the Pershing missile bases . . .'

Morgan stared at the wall, amazed at the simplicity of it. Jesus Christ!

He let go of Hank, and shoved him. Hank staggered across

373

the bathroom, and collapsed onto the lavatory seat. He flung his head back, his eyes screwed up, mouth open, rasping.

Morgan stopped at the door. He said shakily:

'Surprising how soft you hardware merchants are, Hank. So you'd better have a little rest here, for three hours. If you try to leave earlier, one of my boys will stop you outside the door. And stick you back in the wash basin. You don't want that, do you, Hank?'

'No . . .' Hank whispered, eyes closed.

'And don't mention this to anybody, Hank. Because I've got it all down on tape. And if you blow any whistles, Worldarms Limited will be looking for new premises, in the Congo. Just let the Sanchez deal die a natural death, Hank. If you'll pardon the pun.'

Morgan turned out of the bathroom. He picked up his bag and walked out of the room.

He went down to the reception desk and asked about a good messenger service to Paris.

'*Exprès Aujourd'hui*, Daylight Express, sir.'

Morgan went out to his car. He played the tape-recording of Hank Wilcox into his other tape-recorder, making a copy. Then he flagged a taxi and told it to take him to the premises of Daylight Express. Morgan handed over the copy of the tape. The clerk sealed it in a stout envelope and gave Morgan an invoice.

'This will go to Paris today?'

'Tonight, sir, with our regular express delivery. It will be hand-delivered first thing tomorrow morning.'

'Thank you.' Morgan paid the fee. He went outside to the nearest public telephone. He telephoned the British embassy in Paris. He asked to speak to the Military Attaché. He said:

'Make a note of this. The Argentinians are trying to buy exocet missiles from Aerospatiele, with a fake end-user certificate from the Sudan, in order to mount another invasion of the Falklands. I'm sending you today a tape-recording which proves it. Put a stop to it, will you? And warn Mrs Thatcher, please.'

'*Who's this speaking?*' the man demanded.

'Never mind.' Morgan hung up.

He got a taxi back to his car. He drove out of Lyons onto the road for Italy.

52

He spent the night in a truck-drivers' hostel outside Florence, but he hardly slept. The decision he had been avoiding in the last four weeks was now staring him in the face. It was 8.00 am when he parked outside the Holiday Inn, in the suburbs of Rome.

He had prayed for good golfing weather, and his prayer seemed to have been answered, and he felt sick in his guts. It would have been a tremendous relief if it had been pissing with rain, if his mission had been made impossible. It was a cold, fine day. His nerves were stretched tight.

He was wearing the wig and moustache. He checked into the hotel. He ordered coffee to be sent up to his room, and waited feverishly for Rome to get to work. At nine o'clock he telephoned the Tourist Bureau. He asked about a good motorist guide to the beauty spots in the environs of Rome. They recommended a publication. He went down to the hotel foyer, to the newsstand. They had the guide book. He bought it, plus a good road map.

He unfolded the map on his bed, and began to read the guide feverishly, referring to his map. He circled places which sounded appropriate. At ten o'clock he telephoned the golf club again.

Yes, the club was still expecting Cardinal Gunter to play in the tournament this afternoon. About four o'clock they expected him to come off the links. Yes, that would be a good time to call for the book. Goodbye.

Morgan held his face. God, it was all unreal.

He went down to the car park. He got into the car, started the engine. He took up the road map, looking for the easiest way to get to the first beauty spot he had selected.

He muttered: 'Now help me, God . . .'

And maybe God did help him. The first scenic spot he checked out was the best. He went to four others, but they were not nearly as easy and good as the first.

It was eleven miles out of Rome, on the Appian Way, a picnic site in a forest of pine, overlooking a volcanic lake. To get to it, you proceed down the Appian Way for ten miles: then you encounter an intersection. There is a stop sign. Turn left. Drive five hundred metres, and a track leads off to the right. Wind up through the forest. Over a hill. A fork in the track. Down the right-hand fork, to picnic tables. The left-hand fork winds along the lake and eventually loops back to the road.

And something else: half a mile before the intersection was a public telephone. And beyond the intersection he found a truckers' stop called Bar-Restaurant Venezia. He went in. He ordered coffee and cognac. There was also a public telephone in the corner. He lifted the receiver. It worked. He made a note of the number.

He drank the coffee and cognac. He told himself that all this was only a contingency plan. You've always got to have a contingency plan, that's what they'd taught him.

It wasn't perfect, but it was a good place for murder. Nowhere is perfect for murder.

He wanted to weep.

He had over two hours to wait. And he did not know how he was going to stand it. He wanted to be sick. He wanted to get in his car and just drive, drive away. Then he knew what he really wanted to do.

It was two o'clock when he got to Saint Peter's. There was muted organ music, the smell of incense, the chanting of devotions. Way down there the lamps burned around the sunken tomb of Saint Peter, the triumphal baldachin aflicker, the afternoon light gleaming through the stained-glass window onto the throne of Saint Peter. It was magnificent, and Morgan knew all over again that he was a Catholic in his bones, and he stood in awe of the power and the glory which all this material majesty symbolized, and with all his desperate heart he wanted the right thing to happen. He dipped his fingers shakily in the holy water, and crossed himself.

He walked down the long nave, past Saint Peter's tomb, towards the pews below the throne at the apex of the basilica.

He came to the second row, right in front of the altar. He genuflected. He sat down.

He sat, his hands on his knees, looking up at Saint Peter's throne, trying to let the holiness of the place seep into him, calm him. He closed his eyes, and rested his forehead in his hand.

He realized he was trembling. He screwed his eyes up tight and tried to concentrate. It was a long moment before he could think of anything more than *Please God . . .* Then he clenched his teeth:

'*Keep helping me now, God! To do what is right!*'

And suddenly he knew that God would help him, that today would be lucky, that soon all this awful business would be over, and with that comfort the dam bust, and he wept.

It was three o'clock when Morgan got to the Appia Antia Golf Club.

He found a parking space. He sat there a moment, calming himself. Then he got out, and walked across the parking area, up into the club house.

There were Christmas decorations. People in the lounge and at the bar. He turned into the office. The secretary's door was open. The man glanced up, recognized him and smiled.

'Good afternoon,' Morgan smiled. He felt shaky. 'Have I had any luck?'

'Not yet,' the secretary said. 'He came rushing in, but I will catch him when he comes off, in about half an hour.'

'Is it all right if I sit in the lounge and wait? I'd like to thank him, if that's possible, so would you give me a wink when he comes in, in case he goes rushing off?'

'If I can,' the secretary said, 'but I may be rushing myself . . .'

It was a long half hour.

He went onto the terrace: every fairway had players on it. Golfers were trudging back towards the club house. Most of them made for the door beneath the terrace, into the changing rooms. Morgan tried to gauge whether he would recognize Cardinal Gunter from that distance. He doubted it, unless the man played golf in clerical robes, which surely he would not.

He turned back into the lounge, to the bar. He badly wanted

377

a drink, but he did not dare. He ordered coffee, paid, and went to sit where he could see the entrance to the secretary's department. He slowly sipped the coffee, not tasting it. People were coming and going all the time.

If he missed him . . . He had a vivid image of the man, from the photograph on the back of his book, but now suddenly he was assailed by doubt. How long ago was that photograph taken? God – he was a fool not to have gone to the public library and checked through newspaper files until he found a recent photograph of the man! If the club secretary did not tip him off he might not recognize him from this distance! The bar was filling up with golfers joining each other, waving to each other, ordering drinks.

It was a long half hour. Then suddenly the club secretary was coming towards him, holding a book. Morgan began to rise, in panic. *The man had gone!* . . . The secretary handed him the book and whispered: 'The cardinal has autographed it. He is the man in the middle of that group.'

So he had missed him. Cardinal Pieter Gunter was at the bar, his back to him, laughing at something somebody had said. Then he turned sideways, and Morgan could see his face. He was much more impressive in the flesh than in his photographs. He was bigger than he had imagined, six foot two easily, broad in the shoulder. And that leonine sweep of well-groomed grey hair. His cheeks flushed from the cold, he looked a vigorous, confident man in his mid-fifties, in the prime of his professional life. He was dashing in his well-cut clothes. Morgan could almost feel the man's charm and natural authority from where he sat. He was a natural leader. Now he was telling a funny story. His companions craned forward, grinning in anticipation. It was quite a long story, and Morgan had a good chance to observe him. The man was a natural story-teller, a natural actor, using his hands, his eyes. Then he came to the punchline, and his group roared with laughter, and the cardinal laughed as heartily as any, delighted with his own joke.

Morgan sat, pretending to read *Letters to the Mighty*. Glancing up and down, watching the man peripherally. He saw him glance at his watch several times. But for twenty more minutes he hung on with his group. Then, suddenly, he excused himself, and he turned and left the bar.

Morgan looked at the cardinal's drink – it was finished. The man was striding down the bar jauntily, waving to people. Morgan hastened up out of his chair after him. The cardinal turned the corner and disappeared. Morgan turned the corner; and the man was nowhere to be seen.

There were two possibilities. He had either disappeared into the toilet, or down into the changing rooms. Morgan strode for the toilet door, pushed it open. Nobody. He hurried down the stairs, two at a time. Into the changing rooms.

It was full of golfers, changing. He saw the cardinal holding his bag of clubs, talking to somebody. At that moment the two men started walking slowly towards him, talking earnestly. Morgan turned and started mounting the stairs. At the bend he looked back. The two men appeared at the bottom, still talking. Morgan mounted the stairs, to the top.

He walked into the toilet. It was still empty. He kept the door open a crack. He saw the two men reaching the top of the stairs. They stopped, and shook hands. Then the cardinal turned and headed towards the toilet.

Morgan retreated to the wash basins. He slammed on a tap. Cardinal Gunter walked in. He went to the urinal. Morgan turned to him, his heart knocking. He opened his mouth, to say the passwords; and the toilet door opened again, and another man walked in.

Morgan slammed off the tap. He dried his hands on a paper towel shakily, and walked out of the toilet.

He retraced his steps, back to the lounge, without looking back. He picked up his empty coffee cup, and pretended to drink, and he looked back. He saw the cardinal come around the corner.

He walked back down the bar, carrying his clubs, to his group. Morgan sat down. The cardinal waved his finger, refusing another drink. He said a few jolly words of farewell. Then he turned and walked out of the lounge again. Morgan hurriedly got out of his chair.

He hurried across the lounge. The cardinal was entering the hall purposefully. There were some people coming up the steps

379

into the club, smiling. The cardinal stopped, and talked to them.

Morgan turned towards a notice board, his heart knocking. He pretended to read it. He realized he was trembling. He felt as if everybody in the club was looking at him suspiciously. The cardinal was talking Italian. Morgan could stand it no longer. He walked around the cardinal. Down the steps, into the cold dusk. Into the car park. He looked back. The cardinal was saying farewell. He turned and began to descend the steps.

Morgan stooped, and fumbled with his shoelace. He peered around. The cardinal was striding down a line of cars. Morgan scrambled up and strode after him; he called:

'Cardinal Gunter?'

The man strode on. Morgan called again: '*Cardinal!*'

The man looked back over his shoulder. Morgan forced a smile and he waved the book. The cardinal stopped. Morgan called: 'I just want to thank you for autographing my book . . .'

'Oh, a pleasure.' He smiled and turned to walk on.

'Cardinal?'

He stopped again. Morgan's heart was knocking. He slipped his hand inside his jacket and switched on the tape-recorder. He stopped in front of the man. He looked him in the eye. He said:

'The elk is not only a Siberian creature.'

There was a stunned silence.

The cardinal stared at him, as if he could not grasp what was happening. Then he blinked, ashen. He glanced towards his car, then back to Morgan. He whispered: 'Who are you?'

Morgan's mouth was dry. 'You know who I am, Cardinal. I've got instructions for you.'

The cardinal was suddenly agitated. He glanced back towards the club house, as if frightened of being seen. Morgan whispered shakily:

'There's no running away. Not only am I armed, but there's always tomorrow.'

The cardinal shook his head hastily in denial. He took a breath, to control himself. 'Well, what is it, man?'

Morgan said, 'We're going to your apartment in Vatican City.'

The cardinal looked more alarmed. 'Why there?'

It seemed unreal that this was happening. He had rehearsed it all, but he felt a fraud. He did not feel like a KGB agent. 'Because those are the orders. The safest place. And because that's where the computer is.'

'What computer?'

'And I must be officially in your company. With an official permit. My name will be John Armstrong. An old friend of yours from America.'

'Why the official permit?'

'So you can't deny afterwards that I was with you. Now, let's go please, Cardinal.'

The man suddenly seemed more in control. Still ashen, but his shock had turned to grimness. For an instant Morgan thought he was going to tell him to go to hell. Then he said: 'Why would I deny that?'

Morgan did not know what to make of him. 'Let's get on with it, please. I'm coming with you in your car. You'll instruct your driver to stop at Saint Anne's Gate, and get a permit for me. Then have me escorted to your apartment.'

Cardinal Gunter looked at him, then clamped his mouth shut. He jerked his head and turned.

Morgan followed him. He wanted to retch.

53

He'd had over a day, driving to Rome, to rehearse his role, his lines, his cross-examination, to cover every possibility: but he still had to remind himself that it was the cardinal who was on trial, not him. He rode up in the elevator beside the Swiss guard. It stopped on the second floor. A large door was opposite. The guard opened it. Morgan entered a gilded ante-room. He hardly noticed the furniture. Across the room was another door. The guard opened it and stood aside. Morgan walked through.

The door closed behind him. He was alone. The room was richly carpeted. Big windows looked onto Saint Peter's Square.

There was a large, ornate desk, a large, marble fireplace. The walls were lined with books. In the corner was another door.

Morgan put his hand inside his jacket and switched the tape-recorder on again. He waited grimly. He was still shaky. Then the corner door opened, and Cardinal Pieter Gunter, Secretary of State for the Vatican, entered.

He had changed into official robes, and the transformation from the jolly man in golfer's garb was profound. He had composed himself. Gone was the shocked, unnerved man Morgan had accosted at the golf club. Morgan could not tell whether his grimness suppressed anger or fear. And Morgan could feel his natural authority – this was a leader, every inch a man to be reckoned with. The cardinal walked to the high-backed chair behind his desk and sat down. He did not invite Morgan to sit. He looked at him steadily, and said:

'Well? What do I call you?'

Morgan's mouth was dry. 'For the time being just call me English.' The cardinal snorted softly, and Morgan said, 'You didn't expect an Englishman?' He walked to the chair opposite the desk and sat.

'What identification have you got?'

Morgan closed his eyes angrily. Because this was the behaviour of a guilty man, on his guard. And he desperately wanted a frightened, innocent man. 'My identification is: "The elk is not only a Siberian creature". That's good enough for you, Cardinal, or I wouldn't be sitting here now.' He added: 'We half-expected this.'

'Half-expected what?'

'That you might fence with us. Prevaricate. Stop it, Cardinal. It's all on file.'

'What is?'

Morgan had almost stopped being nervous now. He said:

'The class of 1931. A brilliant Russian boy being tutored in Catholicism in a *dacha* outside Moscow. In English. Pieter Otto Gunter. Fictionally German, bound for America.' Morgan waved his hand. 'So let's get on with business.'

The Secretary of State was ashen, but in control of himself. 'Well, spit it out, Englishman!'

Morgan held up two fingers. 'We need to know two things.'

He was not sure whether the man was acting, but now the cardinal was all attention.

'Number one. If the cardinals of the Church were convened tomorrow, what are your chances of being elected pope?'

Cardinal Gunter stared at him. Then he cleared his throat and said:

'When is it to be?'

'What?'

The cardinal said: 'The murder of Pope John Paul II.'

A knot came into Morgan's gut. 'There is no need for you to know.'

The cardinal sat back slowly in his chair. He looked unnerved again.

'I don't know what my chances of election are.'

'We want a realistic answer, not a modest one.'

The cardinal shook his head harassedly.

'No idea. These things are not canvassed in advance.'

'We consider that you'd be a strong candidate. Do you agree?'

The cardinal blinked. 'I don't know.'

'Well, think about it. Add up the votes you think likely. We want an answer the day after tomorrow.'

The cardinal nodded, agitated. 'I'll think about it.' He leaned forward. 'But I *must* know when.'

Morgan stared back at him. 'Why?'

'So I can prepare.'

'Prepare what?'

The cardinal waved a hand. 'Myself. My thoughts. My department. It would be a grave mistake to go at this like a bull at a gate.'

Morgan felt sick. Because he knew now the man would have to die. He tried to say it coldly: 'You'll be told what you need to know when you need to know it.'

The cardinal sat back in his chair. His pale face was wooden. 'And the other thing?'

Morgan pulled out the list of names he had compiled from Klaus Barbie's tape. It was a newly written list, without the passwords.

'Somewhere in the Vatican there is a computer which lists all your priests, all over the world?'

The cardinal blinked. 'Yes.'

'Showing where they are now. Their rank. Their histories, how they've progressed since joining the Church.'

'Yes.'

'And we can punch in these names,' he tapped the list, 'and the computer will print it out for us?'

'Yes. Though I don't know how to work the machine myself.' He held out his hand, for the list.

Morgan did not give it to him. 'There must be somebody available who knows how to work it?'

The cardinal glanced distractedly at his watch. 'At this hour?'

'Instruct your secretary to find somebody, please.'

The cardinal held out his hand again. 'Who are these people?'

Morgan said grimly, 'People we trained as agents and planted into the Church decades ago, as we did you. We want an update on them.' He added: 'We know who's done what, but we want an internal assessment of them.'

Cardinal Gunter was staring at him. Then he blinked.

'I see. Of course.'

'And assuming that our assessment accords with your computer, you will summon them to Rome. And fire them.'

Cardinal Gunter's eyes widened a fraction. '*Fire* them? Why?'

Morgan said deliberately: 'Those are the orders, Cardinal. But if you must know, we suspect a weak link in the chain. And we've got what we want, and we think that too many cooks may spoil the broth.'

'But there are procedures for this sort of thing –'

'Procedures be damned! You're the Secretary of State! You summon them to Rome on the next aeroplane. You haul them up on the carpet, one at a time. They do not know that you are one of them. You tell them that you have incontrovertible proof that they are Russian-trained agents. You say their passwords to them, which I will supply you with. They will know the game is up, as you did. You demand their resignations forthwith. They'll go, without a fight, I promise you.'

'But some of them may protest innocence! They may have found God.' He changed it: 'May imagine they have found God . . .'

Morgan gave a smile he did not feel. 'Occupational hazard, we've found.'

'But if they have found God, they may insist on their legal rights' trial by our ecclesiastical court!'

'Rubbish! If they've found God, they'll get out gracefully to save harming the Church with a scandal. And any who don't go gracefully, we will deal with.'

Pieter Gunter sat back in his chair. He cleared his throat.

'Very well.' He held out his hand again, for the list. 'I doubtless know some of them.'

Morgan kept the list. 'Call in your secretary and tell him you want the computer operator on the job.'

The cardinal said: 'The operator will find it strange if we're standing over him as he works the machine.'

'Too bad. Make up a story. Or better still, tell him to mind his own business.' He stood up. His legs felt shaky. 'Let's get on with it.'

The cardinal pressed a button. A few moments later the corner door opened. A priest of about Morgan's age entered. The cardinal said:

'I want to show my friend our central computer. We're trying to trace a distant relative of his. If the office is closed, have it opened up, please. And find somebody who understands the machine.'

An hour later they returned to Cardinal Gunter's apartment in the papal palace with two copies of the computer's printout. Morgan pulled his chair up to the desk, and spread his copy on it. He said:

'Sit down and we'll go through the list together, and you tell me about them, anything significant that is not on the printout.'

The cardinal remained standing. 'And then?'

'Then you will summon them to Rome. By telephone. You will get their resignations.' He tapped the printout. 'Seven of them are already deceased, so that only leaves ten. And those ten are all in Europe, so they'll be here tomorrow night at the latest.'

'And then?' There was an edge to the man's voice.

'Then,' Morgan said grimly, 'the night after that you will meet me at a place I will specify. You will bring with you

385

photocopies of their resignations, on official Vatican stationery, plus your official acceptance, signed by you.'

'Anything else?'

'Yes. I have further instructions for you but I'll tell you after we've been through the printout.'

Cardinal Pieter Gunter looked at him a long hard moment; then he said:

'Well, I have some instructions for *you*, Englishman! . . .' He glared, then pointed at the door theatrically. 'Get out! . . . Get out of here and tell your masters that I serve only God!'

54

Morgan was absolutely taken by surprise.

Cardinal Gunter glared, then snatched up his copy of the computer's printout and shook it with malicious pleasure: 'I've got what I've wanted to know for forty years! *Thank* you, Englishman. You've served your purpose, now get out! And never darken the doors of the Vatican again!'

Morgan stared. Incredulous relief was welling up inside him. He could hardly believe this. He *daren't* believe this . . . 'Are you trying to tell me? –'

'I'm telling you loud and clear to tell your masters in the Kremlin that I am not one of their agents, nor have I ever been!'

God, this was too good to be true! If this was true all his troubles were over. He leant forward and lifted his finger at the man: 'But you asked me when the Pope was going to be murdered! You asked for time to prepare yourself . . .'

'Of course, you fool! I wanted to know the details of your plot so I could foil it! But I'll talk to you no more! Leave this moment or I'll call the guards.'

Morgan slumped back in his chair.

'Oh thank God,' he whispered. The cardinal's hand moved to the button on his desk, and Morgan said urgently: 'For Christ's sake, Cardinal, if you don't talk to me you soon *will* be talking to the KGB – and MI6 and the CIA!'

The cardinal looked at him, his hand poised on the button. Morgan shook his head urgently: 'Father, I am *not* a KGB agent – nor a British or American agent! But I *do* have the evidence about you – and about the others on this printout. I am the only person in the *world* who has the evidence and I've come to try to do something about it, to save the Church!'

The cardinal's face was a mask.

'You're not KGB?'

'*No.*'

'Then who are you?'

'An ordinary Englishman! But I have the evidence about you.'

The man's eyes did not flicker. 'What evidence are you talking about?'

Morgan leant forward earnestly. 'A microfilm of a KGB file, stolen by a Nazi agent in Russia during the Second World War.'

The man stared. 'And how do you come to possess it?'

'That's too long a story for now! The bottom line is "The elk is not only a Siberian creature".' He held out his hands. 'How the hell would I know that if I didn't possess the evidence?' He pointed at the printout: 'How would I know about these other agents?' He held out his hands. 'I'm here to try to *save* the Church, not to harm it!'

'You've said you're armed. Why do you come into this holy city with a gun if you mean no harm?'

'Because I'm trying to stay alive from other people who want the evidence!'

'Who?'

Morgan controlled his impatience. He had nothing to lose by answering questions now. 'The KGB and the British.'

Surprise crossed the cardinal's face. 'Why should the British want to kill you, Englishman?'

Morgan leant forward. 'Because *they* know, that *I* know, that once upon a time you were trained by the KGB! In the hopes that one day they would have a pope as their agent! And the British – and Americans no doubt – want to use you *too*. They want you in *their* pocket. But they can't pressurize you into doing anything for them *unless* they have the evidence in their hand . . . And I am the only man who knows where that is! And they want to get it from me! And then I think they'll kill me! In case I have made a copy of it and ruin everything for them by shouting it from the rooftops!'

The cardinal's face was gaunt but his eyes were unflinching. He said quietly:

'So if I am to believe you, you believe that you have bearded the most powerful KGB agent, and have uncovered the most monstrous plot ever hatched against Christendom? That I am a ruthless monster defrauding one third of mankind? –' He forced a bleak smile and shook his head. He stood up wearily, and turned for the door. 'This is ridiculous. Go!'

Morgan was astonished again. He could not believe this. The man knew he had the goods on him, or he wouldn't be here! Yet he had suddenly decided to act. To bluff it out. And the incredulous relief that Morgan had felt was sliding away. This was the behaviour of a guilty man! Not a genuinely indignant man, or a penitent man. He cried:

'For God's sake listen to me! And I mean for *God's* sake! This is not something you can bluster your way out of, using your high authority! For God's sake get it into your head that I *possess* this evidence, and that everybody wants it! And at stake is not only my life but yours, because they'll kill you when you don't do their bidding, and if you *do* their bidding the other side will kill you! But that's the least of it! Because what about your precious Catholic Church? It could come tumbling down in disgrace!' He added angrily: '*If* that is precious to you.'

Cardinal Gunter was half-turned towards the door. Looking at him calculatingly.

'What do you want from me? Money?'

Morgan's heart sank further. A guilty man would make a deal.

'Yes! One million pounds! For the microfilm. And I'll keep my mouth shut. But I could sell this story to the press for a million pounds easily!' The cardinal looked at him. Morgan went on: 'It's cheap! To preserve the continuity of two thousand years of religion! Isn't that why Pope Pius made a deal with Hitler – preservation in exchange for Vatican neutrality? When he should have spoken up against the Nazis and their atrocities? One million pounds is laughably cheap compared to the millions of lives that were lost!'

Cardinal Gunter turned away. 'Get out . . .'

Morgan closed his eyes in relief. But he still wasn't sure. He wanted to shout it, but he made himself say it softly: 'I don't want money! I want *you*' – he jabbed his finger – 'to satisfy *me*' – he tapped his chest '– that you are not and never will be a communist agent.'

The Secretary of State frowned scornfully. 'I haven't succeeded in doing that already?'

'Not yet! You were doing a great job while you thought I was your KGB controller and tried to send me packing! But once you heard I'm not KGB you try to bluster it out and pretend something never happened. You've destroyed your credibility, Cardinal!'

'Indeed? I was trying to establish yours.'

Morgan dearly wished he could believe that. 'And in addition to satisfying me of your innocence, you must purge these other agents from the Church.' He smacked the printout.

'And when I've done that? Any other stipulations?'

Indeed there were. But Morgan was not going to tell him yet. He said: 'Then . . . when I am satisfied with all that, I will destroy the evidence.'

Cardinal Gunter said scornfully: 'When *you* are satisfied? A jury of one.'

Morgan cried, 'Yes! And, unfortunately I'm more than that – I'm the prosecutor as well!' He glared at the man: 'It's just so happened that onto my slender shoulders has descended the burden of deciding the fate of the Catholic Church! And the social stability of a huge part of the Western world!' He shook his head at the man. 'I don't want this job! I'm not even a good Catholic! And I *certainly* don't want to be running for my life from Russian and British and American hit-men! . . .' He tapped his chest and leant forward: 'But I'm stuck with the job, and I'm going to do it.'

Cardinal Gunter seemed to change again.

'When you are satisfied, why won't you hand this so-called evidence over to me?'

Morgan was incredulous. '"*So*-called evidence"? Jesus Christ, you know the evidence is real or you wouldn't be sitting here now talking to me! For Christ's sake stop acting, man!'

The cardinal said quietly: 'You threatened me with a gun. I

had little option but to play along with you. A man with a gun shouting his head off that the Secretary of State is a communist agent? What a nice thing to hear. Besides, I'd like to know what I'm being accused of.'

Morgan looked at him furiously. 'Why do you want the fucking evidence handed to you?'

'Doesn't any man who is being blackmailed, however unjustly? So that such a thing cannot happen again.'

Morgan was devastated that the relief he had felt was definitely proving wrong. He pulled the gun out of his shoulder holster angrily. 'This is your last chance.' He threw the gun onto the settee, on the opposite side of the room. 'Now you are no longer threatened with a gun!' He held his finger out at the man. 'Now you have two options. You can either talk to me, or you can press the alarm button and your Swiss guards can throw me out. Unfortunately you cannot murder me, if that is up your street, because I am here officially. You will have got rid of me, but only for the night. Tomorrow you will be dealing with much heavier-weights than me.'

Cardinal Pieter Gunter was still standing, as if he intended to walk out on this nonsense.

'Why are you involving yourself in this? Why don't you just sell your story to the press for a million pounds?'

Oh Jesus . . .! 'I thought I'd made that clear! I don't wish the Holy Roman Church to be manipulated! And I don't want one of the corner stones of society shaken.'

The cardinal considered him steadily. Then he walked slowly back to his desk. But he did not sit down.

'I think I believe you.'

Morgan snorted. There was something studied about the way he had said that, which robbed the statement of sincerity. Like there had been something theatrical in the way the man had first told him to get out once he had the list of other KGB trainees.

The cardinal sat down slowly.

'And if I fail to convince you of my innocence?'

Morgan said bitterly: 'I will hand the evidence over to the British. And let them sort it out. But they will probably try to use you for their own ends. Against the Russians. As a double-agent, probably. And if they can't succeed in doing

390

that, they'll expose you. Because they can't afford to have a KGB agent in the Vatican.'

'Why wouldn't they just assassinate me?'

'They might. But they might not feel sure that the microfilm tells the whole story, whether the next Secretary of State is a KGB agent or not. So they may decide it's safer to expose the whole plot. And discredit the whole Church.'

The cardinal studied him grimly. Then he said:

'Let me assure you of this: not only do I intend dismissing these ten people' – he tapped the printout – 'but I intend launching a full-scale investigation to ensure the rot has not spread any further.' He added: 'If you are in fact an agent, you can tell your masters that. With my compliments.'

Morgan nodded impatiently. All very well. But, even if he believed that statement, no investigation into communist rot conducted by an ex-KGB agent could be trusted. And he didn't like the fact that the man assumed he was going to continue as Secretary of State. Did he take Morgan for a fool? But he only said, 'Good.'

The cardinal laced his hands together. He said:

'So instead of handing the evidence over to the British authorities, who have no jurisdiction over the Vatican, you should hand it over to the Vatican, surely? They are the best guardians of this information.'

'*Quis custodiet ipsos custodientes?* Who will guard the guards themselves?'

The cardinal spread his hands earnestly. 'Maybe, but how can the British conduct a proper investigation? They can't send Scotland Yard into Vatican City – it's a sovereign state, we could bar their entrance.' He spread his hands again: 'Give the evidence to the Pope himself! Let him worry about it.'

Morgan snorted. The Pope? Good man, no doubt, but a man so naive or so misinformed that he confirms Bishop Marcinkus in his post as president of the Vatican Bank after the God's Banker scandal? And who does the Pope appoint to worry about it? But he said, 'I'll consider it.'

'But you *must*. To protect the good name of the Church. And to ensure an efficient investigation. That's what *you* want, if you are who you say you are.' Then he shook his head with finality. 'I will not cooperate with you unless you assure me of that.'

Morgan wanted to rasp, *You're in no position to stipulate anything! – I've got you like that.* He said impatiently, 'All right, you have my assurance, provided I am satisfied you have made a clean breast to me – starting right now.'

Cardinal Gunter looked away, and got up. He paced slowly across the room, his hands clasped. He said: 'And what is going to happen to you after all this? You say they are trying to kill you?'

Was this a diversionary tactic? 'I'll cross the bridges as I come to them.'

'I think the Vatican can help you across those bridges.'

Morgan snapped: 'Provided I hand the evidence over to you? I will not be bribed.'

The cardinal smiled thinly. 'It was not a bribe, Englishman. It was simply a Christian offer to help a brave man.'

He returned to his desk abruptly. He laid his hands flat.

'It appears I have no option but to cooperate with you. So? How do I go about convincing you of my innocence?'

Oh Jesus, Morgan did not know what to make of him. A Christian offer? Or a ploy?

'I need pen and paper. You tell me your story, from the beginning. Then I will cross-examine you.'

The cardinal sighed, then opened a drawer. He produced a pad of paper. He took a pen off the rack. He waited a moment, thinking; then said:

'Very well. But may I suggest that first we pray . . .' Morgan was taken aback. The cardinal paused, then he said: 'But first I want to say this: I found God almost as soon as they started training me. As soon as I started studying the Bible. And, I was overjoyed! And I knew with all my heart that all I wanted to be was a priest.' He turned to Morgan. 'They thought they were going to double-cross the Holy Roman Church. But I double-crossed *them.*'

55

Pray? What was this – more theatricals? Cardinal Gunter leant his elbow on the desk, rested his head in his hand, and closed his eyes. His lips began to move silently.

And Morgan did not know what to believe. With all his heart he wanted to pray too, lift his arms up wide and pray pray pray angrily, for guidance. But he kept his eyes fixed on the man, watching his every expression, his demeanour, desperately trying to assess his credibility. For a minute the cardinal was silent. Then he crossed himself, and opened his eyes.

He said: 'From the very beginning?'

'Yes, please.'

Cardinal Gunter sat back in his chair wearily, and looked at the ceiling. He was silent a moment. Then:

'I was brought up in an orphanage in Leningrad. Evidently I was a bright pupil. One day I was sent for . . .'

Morgan watched him. And he saw it in his mind's eye: the snowclad house in the woods outside Moscow, the orphan boy in his monk's habit sitting on the bench.

Cardinal Gunter seemed to be warming to his story.

'Boris really was an excellent teacher. A razor-brain intellectual. He knew his Bible backwards, and all the usual theological textbooks. And, of course, all the works on atheism. In fact, looking back, I've often thought the man was within a hair's breadth of becoming a Christian himself. He was so *learned*. We often sat up till the small hours discussing obtuse metaphysical points. And the amazing thing is he didn't *believe* any of these Christian principles he was so ardently expounding and making sure I understood.'

'And this was all in English?'

'Oh yes. We were never allowed to speak Russian. I had intensive coaching in German, of course, but all my theology was taught in English.'

'And how did you feel about going to America?'

393

The cardinal smiled.

'I cannot really describe the joy I kept bottled up inside me those years . . . I didn't care where I was sent, as long as I was doing God's work. I suppose I would have been happiest to stay in Russia, and bellow my sermons to all those atheists . . .' He shook his head. 'America? The Land of the Free, where I could really spread my wings for God? – it was a tremendously exciting prospect for a lad of sixteen.'

'They taught you that America was the Land of the Free?'

Pieter Gunter shrugged. 'They knew they could not fool me, because I was going there. They taught me the realities of America, all the fundamentals of capitalism. But they also drummed into me all the principles of Marxism, and *proved* – yes *proved* to me – how *wrong* capitalism all was. How superior Marxism was. How capitalism was doomed to be defeated.'

'And what did you think?'

The cardinal shook his head.

'I remember having an open mind about economics. I *made* myself have an open mind. I could see both sides of the question.' (Morgan didn't believe that.) 'I was sophisticated enough to be able to see some of the . . . shortcomings of communism. Men were drawing ploughs in those days, like oxen. Are you a student of economics?'

Morgan shook his head.

'Nor am I, really. But I know enough to think that the answer – of Justice – lies somewhere between the two systems.'

'Meaning?'

The cardinal looked at the ceiling.

'The world's resources are so finite. And the population is constantly increasing. A third of the world is hungry now. The day will surely come when the world's goods will have to be rationed to all the people.'

That statement begged a question. But he let it go for the moment. 'Apart from theology and politics, what else did they teach you? Espionage work? Like photographing documents?'

'Yes. Cameras weren't very sophisticated in those days.'

'Radio work? Sending messages?'

'Yes.'

'Surveillance? How to follow somebody, how to shake off somebody who's following you?'

'Yes, all that sort of thing. Enough to get us by. After all, we were going to be priests, not James Bonds.'

'Weaponry? Small arms? Knife work? Explosives?'

'Yes. No explosives.'

'Unarmed combat?'

'Yes.' He smiled. 'I could probably still throw you around the room, Mr Englishman. Though I've never had to use my pugilistic skills. Most priests don't, you know.'

Morgan did not smile. '"Us". "We". So you knew that other people were being trained, like you?'

'I presumed that. But I had no idea who or where they were. I asked my instructors, but they would neither confirm nor deny it. In case I defected, I suppose.'

'And how did you feel about such people entering the Church?'

Pieter Gunter sat back. 'I just wished I could share my joy of Christianity with them – so that I could *convert* them. I prayed for them – to see the same light I had.' He added: 'But I was very worried about them possibly corrupting the Church. And I have been ever since. That's why I was so delighted tonight when you told the computer who they were.'

'*Possibly* corrupting it! Having it taken over by atheist communists, you mean! *That*'s what you were all being sent to do!'

The cardinal held up a hand. 'I was only sixteen. I believed the Church was invincible. God would prevail. I did not believe that us young trainees could really do much damage to such a mighty institution as the Holy Roman Church. It never occurred to me that I might one day be Secretary of State. We were but fleas.'

Morgan made a note of this inconsistency with his last answer. 'Well, it certainly occurred to your mentors in the Kremlin.'

'But remember that I was Russian. A Christian, yes, but I had been taught that Marxism was all good, and capitalism doomed. Human Rights was not a great issue in those days – Hitler was yet to come, the West had carved up the undeveloped world into colonies and were grinding the faces of the poor natives without much conscience. I did not know what Stalin was doing to my own people.'

'So?' Morgan demanded.

'So, at sixteen I was only concerned that the Church be not *abused* – that it not be perverted, sullied by having atheists for priests – at sixteen *that* was my anxiety, the *sacrilege* of it.'

Morgan sat back. Had he caught the man out? Or had he honestly talked his way out of it? Hopefully his tape-recorder would make it clear. 'So what did you do about it?'

The cardinal said: 'Shall I come to that in due course? Tell my story my way?'

'Very well,' Morgan sighed.

Pieter Gunter sat back again. 'Then,' he said, 'came the blessed day when my instructors declared I was ready to go forth into the world . . .'

There was no passing-out ceremony, no visit to KGB head-quarters, there was only a bottle of vodka. The young spy-priest did not like vodka, but he gamely took a glass. Boris let his hair down that last night. He was proud of his protégé and convinced he was going to get to the top. 'Your grasp of apologetics is remarkable!'

'What's apologetics?' Morgan demanded.

'Proving the existence of God by argument. Without using faith, or superstition or fear. One can prove God's existence in exactly the same way as one can prove by logic that two and two make four, or that the world is round.' He spread his hands: 'God *exists*, that is provable.'

Morgan watched him. He nodded. The man went on: 'The trouble is that ninety-nine per cent of the world knows no elementary logic. They are either suburbanites rushing around mindlessly making a buck, or they're primitive people who think the world is flat. They don't *think*. So, when it comes to God, they only believe because of vague superstition they learnt at their mother's knee, and call it "faith". If only we could get them to use a few simple rules of logic they would be better Christians.'

'So Boris, your teacher of logic, was being *ill*ogical in not believing?'

'Ah, yes. And that is why he was so nearly a believer. That last night, in his cups, he almost broke down and admitted it. He so badly wanted to pray. And how I prayed for him . . .'

The next day the young man left Moscow by train. He was so excited that he felt no pangs about leaving his homeland forever. His only anxiety was that his forged papers would get him through borders.

'I know the feeling,' Morgan said grimly.

'You're travelling on false documents, Englishman?'

Morgan cursed himself for saying anything. 'My passport reads "John Englishman",' he said curtly.

Two days later Pieter Gunter was at a town on the border. The next day he walked out of the forests, into Germany. Six weeks later, from the decks of an immigrant ship, he saw the Statue of Liberty reaching up into the morning sky.

'How did you find your way into Germany?'

'They had given me a map. A route.'

'How did you make your way to Hamburg?'

'I walked to the nearest village. Then took a train. As instructed. I had money.'

'When you got to Hamburg, did you report to your contact?'

'Yes.'

'Why?'

'Because,' the cardinal sighed, 'he had arranged my immigration to America. The ship passage.'

'But why didn't you just defect once you got to Germany? Hide? Run away to France?'

'Because I wanted to go to America! Get as far away as possible from Russia. I imagined they would track me down easily in Europe. It was safest to get to America before doing my disappearing trick. And America I knew – I had been trained for it.'

'How did the Russians manage to arrange your immigration?'

'I don't know. Immigration to America was less formal in those days. They were taking many refugees from Europe.'

'So you entered America on forged documents. Did you have any trouble on landing?'

'No. It was all pretty chaotic. Thousands of poor Europeans arriving on Staten Island with their pitiful possessions. Long queues. Endless waiting. It was all very rough and ready.'

'And then? You must have had a contact in New York.'

'Yes. A telephone number. I had to identify myself by code words. Then he would give me instructions as to where to meet him. And give me my orders. Thereafter, he would be my local controller.'

'And did you telephone him?'

'Yes.'

'*Why?* You were wanting to get rid of your Russian connections, you said.'

'Because,' Cardinal Gunter said, 'for all I knew he had an agent waiting outside the immigration door. To see what I got up to. To kill me if I put a foot wrong. And I had to know what my controller *looked* like. So I could avoid him in future. I had to identify my enemy. He knew what I looked like, from photographs. And, I also needed to learn what seminary I was supposed to be joining. So I could avoid that one.'

'Why didn't you just walk to the nearest police station, make a clean breast and ask for political asylum?'

'At sixteen years old? . . . Look, I considered that, but I had no confidence that I wouldn't be deported back to Russia. To certain death. And I had entered America illegally, as a trained spy, on false papers – that was presumably a serious criminal matter.' He sat back. 'And I didn't want to risk my precious plans for joining the priesthood.'

Morgan sighed and ran his hand through his hair.

'Very well. So you telephoned him.'

The meeting took place at a coffee stall on Grand Central Station.

Young Pieter Gunter first walked once around the concourse, as instructed: he was in a daze, of fear, of excitement. He could hardly believe that he was in New York at last, and he was tense with worry that he would give himself away. At three o'clock the genial voice said beside him: 'The elm is not only a Siberian creature.'

The man was about forty years old. Blondish hair, brown eyes. Apparently American. He slipped Pieter Gunter a hundred-dollar bill.

'At three-twenty there is a train to Princeton from platform eleven. Go to Saint Joseph's seminary. Ask for Father Watson. Tell him you want to join the priesthood. He will take your application from there.'

Pieter Gunter said, 'Does he know?'

'Of course not. But he deals with newcomers in the first instance. You will call me from a public telephone day after tomorrow to report your situation, using the same passwords. I will then give you further instructions. Well . . .' he took a gulp of coffee, 'nice talkin' to ya, buddie . . .'

Pieter Gunter walked numbly to the ticket office. He dared not look to see if he was being watched. He bought a ticket to Princeton.

'Why *Princeton*?' Morgan demanded. 'That was the place to *avoid*.'

'Because the man might have been watching me.'

He got on the train. He got a seat at the very back of the coach, so he could see if he was being observed. At the first station he got off. He caught the next train to Detroit.

'Why Detroit?'

'It was the next train coming through.'

He arrived two days later. He got a bed in the Salvation Army, using a false name, and took the first job he could find, as a plate-scullion in a hotel. ('Oh, the *food*, I couldn't believe the food. I made a pig of myself on other people's leftovers.') After two weeks he crossed into Canada.

'Why Canada?'

'To do a disappearing trick. I was frightened that the mother-land agents were scouring America for me. I figured that if I disappeared for a year they wouldn't dream of looking for me in a Catholic seminary then – after all, they'd trained me as an atheist. I hoped that after a year they'd forget about a sixteen-year-old defector called Pieter Gunter. At the Salvation Army I'd heard about a mine up in Ontario that was taking on men. So up I went. Got a job.'

'How much were your wages?'

'Eleven cents an hour. Almost a dollar a day, pretty good in the depression. I even enjoyed it. And it's beautiful up there –'

'What was the town called?'

'No town as such, just the mine. Called Moose Head. Just a track leading to it, in the middle of the forests. No women. No booze, because the forest was part of an Indian reservation.' He smiled. 'The mine could only have booze if they held a "banquet". So once a month the mine threw a banquet. You had to pay ten cents. The feast consisted of one biscuit per man. But for your ten cents you got four bottles of beer. You solemnly sat down at the banqueting table and ate a biscuit. Then you could drink your four bottles of beer.'

Morgan rubbed his chin. This was impressive detail. 'Did you go to the banquets?'

'Certainly. Russians are not averse to drinking.' He shook his head. 'And after the beer there were always fights. Somewhere somebody would get into a quarrel, and a fist would fly, and within moments twenty men would be slugging at each other midst crashing tables, just like in a cheap movie.'

Morgan wondered if he believed that. It sound too trite. 'What brand of beer was it?'

The cardinal looked surprised. 'Mollson's, I think. Why?'

'And during this time, did you do any preaching?'

'No. I was keeping a low profile. Besides, who would listen to a youngster? But I did a great deal of praying. And I count that as one of the most profitable periods of my life. Because I observed my fellow man, in the raw. Learned his weaknesses. And a few of my own.' He added: 'And I learned to play the guitar.'

Morgan sighed wearily. 'The guitar? All right. What happened then?'

Pieter Gunter rubbed his face with both hands.

'I spent almost a year on that mine. Then I felt it was safe to poke my head out. I took my money and went back down the track to the railroad. I jumped on a flat car, heading for Calgary.'

'A flat car?'

'A railway car that carries timber. I stowed away on it.'

'Why didn't you pay your fare, like a good boy should?'

'It was a goods train only. And jumping flat cars was a traditional way for miners to get around Canada. The train was going to Calgary anyway. I didn't exactly hijack it.'

Morgan did not smile. 'Why Calgary? Why not back to America?'

The cardinal smiled. 'I wanted to go to the rodeo. My last fling before I entered the priesthood. The Calgary Stampede. I've never seen anything like it, so many horses and cattle. I was enthralled.' He added: 'I've loved westerns, ever since.

Maybe I'm a cowboy at heart. Few things could be nicer than riding off into the sunset, at one with nature, just you and your horse, and your guitar, and God.' He smiled. 'With some people it's flying an aeroplane. With others it's skiing. We all have our little daydreams. And would you believe, I've never learned to ride?'

Morgan smiled despite himself. He could believe this. 'Well, you should.'

'Absolutely right. One day I'll summon the nerve to buy me a hoss. And I'll take a vacation, and I'll ride away into the sunset. Now, then – where were we?'

'Calgary.'

And so young Pieter Gunter came down from the plains of Canada, back into America, across the Rocky Mountains, and he made his way to the Saint Martin's Catholic Seminary outside Portland, Oregon. He knocked on the big door, with his guitar, and he told the man he wanted to become a servant of God.

And what happened with the Russians?

'*Nothing?*' Morgan echoed. 'Not a single contact in the next forty years?'

'Not a thing.'

'Not a breath of suspicion that you were being watched?'

'No. And I kept my eyes wide open for years, believe me. I was hyper-sensitive. Then the Second World War came along. I was ordained by then, and an American citizen. I was a chaplain in the Army, in Europe. Russia went into the war too. I imagined that in the chaos the whole project had been abandoned. Mislaid. Something.'

Well, that was true: Klaus Barbie confirmed that. 'But you were still using the name they had given you. Why hadn't you taken another name?'

'It was the only name I had. The name on my papers. I was used to it. And, I hoped that they'd forgotten about me after I dropped out of sight.'

Morgan made a note irritably.

'But how come they didn't hear about you?'

'There were no computers in those days. I guess they simply did not have access to a central registry of priests, and Oregon was a long way from Moscow. And then, after the war, I was sent to Mexico. I dropped out of sight.'

Morgan frowned. 'But all this time you were living a lie. Your fellow priests must have asked, Who are you, Where do you come from? How did you feel, living a lie?'

'It was a very white lie. I simply said I was an orphan from Dusseldorf. And you're forgetting one very Catholic thing – confession.'

'You *confessed* it?'

'About two years after I entered the seminary. Until then I had not considered it a sin, to tell a white lie about my origins. Nevertheless, after about two years it got me down. I got fed up with the petty subterfuge –'

'*Petty?*'

'To me it had become petty –'

'Then why did it get you down?'

He sighed, 'I was growing spiritually every day, I was growing daily more confident that I had been forgotten by Uncle Joe in Moscow.' He shrugged.

'Finally, I had had enough. I confessed it all.'

Could he believe this? 'And what did your confessor say?'

'I must admit I chose my confessor. He was a lovely old man. He was a Latin expert. Used to read Ovid's odes in Latin for bedside reading. I picked him.'

'And what did he say about having a Russian spy in the seminary?'

Pieter Gunter smiled. 'He was a bit astonished. I could not see his face. He said: "And – *are* you a Russian spy now?" I replied, "No, Father".'

'And he believed you – just like that?'

'I was off to a flying start on credibility, wasn't I? He knew my voice. Why does a spy confess unless he wants to make a clean breast? Particularly if he's a student priest. I told him the story. Or as much as he wanted to hear.'

'And?'

'Well, he believed me, that I was innocent. He simply said I had come to Christianity by an unusual route, and to go in peace.'

'And he didn't report the matter to his superiors?'

'Of course not! Nothing that a priest is told in the confessional may be repeated to anyone.'

Morgan sat back. In wonder.

'And so the matter was laid to rest? And nothing happened for the next forty years? Even though you were rising to international fame. Using the name the *Russians* had given you.'

'Surprising, I agree. I can only believe their plan got buried in the turmoil of the war. And then Russia acquired vast new territories to worry about – the whole eastern bloc of Europe. And then Stalin died and there were more big changes. The plan got forgotten.'

Morgan got up. He paced across the room.

'They wouldn't forget a big fish like you. An important project like getting the Vatican in their pocket. If what you say is true, the Russians were just letting you quietly rise in the Church, until the war came along. But then they lost the file. It was stolen by a Nazi agent in the KGB. He fled to Germany with it.' He turned. 'Without the file, the Russians don't know today the details of the project started fifty years ago. Names. Passwords. Codes. Destinations. All the KGB people who compiled that file are long-since dead. Without the passwords they can't get to you, even if they know that you are one of their protégés. You only knuckled under to me because I knew the passwords.'

The cardinal frowned. 'But why has it all come to a head now? How do you come to have the file?'

'Never mind. All that matters is that I've got it, and my intentions are good.'

The Secretary of State got up. He paced slowly across the room too. He put his hands together. 'I am aware that compliments will get me nowhere. But may I say that this is very courageous of you. And very, very noble.'

Morgan glanced at him. Was that genuine, or was it a ploy? 'So you believe that I am what I say I am?'

'Yes.' The cardinal closed his eyes and massaged his forehead. Yes, he believed Morgan. And he felt faint, because that made it even harder to do what he had to do.

Morgan felt sick-in-his-guts exhausted. Because he could not say the same for the cardinal. He took a deep breath. 'I want all these men got rid of from the Church. Tomorrow. And right now, tonight, you are going to sit down, and write a confession.' He turned to the man grimly. 'Taking the form of an oath to Almighty God. On your official stationery, in your own handwriting, and under your official seal. Briefly confessing the whole story, up to today.' The cardinal looked at him woodenly. Morgan continued: 'That confession I will take away with me tonight, as insurance. Forty-eight hours from now, you will meet me.'

'Where?'

Morgan said impatiently: 'I will telephone you the night after tomorrow at nine o'clock sharp. On your private line. And I'll give you instructions. You will come to that place *alone*. You will hand to me photocopies of each man's resignation.' He paused. 'Is that a deal?'

The cardinal sighed. 'Yes.'

Morgan went on grimly: 'You realize that if you fail to show up at the appointed place, or if there is any subterfuge, I will be armed with both the evidence *and* your confession. I only have to show both to the press, and this whole awful business will become public knowledge. With all the consequences. Or I can give it to the British. With all *those* consequences.'

Pieter Gunter closed his eyes. 'Yes. I realize that.'

Morgan held his head. He felt sick in his guts.

Cardinal Gunter said quietly:

'And then?' He paused. 'Then will you hand this evidence over? To the Vatican?'

Morgan massaged his brow. He knew, now, what he really had to do – the dreadful decision he had been evading since Zurich was finally staring him in the face. It was crystal clear, and with all his sick heart he just wanted to spread his arms to the heavens and have the decision taken from him. But the terrible fact was that he had finished his cross-examination and he still did not know what to believe. And that meant only one thing: *No benefit of the doubt*. The stakes were too high.

'Yes,' he sighed. 'If I am satisfied, then I will give you the evidence . . .'

404

56

It was the longest forty-eight hours of his life. And the shortest. He longed for something to happen which would make his mission impossible; he wanted to stretch his arms up and pray for the Lord to give him a sign. But the Lord did not.

That night he collapsed into bed and slept as if he had been pole-axed, but at three o'clock the next morning he was wide awake staring in the darkness, his heart sinking. He turned over and desperately tried to go back to sleep, but it was hopeless. He swung feverishly out of bed, rang room service for coffee, then went to the shower. He stood under it for five minutes, trying to beat the tension out of his head.

Then he got dressed, sat on the bed, drinking coffee, chain-smoking, and listening to the tape-recording he had made of Cardinal Pieter Gunter. Listening hard to every inflection, desperately looking for every point in the man's favour, trying to remember his demeanour with each answer. He rewound the tape and listened again. Then he collapsed back on the bed.

The judgement was still No.

No . . . If he were sitting on a jury, then, yes, he would have to give the man the benefit of the doubt, as required by law, and acquit him – just. He would have had to find in his favour that it was not proven beyond reasonable doubt that Pieter Otto Gunter had *not* found God at age fifteen and had, for the next forty years, miraculously escaped Russian memory and detective powers – despite continuing to use the very name they had given him, despite becoming a household name. Okay, the Klaus Barbie tape gave that story some credence – the KGB file stolen, turmoil in war-torn Russia, after the dust settled nobody in the KGB could remember the name Pieter Otto Gunter nor the passwords.

Nobody?

Okay, just credible. Maybe there was only one man in the whole KGB in the 1940s who knew the whole file, and he had died. Nobody else knew the passwords. Hence nobody knew how to get at the boys in monks' habits, nor even where they were.

Credible? A big project like getting the Vatican in the Kremlin's pocket, and only one man knows?

Okay, Klaus Barbie's story made that credible. Just.

But who was Klaus Barbie? The Butcher of Lyons, that's who. Was such a man to be believed on every point? All we know for sure is that he came into possession of the file some time after the war, and tried to use it for his own ends. We don't independently know *when* it was stolen from the KGB – it might have been stolen only recently, in which case it was not credible that nobody in the KGB remembered Pieter Otto Gunter's passwords . . .

And there were inconsistencies or improbabilities in the man's story. Several.

Why go to America once he had escaped Russia – why not run away to the nearest place, like France?

Why report to his controller once he was safely in America? Why keep using the same name the KGB had given him?

And why, oh why, confess his 'very-white lie' after he felt he had successfully escaped his Russian mentors. Why does a nineteen-year-old, who counts himself lucky and who doesn't count his 'petty subterfuge' a sin, risk losing all by confessing?

Credible? . . .

And the man had changed his story for a while – after discovering Morgan was not KGB he had tried to bluff it out. To use his high authority.

But the most sinister evidence against him was his question: *When is the murder of the Pope going to be?*

Oh, Jesus. The man had just jumped to that conclusion. And then asked for time to prepare himself. 'It would be a grave mistake to go at this like a bull at a gate . . .'

Okay, he had explained it away, by saying he wanted to know the details of the murder plot so he could foil it. 'You fool!' But anybody would have given that explanation, anybody could have acted that out. And he was an experienced orator.

Morgan pressed his fingertips to his eyes.

But there was one big point in the man's favour, which any lawyer would have hammered home to a jury: Cardinal Gunter, once they had the computer's printout listing the whereabouts of the other KGB trainees, had told Morgan to get out. Said that he now had what he always wanted to know. Said that he served only God. Said 'Never darken the doors of the Vatican again . . .'

Why would the man do and say that unless he was genuine?

Several possibilities. One: Maybe he was testing Morgan. Maybe he suspected that he was not KGB – he did not sound like a KGB man, did he? Wasn't it suspicious that after all these years a strange Englishman shows up from nowhere claiming to be a KGB messenger? So, why not test him? If Morgan stuck to his guns and proved himself to be KGB, what would the cardinal have lost? Nothing.

Two: Develop that argument further. If Morgan was *not* a KGB man, it was quite possible he was a blackmailer, an ordinary crook. In which case, what better way to intimidate the blackmailer than to send him packing, to piously deny being a spy, claim that he served only God? Pretend to be impervious to blackmail?

Three: If Morgan was not KGB, then there was a strong possibility he was an MI6 or CIA man. In which case, it was equally important to Cardinal Gunter to throw him off the scent, to pretend he was a pious defector.

Morgan dragged his hands down his face.

And there was something else about that incident which smelt bad – there had been something theatrical about the way the cardinal had told him to get out. The authoritative stance, the pious finger pointed at the door, the threat to call in the Swiss guards (a hollow threat, when you examine it, because Morgan could have initiated a scandal throughout the Vatican by shouting his head off to the Swiss guards about KGB spies – the cardinal would not have risked that). And then, when Morgan had been overwhelmed with relief that he was dealing with an honest defector, and said he was not a KGB messenger, the cardinal had changed his stance yet *again*. Bluffed. Acted. 'You threatened me with a gun'. Denial of his past. Then, another contradiction: 'What do you want? – money? . . .'

Morgan shook his head. Sick in his heart.

And then the man's whole attitude and demeanour had changed yet again. 'I think I believe you'. And then he had appeared to become totally cooperative. 'I double-crossed *them*'. 'First let us pray'. Then patiently, earnestly telling his whole story. Little anecdotes about the plate-scullion stuffing himself on rich people's leftovers, the fights at the one-biscuit banquet at Moose Head mine, the Calgary Stampede . . . Throughout there had been a certain glibness, as if he had had the matter rehearsed for years. And the man was an experienced talker, accustomed to the pulpit, to wheeling and dealing in the corridors of power . . . And he had brought all these skills to bear with ease on Morgan, an honest Jack Tar, a babe in the woods.

And there was something else that Morgan found almost contemptible: not once had the man offered to, or even *hinted* that he would resign his high office as part of the bargain to save the Church. *Why not?* It was an elementary offer for an innocent man of God who admits his guilty past! But no: Morgan had not stipulated it, even though insisting that the other ten be dismissed, and it was as if the man had seized on this oversight by a country boy and proceeded to consolidate his gain by browbeating: 'You *must* give me the evidence, otherwise I won't cooperate.'

Morgan held his hands to his face.

That left the car park at the golf club – the only other point to be made in the man's favour. The cardinal had been shocked when Morgan first accosted him. He had gone ashen, unnerved, looked as if he wanted to run for it. A complete change from the confident, jolly man he had observed in the club house.

Was he frightened because he was an innocent man?

Oh Jesus . . . Yes, possibly – but wouldn't any man be shocked by being accosted by a stranger mouthing passwords he hadn't heard for decades? Wouldn't any man, let alone an important personage, be intensely worried that an embarrassing scene could develop in a public place? Even a guilty man, a willing KGB agent, would be taken by surprise, and intensely worried by that. And the hard fact was that the man had not tried to bluff it out *then* – he had not stormed off protesting his innocence *then*. But he had tried to do so when he had discovered that Morgan was not a KGB messenger after all.

Morgan lay on the bed, his fingertips pressed to his eyelids.

All right! Two or more explanations for all these points. And if he were sitting on a jury he would probably feel he had to acquit him, declare that the case was not proven that he was *now* a KGB agent. That maybe he had indeed found God, that he was therefore no danger to the Holy Roman Church. But Jack Morgan was not sitting on a jury.

And the terrible fact remained that even if he was *wrong* in convicting the man now, even if the man *was* innocent and would not willingly damage the Holy Roman Church nor Western society, *even if he willingly resigned his high office* – the terrible fact remained that the Russians could still get at him. The fact was that even if the cardinal resigned his office, the Russians could still force him to reveal all he knew about Western diplomatic affairs. About the Church's intentions and secret policies. And once they'd made the cardinal talk they could *still* blow the whole story and bring the whole Catholic Church into disrepute . . .

The terrible fact was that even if the man was innocent he knew too much. He was too valuable to be allowed to live . . .

Morgan sat up, and held his brow. Sick in his guts. An honest man who had just had to sentence another man to death.

Oh God, wasn't there another way?

Couldn't he just hand this whole problem over to the Pope? Tell Cardinal Gunter to take him to Pope John Paul II, and tell His Holiness to conduct a full-scale investigation, weed out the rot, set his house in order? Wouldn't that be enough?

He sat, holding his head. And the terrible answer was No.

No, for two reasons.

Firstly, how could Pope John Paul be trusted to conduct a complicated investigation of his own vast Church? A man so misinformed, or so naive, or so easily led that he rescinds his predecessor's orders and re-instates a man like Bishop Marcinkus as head of the Vatican Bank after the God's Banker scandal? Pope John Paul was doubtless an honest man, a wonderful spiritual leader, maybe the best the Church has ever had, but 'horses for courses'. How good a detective would he be, how bad a judge of confused, labyrinthine evidence, the tangled webs and dupes of modern espionage, if he was so dumb as to re-appoint Bishop Marcinkus? *Would he not even re-appoint Cardinal Gunter as Secretary of State?* Or be persuaded to whitewash the whole thing? . . . You do not put a rabbit, not matter how well intentioned, in charge of investigating a lettuce patch . . .

And the second terrible reason was the old one: even assuming His Holiness did fire Cardinal Gunter, the Comrades could still get at him, make him talk, do tremendous damage and bring the Church into calumny and the West into disarray.

Morgan took a deep, trembly breath.

Oh God . . . That left only one last question.

Who? *Who* was going to do it?

Now don't flinch from the final decision: Who?

No, not Danziger for an accomplice.

Then who?

Himself?

Could *he* do it? Have the courage of his convictions? In cold blood?

He slumped back on the bed.

Sit up and review the evidence again. Try to find something more in the man's favour.

Then suddenly he thought of another question he could ask the man. He was surprised he had not thought of it before. A trick question! He stared across the room, thinking it through. He almost felt excited.

A trick question. It could save the man's life. If he answered Yes, and agreed, then Morgan would *know* he was not to be trusted. And it would be that much easier to get rid of him.

And if he answered No and refused? Would that mean that he *was* to be trusted? That his life could be spared?

Morgan stared across the room, trying to think straight.

Then he collapsed back on the bed again, in despair.

No. It didn't make any difference to the final result. Because even if the man anwered No, it may be because he saw through the question, saw the trick – but, even if that wasn't so, the fact remained that the KGB could still find him and force him to reveal all he knew . . .

But he should still put the question. If only in the hopes the man answered Yes. And thereby made it easier.

But oh God, if he answered No it was going to make it even harder . . .

Morgan squeezed his eyes closed. At the end of his tether.

Who? Danziger?

And all he had to do was pick up the telephone and call Danziger in Marseilles. And it would all be over.

He took a deep breath, sick in his guts.

That terrible day went that way.

At eight-thirty that night, he left the hotel. At nine o'clock he drove past Saint Anne's Gate at Vatican City, and began to time himself.

He drove along the route he had selected, across Rome, and out onto the Appian Way towards the beauty spot. He passed the public telephone half a mile before the intersection. He drove on, to the intersection. He timed it: about thirty-five minutes.

He turned around, and drove back towards Rome.

Tomorrow he had to buy gloves. And binoculars.

57

The next day was the longest of his life.

At eight o'clock that night he paid his bill, up until the next day. He explained that he might be leaving very early in the morning. He returned to his room, packed everything into his handgrip and left the hotel with it. Then he drove carefully across Rome, and out onto the Appian Way.

It was a few minutes before nine when he came to the public telephone, half a mile before the intersection. He waited until exactly nine o'clock. He went to the box.

He dialled Cardinal Gunter's private telephone number.

The cardinal answered immediately. He sounded very tense. Morgan said: 'What kind of car do you have? Your own private car, not your official one.'

The cardinal said nervously: 'A Citroën.'

'Colour?'

'Blue. Dark blue.'

'Number?'

The cardinal told him. Morgan said: 'Leave the Vatican immediately, driving this car. Drive out onto the Appian Way. About sixteen kilometres from the centre of Rome you will encounter an intersection, in the forest, with a stop sign. There're some street lights there. About five kilometres further on you will see a truckers' hostel, called Bar-Ristorante Vene-

411

zia. Go inside and get something to drink. You'll see a public telephone in the corner. Sit near it. When it rings, answer it. Got that?'

'Yes,' the cardinal whispered.

Morgan hung up. His face and hands felt clammy.

He got back into his car and he drove on down the dark Appian Way. He came to the intersection and turned left. He drove five hundred metres, then came to the track leading up into the forest. He swung onto it. He drove up through the forest. Over the hill. He came to the fork. He first turned down the right fork. He drove to the picnic tables. He switched off his lights and peered around. There were definitely no other cars. He turned and drove back, up to the fork. He turned down the left fork. He drove for a hundred yards, then pulled into the trees. He got out of the car. He left it unlocked. He started running back up the track, towards the tarred road.

He walked back to the intersection. Then he scrambled up the bank, into the forest again. He crouched down, and peered down the Appian Way, towards Rome. He could see the road well.

He sat down, and pressed his hands to his face. They trembled.

He looked at his watch. He had at least fifteen minutes to wait. With all his sickened heart he wanted to pray. But for what? For help? For forgiveness? He could not bring himself to try.

He put his new gloves on.

Four cars passed. Each time Morgan's stomach turned over. He peered through the binoculars. But as soon as each car came within a hundred metres, into the lamplight, slowing down for the stop sign, he could see it was not a blue Citroën. And he untensed, sick in his guts. Then, after seventeen minutes he saw new headlights coming. And this was a Citroën.

The car came up the hill, slowing for the stop sign. Morgan crouched, his heart pounding, peering through the binoculars. Then he could make out the car's number. Only one person in it. It came rolling to a halt, abreast of him. And Morgan came bursting out of the trees, onto the road.

He flung open the front passenger door. Pieter Gunter

jerked, shocked, his face ashen in the panel lights. 'It's me,' Morgan snapped. He got in and slammed the door. 'Go. Turn left here.'

The cardinal hastily surged the car forward. 'I thought you were going to telephone –'

'Change of plan. Just drive.'

The car swung left, down the road. The cardinal looked ill. 'Why the change?' he said hoarsely.

'In case you have people covering the bar. To jump on me.'

'I see. Well, I haven't.'

'Good.' Sick in his guts. He looked through the rear window. There was nobody following. He said, 'There's a turn-off into the forest, on the right. Take it.'

The car turned off the tarred road, onto the forest track. It ground up the hill. Then came the fork. 'Take the right.'

The cardinal obeyed. Two hundred yards on they came into the picnic area.

'Stop. Switch the headlights out. Put the interior lights on. Leave your safety strap on.'

The cardinal obeyed. He turned to Morgan. He was haggard. 'Now?' he said.

Morgan opened his door and climbed quickly out. He crouched on his haunches in the open doorway. He took a trembly breath. 'Have you got the resignations?'

Pieter Gunter was very frightened. 'Why have you got out?'

'Elementary self-defence. Have you got the resignations?'

Pieter Gunter put his hand in his pocket. He pulled out a large envelope. It trembled in his hand. He passed it over.

Morgan fumbled it open. He pulled out a sheaf of photo-copied documents.

There were twenty sheets, stapled together in twos. The top copy was in Italian. The second was in English. All on official Vatican paper. Morgan speed-read the English copies. They were exactly as he had ordered: a simple, one-line confession; a simple, unequivocal resignation. 'Was there any trouble?'

'Some.'

'Meaning?' He did not care.

'Meaning I'm convinced that some of them are holy men, to whom an injustice has been done.'

413

'They all protested their innocence? Claimed to have found God?'

Pieter Gunter closed his eyes briefly, and nodded. 'True.'

'But in the end they all accepted the inevitable? And agreed to resign quietly.'

'True.'

Thank God he had been right. And please God he was right in what he yet had to do. Pieter Gunter said:

'And now? Have I satisfied all your conditions?' He held out a trembly hand: 'Have you got the evidence?'

Morgan felt sick anger flare that this had been thrust upon him. He said: 'Yes. But I have another condition to impose first.'

Pieter Gunter closed his haggard eyes again. 'What is it now?'

Morgan's mouth was dry. God, now he wanted the answer to be the wrong one, to make it easier: if the answer was the right one it was going to be even more terrible. Perhaps it would be easier not to know, to execute judgement on what he already knew, but he had to ask it. He said:

'The world is rapidly becoming over-populated. A big part of it is starving already. In a hundred years there will be chaos.' He cleared his throat. 'I know that you cannot countermand the Pope's ruling on the subject. But as Secretary of State you can lead a powerful movement to persuade him to lift the Catholic Church's prohibition on contraception . . .'

There was a silence. Pieter Gunter looked at him, his eyes haggard. Then he said:

'And if I agree, you will give me the microfilm?' He cleared his throat. 'And if I then break the agreement, you will blackmail me, by using my hand-written confession. And if I still don't do your bidding, you will expose me.'

Morgan's nerves were near breaking. 'Just answer the question!'

Cardinal Gunter went on unsteadily: 'And if I refuse this new condition, you will *not* give me the microfilm? And I, and the Church, will ever more be liable to be blackmailed by you – we'll live under the constant sword of Damocles that you will use the microfilm against us, for whatever purpose, expose this

414

whole sordid story and bring the Church into disgrace. So I cannot trick you. You have all the cards.'

'Correct.'

Pieter Gunter said shakily: 'So all is lost. So I have nothing to lose, my friend. Nothing to lose by giving you a truthful answer. And that answer is No.'

Morgan wanted to bellow his fury to the sky because this answer made it harder. The cardinal went on grimly:

'This may be wasted effort, but I also have nothing to lose by trying to persuade you.' He took a tremulous breath. 'This matter of contraception has been a bitter bone of contention between the Church and modern man for decades. And the arguments in favour of contraception are weighty. But the hard fact is that human life is sacred. It is God-given, for His purpose. And I will not now, nor ever, allow that divine purpose to be frustrated by man.'

Morgan did not know why he was arguing with the man because it made no difference but he cried, *'But the world's only so big – how can we keep filling it with people who're going to starve?'*

'I am familiar with all the arguments, believe me. And if you like I will debate them with you till the cows come home. But the end result will be the same: as long as I have any power I will not permit the matter to be bargained about . . .' He looked at Morgan, his exhausted eyes liquid. Then said with controlled anger: 'You may expose me for what happened in my youth! You may shake the Holy Roman Church to its foundations by so doing, but I will not bargain about the sanctity of human life! God's will is not negotiable!'

Morgan wanted to retch. His task had not been made easier for him. Cardinal Pieter Gunter said, white-faced:

'So? Now you are not going to give me the evidence?'

Morgan wanted to break down and weep. Before he could answer, the cardinal said: 'And now you're going to kill me?'

Morgan's throat was thick. He said: 'You are the Secretary of State. You know so much. The Russians can make you talk if they ever catch up with you . . .'

The cardinal interrupted shakily: 'I anticipated this. So I have something further to offer you . . . My last card . . .'

He put his hand into his pocket, and pulled out another envelope, sealed. It trembled in his hand.

Morgan took it. He began to open it. The cardinal's hand shot back inside his jacket and he pulled out a gun.

He pointed it at Morgan tremblingly.

Morgan crouched in the open door, astonished, staring at the gun. The cardinal clutched it in both hands, his face a mask of horror at what he was doing. He whispered:

'*For God's sake let me spare your life, Englishman. Give me the microfilm* . . .' Morgan's mind was stammering. The cardinal blurted: '*If you don't, I've got to kill you, Englishman! And damn myself* . . .'

Morgan whispered: 'You said human life is sacred.'

The gun trembled three feet from his face. 'But so is the Church! The Church is worth much more than your life and my immortal soul in purgatory. The Church must live so that mankind can live, and you have the evil power to destroy the Church!'

'I do not want to destroy it! – I'm trying to save it!'

'Then in the name of God give me the microfilm, Englishman! And save the Church and your life and my immortal soul!' The gun trembled in his clasped hands.

Morgan blurted: 'I haven't got it on me –'

The cardinal cried desperately: 'You're lying! You said you had it on you!'

'I'm not!'

'I can't afford to believe you, Englishman! Nor can the Church! Nor can mankind! If you don't give it to me now I've got to kill you! I can't take the risk on behalf of God and the whole of mankind! Your life isn't worth that risk! So in the name of Jesus Christ I beg you to remove the risk and give me the evidence now and save your precious life! This is the last time I ask!'

'Tomorrow! – I haven't got it with me now . . .'

And Pieter Gunter's eyes widened and his face seemed to swell with horror and Morgan stared at the gun aghast; Pieter Gunter's clutching hands tremblingly tightened, and the bile welled up in his throat. And he could not pull the trigger, and Morgan flung himself sideways.

416

He flung himself wildly onto the ground beside the car. He scrambled up and pulled out his gun and crouched against the rear mudguard, his heart pounding. He heard the driver's door burst open and the cardinal scramble out. Morgan looked desperately at the trees, for cover to run to. But the car was stopped right out in the open. He raised his head and peered through the rear-door window. He jerked his head down again. He could not see the man. He looked frantically behind him, then peered under the car, looking for the man's feet. He could see nothing. Blackness. He scrambled to the very rear of the car. Gun up. He peered around the rear light.

Nothing. He dashed to the other rear light. He crouched there, gun ready. Then he peered around the corner.

Again nothing! He swivelled and faced the other way, then scrambled backwards to the rear left mudguard, his heart hammering: then he peered through the rear passenger window, and he saw the man. Saw his horrified face looking back at him, and they both jerked their heads down simultaneously. Then Morgan heard the man vomit.

He heard a heaving sound, and a retch, then out it came in a gush. Morgan was amazed; then he scrambled back around the rear of the car. Then he leapt out into the open, his gun clasped in both hands in front of him, his heart pounding.

He stared. Cardinal Pieter Gunter was on his hands and knees, his head hanging, his gun on the ground. He retched once more, then coughed, and shuddered; then he raised his head.

His haggard eyes were streaming, his face suffused. Vomit on his chin. He seemed quite unsurprised to see Morgan covering him with the gun, quite unafraid; just exhausted, nauseous, finished. He raised his wrist to his chin, and wiped the vomit off. He looked at Morgan, his eyes wet, and he said: 'Forgive me . . .'

Morgan stared, the trembling gun trained on him. The man lifted his other wrist and wiped his eyes.

'Forgive me,' he repeated, 'I'm not man enough for the job. I thought I could, but evidently I haven't the guts for it.' He clambered shakily to his feet. He left his gun on the ground. He had flecks of vomit on his jacket. He slumped back against the car, his arms hanging, utter exhaustion on his face.

'Well, get on with it, man. I know I should fight to the last drop of blood for the Church but I've done my best and you've outgunned me.' He added, almost wearily: 'I made my last confession before I came here, so make it quick.' Then he closed his eyes impatiently, buried his fingers into his shirt and pulled out a crucifix. 'Don't worry, I haven't compromised anybody, I said my confession to this.'

Morgan stood there, knees bent, both hands training the gun on the man, and with all his sick heart he just wanted to break down and weep. He said hoarsely,

'You understand why I've got to do it?'

'Yes, yes, man, I'm not a fool – for the same reasons I had to kill you. For the sake of the Church. I can be made to talk by the Russians. Et cetera, et cetera. I know that. If one sticks one's nose into politics, one must expect to get it bloodied. So get it over, Englishman. Quickly please!'

And Morgan wanted to vomit also, and bellow his anguish to the skies, and before he could lose his nerve he strode at the man. He pulled out the canister of nerve gas and thrust it at the cardinal's startled face, and he pressed the plunger.

Pieter Gunter's knees buckled, and he collapsed, unconscious.

Morgan grabbed him up by his armpits, and he dragged him.

Dragged him round the front of the car, gasping, rasping, the tears running down his face. He dragged him to the driver's door. He dropped the man, opened the door. He heaved him up again, and he wrestled the top half of him onto the driver's seat. Whimpering. He then ran around to the passenger door and scrambled in. He heaved the cardinal into the car. Then he ran back to the driver's door. He shoved and wrestled his legs in. Then he heaved the man up, into the seated position. The head hung forward. Morgan wrestled his seat-belt on. Then he ran back to the passenger side.

He picked up the cardinal's gun. The tears were running down his face. He scrambled into the back seat of the car. He leant over and grabbed the cardinal's right hand. He fumbled the pistol into the palm. He closed the fingers around the butt. He bent the elbow and brought the pistol muzzle against the man's temple. He closed his gloved finger around the trigger. He screwed up his eyes, and he wanted to bellow his anguish.

418

He cried: '*God, forgive me* . . .' And his finger tightened on the trigger.

He felt it click, and tighten. And a retch of horror welled up in him. One more hair's breadth and the man was dead.

And he could not pull the trigger.

He could not pull it, and he let the arm drop.

Morgan scrambled out of the car, and the dam of tears broke. He staggered back against the car and he dropped his head, and he wept.

And oh God they were tears of happiness, of overwhelming relief, and he wept out loud:

'*Okay, God* . . . *It's up to You now* . . . *I've done my best* . . . *Just get me to the Pope* . . .'

Part Ten

58

The snow lay crisp on the rocky orchards, thick upon the old tiled roof of the farmhouse, and smoke curled up the chimneys.

It was a wonderful feeling coming back to his beautiful woman in this beautiful house, knowing that his work was done. He was not even worried that she would be furious with him for tricking her again – he had the best news in the world to tell her. He hooted from the top of the land, and rolled down his window and hollered, but he did not expect her to come bursting out of the door this time. He rolled the car down the track. As he got to the house, the door opened and Makepeace came out with the rifle. He looked very worried. He came to the window and said: 'She's in the bedroom.'

Morgan walked into the courtyard, a smile all over his face.

She was standing by the fire in the bedroom. She turned, unsmiling. Morgan walked up to her, a grin all over his face. He wanted to take her in his arms and laugh. He put his hand in his pocket and pulled out the envelope containing Cardinal Gunter's confession and all the resignations. He said:

'It's all over. I've confronted the Secretary of State, and got everybody's resignations, including his. And I've seen the Pope. He's going to do a full investigation. And he's going to see that the British leave us alone.'

Her eyes were wide.

He had told her everything, in detail. They lay on the double bed, the confessions and resignations scattered on the floor; she felt absolutely limp and laughy with relief. She wanted to throw her arms wide and laugh her praises to the Lord.

'And the great man himself?'

Morgan smiled.

'Very impressive, even in his dressing gown. Had a dragon on it. His English is a bit awkward. Very formal.'

'A dragon?'

'A gift from somebody in Korea, he said.'

'Popes shouldn't sport dragons, should they? And how did he take all this, you and the Secretary of State walking in at midnight?'

'Thunderstruck when the cardinal confessed. Couldn't believe it.'

'But he took notes, and all that?'

'Of course.'

'But didn't want the microfilm?'

'Of course. Very anxious. But he finally accepted that I couldn't hand it over until his papal investigation was satisfactorily finished.'

'And how did the cardinal really behave throughout all this? Except "very correctly"?'

'Really, very correctly. He had recovered his composure. A man of great fortitude. Made a clean breast. Gave in his resignation, et cetera.'

She said, 'And, you're satisfied he'll cooperate fully with the investigation, and accept banishment to some obscure outpost of the Church's empire?'

'He has no choice, because I've got his confession. And for the same reason the Pope must make him go. The Pope won't risk a scandal like that.'

'But do you think he's innocent now?'

'Yes. I wasn't sure before. Not at all. But when he couldn't bring himself to shoot me, and then vomited and surrendered – no man could have acted that out. And when he regained consciousness, amazed to be alive . . .' He shook his head. 'We were both very emotional.'

She closed her eyes and squeezed his hand. 'Thank God he couldn't pull the trigger. And thank God you couldn't either.' She sighed. 'But you said he knew too much, the Russians could still get at him? Do you think it's safe now, if he's sent to some obscure outpost?'

Morgan hardly cared any more. He had done his best.

'The Church must be able to spirit him away somewhere. Like the Congo. Or the Outer Hebrides. It's safer to keep him within the cloisters than throw him out into the big wide world.'

She smiled at the ceiling. 'Oh, just thank God . . .' Then she turned to him with a smile from all her heart. 'I admire you so much. And love you so much.'

He had never been happier in his life.

'I love you too. And admire you.'

She sat up and shook her fingers through her hair.

'So, we're full of mutual admiration. And it's all over! . . .'
She held her happy face with both hands a moment, then said:
'Now all we've got to do is get the British and Russians off our
backs.'

'The Pope guarantees that. "They'll have me to deal with",
he said.'

She smiled. 'You think he likes you, huh?'

'There'll always be a bed for us in the Vatican.' He added,
'If we're married, of course.'

'Oh, I'll marry you, Jack Morgan, RN Retired . . .'

Makepeace left the next day, carrying a letter to post to
Carrington from London, telling him to get off their backs:

*'You can tell the French government that they can go ahead
and prosecute Klaus Barbie. Because the microfilm has been
destroyed. And you can tell Her Majesty's government that I
have written a lengthy account of what they tried to do, sparing
no sordid details, and I have placed this, sealed, in the hands of
a very competent lawyer to be published if we suffer any further
harassment whatsoever. It will make Watergate look like a caper.
So tell Brink-Ford and Her Majesty to call off their goons, and
tell our ambassador in Moscow to tell the Kremlin to call off their
goons too. And never darken my horizons again, Carrington, or
you and Her Majesty's government will come tumbling
down . . .'*

In fact he had not yet written the story for the lawyer to hold:
he had intended doing so that very night, for Makepeace to
deliver, but he had been too tired and too happy to face the
task. However, he fully intended doing so, when they returned
to England. But for the time being he was sure that his letter to
Carrington, plus the Pope's message, was enough to intimidate
them. And he was sure that nobody would find them.

But, after Makepeace left, Morgan did work out an escape
route, in case they ever needed it. He went to a village and
bought a second-hand motorcycle, a Guzzi 350cc track cycle,
with a pillion. About a mile downstream from the farmhouse,
the forestry road crossed the river at a small bridge. He hid the
motorcycle under the bridge, covered in a plastic sheet and

shrubbery. They went over the escape route together. They would jump into the stream that ran past the house and make their way down to the river, leaving no tracks. Once in the river, they would make their way down to the bridge, still leaving no tracks. They would get on the motorcycle and ride away down any number of forestry trails, to the main road. It was a good plan but he did not think they would ever need it. They practised it once, then put it out of their minds: they did not want to think about anything but each other until the new year.

They had a lovely time that December, without the fear any more. It felt as if the weight of the world had fallen from their shoulders. He still went out every day, with the FN rifle, to check the snow for footprints, but he was sure that they were safe. Every second day or so they drove to one of the villages to buy groceries, and now they no longer dashed in and out; they stopped in a bar if they felt like it, or a restaurant and had lunch. It was nice way out here in the country, the snow-clad Alps rearing up, the narrow streets white with snow, the fires in the hearth, the good smell of cooking, the red-cheeked children playing with their sleds, the innkeeper jolly. A week before Christmas they went to buy a suckling pig for dinner; but when the butcher produced a piglet, squealing, for her admiration before slaughtering it, she squealed herself and insisted on buying the animal on the hoof, alive and well.

'What're we going to do with it when we leave?' Morgan sighed.

'*He was going to kill it!*'

She bought a chicken instead, already deceased. That same day, in the market, she saw two forlorn geese, and she bought them as well. Then, her appetite for conservation whetted, she bought two ducks, male and female.

'What're we going to do with all this livestock when we leave?' he said.

'We'll board them with a farmer until we come back. Which will be soon.'

There were other signs of that intention. She had started whitewashing the walls, and Morgan was set to work repairing things; and now every time they went to the village she came back with this vase and those pretty dishes and that nice set of brass oil lamps, and all kinds of household gear, new buckets and brooms and mops, and paint for stripping old furniture and preserving wood. Two days before Christmas he went into the forest to get a Christmas tree, and to check the snow for footprints, and when he came back she had got stuck into an uncobbled corner of the courtyard with a spade, digging a duck pond. 'In the new year we'll build them a proper one.'

'Anna, in the new year we've got to go back to work and start making a living.'

'How can we? What'll we do with all these animals?'

But work was going to be fun. She was going to sail with him, for the first year the ship would be their home, the sea would be their garden, every evening they would have their sundowners on the bridge, watching the sun go down. But all that was in the new year, and maybe not before February, what with all these animals. Morgan helped her dig the duck pond, and then mixed up a sack of cement, and lined it. The ducks and geese thought it was terrific.

'Oh, it's going to be lovely here in summer . . .'

It was a lovely Christmas Day. She decorated the Christmas tree with tinsel and candles. She pot-roasted the chicken with potatoes and pumpkin. She had been unable to buy an English Christmas pudding but she had made a splendid drunken trifle, and to make it set she had left it outside overnight. And there was cherry brandy and champagne and nuts. It was beautifully jolly sitting round the kitchen table, the candles flickering, the fire crackling, the snow outside, and the sounds of great splashing in the duck pond. When she began to get along with the cherry brandy she wanted to bring the geese in because it was so cosy, but they refused. It was lovely, the fire, the wine, the tree, the dinner, her rosy cheeks and her smiley, happy face. They drank a toast to absent friends, and for a sentimental minute they even wished Makepeace was still here. 'Here's to Makepeace,' she said. 'Good man.'

'I just hope we never see him again.'

'Are you quite sure he won't tell anybody where we are?'

'He's not very bright, but he's not stupid, and he means well.'

'He was very sweet to me. Very worried how I was feeling.'

'Nice guy, Makepeace.'

427

'Who else can we drink to? Cardinal Gunter?'

Morgan smiled, and for a moment he felt his eyes burn. He raised his glass. 'To the cardinal. Good guy, too.'

She thought a moment, then took his hand across the table. She smiled and said: 'I have a confession to make.'

She considered her words, then said: 'When you first got involved in this, I thought you were out of your depth. No, I'll rephrase that . . .' She paused. 'I have always thought of you as a most honourable man. British public school, Royal Navy, the best of the British virtues. And you are, indeed. But I thought you were out of your league in the big bad world of politics as I knew it, through Max – an honourable schoolboy approach to life. And so, I had no confidence that you would be able to handle all this. I thought you just wouldn't be . . . devious enough. And so when you said we were going back to Switzerland to get the microfilm, I was going to get it from you, and do it my way.' She paused. 'And so when we were together here before you went away, and we were so happy, it was a sort of . . . sad, fatalistic happiness. Because I knew it could not last. We could never be really safe, because you did not know about the big bad world and had not thought it all through. So I was just grateful to be happy for a little while. But now . . .' She smiled with all her heart, and suddenly her eyes were glistening. 'Now I've seen that you *are* clever enough. You thought of everything. And, on top of it all, still honourable . . .' Her eyes glistened. 'You don't know what a remarkable achievement that is, in this rotten world.'

He smiled at her, but did not believe he deserved such happiness; after all these years here they were together, the dream he had never believed would come true: and the last nine weeks was just a bad dream from which they had woken up. He got up, and walked around the table, and he picked her up from her chair. And he carried her out of the kitchen, and bumped her through the doorways, into the bedroom, and he dumped her on the big double bed and collapsed beside her, and they were both laughing.

December went like that. They laughed a lot, and drank a lot, and loved a lot, and slept a lot, deep in each other's arms. They felt wonderful, and safe. Each day he still went out to look for strange footprints. But each day he left it later and later, and he only did it when he felt like a walk, or had to collect some firewood. Each day he saw nothing. Each day he grew more relaxed.

December went that way. It was on New Year's Day that he saw the footprints in the snow.

59

He stopped in his tracks, his heart knocking: then he unslung the rifle and crouched down, every muscle tensed. He peered through the forest, all around.

He examined the footprints again, feverishly. There had been no fresh snow that day. The prints were crisp. Several hours old. He stood up slowly.

The footprints stopped here. From here the man could have seen the house clearly. He had come through the woods to this point, stopped, then retraced his steps. Morgan looked at his watch shakily. It was after two o'clock. About another two hours of daylight. He started following the footprints.

They were as clear as a tramtrack. They headed through the trees for the forestry road a mile away. He followed them fast, striding, running, striding again, his eyes darting through the trees. Ten minutes later he could see the road. He went creeping forward.

There were car tyre marks on the road. The footprints disappeared at the car tracks. The car had turned around and driven off the way it had come. He examined the snow all around. There was definitely only one set of footprints.

Morgan started running flat out through the forest, back towards the house.

He burst into the courtyard. He locked the big door behind him. '*Anna?*'

There was no answer. He ran into the house. 'Anna!'

She answered from the kitchen: 'Yes?'

He burst into the kitchen.

'Go pack our things.' She was astonished. 'A man was here

429

a few hours ago. He's gone to fetch reinforcements. You've got fifteen minutes. I'm going up to the water tower to keep watch.' He snatched up the pistol and the machine gun. He ran through the house.

He clattered up the steps, into the tower. He clambered up through the trapdoor. He crouched between the two water tanks and peered over the top of the wall.

He could see all the borders of the farm. He swept his eye along the edge of the forest. There was only the silent stillness of the snowy trees.

He turned feverishly and looked down towards the river. He moved his eyes slowly along the winding banks. Nothing. He turned, and peered all along the other two boundaries, searching the old fruit trees on either side.

He sat back on his heels. He looked at his watch feverishly. Almost three o'clock. Only one hour of reliable daylight left. He scrambled back down the ladder.

He ran out of the house, into the courtyard, then to the stable and scrambled into the Fiat. He started it, and reversed out. He lined the car up with the wooden door. He scrambled out, started back towards the house; then he remembered the geese. *They couldn't leave the animals locked in . . .*

He opened the big outer door, then ran for the back of the barnyard. The ducks and geese were floating in their pond. He went to the pigsty and chased the piglet out. He ran back to the pond. The ducks and geese came flapping out. He waved his arms and they started running, their webbed feet padding and their heads up high. They ran worriedly towards the big wooden door, honking and quacking. The gander shied away from it when he saw the big wide world out there.

'*Out! Get out!*'

The gander plunged ponderously through, looking alarmed. The female blundered flappily after him. They went honking and quacking out into their new hinterland. Morgan slammed the door behind them. He turned and ran back into the house.

'*Hurry up and load the car!*'

He ran up the steps of the water tower again. He scrambled up the ladder, back to the water tanks.

He snatched up the FN rifle. He looked at his watch. Then peered over the ledge.

He swept his eyes along the forest. Nothing. Then, as he was about to turn and look down to the river, he saw the movement.

He froze, his heart pounding.

All he had glimpsed was a movement in the trees. But had he seen a man? Or a fox? The form had gone behind a tree. He stared at the place, desperately waiting for it to show again. Then he saw it again, and his stomach contracted.

It was a man, creeping. Then, he saw another movement, twenty yards away. It was another man. He swung around frantically and looked down at the river.

He stared at the river, keeping his eyes still, to catch any movement. Nothing. He swept the banks. Not a movement. But the banks were thick with trees and shrubs. He scrambled around and looked up along the borders of the land. Nothing. But there were all those gnarled fruit trees, black and grey against the snow. He looked desperately back up to the forest again.

He could not make the escape by car. That left the river route. But if there were men up in the forest there were probably more, covering the orchards. That meant the only hope was darkness. He looked feverishly at his watch again. He scrambled over to the ladder and called down: 'Anna!'

She came running up the steps. He thrust the pistol down to her.

'They're here. Take cover at the main front window onto the courtyard. If they come over the wall, shoot the moment you see their heads.'

She looked aghast; then snatched the pistol and ran back down the stairs. Morgan snatched up the FN, and slid off the safety catch. He peered over the wall, up towards the forest.

Then he saw the car coming.

For a wild moment he thought it was Makepeace dropping back like a guardian angel. An emissary from the Pope . . . Then he knew it was too much of a coincidence. It was a trick! These were the guys come to take them alive, to get into the house posing as visitors . . .

The car was coming through the forest towards the top of

431

the orchard. Morgan looked along the treeline for the men – he could not see them. Now the car was coming out of the forest. It began down the track towards the house.

Morgan slid the rifle up, the barrel on the wall. The car was a Ford. Blue. Two people in it. It rolled down the track towards the big main doors; then it stopped. Morgan waited, heart pounding. Then both doors opened, and two policemen climbed out.

Morgan stared, astonished. *Police . . . The police had arrived in the nick of time! . . .*

The two *gendarmes* walked towards the big door. Morgan thought: Ford . . . *Since when do French police drive around in blue Fords?* Everybody opens the door for a policeman . . . Take us by complete surprise . . . The policemen disappeared from his line of vision. Then there was a loud knocking on the outer door.

'*Allo? Police. Allo?*'

Morgan's heart was knocking. His eye swept the orchards, up to the forest again. Then two men came running out of the forest. They disappeared into the fruit trees.

'*Allo! Police!*'

Anna came scrambling up the ladder: '*They're police*,' she whispered.

'It's a trick! They're Russians! Get back! As soon as it's dark we're making a run for the motorbike at the bridge!'

She disappeared back down the ladder. There was knocking again. This time the big door shook. '*Police! Open up!*'

Morgan crouched, waiting. Silence. Only the pounding of his heart. Waiting for a head to show over the wall, for somebody to show himself in the orchard. But nothing moved. The two men could be creeping around the outside of the wall and he would not see them from here. Then he heard a crash against the outer kitchen door. He jerked around. Another kick. But the door held.

Another silence. Ten seconds. Twenty. Then out of the corner of his eye, he saw a hand appear over the top of the wall at the corner of the house, and he swung his rifle onto it. He could not see the other hand. Then a leg swung up on top of the wall. Morgan waited, his gun sights trained on it. Then out of the corner of his eye he saw two men break cover from the fruit trees, and he fired at the leg on the top of the wall, then swung the rifle across the orchard and fired blindly, *crack, crack.*

He swung the rifle back to the wall top. He saw a foot protruding around the corner of the house, inside the courtyard. The foot of a man lying down. Then a shot rang out and chips of masonry flew and he jerked his head down.

He crouched behind the water tanks. *That bastard was inside the courtyard, wounded.* And where was the other one? They knew he was up here now . . . He snatched up the sten gun, turned for the ladder, and scrambled down it.

He ran down the narrow steps, and burst into the hall below. Anna was crouched at the window. He rasped: 'There's a man in the yard, wounded. Maybe another one. Stay here.'

He ran through the dining room to the living room door. He pressed himself against the wall, his chest heaving, and peered round the corner. He could see the french window overlooking the courtyard. That was where the bastard had fallen. But he could see nothing. He dashed across the living room, to the window, and peered.

There was blood on the cobblestones. But no body.

He unlocked the french window. He clutched the sten gun to his hip, and he burst out into the courtyard.

Nobody . . .

But the trail of blood. It led up the side of the house, past the front door, past the bedroom windows. It disappeared around the corner.

Morgan ran up the side of the house. To the corner. He stopped, flat against the wall, his chest heaving. He peered around the corner.

Nobody. He swept his eye across the courtyard. The blood trail disappeared across the snow and from here he could not see where it went. He came out from behind the corner. Then there was a crack and a blow knocked him sideways, and he sprawled.

He hit the cobblestones and the same instant he scrambled up, and ran. He ran flat out for the car and flung himself behind it.

He crouched, rasping, gasping. He feverishly felt his thigh. There was no real pain. He felt warm blood. He looked down at the wound. His thigh was sodden. He feverishly looked along the outer wall top. They would be closing in on them out there. No, they thought he was still up in the tower, with a good field of fire – they would wait till dark now. The light was going already. In twenty minutes they would close in . . .

Suddenly the pain came into his thigh. He screwed up his eyes, trying to think. He did not know where the wounded man was. He could be in the stables, in the cowstalls, in the pigsty, behind the barrels in front. But *he* knew where Morgan was, behind this car . . . Get back to the house. The bastard had a bad leg wound, he couldn't do much. And just then he saw him.

Suddenly a barrel tipped over, and the man scrambled. He hobbled for the cowstall and threw himself behind the wall. Morgan swung his gun on him – but too late.

Danziger . . . That was fucking Danziger! . . .

He yelled, full of hate: '*Danziger, you bastard, I saw you! . . .*'

And oh God, God the fury. And oh God, God, Makepeace . . .

He scrambled down the side of the car, towards the rear. He really felt the pain in his thigh now. He crouched behind the rear wheel a moment, then clenched his teeth and ran.

He ran flat out for the bedroom corner, and flung himself around it. He stopped, pressed against the wall, gasping, trying not to feel the pain. Then he ran back to the living room. He slammed the door shut behind him, and bolted it.

It was almost dark inside. He hurried into the dining room, into the hall. She was crouched by the front door, her gun pointed at the window, ashen. She whispered: 'Is it really Danziger?'

'Makepeace must have opened his big mouth!' He took a trembling breath. 'We'll make a run for it in ten minutes, when it's dark. Get our passports and money, and the diamonds and the confessions, that's all. Then come up to the tower.'

He turned and made for the steps. She gasped: 'Your leg . . .' He ran up the narrow steps, wincing at the bloody pain.

He crouched between the water tanks, getting his breath back. Then he raised his head.

He looked up at the forest. Nothing moved. Down the orchard. Nothing. He turned and peered down at the river. Not a thing moved.

The light was going. He checked the rifle, then slid it over the wall. He aimed at the treeline of the forest. He squeezed the trigger.

His shot rang out, sharp and shocking, and he shifted the barrel and fired twice more, *crack – crack*. Then he swung the barrel and he let go down the middle of the orchard in a sweeping, shattering line, just to impress them. He pulled the rifle back and crouched down again. He rammed in a new ammunition clip.

Anna whispered: 'I'm here.'

He turned, on his haunches. She was crouched against the tanks, her face white. He said: 'We're safe up here. We dominate the field of fire. If they break in, we'll hold them off on the stairs.'

She unzipped her tracksuit blouse and pulled out a cognac bottle. She uncorked it and took a swig. She closed her eyes as she swallowed. Then held out the bottle to him.

He put it to his mouth and took a big swallow. It burned down into his gut. He took another mouthful. She was holding a newly lit cigarette out to him. He took a drag, and inhaled deeply. 'All right,' he said.

He crouched up, and peered. The light was going fast. He swept his eyes over the snowy orchard, up to the forest. Nothing. He turned and peered the other way towards the river. Nothing moving. He dared not put his head right over and look down into the courtyard below. He crouched down again. He said:

'All right. We're going to get out of this. Remember, they are not trying to kill us now. They want to take us alive.'

Her eyes were suddenly glistening. 'I love you,' she whispered.

He felt his eyes burn.

'I love you too.'

She whispered: 'With all my heart.' Then two tears welled over and rolled down her cheeks. 'We had a lovely time here, didn't we?'

He wanted to weep. 'We did . . .'

She said: 'We're going to come back here, aren't we? After this is all over.'

'Yes. We are.'

'And we'll do the house up properly, won't we? And build a proper duck pond. And get two horses?'

'Yes. We will.'

Two more tears rolled over her eyelids and down her cheeks. 'Do you promise?'

His throat was thick. 'I promise.'

She wiped her eyes, then took his cigarette from him and took a deep drag. She blew it out.

'Okay. A promise is a promise. So let's get on with it . . .'

He crouched up one last time, and poked the sten gun out into the dusk, and he squeezed the trigger. There was the shattering clatter of it, and he swept it through the dusk, *da – da – da – da* – raking the orchard blindly, then he swung around and swept the fire down towards the river, *da – da – da – da* – and the shattering noise and the stink of cordite filled the cold dusk.

Then he turned, and scrambled down the ladder.

He clattered down the steps, into the hall. Anna was behind him, with the pistol. He strode through the dining room, into the kitchen. It was dark inside the house, now.

He peered through the kitchen windows, into the back yard. He could not see Danziger. He turned to the outer kitchen door. He lifted out the iron bar.

He turned to her. Her face was white. He took the pistol from her, checked the magazine, handed it back to her. He put a new ammunition clip into the sten gun.

'Ready?'

She nodded, gaunt.

He took a shaky breath.

'Okay. Side by side. We run down to the river on the path, not in the stream bed. No point, now it's dark. Once we get onto the path you run ahead of me.'

She nodded.

He took her in his arms and clutched her tight. Her breath trembled. He squeezed her once more, then let her go.

'Okay . . .' He slipped the catch back on the lock. He

436

clutched the sten gun in his right hand, and flung open the door.

They came bursting out of the door, into the darkness. They ran flat out through the walnut trees, onto the path. He looked desperately behind and she ran ahead.

She ran flat out down the path, her hair flying, the pistol in her hand, every moment expecting the shattering gunfire. She ran and she ran, the snow flying from her pounding feet. He ran five yards behind her, eyes darting desperately ahead in the darkness. They ran, and ran, the black banks of the river only sixty yards ahead now. Now fifty, now forty. *Please God Please God Please God* – now the black river was only thirty yards ahead, now twenty, now ten . . . When they were five yards from the river the shot rang out, and Anna lurched and contorted, her arms upflung, and she crashed.

The shot that got Anna Hapsburg was not intended to kill her, only to pull her down. She sprawled headlong, ploughing up the snow, and Morgan crashed over her. He scrambled up, shocked, horrified, and cried '*Anna!* –' He snatched up her pistol and he seized her arm and he tried to heave her up, and she was a dead weight. He shouted '*Get up!*' and he wrenched, and he dragged her.

He dragged her through the snow, grasping and heaving, stumbling, slipping, and he came to the bank. He plunged her down it. He crashed into the shallow icy water, feet first, and she crashed in after him. He crouched down and tried to wrench her up into his arms. He shook her: '*Anna!* –'

She lay in the water, in his arms. She whimpered, '*Go – you go . . .*'

And he wanted to weep his relief that she was alive. '*Where're you hit?*' His hands clutched over her body.

'In the back – you go –'

His hand was bloody, and he felt the wound in her spine. And he wanted to bellow his hate and outrage to the sky. He crouched and heaved her arm over his shoulder. He slung his arm holding the sten gun around her waist, and he heaved her up. She hung from his shoulder, her legs limp.

He staggered through the icy water, slipping and stumbling

437

on the stones, half carrying her, half dragging her, rasping, gasping.

60

He staggered with her to the edge of the waterfall. He released her, and she collapsed in the icy rushing water, and he jumped down into the shallow pool below. He reached up frantically and grabbed her arm. He heaved her over the waterfall.

She came with a splashing crash. He wrenched her arm up around his neck again. He ploughed her across the pool, grunting, gasping, stumbling, praying *Please God Please God* . . . He looked wildly over his shoulder. He plunged her on. Then the pool shallowed off, and the bend in the river was only twenty yards ahead. He went stumbling across the pool, dragging her; then he was in rapids. He staggered and lurched her on, his heart pounding from the exertion. Now the bend was ten yards ahead, now eight, now six, and he prayed *Please God only ten more seconds.* He dragged her, and dragged her – and then they were at the bend, and he staggered around it.

He collapsed back against a big rock, gasping, clutching her, the water swirling around his knees.

Then he crouched down again. He slid one arm under her knees, and he heaved her up in his arms.

He laid her on the cold stones between the boulders, whimpering; then he furiously grabbed the sten and scrambled across the rocks. He crouched behind the big boulder. He peered through the darkness, upriver, rasping. He did not feel the icy cold, all he knew was the desperate fury and the fear for her. And with all his furious heart he just wanted the bastards to show themselves so he could just blast out his hate hate hate and kill kill kill. *And oh God God God just help me now to save her, save her* – he swept his eyes furiously, desperately up and down the banks, and he saw nothing.

He scrambled back across the stones. He whispered hoarsely:
'Anna? . . .'

She opened her eyes. She gave an exhausted smile and she
whispered:

'What's the plan?'

He felt desperate tears burn. 'Are you in pain?'

'No pain. I can't feel a thing. I'm cold, that's all. Now tell
me the plan . . .'

And the rage welled up in his breast, the red-black fury that
the bastards had done this to her, smashed her spine and now
she was cold, and he wanted to bellow his outrage to the sky
and go charging out there to kill kill kill . . . She whispered:
'We've had it, haven't we, darling?'

He shook his head and started to deny it, to say he knew not
what, oh God, just anything to make her feel a little better,
and she smiled: 'Okay, I've got a plan . . .'

He half-sobbed: 'What's your plan?'

She whispered: 'Central Africa . . . They'll never find you in
Central Africa . . .'

A sob choked his throat and two tears rolled out and she
gripped his shirt and she whispered urgently: 'You must do it,
then run, darling.'

And he wanted to shake her and bellow that he could never
do that, *never never could he do that* – and she whispered:
'They've got us nailed down here, they just have to wait it out
and then take us alive, and they'll do terrible things to us, and
then they'll put a bullet through our heads – so what's the
point? . . .' He started to speak and she went on urgently:
'*Listen to me* . . . I can't run . . . But you can . . . You can get
out of here, with your kind of luck . . .' She closed her eyes
and she shook her head: 'And I'm not going to live with you
with a broken back . . .' He opened his mouth and she cried:
'No way! . . . And it's not going to happen anyway because
after they've taken us alive they're going to kill us . . . So let's
finish it now, and then you run, darling . . .'

And he felt the love and the anguish rage up and he wanted
to seize her and shake her and shake her to make her run run
run with him, *make her run* – he pulled her up in his arms and
clutched her tight and he rasped:

'*I'm going to get us out of this . . . I'm going back up the river*

439

to finish the bastards and then we're going to live happily ever after . . .'

And he turned on his haunches, and she grabbed his wrist and gasped, 'No! Run!' He pulled his arm free and he scrambled furiously across the rocks. He snatched up the sten gun, and he leapt over the boulders, back into the river. She cried:

'*Run, Jack . . .'*

And she knew there was only one way to make him do it; she heard him splashing back up the river, looking for the bastards: and she lifted her frozen fist to her head, clutching the pistol, the tears rolling down her face. She cried out once more, '*Run, Jack . . .'* and she closed her eyes tight and she whispered, '*God forgive me . . .'*

She squeezed the trigger.

The shot rang out, and he gasped, as if he had felt the blow himself; then he turned around, aghast. He went plunging wildly back down the river to the boulders. He scrambled up over them, whimpering: then he saw her lying on the stones, her arm outflung, clutching the pistol, the blood running out of the hole in her temple.

Morgan stared, horrified, uncomprehending. Then he felt it roar up from inside him, the outrage and the grief grief grief. And his mind reeled red-black with hate hate hate, and he filled his lungs and bellowed his outrage and grief to the sky. He clutched the sten gun and turned to go charging up there blazing to kill the bastards who had killed her – and a voice shouted out of the darkness:

'*Jack! Don't be a fool, man! We've got you surrounded!'*

Morgan crouched, the tears running down his face.

Carrington! That was Carrington's voice . . . And he felt his mind reel in hate and outrage again. He filled his lungs and bellowed:

'*I'm going to kill you, Carrington! . . .'*

Carrington shouted out of the darkness:

'*Jack – what do you think you're doing, shooting policemen? They'll hang you for that!'*

'*They aren't policemen – they're your hit men! And I'm going to kill every one of them and I'm going to kill you! . . .'*

Carrington shouted: *'Jack, I haven't come to kill you! I've come to talk some sense into you! But if you fight you'll be gunned down like a mad dog!'*

Morgan crouched, sobbing; he bellowed: *'You're the mad dogs, Carrington! Didn't you get the message from the Vatican?'*

'I don't know what you're talking about, Jack! See reason, man! You've got the goods we sent you for! We must have them! We've got to know you're on our side!'

Morgan bellowed: *'The goods are destroyed, you fool! You got my letter!'*

'Jack, we can't believe you, man. We can't afford to leave this hanging in mid-air, it's too important! See reason! And the Comrades won't believe you either, they're coming for you too, Jack! So join our side, where you belong, man.'

The sobs choked up in Morgan's throat again. Carrington shouted:

'Jack – think about it . . . It's cold out here, man! We'll give you fifteen minutes to talk about it with Anna.'

The tears choked up, and he dropped his head. He turned and crouched back to her body, the tears running down his face; he knelt beside her, and he pulled her up in his arms. He clutched her tight, and his heart broke.

He dropped his head over hers, clutching her, his sobs choking and racking.

For a minute he held her, rocking her, weeping; then he laid her down on the cold stones. He filled his lungs and he shouted hoarsely into the night:

'Fifteen minutes you'll give us to talk it out?'

'Yes.'

He sobbed out loud. He turned her over, onto her back. He folded her hands across her chest, one by one, in the sign of the cross. Then he took a lock of her hair, and draped it across the bullet hole in her temple. And the sobs racked up him once more, and he bent and kissed her one last time. He clutched her, and rocked her, and rocked her, and the grief and the pity, pity, pity came sobbing out.

Then he laid her down, and turned away. He picked up the

441

sten gun. He scrambled blindly across the rocks; and between the boulders; and he scrambled down into the water.

He started blindly down the river, towards the bridge and the motorcycle, the tears running salty into his mouth.

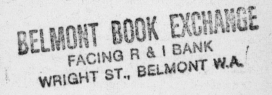

Embassy
Leslie Waller

July 4th is only seven days away. The élite of Washington and London will assemble at the American Ambassadorial residence to celebrate the day. So will a cadre of terrorists.

To Intelligence Officer Ned French falls the task of averting an international catastrophe. But he has problems of his own – a guilt-ridden past; a beautiful wife who is restless; a mistress who becomes his wife's confidante . . .

'*Embassy* is realistic, complex, gripping and satisfying. Waller at his best!' Ken Follett

FONTANA PAPERBACKS

A Thunder of Crude
Brian Callison

Caluria is a supertanker, a giant of the sea. But years of neglect have turned her into a floating powder keg.

The Panoco oil terminal is the last word in technology. But greed has allowed safety systems to run down.

Together, a powder keg and an open fire spell disaster and death. Add an overage captain, an inquisitive lady reporter and a group of teenagers out to make trouble, and the countdown begins . . .

FONTANA PAPERBACKS

Fontana Paperbacks: Fiction

Fontana is a leading paperback publisher of both non-fiction, popular and academic, and fiction. Below are some recent fiction titles.

- [ ] GLITTER BABY Susan Elizabeth Phillips £2.95
- [ ] EMERALD DECISION Craig Thomas £3.50
- [ ] THE GOLDEN CUP Belva Plain £3.50
- [ ] A THUNDER OF CRUDE Brian Callison £2.95
- [ ] DESERT QUEEN Julia Fitzgerald £3.50
- [ ] THE GREEN FLASH Winston Graham £3.50
- [ ] UNDER CONTRACT Liza Cody £2.95
- [ ] THE LATCHKEY KID Helen Forrester £2.95
- [ ] IN HARM'S WAY Geoffrey Jenkins £2.95
- [ ] THE DOOR TO DECEMBER Leigh Nichols £3.50
- [ ] THE MIRROR OF HER DREAMS Stephen Donaldson £3.95
- [ ] A SONG IN THE MORNING Gerald Seymour £2.95

You can buy Fontana paperbacks at your local bookshop or newsagent. Or you can order them from Fontana Paperbacks, Cash Sales Department, Box 29, Douglas, Isle of Man. Please send a cheque, postal or money order (not currency) worth the purchase price plus 22p per book for postage (maximum postage required is £3.00 for orders within the UK).

NAME (Block letters) _____

ADDRESS _____

_____

_____